Dedalus Europe
General Editor: M...

*The Tragedy of the
Street of Flowers*

Eça de Queiroz

The Tragedy of the Street of Flowers

Translated and with an introduction
by Margaret Jull Costa

Dedalus

Funded by
THE
ARTS
COUNCIL
OF ENGLAND

Dedalus would like to thank The Arts Council of England in London, The Portuguese Book Institute and The Camões Institute in Lisbon for their assistance in producing this book. Special thanks go to The Portuguese Arts Trust for all their advice and support.

Published in the UK by Dedalus Ltd, Langford Lodge, St Judith's Lane, Sawtry, Cambs, PE17 5XE
email: DedalusLimited@compuserve.com

ISBN 1 873982 64 X

Dedalus is distributed in the United States from the 1st January 2001 by scb Distributors, 15608 South New Century Drive, Gardena, California 90248
email: info@scbdistributors.com   web site: www.scbdistributors.com

Dedalus is distributed in Australia & New Zealand by Peribo Pty Ltd, 58 Beaumont Road, Mount Kuring-gai, N.S.W. 2080
email: peribo@bigpond.com

Dedalus is distributed in Canada by Marginal Distribution, Unit 102, 277 George Street North, Peterborough, Ontario, KJ9 3G9
email: marginal@ptbo.igs.net   web site: www.marginal.com

Dedalus is distributed in Italy by Apeiron Editoria & Distribuzione, Localita Pantano, 00060 Sant'Oreste (Roma)
email: apeironeditori@hotmail.com

First published by Dedalus in 2000
First published in Portugal in 1980
The translation and introduction copyright © Margaret Jull Costa 2000

The right of Margaret Jull Costa to be identified as the translator of this work has been asserted by her in accordance with the Copyright, Designs and Patents Act, 1988.

Typeset by RefineCatch Limited, Bungay, Suffolk
Printed in Finland by WS Bookwell

A C.I.P. listing for this book is available on request.

MINISTÉRIO DA CULTURA

INSTITUTO PORTUGUÊS DO
LIVRO E DAS BIBLIOTECAS

INSTITUTO
CAMÕES

Portuguese Literature from Dedalus

Dedalus, as part of its Europe 1992–2000 programme, with the assistance of The Portuguese Arts Trust in London, The Portuguese Book Institute and The Camões Institute in Lisbon, has embarked on a series of new translations by Margaret Jull Costa of some of the major classics of Portuguese literature.

Titles so far published:

The Mandarin (and other stories) – Eça de Queiroz

The Relic – Eça de Queiroz

The Tragedy of the Street of Flowers – Eça de Queiroz

Lúcio's Confession – Mário de Sá-Carneiro

The Great Shadow (and other stories) – Mário de Sá-Carneiro

The Dedalus Book of Portuguese Fantasy – editors Eugénio Lisboa and Helder Macedo

Forthcoming titles include:

The Crime of Father Amaro – Eça de Queiroz

Cousin Basílio – Eça de Queiroz

THE TRANSLATOR

Margaret Jull Costa has translated many novels and short stories by Portuguese, Spanish and Latin American writers, amongst them Mário de Sá-Carneiro, Bernardo Atxaga, Ramón del Valle-Inclán, Carmen Martín Gaite, Luisa Valenzuela and Juan José Saer. She was joint-winner of the Portuguese Translation Prize in 1992 for her translation of Fernando Pessoa's *Book of Disquiet* and was shortlisted for the 1996 Prize for her translation of *The Relic* by Eça de Queiroz. With Javier Marías, she won the 1997 International IMPAC Dublin Literary Award for *A Heart So White* and, in 2000, she won the Weidenfeld Prize for her translation of José Saramago's *All the Names*.

ACKNOWLEDGEMENTS

The translator would like to thank Maria Manuela Lisboa and
Ben Sherriff for all their help and advice.

INTRODUCTION

José Maria de Eça de Queiroz was born on 25th November 1845 in the small town of Povoa de Varzim in the north of Portugal. His mother was nineteen and unmarried. Only the name of his father – a magistrate – appears on the birth certificate. His mother returned immediately to her respectable family in Viana do Castelo, and Eça was left with his wetnurse, who looked after him for six years until her death. Although his parents did marry – when Eça was four – and had six more children, Eça did not live with them until he was twenty-one, living instead either with his grandparents or at boarding school in Oporto, where he spent the holidays with an aunt. His father only officially acknowledged Eça when Eça himself was forty. His father did, however, pay for his son's studies at boarding school and at Coimbra University, where Eça studied Law. Like the character of Vítor in *The Tragedy of the Street of Flowers*, Eça was not at all drawn to the legal profession. Instead, he joined the diplomatic service, working as consul in Havana (1872–74), Newcastle-upon-Tyne (1874–79), Bristol (1879–88) and, finally, Paris, where he served until his death in 1900.

He began writing stories and essays, which were published in the *Gazeta de Portugal*, and became involved with a group of intellectuals known as the Generation of '70, who were committed to reforms in society and in the arts. The novels he wrote in the next thirty years were all biting satires on, for example, celibacy and the priesthood (*The Crime of Father Amaro*, 1875), the romantic ideal of passion (*Cousin Basílio*, 1878), religious and social hypocrisy (*The Relic*, 1887) and, in what is generally considered to be his masterpiece, *The Maias* (1888), the disintegration and decadence of Portuguese society. Only in his last novel, *The City and the Mountains* (1901), did he appear to soften, praising the simple rustic life and condemning life in the city.

*

The Tragedy of the Street of Flowers was only published in Portuguese in 1980, when Eça's work went out of copyright. Three editions came out almost simultaneously, all based on a manuscript in the Biblioteca Nacional in Lisbon. Many Eça scholars were horrified that what they considered to be an unfinished work by Eça should be made public. Eça, they argued, had clearly chosen not to publish it during his lifetime and his wishes should be respected.

We do not know definitively why Eça chose not to publish the novel. It was part of a planned twelve-volume series entitled *Crónicas da Vida Sentimental*, intended to be a gallery of nineteenth-century Portugal, a project that came to nothing. It is possible that his heirs may have been put off by the apparently unfinished nature of the manuscript or possibly by the subject matter, but Eça himself wrote of the novel in 1877: 'It's not immoral or indecent. It's cruel.' He added that he thought it 'the best, most interesting novel I have yet written', infinitely superior to his *Cousin Basílio*, and 'a real literary and moral bombshell'.

Could Eça have decided not to publish the book because the feelings and incidents described in it were simply too close to home? Eça's novels, unsurprisingly, abound in orphans being shuffled off to live with aunts and uncles; here, Vítor's childhood trajectory – wetnurse, aunt, friend of family and, finally, uncle – is the one that most closely follows Eça's own. But there is also the secrecy and shame surrounding Vítor's birth and, possibly more importantly, the void at the centre of Vítor's life which only Genoveva can fill. When he wakes up after Genoveva's first soirée, the memory of her fills his soul 'with all the sweetness of a mother's kiss', and, later, life without her affection seems to him unacceptable, her affection being 'the sweetest thing he had ever known, an affirmation of his self-worth'. These deep longings for the love of a mother, however unconscious, are complicated by the fact that the woman who becomes his lover is not only his mother but also a high-class prostitute. There is something deeply unsettling and possibly vengeful about this conjunction in one character of what are traditionally regarded as the highest and lowest of female roles. The mother who abandons her child is portrayed as selfish, immoral, unnatural and doomed to a terrible death. Although no one would suggest that there was an incestuous relationship between Eça and his mother, nevertheless, given the similarities between his and Vítor's background, would incest between mother and son – with the mother depicted as a corrupt, mercenary courtesan – have violated too great a taboo and been too potentially wounding to his own family? Could Vítor's longing for a mother's love have been seen as an implicit criticism of Eça's own mother? Was there a danger of fact and fiction becoming dangerously blurred? We will, of course, probably never know. It is interesting to note, though, that when Eça returned to the theme of incest in *The Maias* (which he began writing shortly after abandoning *The Tragedy of the Street of Flowers*), the incest is between brother and sister, rather than mother and son.

As to the unfinished nature of the book, while it is true that Eça had still not settled on a title or even on the names of one or two minor characters and that there are occasional non sequiturs or redundancies, in my view, the novel still stands as an utterly convincing whole, providing us with an acid portrait of a society in which everyone and everything has its price. It gives us, above all, the truly extraordinary figure of Genoveva, a self-made woman if ever there was one, who knows almost to the date when her looks will cease to be saleable. Genoveva is, it is true, a rapacious schemer, and yet while one is repelled by her lack of scruples, one cannot but be seduced by her sheer energy and by her passionate commitment to grasping what she perceives as her last chance of happiness with Vítor. She is, ultimately, a tragic figure, for, having rejected motherhood and motherly love when she abandoned Vítor as a baby, she is ultimately destroyed when that love reappears in perverted form.

In Vítor, on the other hand, we have a brilliant portrait of a man in search of definition, an emotional orphan, whose feelings change with the wind. He is full of bravado and ambitious plans – he will run away with Genoveva, he will be a successful lawyer or a famous writer. When he does become a published poet, his poetry is a poor imitation of a minor French writer and is published in a women's magazine.

Eça also gives us a gallery of vividly drawn minor characters, particularly at the two parties held by Genoveva – Dâmaso, the plump fool soon parted from his money, blunt-speaking, honest Uncle Timóteo, the tender extrovert, Sarrotini, the unctuous João Marinho. These 'soirées' are provincial caricatures of their Paris equivalent and give Eça plenty of scope for poking fun at what he perceived to be third-rate bourgeois Lisbon society. Eça, as always, finds gold in the very mediocrity he is mocking, and the result is a novel that is both tragic and richly comic.

THE TRAGEDY OF THE
STREET OF FLOWERS

I

It was in the Teatro da Trindade, at a performance of *Bluebeard*.

The second act had already begun, and the chorus of courtesans were just bowing and retreating in an arc to the back of the stage, when, in a box to the left of the circle, the rusty creak of a stiff door lock and the scrape of a chair drew a few distracted glances. A rather tall woman was standing in the box, slowly undoing the silver clasps on a long black silk cape lined with fur; the hood of the cape was still up, but nevertheless afforded an impression of large, dark eyes in an oval, aquiline face; whether natural or artificial, the faint shadows beneath her eyes lent seriousness and profundity to her gaze. With her was a thin woman, wearing a gold watch chain strung across a vulgar silk bodice; the thin woman took her companion's cape from her, and she, with a light, delicate movement, turned and stood very still, studying the stage.

The lethargic audience immediately stirred into life. Opera glasses were trained on her – 'a veritable fusillade', to quote Roma, the esteemed author of *Idylls and Dreams*; a fat fellow, standing just below her box, was so anxious to get a look at her that he turned round rather too suddenly, slipped on a step and fell over, to loud guffaws; while the fat man, very angry and red in the face, was rubbing his rear, the woman leaned forward and spoke to her thin companion, who remained perched on the edge of her chair, respectful as a maidservant, stiff-backed as a religious zealot. She had a large red nose, her hair was combed flat to her head, and her submissive smile revealed long, carnivorous teeth; in order to view the stage, she carefully donned a pair of spectacles. She was clearly some sort of ageing English governess.

The talk in the circle was that the beautiful unknown woman must be the Princess of Breppo, a poor, distant relative of the House of Savoy. The withered old Countess de Triães, sporting a white camellia in her grey hair, even wondered if 'the king would notice'; but the king sat motionless, leaning on the edge of the box; he was wearing blue-tinted pince-nez and an admiral's uniform with vast gold epaulettes; the queen, looking lovely in purple, her bejewelled fingers resting on her cheek, was still smiling at the grotesque stage antics of 'Count Oscar'. They did not even notice 'the princess'. Some said she had been expected to stop off in Lisbon on her way to Brazil, where she was going in order to escape importunate creditors or to pursue an interest in the flora of the Americas or to shake off the tedium of Europe.

That night was a benefit performance, and the theatre was packed. In another box, in a lilac dress, her hair like a stiff helmet, sat the plump, white Viscountess de Rosarim, whose virtuous nature was the talk of Lisbon and caused people to mutter angrily and impatiently: 'The woman must be stupid!'

Beside her, hiding behind a large, black fan, was Miss Ginamá from Bahia, a glimpse of whose silk stockings was enough to provoke uncontrolled lubricity amongst the populace. Opposite, sitting in the midst of her devout, respectable family, was Mercês Pedrão, whose habit, so it was rumoured, was to bestow on any man under fifty-five who came near her the knowing but prudent caresses of a voluptuary. And in the farthest-flung box sat two sad negroes with diamond pins in their shirtfronts.

Slender Father Agnaldo was up in the circle, wearing gold-rimmed pince-nez and with his hair combed carefully over his bald pate; he was a great success in the Café Martinho where he would spend the nights making mock of church dogma and drinking chartreuse; there too was Carvalhosa, now a deputy, but who still bore the traces on his jaundiced skin of the vices he had loved too well at university; also present was the esteemed poet, Roma, who, when he was happy, would invent comical words and, when in more splenetic vein, would sing of the moonlight in the valleys and of his love for certain duchesses, and who, whether sad or gay, was always running grimy fingers through his scurf-ridden hair.

Dear, kind Baldonísio, clean-shaven and bald, teetered from one box to another, his hips swaying, his voice trilling out soft as a cricket's; he observed all the fast days and was much loved by devout aristocrats. The ladies beamed at the illustrious pianist, Fonseca, who kept fiddling with his glasses and who, the day before, had published a waltz called 'The Throne Waltz', which he had dedicated to their majesties. Padilhão, sociable as ever and much in demand for his ability to imitate actors, animals, the whistling of a train and the sad sound of an oboe, was also much in evidence.

One noisy box was packed with heavily made-up Spanish women, whilst in the stalls down below, amidst the drab of army uniforms, one caught the occasional faint glimmer of an officer's insignia. The heat and the mingled breath of so many people crammed together made for a suffocating atmosphere. The more obese members of the audience were perspiring and fluttering their fans. Hands wearing gloves made of oxblood, bottle green or mustard yellow leather smoothed trim goatee beards. In the balcony, a child was crying obstinately. And the anonymous masses – people who eat, procreate and die anonymously – looked blankly about them with dark eyes.

The unknown woman took up her opera glasses and trained them for a moment on the queen, on the stiff, flowery coiffures of the ladies, on the fine, gallant profile of Dom João da Maia and on the Spanish girls. Occasionally, she would smile and talk to the scrawny governess. She was blonde, either natural or dyed, and was wearing a dress in pearl-coloured silk, with a modest, square neckline; a black enamel pendant set with tiny diamonds and threaded onto a pale ribbon nestled on her breast, which was the colour of warm milk.

Two men in the circle seemed particularly fascinated by her. One of them kept smiling broadly, fidgeting in his seat, polishing the lenses of his opera glasses and staring up at her, elbows akimbo; he was a short, chubby man in his thirties, with a fuzz of black beard on his plump face. His name was Dâmaso Mavião, but he was known to everyone as Dâmaso. He was rich and well respected. His father had been a money-lender, but Dâmaso wore a ring bearing a coat of arms; it was, almost without modification, the coat of arms of the Count de Malgueiro, a decrepit gambler and hardened drinker, to whom Dâmaso, believing it the chic thing to do, gave the occasional silver coin. He was wearing beige trousers, and beneath his waistcoat gleamed a shirtfront with coral buttons in the form of little hands each holding a golden pencil.

The other fellow, a young man of twenty-three, stood motionless, his arms folded, studying her as intently as one might a famous painting. He was doubtless thinking that he had never before seen such alluring, desirable beauty, such splendid, warm, white skin, such long eyelashes so gracefully lowered and raised. The curve of her throat and breast was lovelier than anything he had seen in statues or engravings, and her mass of golden hair must, he thought, be silken and heavy to the touch and have the soft warmth of living things. Her flesh must exude a subtle perfume and be so exceptionally sensitive and supple as to make any man tremble. He imagined that the silk dress she wore would have its own vitality, as if it were another skin. He marvelled at the smoothly elegant way she turned her head, and when she removed her long eighteen-buttoned glove, he stared in wonderment at her bracelet – a snake which coiled five times about her arm and seemed to rest its flat head, set with two large rubies like two bloodshot eyes, on her white flesh.

Dâmaso had stated categorically that 'she must be a princess' and that idea made her feel infinitely distant from the young man, as if she were lost in some glorious long ago, with all the haughty pride of an historic family and the inaccessibility of queens. What had her past life been? What would her voice be like? What feelings did she have? Had she ever been in love? With whom? He could only imagine her lavishly dressed, striking stately poses; he could not even think of her in a bedroom, wearing a simple white nightgown; she belonged in high-ceilinged, damasked salons hung with standards, where phalanxes of pages bowed as she passed.

What was she doing there, then, in a box at the Teatro da Trindade, with an ugly paid companion? Would she have the candour of a poetic soul? Could she love just anyone? What form would her love take? What delicate gestures would she make when she gave herself to a lover, what fine words would she utter? Surely she would inspire a fanatical, almost religious devotion. Who could possibly ever possess such a creature?

These vague thoughts came naturally to a young man of a sentimental, melancholy turn of mind. His name was Vítor da Silva, a law graduate, who lived with his Uncle Timóteo and worked in the offices of the lugubrious Dr Caminha. He had brought back with him from university, and from his literary acquaintances there, a kind of hazy romanticism, a morbid sadness, a dislike of all activity and a distaste for his profession. He had read a great deal of Musset, Byron and Tennyson; he himself wrote poetry and had had some poems published in newspapers and magazines: *The Dream of Dom João*, *Flowers of Snow*, a few sonnets. He had recently been working on a short poem about King Arthur and the Round Table, the Holy Grail and Lancelot. The brute imperfection of everyday life filled him with melancholy. He still lived in hope of finding a lover like Juliet and, although contact with blunt reality had made him lose some of his romantic ideas, his complete lack of any sense of irony allowed him to continue to venerate the ideal. He got up late, loathed the legal profession in which he worked, was a republican and a dandy.

'Look, she understands Portuguese,' Dâmaso suddenly exclaimed, elbowing Vítor.

'How do you know?'

'Can't you see, she's laughing at Isidoro.'

The second act was drawing to an end. The conductor was bouncing up and down, brandishing the baton, the violin bows rose and fell as the violinists sawed away; the piccolos sang out shrilly, while the bespectacled man playing the bass drum, with a scarf over one shoulder, dealt the drumskin soft, sleepy blows with his drumsticks. On stage, Carlota, in a terrible state, the train of her dress all dirty, was dragging herself through the court, whining:

> I bet that fat old fishwife
> Was once the bane of his life

19

And the ladies of the chorus, their hair dishevelled, pretended to be deeply shocked, raising now one arm, now the other, as stiffly as puppets. The fat, scarlet 'queen' was sweating; 'El-Rei Bobeche' was drooling; and the audience burst into laughter and applause when he and 'Count Oscar', playing the fool on the royal armchairs on stage, suddenly swung round and put the soles of their feet together to form the converging legs of a ludicrous W.

The curtain fell. There was a rising murmur of voices; people puffed out their cheeks in the heat; fans fluttered, and the people in the boxes and the circles gradually fell silent and stared into space, hot and weary; people yawned or peered vaguely round the theatre through their opera glasses.

A group of men standing at the door to the circle were examining the unknown woman; speculative comments were made: Was she really a princess? But someone said that the princess in question was a little old lady with a chignon. Perhaps she was the new leading lady at the Teatro de São Carlos. Then a grey-haired man with a slight stutter joined the group and said knowledgeably:

'She's a tart!'

Since he was a person who had visited both Madrid and Paris on government business, his opinions, whether on debauchery or cuisine, were always highly respected. And two broad-backed Brazilians left the group disconsolately, muttering:

'She's one of those French women on the make. Rio's full of them.'

But everyone agreed that she was certainly a tasty piece, and her décolletage was highly praised. A pale gaunt youth, jacket tightly buttoned, narrow-brimmed hat flat on his head like a plate, and carrying a murderous-looking walking stick, made all eyes glitter when he muttered hoarsely:

'I wouldn't mind getting her alone!'

They discussed loudly whether her hair was natural or dyed. They were all good friends and so addressed each other as 'old fool' and 'idiot'. One lawyer got very irate and bet two *libras* that her hair was dyed.

She, meanwhile, had gone to sit at the back of the box, talking now and then to the Englishwoman and looking rather tired, smothering yawns with one small hand, the rings on her fingers glinting in the semidarkness. Vítor da Silva, who could not now see her from his seat, was about to get up and sit further forward, at the front of the circle, when he saw a man he knew, Joaquim Marinho, go into the box.

Marinho was from Trás-os-Montes in the far north of Portugal, but had lived in Paris for years. He had inherited a strip of impoverished land near Bragança, but according to his friends – who said of him respectfully and with a lift of the eyebrow: 'He's a sly one, Marinho!' – he had got rich in Paris, and people spoke gravely of 'Marinho's fortune'. He was short, slightly built, almost bald and sported a fine blonde beard; he had small feet and moved almost noiselessly; he smiled easily and, when he spoke, had a habit of rubbing his hands together. He was so extravagantly polite, it was almost embarrassing. He called everyone 'my dear friend' and always had a few chocolate bonbons in his pockets for the ladies. He was so eager to please that he would quite happily post a letter for someone or deliver a package to the customs office. Should a peer of the realm or a director-general speak to him of the weather or about the latest bullfights, he would listen, eyes wide, biting his lower lip, as if astonished at such rare words of wisdom. He would buy beer for the capitalists in Balthreschi's patisserie and say a few paternal words to the younger men, slipping his arm around their waist and whispering lubricious comments about dancers. He always wore magnificent overcoats, and if anyone complimented him on this, he would immediately take off the coat and display the cloth in a favourable light, showing off the lining and the excellent seams, and say quietly:

'A bargain. It's the first time I've worn it – it's yours for five *libras*.'

He was always doing deals. People said of him: 'Marinho has a very sharp eye for business!' He almost always dined out and claimed to suffer from neuralgia.

Vítor was surprised at his familiarity with the stranger. Marinho had grasped both her hands, smiling broadly. He had picked up her opera glasses and muttered something to her that made her laugh. She was certainly no princess, and the thought made Vítor feel suddenly strangely happy.

Dâmaso agreed and, standing at the circle door with the others and stroking his beard, he said:

'If she's so very friendly with Marinho, she's clearly no princess.'

And they all decided that she must be the new leading lady at the Teatro de São Carlos.

'We've got ourselves a woman, then,' exclaimed Dâmaso. 'If she tries to play the fine lady, she'll be booed off.'

And turning to the gaunt young man with the murderous walking stick, he said:

'Are you dining afterwards, Viscount?'

'Hmm,' the Viscount said in his nasal tones, which meant 'Yes'.

But the stocky, illustrious pianist Fonseca said that the new leading lady was thin and short, with jet-black hair.

Marinho would enlighten them. And since he was at that very moment emerging from the unknown woman's box, they gathered round him in the corridor.

'Who is she? Who is she?'

'Wouldn't you like to know!'

'Come on, Marinho!'

He stroked his beard, laughing to himself. Then, head on one side, he said confidentially:

'A lady of the best society, the very best!'

'Is she French?'

'Oh, really . . .'

He smiled, warding off their questions. People stood on tiptoe around him; one of the king's courtiers, a pleasant, witty fellow, put his hand to his ear; a decrepit, deaf old gentleman, wearing an enormous top hat, asked a great hulk of a man with a pointed goatee beard to tell him what Marinho had said. The hulk bowed respectfully and addressed him as 'Count'.

Finally, Marinho, hemmed in, pressed up against a wall beneath a gaslamp, scraping the whitewash with the sole of one of his shoes, told them everything. He had met her in Paris, in the house of Baroness de Villecreuse, a most respectable lady, separated from her husband, who lives in the Champs-Elysées, near Madame de Sagan. Turning to a pompous, potbellied man with a grey beard, he said:

'You know the place, don't you, Vasconcelos?'

The man replied in the shrill tones of a cricket:

'I adore it.'

'Well, that's where I met her. She invited me to dine at her house a few times. Her name is Madame de Molineux. She's Portuguese, from Madeira. Molineux, the old devil, was a senator of the Empire. God, you ate well in that house!' And he rolled his eyes in delight. 'The Molineux are a very old Normandy family. After that disastrous business at Sedan, the old chap went to Belgium, where he died. And that's all I know about her. She's called Genoveva.'

Then someone asked:

'Who's the other woman?'

'A companion, a kind of maid. An Englishwoman. I'm coming, I'm coming!' he said in response to Dâmaso, who was beckoning to him.

The bell was ringing; the group dispersed. And Marinho, putting his arm about Dâmaso's waist, said:

'What is it?'

'That woman, is she with anyone?'

Marinho opened his arms wide and, lowering his voice, said:

'*Chi lo sa?*'

And Dâmaso, in a still quieter voice and grasping Marinho by the lapel of his jacket, said:

'You couldn't introduce me, could you?'

'Why, of course. She even asked me to bring someone along in the next interval! It's not strictly etiquette to introduce anyone at the theatre . . . but here . . . and, besides, she did ask me.'

The orchestra was accompanying the aria:

Fresh young loves,
I plucked them like flowers . . .

'I'll see you later, then,' said Dâmaso.

But Marinho held him back and walked the length of the corridor with him, arm in arm, bending towards him, talking urgently.

'But when do you need it?' asked Dâmaso.

'If possible, tomorrow,' replied Marinho. 'I'll drop by your house. I do apologise, but I'm really strapped for cash . . . And it's all a complete fuss about nothing. It could only ever happen here. A hotel in France would never pester a gentleman, a person known to them, for the miserable sum of 62,000 *mil réis*. Ridiculous! So tomorrow it is, eh? And we'll go and see that woman at the end of the next act. And, remember, don't hold back!'

He rubbed his hands vigorously, laughing silently, then, with a bow, went back into the box belonging to the Viscountess de Rosarim, 'our virtuous beauty', as he called her.

Dâmaso returned to the circle triumphant; he eyed Madame de Molineux as if taking possession of her, and began putting on his gloves. Leaning towards Vítor, he said:

'Marinho's going to introduce me!'

And he told Vítor that she was a countess from Paris and very chic! And she was Portuguese too! Who would think it? 'What a woman, though. I'd give her anything she wanted!'

He was very sure of himself. Generally speaking, he was thought to be a bit of a dandy and people said of him: 'That lucky devil Dâmaso is never without a woman!' A fat actress from the Teatro Príncipe Real, a magician's assistant, had tried to kill herself by eating the heads of matches, and all because of him. He was much in demand amongst the Spanish girls, and his sentimental curriculum vitae even included an aristocratic episode in Sintra, where he was caught in flagrante with the Countess de Aguiar in the Capuchin monastery. The countess was, and still is, like a dish served at table, which you received from the person on your right and passed to the

24

person on your left. Since then, Dâmaso had looked women straight in the eye, pulling at his beard, and when, at three o'clock each afternoon, he pranced across Largo dos Mártires on his horse, he felt that Lisbon was his to command.

Vítor, who said nothing, now found her even more captivating. She had lived in Paris, he thought, amongst lofty, original beings; she had visited the Tuileries; and the weary, defiling gaze of the old Silent Emperor had doubtless fallen on her beautiful shoulder blades. She had met famous authors, visited notable artists' studios, and everything he had read or heard about Paris clustered around her like a natural adornment, and she became associated vaguely in his mind with the spirit of Dumas *fils*, with Doré's engravings and Gounod's music, with the old generals of the Jockey Club and the refinements of the Café Anglais – the whole wonderful framework of a superior civilization.

Meanwhile, on stage, five grubby women, with inelegantly curled hair and low necklines revealing bony clavicles, were standing in a line shrilly singing to a jerky rhythm:

> Left for dead in the grave,
> I came straight back to life,
> Straight back to life, back to life . . .

Then from the door of the circle, Marinho, on tiptoe, was signalling to Dâmaso. In his haste, Dâmaso stumbled over a child, who started to cry, and knocked the opera glasses out of the hand of an extremely large woman. He was very pale.

An old lady, slumped in her seat behind Vítor, remarked with satisfaction:

'He must have got the colic.'

'It's those sorbets they eat,' muttered her neighbour sourly.

And the five scrawny women standing in a line, once more took up the shrill refrain:

> Left for dead in the grave,
> I came straight back to life,
> Straight back to life . . .

Marinho led Dâmaso into Madame de Molineux's box, introduced him and left discreetly. She bowed her head gracefully and, indicating the Englishwoman, said:

'Miss Sarah Swan.'

Dâmaso bowed again. His face was now bright red.

'Do you speak English?' asked Miss Sarah.

'I learned at school, but I've forgotten it all.'

Miss Sarah bared her teeth in a smile, coughed, and adjusting her glasses, looked back at the stage.

Madame de Molineux turned slightly towards Dâmaso, who asked her hurriedly:

'Are you enjoying yourself?'

'Oh, yes, very much.'

She affected a slight foreign accent.

'Have you seen the operetta before?'

'Yes, I think I have, at the Variétés in Paris, I believe.'

'A very different experience, I imagine,' remarked Dâmaso.

She agreed politely, smiling.

There was a silence. Dâmaso, who had grown still redder, was slowly stroking his beard; sweat was trickling down his back. Then the curtain was lowered, and the interval hubbub started up again. Madame de Molineux withdrew to the back of the box and, as she brushed past Dâmaso, the noble beauty of her person, the rustle of silk, her penetrating perfume, made him bow slightly.

He saw that several pairs of opera glasses were trained on him; he wanted to appear animated, chic, and in an over-loud voice and making a sweeping gesture, he asked:

'Have you been in Lisbon long?'

She conferred with Miss Sarah and said:

'Just five days.'

And Dâmaso, in a sudden verbal flurry, plied her with questions:

Was this her first time in Lisbon?

It was. She had gone straight from Madeira to London and from there to Paris . . .

Did she like Lisbon? 'Very much!' Had she been to the

gardens in the Passeio Público, to the Teatro de Sâo Carlos? 'Yes.' Had she been to Sintra? 'No.'

She was sitting slightly slumped in her chair, her hands in her lap, holding her closed fan. Her hands were slender and white, but strong, as if accustomed to holding the reins of a horse and to an active life.

Dâmaso then offered her his house in Colares, should she wish to visit Sintra. It was a student's house . . . But seeing her slightly surprised look, he blushed and added:

'I myself am living in Lisbon at present; I always spend the winter in Lisbon.'

'I'm sorry,' she said, interrupting him, 'but who's that lady in dark blue opposite us?'

It was the Countess de Val-Moral. Dâmaso pretended he was an intimate friend of hers. 'I could tell you about everyone in Lisbon,' he declared. 'Oh yes, I know absolutely everyone.'

He was growing animated. He mentioned a number of ladies; he thought it witty to speak of scandals; he pointed out a few well-born young men; he spoke of bullfighting; he even imitated the actor Isidoro.

Opening her fan with a weary gesture, she murmured:

'Hm, interesting . . .'

Dâmaso was convinced he was making an excellent impression. He grew excited; he pulled off his gloves; he asked to have a look at her fan. And, leaning on the edge of the box, he half-turned his back on the circle.

'Of all the ladies here,' she was saying, 'the only real lady is the Queen.' Putting one finger to her brow and frowning slightly, she asked: 'Now what family is she from?'

Dâmaso was quick to remind her that the Queen was the daughter of Victor Emmanuel, from the House of Savoy.

'Of course, how silly of me! She's the sister of Humberto. Such a fine young man, don't you think?'

'So people say . . . yes, so everyone says . . .'

'Two years ago in Paris, I often used to go riding with him in the mornings. Isn't it the custom in Lisbon to go riding in the morning?'

27

'It certainly is!'

He then listed his own horses; he had three: one for riding, one for the phaeton, and one for the coupé, at night.

They discussed horseracing. She had been to the Derby, at Epsom. Dâmaso praised the course at Belém. He had heard foreigners say there was no better view from the stands in the world; it was as good as anything anywhere.

'They even speak English at the weigh-in.'

And leaning back, he smoothed his moustache.

Then Madame de Molineux wanted to know who the ladies were in box . . . box 20 in the second row. They were the Spanish girls, who wore camellias in their monstrous coiffures and layers of powder on their small, round faces. There were constant bangings on the door of the box, which would fluster the girls and set them whispering. They would fan themselves furiously and, leaning forward, scrutinise the circle and the stalls with devouring eyes and then, suddenly, for appearance's sake, freeze in ridiculously rigid poses.

Dâmaso looked, smiled, pretended to be embarrassed and then, hoping to be witty, said in mangled French:

'They're the *demi-mondes*.'

'Ah!' And Madame Molineux calmly picked up her opera glasses to get a good look at the Spanish contingent. 'One of them's not bad-looking,' she said.

'Oh, that'll be Lola!' Dâmaso exclaimed involuntarily, then bit his lip and blushed scarlet.

Madame de Molineux merely asked:

'Are there restaurants where one can dine after the theatre, something like the Café Anglais at the Maison d'Or?'

'Alas, no. We're a very backward country. There's Silva's of course, and the Malta.'

'And what mass do people attend?'

Dâmaso recommended the one o'clock mass at the church of Loreto. A lot of people went there.

The Englishwoman had remained silent all this while. Sometimes, for no reason, she would turn to Madame de Molineux and bestow on her a humble smile, or she would peer through her opera glasses at one particular man, before

28

returning to her strict immobility, fixing her dull blue eyes on some point in space. Madame de Molineux yawned.

'I'm afraid I'm rather tired. I got up very early to see off a friend on the ship bound for Brazil.'

'Ah, of course, it left today.'

Then, since the orchestra was tuning up, Dâmaso prepared to leave:

'Your humble servant, madam.'

'I receive visitors at the Hotel Central between two and four,' she said with a curt nod.

Dâmaso returned to the circle, radiant, and dropping into his seat beside Vítor, muttered:

'I've got myself a woman.'

Then, leaning back, he started 'giving her the eye'.

But Madame de Molineux was standing up and, in an instant, she was wrapped in her silk pelisse, the hood again almost covering her face.

Dâmaso leaped to his feet, very agitated.

'Come on,' he said to Vítor, 'come on, man.'

They ran downstairs and stood by the door. The lanterns on the waiting carriage lit the dark street; young lads, each with a cigarette in the corner of his mouth, were also waiting; the colonnade was deserted, its walls plastered with cheap advertisements, offering translation services; in the café, a waiter was leaning against a column, reading a crumpled newspaper by the light of the gaslamp; another waiter was stretched out on one of the marble-topped tables, dozing; and from the back came the monotonous click of billiard balls. Then there was a rustle of silk; it was Madame de Molineux. She was quite tall and the pelisse she wore was very full; picking up the train of her dress, she revealed the lace of her petticoats and the black silk of her stockings.

Dâmaso stepped forward, and they stood chatting at the door while a boy raced desperately down the street, calling for the coachman for the Hotel Central.

Vítor, standing out of the wind, his heart pounding, was fumbling nervously with a cigarette. The whiteness of the petticoat, as well as the woman's noble stature and the lavish embroidery on her pelisse all troubled him as if he were in the presence of some superior being. Dâmaso was swaying back and forth, beating his stick against his trousers; he was apparently talking about the weather; it was a dark night of shivering stars.

But then Madame de Molineux turned and appeared to notice Vítor for the first time; for a moment she rested on him her dark, shining eyes, which seemed even larger beneath her hood. But the boy came running back, out of breath, in the wake of the hotel coupé. Dâmaso bowed and she, on the pretext of getting a better grip on her train, turned again and looked directly at Vítor.

He stood there in suspense, surprised. The carriage door closed and the carriage bore her away.

Dâmaso said to Vítor: 'Let's go and have supper at the Malta, shall we?' And as they walked down the street, he was smugly whistling the march from *Faust*.

Vítor said nothing. He could feel the blood flowing unusually fast in his veins. Carriages were leaving the Teatro de São Carlos, groups of people passed them, women's cloaks gleamed white in the night. And he found Lisbon interesting; he wanted to publish a poem, or be applauded in a theatre and generally be considered an important person.

When they entered the Malta, the waiter approached them, yawning, and turned up the gaslight; a crude, tremulous light struck the walls and the low ceiling; in a bored voice, he asked:

'And what can I do for you, gentlemen?'

Dâmaso was studying himself in the mirror opposite, fiddling with his beard; he felt bohemian, alive and full of energy.

II

When Vítor came down to breakfast the next day at eleven o'clock, his Uncle Timóteo was in the living room, in his armchair by the window which stood open to the luminous morning; he was reading the papers, with one leg curled beneath him, oriental fashion, and the other, which was made of wood, resting on the window sill.

They lived in a third-floor apartment in Rua de São Francisco, a little way down from the Writers' Guild. It was early December and the winter had so far been very dry, the air clean and clear, the skies intensely blue and with plenty of good sun for old men.

Uncle Timóteo was sixty years old; he was small and thin, talkative and enthusiastic. He had dark, mobile features, prominent cheekbones and sparkling eyes, a white mane of hair and bold white sideburns which stopped half-way across his cheeks. He was a retired judge and had spent all his working life abroad; he had lived longest in India, where he had lost his leg while out hunting birds, which annoyed him, because – according to him – he should, at the very least, have left his leg in the jaws of a tiger. He had always been more of a soldier than a judge. As a student at Coimbra University, he had been a troublemaker and a fighter, and, later on, in his courtroom, he had often thumped so hard on the table that the dark-skinned native lawyers had turned pale. Wherever he went, he was in permanent conflict with the authorities; he had even given a beating to a secretary-general of India, a peace-loving fellow who wrote odes and suffered with his digestion. But people respected his severe brand of honesty because, beneath that impetuous exterior, he was also extremely kind and compassionate and even susceptible to certain finer feelings.

He was a great supporter of the underdog and would ride to the rescue as boldly as any paladin. A nursemaid shaking a child in the street, a carter tyrannizing an ox, a boy scalding a

31

cat would immediately find Uncle Timóteo bearing down upon them, with his thunderous voice and his silver-tipped cane.

His wife, an excellent lady from Macau, had left him eighty *contos*, which, he said, meant that he could afford to keep both a carriage and a nephew. He gave all his love to Vítor and all his admiration to England; he subscribed to *The Times* and read it from cover to cover. His main companion was a dog, an English retriever called Dick. Timóteo was an early riser, a believer in cold baths, as well as an inveterate smoker of pipes and drinker of grog. He hated priests and said that any young man of twenty-five who had neither a wife nor a mistress was not to be trusted.

'Who's this Princess of Breppo, then?' he asked irritably when Vítor came into the room; he was peering severely at the local paper through his horn-rimmed pince-nez.

'Why? What do they say about her?'

Timóteo read:

'"We have just returned from the Teatro da Trindade, where the benefit performance, etc. etc.". . . here we are . . . "In one particular box was a very beautiful foreign lady, whom some declared to be the Princess of Breppo."'

'No, that's what people were saying, but it wasn't true. She's a French lady, Madame de Molineux."

'These papers are nothing but gossip-sheets,' complained Timóteo.

Vítor went over to the window, yawning. He had slept badly. He had left the Malta at two o'clock, and with his mind troubled and his belly still full of food, he had dreamed all night of Madame de Molineux, but mixing her with characters from Michelet's *History of the French Revolution*, which he was reading at the time, and snatches of Tennyson's poetry. He was in a street in the Bairro Alto, and someone was trying to introduce him to Madame de Molineux, but just as they were about to shake hands, something would push roughly past, separating them. First, it was Sir Galahad of the Round Table in his silver armour, a white feather in his helmet and a lily on his shield, who passed by saying: 'I am strong because I am pure: I am searching for the Holy Grail and I destroy all shameful loves.'

Then it was a flock of very white sheep with fleecy backs, crushed together and bleating sadly, smelling of the meadow. And he and she stretched out their arms over the sheep, but their hands did not meet. Then, again, they were just about to embrace when a cart came trotting loudly down the narrow street; people were crowding round it, shouting, and, jolting about in the cart were three men, their heads held high; one was Camille Desmoulins, who kept crying out: 'Lucile! Lucile!'; another was Danton, smiling proudly; and the third was his father, whom he knew only from the portrait in the dining room: a conventionally dressed man with a sepulchral look in his eyes and a lock of a woman's dark hair clutched to his chest.

Vítor stretched, worn out by his dreams. A canary in a cage hanging in the window, started singing stridently.

'Be quiet!' bawled Timóteo.

The canary fell silent. And Timóteo, got to his feet, his wooden leg dragging on the floor.

'Honestly, the poor creature has no millet and no water. Clorinda!' he yelled.

A brisk, chubby woman appeared.

'It's eleven o'clock and these birds have had no fresh water and no food. Sort it out at once, Clorinda. And bring us some food.'

Going over to the table, leaning on his stick, with the newspaper still in his hand, he said:

'So she wasn't a princess, eh? As if she would be. What do they know!' And he glanced at the paper again, shaking it. 'This is supposed to be a newspaper. It's got articles, reports, reviews: Special Tariff No.1 has been approved. A boarding school boy, Master someone-or-other, was dismissed from school. It seems that so-and-so wants to stand in Mirandela as a conservative. Someone else is auctioning off his pawnbroking business. A proposal put forward by the cattle-dealer Fernandes João was accepted by the council of Vila Nova de Famalicão, etc. etc. It's extraordinary. Everything is there, including two columns listing 'arrivals and departures': he died for love . . . Idiots! And I haven't had a copy of *The Times* for three whole days. Call this a country! Clorinda, surely those eggs have boiled by now!'

He had placed his stick between his knees, tied his napkin round his neck and was feeding toast to Dick, who was sitting beside him, staring longingly up at him, his tail beating against the floor. Then Uncle Timóteo, looking at Vítor, said:

'What the devil's up with you, man? You look positively yellow! What time did you get in last night? What time did you hear him come in, Clorinda?'

The excellent woman smiled and said:

'He came in at two o'clock, sir, and then he sat up reading.'

'He'll ruin his health!' exclaimed Uncle Timóteo, banging his knife on the edge of his plate. 'You'll be a hunched old man before your time! You'll wear yourself out, man. By thirty-five, you'll have crow's feet, a hunchback, problems with your kidneys and you'll just gaze at women from afar, having completely lost all interest.'

Vítor laughed: 'I was reading about what your friends, the feudal lords, abbots and bishops used to do to the serfs before the revolution: beatings, torture, hangings, terrible.'

'That was quite wrong,' growled Timóteo. 'The serf, the worker, is a man like us and deserves respect. Now, if they were Blacks or Indians . . .'

Vítor protested, scandalised. The Indians were a noble race!

'Rubbish! Anyone who calls an Indian a man, has either never seen a man or never seen an Indian! I was there at the Goa rebellion, leading regiments . . . It's odd, you know, I could have taken the whole of India with just two men each armed with a stick! Look at the English. A handful of police against millions of men. It's a question of nutrition, my dear boy. What can people who live on watery rice do against hulking great soldiers who dine on roast beef? Why, bend the knee!'

Vítor had only very vague political beliefs. He hated the Spaniards crushing Cuba and the rebels in Managua, the Tsar whipping Poland into submission and the English punishing Ireland, that Celtic land of bards. He shrugged and said:

'Tyrants!'

'Tyrants!' exclaimed Timóteo, his eyes flashing. 'Do you know, sir,' (whenever he got into any heated discussion about colonial politics with Vítor, he always addressed him as 'sir'), 'do you know what they've achieved in India? They created everything! Cities, railways, bridges, docks, navigable rivers, plantations. Before, when there was famine in India, they would die in their millions! And now they never lack for rice because the Englishman is there to give it to them.'

But Vítor considered the Indians to be more poetic than the English. He talked about idealism, about their architecture, their marvellous poetry.

'Poetry? Rubbish! You should go and see the cotton business in Calcutta and Bombay! Now that's real poetry! When all they had were their poems, they lived in the fields and went around naked. And now they're well housed and well fed. When the English first went there, they found the people covered in lice, and the Indian louse, my boy, is a creature this size.'

He indicated the tip of his finger.

'Uncle please!' exclaimed Vítor, pushing his plate away with a grimace of disgust.

'What's wrong, man? Nothing in nature is disgusting. A man should be able to talk about anything and eat anything. I'll tell you something. Between the ages of twenty-four and twenty-five, I breakfasted every morning on snake soup. Excellent stuff. For a whole year . . . when I had pleurisy.'

Vítor looked at him, fascinated:

'You had pleurisy?'

Timóteo mumbled, looking down at his plate:

'Yes, I did succumb . . . once . . . when I was in love.'

Vítor laughed out loud.

'Even better! But who with, Uncle?'

'Bring the coffee, Clorinda. And my tobacco.' Then slowly removing his napkin, he went on: 'When I say 'in love', I mean 'infatuated'. It wasn't love. I was over it in two months. But it was the one great romance of my life – I've had nothing more to do with romance since, not even in books.'

'But who were you infatuated with, Uncle?' asked Vítor, interested, his elbows on the table, a vague smile on his lips.

'With your mother.'

Vítor was astonished. Timóteo dropped his last bit of meat into Dick's eager mouth.

'Your mother was fourteen then. But she was so tall and strong, and with such long, long, hair, she looked more like twenty-two. She was damnably beautiful! You wouldn't know, since there's no portrait of her. But, God, she was lovely. She lived next door.' He smiled. 'How time passes! She kept two blackbirds in a cage at her window. And there was a song we used to sing then:

> A pretty blonde girl sits at her window
> Tending her two little birds.

The moment I'd see her at the window, I'd start singing that song. I think that's why she took against me.'

Clorinda came in with the coffee. Uncle Timóteo spent a long time stirring in his sugar and then lighting his pipe. Finally, he leaned back and said:

'I'd get annoyed, she'd get annoyed, I started to fall in love with her and she couldn't stand the sight of me. And that is when my infatuation began. She did everything she could to dissuade me. Slammed the window on me, turned her back, hid from me behind her sunshade. She was an insolent, cruel little devil! One night, I'll never forget it, I had the ill-fated idea of serenading her in Spanish. There was a Spanish song that was popular at the time:

> *Señorita, usted que tiene*
> *Amarilla la cola . . .*

I stood underneath her window with my guitar, I used to play the guitar then, quite well actually, because one thing I've never lacked, thank God, is confidence . . . and I started strumming away and singing:

36

Señorita, usted que tiene
Amarilla la cola . . . .

The window opened and a little voice said: "Is that Senhor Timóteo?" You can imagine how I felt. I immediately started working out how I would climb up to her balcony. It was dark, in the middle of winter, and very cold. "Is that you, sir?" "Yes, my love, it's me!" "Here you are, then!" And she emptied a bucket of dirty water over me. Can you believe it? "That'll cool you off!" shouted the voice from above, the voice of that shame . . . of your mother, Joaquina.'

'And did it cool you off, Uncle?' asked Vítor, engrossed and surprised, his eyes fixed on the old man.

'It certainly did, I caught pleurisy! I spent two months in bed getting over it. That's where the snake soup came in. It was considered a sovereign remedy for tuberculosis in my day, and I think it still is in Trás-os-Montes. As soon as I recovered, I applied to go abroad and I embarked on the *Santa Quitéria*. The captain was from Tondela, a short, red-haired chap, but very brave. No sooner had we crossed the bar, than a storm hit us! I thought we were lost. The waves! I can see him now, in his oilskin hat, boots up to his knees, slithering about on the deck, shouting, and the waves pounding the boat. I was clinging on to one of the masts. He saw me and bawled out: "Get away from there, you pathetic devil!" After that, we were the best of friends. And within a month, I was cured and hauling in the jib with the best of them. I'd forgotten all about my infatuation. But that's the way we were then. Not like men nowadays.'

'And what happened then?' asked Vítor.

'Then? Nothing. After that, your father went to Coimbra, saw her, as I had, at the window, feeding her birds, and he sang her the same song. I don't know if he tried serenading her too, but he didn't get a bucket of water thrown over him, he got her father's blessing instead, and they were married . . . and then you made your appearance in this vale of tears, a real vale of tears as it turns out . . .,' he added solemnly, falling silent.

'And my mother died a year later.'

Timóteo studied his pipe for a moment, then said slowly:

'Yes, a year after you were born, she fell ill. She went to the Pyrenees with your father and . . . never came back.'

Then, after clearing his throat loudly, he got up, leaning on his stick, mumbling:

'That's the way things are in this hellhole of a world!'

The clock in the living room struck midday.

'Oh no, I promised I'd be in the office by eleven!' said Vítor. He got up and stretched. 'Well, I've certainly learned a few things this morning. There's so much I don't know about our family.'

And after lighting another cigarette, he went out, adjusting the buckle at the back of his waistcoat, while Timóteo, slumped in his armchair, was muttering:

'Yes, there's a lot you don't know.'

Timóteo stayed sadly smoking his pipe, glancing up now and then at the portrait in oils of Vítor's father that hung on the wall. He had a long, pale face, a high, white forehead, long hair, a long, black moustache covering the corners of his mouth, and he was wearing a black satin cravat. It was painted in 1846 or 1847, years of great civil unrest in Portugal and the time of his unfortunate marriage. What a shock for Timóteo when he got the news in Angola that his brother Pedro had married Joaquina. 'The fool!' he had exclaimed, screwing up the letter and thumping the table. Timóteo had the greatest respect for his brother: he was so intelligent, so brave, such a gentleman. And he was going to marry Joaquina, Maria Silvéria's daughter, to whom he, Timóteo, had said: 'If you come to Oporto with me, I'll set you up in a house and give you an allowance of two *meias-moedas* a month.'

It's true she had thrown a bucket of water over him, but there were people in Guarda, Telmo Santeiro amongst them, who had seen a second lieutenant in the cavalry climb up to her window one snowy night. And his brother was marrying her! Stupid fool! Such a fine lad too; he had written that lovely short poem, *Night in the Cemetery*. And then, one morning, a year and a half later, when Timóteo was breakfasting on his usual beef stew, the black servant announced: 'There's a gentleman to see you, sir.'

The 'gentleman' was his brother Pedro, all dressed in black. 'Has Joaquina died?' Timóteo had exclaimed. 'No, she ran away,' said Pedro, without so much as a tremor. Two Africans came in carrying two trunks. Pedro drank a large cup of coffee and told Timóteo his story. After he and Joaquina were married, they went to Lisbon. In Guarda, she would always be Maria Silvéria's daughter; in Lisbon, no one would know her. They lived in Rua do Crucifixo, and opposite them lived a young man, a Spanish emigré. One morning, two months after the baby was born, even before he had been baptised, Pedro had gone off hunting alone and when he came back, he found a note in Joaquina's large handwriting: 'Goodbye. Forget me; my destiny is carrying me far away.' And that was all. The servant and nursemaid said their mistress had left at midday with a small bundle of clothes. 'During those first rather bitter moments,' he went on, 'I made all the necessary arrangements. I took the baby to Aunt Doroteia's house; poor thing, how she cried when I told her what had happened, how she clung to the "little angel" who bestowed a period of unexpected motherhood on her old age. I had him baptised. His mother had wanted to call him Caetano, but I called him Vítor. It was our father's name. To the maid – an emptyheaded girl from the Algarve – I gave a bit of money which she tied up in a handkerchief and took to her husband in Olhão. She never knew what had really happened; the nursemaid stayed with the baby and, a few days later, I left for Madrid. This wasn't some kind of hunt, of course. I spent a few gloomy days and hours in Madrid, in a gloomy room in La Fonda de la Nobleza. Every Spanish cape that brushed my shoulder, every "*caramba*" I heard, made my pulse beat faster. From Madrid, I wrote to a few friends in Guarda – the Magalhães and the Vaz family – to tell them I was leaving for the Pyrenees with my wife, who was ill, poor thing . . . And I went to the Pyrenees, where I spent eight months fishing for trout in the Gave river; odd, eh? At last, I wrote again to the Vaz family and to the Magalhães, etc. to tell them my wife had died. In fact, for me, she was dead. I doubt they gave the matter much thought, what with the political upheavals at the time. They probably said: "Lucky Ega!" I went back to Lisbon. The little boy had one tooth by then and was weaned. The nursemaid, a sweet girl, silent and strong as a tree, had died. But I began to grow bored with the city; I got on a ship bound for Africa and here I am.' 'To do what?' Timóteo had asked. 'Anything. Perhaps just to catch a fever.' 'He still loves her,' Timóteo had thought then.

Pedro had brought some money with him, but he got into some unprofitable business deals; he spent his time studying plants, he learned how to stuff birds and he began drinking spirits. The doctor, who lived in Luanda, restless as a caged cat, warned him: 'My friend, once you start drinking spirits, that's it, you'll be buried in this godforsaken place.' One night, Pedro and Timóteo had gone for a walk outside the city. Timóteo had never forgotten that night; the huge African stars, innumerable as dust; the silent sea gleaming phosphorescent in the dark; gusts of woodsmoke in the air and the smell of hot, humid lands . . . 'Listen,' Pedro said suddenly. 'I don't want my son to know what his mother did. It's quite enough that I should bear that shame. As far as he and everyone else is concerned, she's buried in a cemetery in Barèges. Aunt Doroteia, the dear woman, certainly won't tell him, and his nursemaid is dead. The other maid is too stupid and, besides, she's living somewhere in the back of beyond in the Algarve. Give me your word of honour you won't tell him.'

Timóteo had given his word of honour. 'Another thing,' said Pedro, 'I don't want him to bear the same name as his mother. She's known as Joaquina da Ega, and she can keep the name; it's an easy name for foreigners to pronounce; it's her name and a good one. But for myself and my son, the name Ega doesn't exist. It's a dirty name. Joaquina never knew this, but I baptised him with our other family name, one we never use: da Silva. Vítor da Silva, son of Pedro da Silva.' He stopped, placed his hand on Timóteo's shoulder and said in a low, hesitant voice: 'Will you call yourself Timóteo da Silva?'

Timóteo had cleared his throat. 'Ega is my father's name!' he muttered. 'Look, Timóteo,' Pedro had said, 'I'm not going to live much longer. Do it for me.'

Timóteo had struck the trunk of a coconut palm with his walking stick so hard it set the whole tree swaying. 'Damn that Joaquina woman!' he said. 'All right, Timóteo da Silva it is.' 'Thank you,' said Pedro, 'now we'd better get back, I'm starting to feel cold.'

And within a matter of days, he was dead from a fever. His body was taken to the old São Jacinto cemetery. A smooth stone and a cross marked his grave. He was thirty-three. That night, a windy night, Timóteo went to visit his grave; he walked around it, spitting and cracking his knuckles; then, looking down at the gravestone, he said out loud in the silence: 'Damn the woman!'

He went back to Lisbon. Vítor was four by then and already a proper person. His Aunt Doroteia would watch him running about and she would weep. That winter was a hard one, and Aunt Doroteia died of a cold. 'God, they're all leaving me!' exclaimed Timóteo angrily. 'What a life!'

Since he had to go to India as a judge, he had left the lad with his friend, Gouveia Teles, an old widower, who lived in Almada where he did good works and read Horace.

It was at that time, when they were selling off Aunt Doroteia's furniture, that he received a letter from Spain, addressed to Senhor Pedro Ega, c/o Dona Doroteia de Ataíde, Rua da Oliveira, 50 or 60. He opened it and found two lines written on blue paper: 'Your wife is dead and was buried this morning in the cemetery in Oviedo.'

'And a good job too. So that's one episode over and done with. Time to start afresh.'

And he had embarked for India on the *Trafalgar*.

By the time he came back, Vítor had finished school. Timóteo had got married in India, been widowed and lost his leg on a tiger hunt. 'I was shooting birds really,' he told Teles, 'but I say "tiger hunt" to impress the boy.' The boy went to live with him, much to old Gouveia Teles' distress, who muttered: 'Honestly, Timóteo, you give me the boy one minute, then just take him away the next.' But old Teles was very old, and he died a year later, suddenly, as he was sitting by the window reading 'Ode to Célia'.

At around that time, when Vítor was at university in Coimbra, Timóteo saw a most unusual announcement in the paper: 'Anyone knowing anything about Pedro da Ega is asked to leave their name and address at the Hotel da Europa, as well as a time when they can be contacted. Ask for Mr A. Fornier.'

Surprised, Timóteo sent a visiting card to the Hotel da Europa and the following day, at the appointed hour, Mr Fornier came into his living room. He was a large, plump man with prosperous, rosy skin, a fringe of blonde beard and two ringlets of hair over his ears; he wore gaiters made of yellow drill and minced about on tiny feet shod in shoes polished to such enamel perfection you could see the furniture reflected in them. He placed his tall white hat, with a very curly brim, on a chair and bending slightly at the hips, said in an odd, garbled Portuguese: 'Have I the pleasure of meeting Senhor da Silva?'

Timóteo conceived an immediate hatred for this person. He cleared his throat and growled: 'Yes, I'm Timóteo da Silva.'

The plump gentleman smiled and slowly rubbed his hands. 'Perfect. Could the gentleman inform me about . . .,' he rummaged in his pockets, pulled out a notebook, perched a pair of gold-rimmed pince-nez on his nose and read, 'about Pedro da Ega, of Guarda, married and since widowed.'

Timóteo fixed him with a glittering eye. 'Who wants to know and why?'

The plump gentleman bowed and, with one hand on his chest, said: 'I am not authorised . . .'

'Right then, you'd better leave this instant, my friend.'

With his eyebrows arched, his lower lip stuck out, the man stared down at his own polished shoes, and muttered: 'Really, really . . .' He went to pick up his hat. 'Listen, my French friend,' Timóteo said, 'Senhor Pedro da Ega died in Luanda. If you need a death certificate, write to the parish of São Jacinto.'

The man was scribbling rapidly, joyfully, in his notebook. 'Perfect, perfect! Could you, sir, also inform me about a small child . . .'

Timóteo, who was looking at him, arms folded, exclaimed: 'The small child died too. The whole bloody family kicked the bucket!'

'Most unfortunate, most unfortunate!'

'But, since I'm answering your questions,' said Timóteo, 'I think the least you could do is tell me who sent you, who wants to know . . .'

The man methodically put his glasses away and said that Timóteo was most kind. He was a buyer of antique china and Gothic furniture. And when his friend, his very good friend Lord Lovaine, had learned he was coming to Portugal, he had charged him with finding out about Pedro da Ega. As far as he could tell, Lord Lovaine had met him, probably while he was travelling. 'Yes, they must have met in the Pyrenees,' mumbled Timóteo. Then out loud: 'I thought the interested party might be Joaquina dos Melros.'

The well-fed gentleman opened wide, astonished eyes. 'No, Lord Lovaine, Lord Lovaine!' he said, smiling. 'Right, then, if you require nothing further . . .,' said Timóteo.

The man gave two tugs on the lapels of his blue suit and recited, in one breath, in a rather more practised Portuguese: 'If you have any vases from India, porcelain from China or Japan, leather chairs, Arabian chests of drawers, carved bed-steads, ivory, Renaissance cribs, chests, satin bedspreads, tapestries, which you would be interested in converting into cash . . .'

Timóteo interrupted him: 'All I have is this walking stick, now, goodbye.'

The plump gentleman stopped dead, scratched his beard in various places with one finger, then picked up his hat, and left, muttering: 'Really, really . . .!'

That was the last time Timóteo had heard Pedro da Ega's name. But why should he remember all that today?

'What's done is done,' he murmured, filling his pipe again and stroking the dog's muzzle.

III

A few days later, at 18 Rua de São Bento, Uncle Timóteo was leaving the second-floor apartment of Colonel Stephenson, an old English friend of his, who had enlisted with the Portuguese army after the war of 1832. The colonel was a robust old man, a great drinker of brandy and teller of anecdotes, who still spoke Portuguese with a strong English accent. Timóteo visited him often, since the colonel's gout prevented him straying far from his huge armchair, his 'shell' as he called it, and they would sit and smoke large pipefuls of tobacco together, discuss politics, social mores and English cuisine, drink a bottle of brandy between them and remember the past, occasionally uttering a few of their favourite oaths.

As Uncle Timóteo was making his slow way down the last flight of stairs, his wooden leg thudding on each step, a little girl of about eighteen months, very plump and blonde and precariously balanced on chubby, red legs, came tottering across the courtyard on her own, squealing with laughter and waving her arms in the air, her tiny fists tight shut.

Through a side door off the courtyard was a mercer's shop; the child's mother, a kind, healthy, cheerful young woman, who owned the shop and was known to Timóteo, had doubtless become distracted for a moment and allowed the little one to wander out into the courtyard alone. Just then, Timóteo heard the sound of horses' hooves departing, and saw a tall, blonde woman, Madame de Molineux, come hurrying into the courtyard, with the black train of her riding habit draped over her arm. A white veil on her hat covered her face, and she wore a bunch of violets in a buttonhole in her bodice.

As she was crossing the courtyard, heading straight for the stairs, the child teetered unsteadily into her path. Madame de Molineux impatiently kicked her to one side; the child fell face first, her hands outstretched, and lay on her belly on the flagstones, screaming and unable to get up.

Madame de Molineux had moved on. A woman rushed

out from the shop, scooped the child up in her arms and ran back in with her, covering her with kisses.

Madame de Molineux was already on her way up the stairs, when Timóteo, who was just two steps down from her, said, frowning:

'You'd have to have a heart of stone to kick a child.'

Madame de Molineux stopped dead; beneath her veil, her face had flushed scarlet, but, turning round, she said in a cold, cutting tone:

'Are you addressing me?'

Timóteo, standing very erect, also turned round:

'Who else would I be talking to? Is that any way to treat a child who can barely walk? If I were the child's mother, I'd give you a good slap!'

Madame de Molineux instinctively raised her whip. Timóteo's eyes were now fixed on hers, with a strangely insistent, increasingly angry look in them.

'You insolent man!'

At that, Timóteo coloured and said slowly, with his cane at the ready:

'Call the man of the house, if there is one; tell him to arm himself to the teeth and come out here right now.'

Madame de Molineux looked at him, shrugged and muttered:

'You're mad.'

But Timóteo shouted up at her:

'I don't know who you are, madam, but one thing's certain, you're no lady!'

And with that he stormed off. Still shaking, he scrambled into his carriage and struck the floor repeatedly with his cane. Yet, despite the storm of anger roaring inside him, he was thinking: 'Now where the devil have I seen that face before?'

As soon as the maid opened the door, Madame de Molineux strode across the entrance hall, revealing black, ankle-length breeches beneath her skirt. With the train of her riding habit still draped over one arm and her whip clutched angrily in her hand, she rushed over to the living room window; she wanted to see the man who had insulted her, but the carriage had already pulled away and she saw only the back of the driver, with his hat pulled down over his ears.

She threw her whip down on a chair and unfastened her hat; her hands, in their suede gloves, were still trembling slightly; she took a few agitated steps about the room. The close-fitting, black riding habit emphasised the line of her bust, the curve of her slender, supple waist, the slightly lascivious tilt of her hips. Anger made her already tall figure seem even taller; there was a cold glint in her dark eyes, and beneath her face powder, her cheeks were blazing. She stopped pacing, hurled down her gloves and, going into her bedroom, shouted:

'Mélanie!'

She had rented the apartment fully furnished, and her bedroom had the mean banality of a hotel: the rug by the dressing table was worn with use; the drapes around the bed were made from thin, cheap cotton, and the other curtains in the room were of blue rep, bleached and faded by the sun; and there was a crack in the ceiling plaster. However, just as an artist, with a little skilful shading, can lend charm and originality to a banal lithographed figure, so Genoveva had succeeded in making her room seem rich and interesting, simply by adding here and there a few refined, luxurious touches. A magnificent plaid coverlet lay across the bed; the linen sheets bore her bold monogram and a countess's coronet, both embroidered in scarlet silk; her sumptuous lace nightgown was folded away in a blue satin case; the gold tops of various glass bottles glinted on the chest of drawers; on a round table covered by an ugly bit of felt cloth, cheaply dyed, lay a snakeskin blotter bearing a silver crest, as well as an elegant paper knife and fine writing paper with an expensive watermark; on the dressing table, in boxes lined with cherry-red velvet, was the bright steel of her scissors, the gleam of tweezers and the golden brown of tortoiseshell combs; a pair of long, buttoned, pale suede gloves had been flung casually down; some lace hose overflowed from a drawer crammed with silk stockings, so light they might blow away; and wafting on the air, like her personal signature, was the vague, subtle aroma of opulence, of opoponax and Tanglewood.

'Mélanie!' she shouted impatiently. 'Where were you? Come and help me undress!'

And she began unbuttoning her riding habit, her fingers still trembling with rage.

Mélanie was twenty-five and came from Plancus, in Provence, but all she retained of that hot land, where the blood burns, were her dark, avaricious eyes and the supple, sensual movements of her tall, skinny body. Paris, where she had rolled about like a pebble on a river bed, had smoothed, polished, refined and perfected this tall, handsome girl, who had arrived, some years before, weeping bitterly, having left her family and run away with a Catalan. Now she had a slim, expressive, bold nose, dry lips which she constantly moistened with her tongue, hips as narrow as a boy's, and a light, quick step. She had led a complicated life: after the Catalan, she had moved on to a Carlist, who had been followed in turn by a Brazilian. For many years, she had worked as a maid in the gloomy Hotel Português do Meio-Dia de Pernambuco in Rue Lafayette; then she had got lost in the depths of Paris, where she had lived in one miserable garret after another and danced frenetically in dance halls, where she was paid for her pains by some and cheerfully beaten by others.

She had been passed on to Genoveva by the mother of Madame de P., a Portuguese *cocotte* married to a German who had been governor of Metz in 1870. Mélanie had been trained by Madame de P. and she was an excellent chambermaid, astute, clean and discreet, and she spoke Portuguese as if she were a native of Lisbon, apart from a slight Brazilian lilt picked up from her days at the Hotel Pernambuco.

Genoveva had got into the habit of always speaking to her in Portuguese, the better to confide in her, for she had no secrets from Mélanie, indeed, she poured out to her, as if into a bucket of dirty water, whatever passed through her head, however evil, outrageous or immoral. Mélanie adored her; she even felt rather attracted to Genoveva, with her lovely figure, for Mélanie was becoming more of a sensualist with each night that passed, rather as a drunk grows drunker with each fresh glass of wine; a kind of greedy hysteria dulled her eyes; not that these libidinous preoccupations prevented her from zealously carrying out her duties. She was an excellent maid of vice, for she was the soul of discretion, treated Genoveva's clothes as devoutly as a sacristan would the vestments of a priest, and had a real gift for duplicity and pretence; there was no one like her when it came to putting off a pressing creditor or an importunate lover. Her small, pink tongue, so prodigal in Provençal words, could produce a lie as naturally as it produced saliva. She was also very careful with money, an invaluable quality in a chaotic household, for she would scrutinise the cook's accounts, question her about prices and haggle over every last penny. She combined the suspicious nature of a policeman and the acuity of a second-hand dealer. With her small feet, her feline gait, like that of a cat on heat, she would bustle about in her bonnet, darting lewd glances, coming and going, telling lies, sorting things out, gulping down large glasses of water, eating almost nothing and using men like the most refined of gluttons, first one, then another and another and another, sometimes several at the same time, though she never mixed them up, savouring in each man some particular pleasure: this one she liked for his twinkling eyes, that one for his honed muscles, others for their sheer talent for debauchery. Of love she would say: 'Ça c'est de la fichue blague et v'là!' It was just a lot of hot air.

Genoveva was shocked to learn that during their last year in Paris, Mélanie had had eleven men! Renaming her Mélanie the Maneater, she took her unreservedly into her confidence.

Genoveva was sitting on the bed, her admirably white neck and arms bare. Her pampered skin, subject to a regime of milk and ice water, seemed to absorb the light like the bold, fresh petals of a camellia; her rounded legs glowed palely like burnished ivory; her arms were slender, vigorous, with something marmoreal and sculptural about them, their milky softness and firm muscles betraying a sensual vigour. Her neck too was proud, strong, noble, and the two globes of her full breasts, visible beneath her camisole, had a robust, virginal firmness.

She stretched out her feet to Mélanie, who removed her mistress' boots and the tight underbreeches she wore for riding; then Genoveva donned a long robe in dark silk and put her feet, encased in black silk stockings, in a pair of blue velvet slippers.

'Here I am, all alone, with no husband, no son, no brother, no one!'

'Whatever's wrong, madam?' asked Mélanie, puzzled, folding her thin arms.

'I should have taken my whip to his face!'

And she told the astonished Mélanie about how Timóteo had insulted her. An old man, with a wooden leg and a carriage and a filthy old driver . . . he looked quite mad . . . and he had taken it upon himself to tell her off, and all over some child she had pushed out of way because it was getting tangled in her skirts. The brute had been coming down the stairs just as she was coming up.

'He'd probably been to see the English colonel. I've bumped into him before, the other day, in fact; Senhor Dâmaso was going down the stairs with him. Yes, the wooden leg, the carriage . . . I'd say that's him all right.'

'Senhor Dâmaso is an ass,' Genoveva said, getting to her feet and nervously fastening the silk buttons on her robe. 'Bring me the bottle of gin, Mélanie, and some water. Where's the Englishwoman?'

'She's in her room, madam.'

Mélanie bustled about nearby, her shoes creaking slightly as she crossed the carpet.

Genoveva, reclining in her armchair, was slowly drinking her gin. She seemed gradually to grow calmer. She lit a cigarette, blew out the smoke and relaxed, her legs crossed; her pale, rather narrow brow grew smooth, serene; she stretched and said:

'I went for the most stupid ride today, along some ghastly road, all walls and gardens!' She raised her eyes to heaven, exasperated. 'And that bore, Dâmaso, he's such an imbecile, such a fool!'

Putting her glass down on the table, she got up, her eyes suddenly hard and dark:

'I feel like catching the next boat straight back to Paris! Stupid country, stupid people, stupid life!'

Mélanie made some comment about the climate and the city.

'Oh, shut up and go away. I hate you. I hate everyone. Tell the Englishwoman to go into the living room and play the piano. After all, that's what I pay her for. And pour me some more gin.'

Mélanie hesitated:

'You know lately, madam, you've been drinking far too much. It's terribly bad for the skin.'

'Don't you start preaching at me too!' Genevova yelled. 'I've had quite enough of that for one day. Go on, Mélanie, hurry up. Call the Englishwoman.'

She spoke with a brusque, impatient vivacity, in marked contrast to her aquiline face and her statuesque figure, which seemed to indicate a cool, serene temperament. She continued sipping her gin. It was a habit she had acquired in London when she had lived there with Lord Belton amongst the dank, viscous fogs in which everything fades and merges into a dull, dingy, impenetrable ink, and in which the gaslamps are just blurred, muddy points of light. Her southern nature, then, had been gripped by such a terrible sense of ennui that she had got into the habit of drinking gin to keep the cold out of her soul. Then she had convinced herself that gin warmed her temperament and lent a slightly violent, but pleasing madness to sensual excitements; she had continued to use it, but she never got drunk; she drank it with lots of water, but just enough of it to feel a warmer, more intense vitality circulating brightly through every muscle.

But Mélanie's remark had clearly hit home, because Genoveva got up, dabbed her face with a damp towel, picked up an ivory-backed mirror and looked at herself. No, her skin was still soft, white, a little coarse at the sides perhaps, but not a wrinkle in sight; the only thing that betrayed her age was a barely perceptible graininess about her nostrils, like that left by cheap face powder. Her forehead was still smooth and unlined, and despite her thirty-nine years, her durable beauty was still at its peak; she just needed a little colour on her lips sometimes, when she feared they might look cracked.

She would be beautiful until she was forty-five, 'with the help of plenty of cold water and a little peace of mind', she thought, smiling.

At that point, however, Mélanie came in with a piece of paper in her hand; it was from a man wanting money for the hire of the carriage.

Genoveva was furious. Why hadn't she put him off? What right had creditors to come bothering her like that? And seeing Mélanie still holding out the piece of paper to her, she said:

'Take it away! What do I want with that? Why should I pay him? I'd rather die.'

'I just thought that seeing as how you got some money yesterday . . .'

Genoveva stamped her foot.

She had received some money yesterday, but that didn't mean she wanted to spend it. She was amazed at Mélanie, really she was. Was one supposed to line the pockets of thieves? And, her mirror still in her hand, she added:

'You know, Mélanie, you're a different woman since you left France. You've grown positively stupid. It must be the Lisbon air.'

And she leaned back calmly in her chair, as if abstracted, as if mesmerised by the jumble of inner visions that came back to her from her past; they paraded before her, like scenes in a play. She had been prey to such moments of remembrance and meditation ever since she had arrived back in Portugal; and in that nascent habit of looking back, of staring into space, she had experienced for the first time a vague premonition of old age. Her life up until then had been so full, so difficult, so intense, so packed with events, worries and sensations that she had always lived in the excitement of the moment, had concerned herself only with living, but during the enforced quiet of her life in provincial Lisbon, she would sometimes examine her past, rather as a man might climb a tall tower in order to spy out the land.

She would picture herself, delirious with fever, in a sad, ancient town in the north of Spain, in a room in an inn right next to a church, whose bells, which tolled at every hour of the day, came to represent for her the gloomy sound of eternity. She was being tended by an old woman with skin the colour of parchment, and who wore a large tortoiseshell comb in her hair and passed the time laying out cards on the bedside table, by the light of a tall brass oil lamp, in order to divine the fate awaiting her son, who had recently embarked for Manila.

Then, when she was better and able to sit by the window alone, Genoveva would peer out at the sad street with its broad paving stones, at the narrow shutters of the windows opposite, and at the muleteer with a silk scarf tied about his head, who stopped outside the inn, his mules laden with wineskins. Girls would walk briskly past, gesturing or turning languidly, a scarf wrapped tightly about their shoulders; men swathed in cloaks adorned with bands of scarlet velvet would go into the inn, cigarette in mouth; and canonesses, in sweptback veil and curved headdress, would pass by on their way to the cathedral.

Then she was in a village in northern France, near Rouen, in the low house where she had lived with a man she detested, but to whom she was bound by poverty, ignorance of the language and a lack of family. It was winter; every morning the windows would be covered in frost, and she would sit by the stove watching the constant snow or drizzle and the open umbrellas passing by accompanied by the rustic laughter of some villager. At night, her lover would return, ground down by his fate, worn out with visiting the sick in villages and houses; he would eat his soup with his head bowed, casting her an occasional malevolent glance.

When the weather was fine, she would open the window. Opposite, a barber, who wore a frogged jacket edged with astrakhan, and who had a look of the south about him, would be strolling up and down, waiting for customers, staring up at the pale sky; and they would occasionally catch each other's eye, like two exiles, their faces filled by the same longing for sun and hot countries. Then, as darkness fell, she would sit at the piano and play songs from Portugal or Spain, and the village schoolteacher, on his way home from school, hearing those sweet melodies, would stop and listen, stockstill in the street, his textbooks in his hand.

Then she saw herself leaving in a coach, heading for the Pyrenees and another life in Luz: walks along the road to St-Sauveur, across the bridge over the Gave, along an avenue of elms. And there she would stand, watching the foaming torrent gushing forth from the dark rock whose darkness was relieved only by sudden patches of dull green vegetation that grew, dishevelled and wild, along the steep banks; watching the laughing foreigners pass by on sadly trotting donkeys. She found in the broad, open syllables of the mountain patois something of the sweetness of her own language. Would that sad, mean life never end? The whiteness of the snow, the proud beauty of the dark vegetation made her long for cities, for narrow streets flanked by tall buildings; nature bored her, and she yearned for the theatre and for the hubbub of café life.

Then she had met Lord Belton, and she saw herself once more in the lovely house in St John's Wood, London, where she had lived for several years. Every morning, the maid, her plump, red arms all bare, would have to whiten the three front steps; it was summer and the trees in the garden were a sweet, tender green. Cabs would drive silently by over the white, surfaced roads and, beyond, she could hear the vast, unceasing, monotonous hum of London.

There she was out for a gentle morning ride in Hyde Park, trotting over the black, churned-up earth, hearing the creak of new leather on her saddle and watching the grass growing green amongst the solemn trunks of the chestnut trees; or else strolling beneath a pale silver sun in Regent Street with its broad, cream-painted façades on which the gold on black lettering glittered like new. A lively, impatient crowd fills the pavements; there are boats plying the wide river; ranks of carriages progress sedately down the street: landaus occupied by white-haired old men and driven by fat, apoplectic, bewigged coachmen, and slim, speedy coupés that afford an occasional glimpse of a camellia-white profile.

Noisy cabs; huge, packed omnibuses, manned by red-uniformed conductors, meandering down the crowded streets, bearing the tall, black letters of advertisements; phaetons passing by at a nonchalant trot; a serving boy with the blond curls of an angel; tilburies driven at a cracking pace by men with hard features, their minds on money, frowning as they talk, impatient, whip at the ready; then everything stops; people run, women carrying parcels gather up their skirts, open their sunshades, and they all cross the road; the policeman lowers his arm again, and the queues of carriages roll serenely by, the sun glinting on harnesses and silver axles; and on either side, behind the shop façades, jewels glitter in black velvet display cases, glossy lengths of silk fall in rich folds, black or brilliantly coloured; cashmere shawls from India hang from ivory hooks; the colourful ranks of hats, with their fluttering plumage, gesture like rare birds; the velvets lie dark and soft to the touch; in the depths of the shop, prodigious armchairs proffer seats of embroidered satin; Venetian mirrors throw back disparate glittering reflections; and, outside, the harsh voices of newspaper boys bawl out the world's news: the price of shares, the echo of some distant war.

Then she seemed to see London on a rainy night. The rumble of carriages makes the city buzz; the shopwindows grow suddenly blank; thousands of cabs cut through the darkness of the streets with their lanterns, like so many bloodshot eyes; the ginhouses blaze, and drunks stagger out of them; the policemen wield their truncheons to control the crowds; the sound of a post horn announcing the arrival of a coach echoes out above the noise; beneath the portico of the opera house there is the clack of carriage steps being lowered and, inside, the discreet rustle of silk along velvet-floored corridors; the special escort of grenadiers, wearing shakos, stand motionless in one corner; and, in the auditorium, a sudden silence falls; bare shoulders glisten in the light; there is a subdued murmur, a breath of perfume, and the white feathers worn by occupants of the ladies' gallery in the boxes tremble slightly; Patti sings, and the gentlemen, always so correct, silently hold out to their companions programmes printed on shiny, expensive-smelling paper.

Then, it's time to go home, and, by eleven, the city is a vast, darkened room; the tobacconist's windows are lit with bright lights that illuminate the dark cigars within; the oyster bars are open, selling scarlet lobsters and prawns on beds of gently melting ice . . .

Yes, she had grown fond of London . . . and there she had found love. She remembered her escape with cruel George de l'Estrolies, crossing the Channel on a stormy night, she downstairs in the salon, wrapped in a shawl, barely able to speak, in an agony of vomiting; she could hear the waves thudding onto the deck, the siren whining, the captain's calm, husky voice booming out; and it seemed as if the fog would never lift; a mournful bell kept ringing at the prow; and she could hear the siren even when, still queasy, almost asleep in George's arms, she finally arrived in Paris.

Ah, those first days in the Hotel Mirabeau, in Rue de Pau! What bliss! The air seemed sweet to her, buildings smiled, faces beamed, voices cooed; gone was the brute violence of monstruous London; in its place was a charming, small city, full of flowers, sun and perfume, wrapped in blue sky, like a jewel in cotton wool.

Then came the day when he left her − ah, the tears, the jealousy. Like a heroine in a novel, she too had looked longingly down into the Seine and imagined how her corpse would look laid out in the morgue, on the cold, smooth slab, with a tap dripping onto her green, drenched body.

The city which, until then, had seemed so friendly, cheerful, festive, welcoming and easy, now terrified her with its frank egotism, and faces which, before, had seemed to exude a bright serenity, now seemed colder than the façades of the houses; she loathed the sight of the satin-upholstered carriages, while she had to walk along in the mud, in her last pair of shoes; she loathed all those rich foods on sale in the grocery stores, all those silver platters in the restaurants, when she could only afford a bit of bread and sausage. But, like a good Portuguese girl, she prayed every night for Our Lady of Joy to send her a rich man.

Then came the long nights on the boulevards, the search for money, for a *libra*, even twenty *mil-réis*. She would never forget those nights: at first, she would sally forth hopefully: on either side of her, the boulevard was ablaze with the harsh lights from restaurants and cafés and the glint and glimmer of jewels and silks in the shopwindows. The *petite brune* brimmed with eager excitement to see the café tables filling the pavements, the thousand points of light from the carriage lanterns, the glow of the newspaper kiosks, to hear the muffled sound of footsteps running, the occasional blurred chords from a theatre orchestra. Everyone seemed happy, pleased. In the midst of all that money, all that joy, how could one gold coin, just one, fail to fall into her outstretched hand?

She was in no hurry. It seemed to her that all those men were bound to come up and speak to her, but, since she was shy, timid and inexperienced, she did nothing to overcome that shyness; rather, she withdrew into it and sat on a chair beneath the lofty branches of a tree and waited.

The streets full of cafés gradually emptied, and large, bare stretches of pavement appeared, filled only by pools of light from the café windows. At that point, she would get up and walk down the boulevard, but if a man so much as glanced at her, the sense of shame would return, and she would look away, offended and grave-faced. Eventually, the lights in the shops would go out too; the darkness would spread; the plump waiters from the cafés would begin to close their doors; then she felt impatient, a need to act, move, do something; there were fewer carriages now; the last omnibus went by; all the lights were out, and in the deserted streets all that could be heard was the slow step of some *sergent de ville*.

Then she would go in search of her one friend, an English-woman called Miss Maguire, tall and thin as a tree, and with the waxen pallor of the tubercular. Every day, in the morning, she coughed blood; every day, she would get drunk; and then a kind of rage would enter her, a need for disorder, noise, debauchery; she went to bed with men for free, out of despair, her face almost green, the palms of her hands sticky with sweat.

Often she did not eat all day, and she would sit on the benches in the Café Roch, or walk along the Boulevard des Capucines, her hands shaking, her stomach empty, a vague smile on her lips, hoping that someone would invite her to supper, but she would find instead some foreigner with a penchant for cheap French women, who would offer the poor, starving girl only prawns and beer!

At last, though, Our Lady of Joy took pity on Genoveva; the rich man she had been praying for suddenly appeared out of nowhere, as if by magic. She could hardly remember how they had met; her poor brain, grown stupid on hardship, debauchery and gin, scarcely retained any sensations at all, and ideas flowed through her mind like water. But she did meet him, and he took charge of her life. He was the Comte de Molineux, her husband.

She lived with him for twelve years. He was very old and utterly repellent! He made disgusting noises when he ate; the skin on his face was flaccid and wrinkled; he had no teeth; his bald head was tinged with yellow. But, as well as being a cynic and a vile libertine, he was extremely wealthy. He had served every regime, had had a hundred masters: Louis XVIII, Charles X, Louis Philippe, the Republic, the Empire; he so loved authority that he would prostrate himself before anyone who came to power, his tongue lolling out of his mouth, ready to lick the boots of the new arrival, regardless of what was on those boots, be it mud or blood.

He felt a boundless love for the Empire, for it had perfected the two arts crucial to a life of sensuality – cooking and debauchery. And he loved it too for the advantages it brought him: he loved the constitution, the Emperor, the Emperor's son, even the Emperor's dog. The high point of his day was supper, which was served in his bedroom. He would linger over it, grunting as he chewed, licking his fingers, his head lolling and loose, his hands planted on the table, his eyelids drooping, his lips greasy; and she, poor thing, had to be standing by, half-undressed, all fresh and exotically perfumed, just so that he could run his hands, still sticky with sauce, up and down her legs.

Ah, but, otherwise, life was sweet! What she loved most were the evenings spent in the Bois in spring, riding in her calèche drawn by her English horses; she would sit smiling beneath her silk parasol, suffused with a sense of intense well-being, conscious of a vague happiness emanating from everything about her: from the soft night, from the chestnut trees in the Champs-Elysées, from the delicate aroma of face powder, from the fine, polished surface of the lake – a constant happiness, continuous and sweet, that filled her heart the way water fills a sponge.

She lived on Rue de Balzac; she had money invested; her horses were known and recognised. She adopted the reserved manner of a married woman, but received, with extreme caution and a flurry of modesty, a civil servant from the Ministry of Foreign Affairs, the Vicomte de La Rechantaye – just to put a little romance in her life. All dressed in black, carrying her prayer book, like a devout libertine, she would visit him in a hired carriage; she attended the church of St Thomas Aquinas; she was a supporter of the Empire, and never neglected to wear the requisite bunch of violets; she had the air of a well-fed pigeon; she kept an excellent table, and she was proud of her groom, a lad of sixteen, pretty as an angel and so corrupt he was already living with a woman of fifty and had caught an obscene disease so frightful that Dr Ricard had turned pale, fearing it to be some form of the plague passed down from the sixteenth century, from the time of Jubileu. Laughing, she would recount this fact to her female friends, pleased and proud to be the possessor of such a monster.

And all the other ladies envied her. Then came the terrible year of the war. A moment of supreme joy. On the day the Senate voted to go to war, the Comte de Molineux gave a supper; it was one of his happiest days too. She wore her cream dress all sprigged with violets. Her lover, the Vicomte de La Rechantaye, was to accompany the minister who was bearing the declaration of war to Berlin. And when she thought of her beginnings in an obscure, forgotten little town in Portugal, she was filled with pride to find herself there, on that historic day, and to have, round her table, diplomats, two captains eager for the fray, and two senators who, that very morning, by acclamation, had voted for war. How she had talked, in her bad French accent that she never quite lost! Everyone was certain of victory and, with a smug smile, they kept repeating the Emperor's words: 'It's my little war.'

Yes, it was His Majesty's little war, and they all smiled ecstatically, indulgently. Not long afterwards, she and the Count had to pack their bags and flee to Brussels.

There they had spent a bleak winter in a hotel; she learned of the Viscount's death in the battle of St Privats; and when they returned to Paris after the Commune, on the very day when they were to prostrate themselves at the feet of the Republic, the Count suffered an apoplectic fit and fell dead on the carpet, his mouth fixed in a leer, the old reprobate!

And he had made no will; all his property went to some distant nephews in Normandy; and Genoveva was left with her furniture, her jewels and an income of three thousand francs. Poor thing!

For a year, she withdrew into obscurity, living on next to nothing. However, just as poverty seemed about to beckon again, Our Lady of Joy sent her the Brazilian, Gomes. He was extremely wealthy, but skeletally thin, with small, dark eyes, a black beard and skin the colour of morocco leather; he restored Genoveva to her life of luxury; they travelled throughout Europe, as far as St Petersburg; and he offered to take her to Brazil with him. She accepted in a moment of boredom, feeling suddenly too tired to start all over again, and hoping perhaps to marry; but she hated him, she had a horror of his flesh, which the skin disease he suffered from left covered with red blotches; and when they arrived in Lisbon, when she was confronted by that ocean to cross and by the prospect of seasickness, Brazil and continued contact with that odious man, she baulked, like someone who, on touching a piece of meat, feels the bile rising in her throat. The Brazilian, who was perhaps already regretting having made the offer, accepted her change of heart almost gratefully, gave her three hundred *libras* and left.

And so there she was in Lisbon. But for how much longer? She shrugged her shoulders and downed the rest of her gin.

The door opened slowly and Miss Sarah's shrill voice asked: 'Are you decent, my dear?'

Genoveva told her bluntly that she was not. She merely wanted her to play a little music; she would join her in the living room shortly.

Miss Sarah glided through to the living room, sat down on the piano stool, cleaned her glasses on her handkerchief and put them on; then, sticking out her sharp elbows and straining her neck muscles, she began singing in a sour voice, accompanying herself monotonously on the piano:

The last rose of summer . . .

However, when Genoveva still did not emerge from her room, she stopped, looked around her, removed her glasses, and resting her thin, mannish hands in her lap, gave a deep sigh.

In the light of day, her skin seemed coarser and drier, with red blotches on her cheeks and on her long, bony nose; her high, prominent forehead was pale and shiny; she wore her hair combed back from her somewhat receding hairline and coiled around her head.

Her black silk dress seemed to clothe a body of wood, devoid of soft contours. There was something icy and accusing about her hard, cold blue eyes. She poured all the servility imposed on her by necessity into chilly smiles that revealed large, carnivorous teeth.

She was sad. She spoke little, uttering only brief, rather sententious statements. She made vague, enigmatic references to her obscure, mysterious past, occasionally mentioning English names from the world of finance or from the aristocracy, every gesture and look imbued with longing for those illustrious acquaintances. Whenever Genoveva appeared in some unusually sumptuous outfit, Miss Sarah would regard

60

her with a slight shake of the head, her lips pursed, as if remembering luxuries long since lost. Her conversation often grew misty with melancholy longing for the days when she depended on no one and had a house of her own, a home. Otherwise, she had all the blunt reserve of the great British Isles, as she called them. She made herself utterly inaccessible, like some bleak, steep-sided island. She stood very erect and wore a permanently martyred look; her hatred of the Catholic countries she had lived in only accentuated her rigid Protestantism. The most innocent lithograph of saints or of Christ would make her dry lips curl in a sneer of utter scorn for such idolatry. She found everywhere, apart from England, most uncomfortable; the windows never shut properly and every meal upset her stomach. In France and Portugal, it was the French and the Portuguese who were the foreigners; she was never a foreigner, because she was English. She had a secret weakness for alcohol and a vast appetite for childishly sentimental English novels; and when she spoke of men or of love, with the disdainful reserve of an ascetic virgin, she experienced a few murky moments of cold lust.

She detested Genoveva because of her clothes, her affairs, her post-coital pallor, her carriages . . . and, above all, because she received a salary from her. Being the servant of a foreign woman added the bitterness of humiliation to the sadness of poverty. She did not rebel, though, but accepted her fate and meanwhile grew thinner and spoke more frequently of 'duty'.

Genoveva had been Gomes' mistress when she first met Miss Sarah and had taken her on in an attempt to put her own life on a more solid footing, and in the belief that having a grave, serious paid companion might give her life some semblance of normality. Miss Sarah had been recommended to her as a person who had known misfortune in her life, who was quiet, very frugal, religious and a good pianist.

Genoveva soon realised that Miss Sarah knew little about religion and even less about music; beneath her bony fingers the vaguest, most languid of melodies shrivelled and became harsh, sharp marches in which the notes fell like axe-blows. She played as she walked – precisely, mechanically, lifelessly.

Genoveva kept Miss Sarah on because her prim clothes, tinted glasses, immaculate cuffs and severe nose were all evocative of a household of grave habits, regular hours and promptly paid bills, things which all worked to her advantage in shops. Seeing the lanky, black-clad figure in Genoveva's parlour gave men confidence. She was like the saintly image placed at the entrance to a brothel. 'She's a substitute for my mother,' Genoveva had said one day, 'only much cheaper.'

The moment Genoveva came into the room, Miss Sarah put her glasses back on and began hammering the keys of the rented piano with her long, red fingers, like lobster legs, and again took up the melancholy Irish tune.

The last rose of summer . . .

'Oh, no, please, no more last rose of summer! I've had quite enough of that.'

Miss Sarah stopped singing and, riffling through the sheet music on the piano, immediately began singing in plangent tones:

Dead leaves! Dead leaves!

'No, not that either!'

And striding about the room, her silk gown rustling, Genoveva told her off for always choosing sad, gloomy songs. She had had enough of sentimentality. She wanted something happy, something jolly . . .

Miss Sarah removed her glasses and, spinning round on the piano stool, declared that she was pleased to say it had never been her custom to sing or to learn such wicked tunes.

'Oh, go to the Devil, you old hypocrite!' said Genoveva in Portuguese.

And Miss Sarah, sensing the anger in Genoveva's voice, rose to her feet with great dignity and walked over to the door, where she turned and remarked that Genoveva was clearly out of humour.

'Yes, I am as it happens,' said Genoveva.

The Englishwoman felt it was her Christian duty to sit down and console her. She too was sad; we all have our sorrows; she herself had just received some letters from England.

Genoveva interrupted her again. She did not want to hear about them; she had quite enough sorrows of her own without hearing about other people's.

Genoveva sat down at the piano; she had studied in Paris, but had never got beyond playing the scales, which she had calmly and stubbornly inflicted on everyone she knew, but she knew the accompaniment to a few slightly risqué songs; there was one in particular she was especially fond of: 'L'Amant d'Amanda', 'Amanda's Lover', which, one summer, the whole of France had been singing; and in a warm, thrilling voice, she sang:

> *Chaque femme a sa toquade,*
> *Sa marotte et son dada.*
> *Amanda me demande*
> *Un jour entre deux œillades . . .*

Miss Sarah had got up and silently left the room. Genoveva, her head high, a mischievous smile on her lips, sang on in the rough, vulgar French of the music hall. She substituted the words she did not know with a lot of la-la-la-ing, then, slurring the words, in a bold, crude voice, finished with:

> *Voyez ce beau garçon là,*
> *C'est l'amant d'A*
> *C'est l'amant d'A*
> *Voyez ce beau garçon là,*
> *C'est l'amant d'A*
> *. . . manda!*

She practised her scales once, quickly and inexpertly, then got up, shaking her hands, irritated and sad.

That refrain brought back to her memories of Paris, of the summer, when the parks are full of flowers, the trees grow green and the fountains sing in their marble basins. The whole of life glows and women's pale dresses exude cool perfumes; then there are the joys of the countryside, the cottages overgrown with greenery, fishing on the Seine, wearing a straw hat, the social club where people sing with the windows wide open, the breeze from the river on hot mornings, when the sand glitters and gleaming yachts cut through the still water.

And everything around her made her feel sad and bored: the room with its cheap carpet, the balcony door with its tiny panes, barely letting in the light, the banal console table with its two ceramic dolls from Vista Alegre, the low bed with its coverlet in white fustian, the chandelier decorated with red, slightly fly-blown gauze, all saddened her.

A lugubrious sadness hung over the street, as if it were swathed in a dull merino cape. She was living near Arco da Bandeira, where there was a constant coming and going of errand boys and the clink of beakers on the fountain edge; the water left little muddy rivulets on the ground; at the door of the mercer's shop opposite stood a large barrel of rancid-looking butter; there were hams hanging there, white with fat, and bunches of tallow candles; and above the houses, she could see part of the blank, vulgar façade of São Bento.

Genoveva yawned. The days seemed to her enormous, empty, and the sun progressed in monotonous splendour across the skies; but she preferred solitude to the company of Dâmaso. His fat, smug face, his small, plump, tremulous body, his lustrous hair pomaded into place, his garishly coloured gloves, his vain, rich man's manners, all exasperated her. Sometimes, she felt like driving him from the room with a whip. Dâmaso, accustomed to easy conquests – Spanish girls and matronly mistresses, or some bourgeois wife dazzled by his phaeton – had at first been over-confident. Believing himself irresistible, he had spoken to Genoveva in terms worthy of Don Juan.

Genoveva had demolished him with an alarmed, ironic look and a few barbed remarks. The lion who had entered the room with mane flowing left with his tail between his legs. When he came back, Genoveva very calmly told him that, if she was to stay in Lisbon, she needed to pay off certain debts, and that would require a sum of one *conto* two hundred *mil réis*. Dâmaso did not return for two days, but passion and vanity urged him back, and after forty-eight hours of reflection, many cigarettes and much nervous running of fingers through hair, he returned humbly with the money in his hand.

Genoveva sensed that here was a bird ripe for the plucking, and on the first night that she loftily received him into her bedroom, she left him stunned and stupefied by the scientific application of her sensual skills. Dâmaso heard her utter ardent words that left him tumescent with almost painful pride; he received kisses that made him tremble and close his eyes with pleasure; he saw exquisite dresses, laces, silks that made him think nervously: 'I'd give her my last penny.'

There was, however, one unfortunate incident in the morning. Mélanie led him to a small room where he saw, with a shudder, a long, shallow bath full of water and with two large blocks of ice floating in it. Mélanie, with all the gravity of a priestess, poured half a bottle of Eau de Lubin into the water, placed a Turkish towel nearby, along with a scrubbing brush for his feet and a mug foaming with amber soap; then she left him alone saying:

'Call me when you're ready for your rub.'

Dâmaso stood there, astonished, scratching his head, staring at the bath; he fearfully tested the icy water with his fingertips and immediately withdrew them, muttering:

'She must be joking!'

He felt genuinely embarrassed; this was obviously some chic Parisian ritual, he thought, and he did not want to appear ungrateful, but the idea of immersing himself in that ice-cold water – never! He moistened one corner of the towel, dabbed it on his face and shivered. Sitting by the bath with all the foolish melancholy of a stork, he smoked two cigarettes and left, calling down the corridor:

'Thanks for the bath, it was wonderful!'

When Mélanie reported, after he had left, that the gentleman had left the water untouched, apart from two cigarette butts floating in it, Genoveva exclaimed angrily:

'The brute! That will cost him another hundred or so *mil réis*.'

And it did. A fortnight later, Dâmaso had, as Genoveva put it, 'shelled out' two *contos* and five hundred *mil réis* and was beginning to find it all a bit much. But he was idiotically in love, and it was as if all his bourgeois instincts – prudence, distrust, egotism, self-interest – had been chloroformed; he had only to moan or turn away and Genoveva would slip her soft arms around his neck and utter sweet words which had for him a hypnotic charm:

'My little kitten, my darling, my mousikins, my little lamby-wamby!'

The classically eloquent vocabulary of the libertine were enough to quiet all his worries and for love to roar within him with Lusitanian impatience.

Meanwhile, Dâmaso carefully concealed his prodigality from his friends. He passed himself off as a romantic lover; he told everyone that she was rich, generous and uninterested in money; he secretly bought some coral buttons which he wore, claiming they were a present from her:

'She just can't stop giving me presents! The woman's quite mad about me!'

He said this in cafés, in the Teatro de São Carlos, in brothels, and was even looking for a way of having it published in the society columns of the *Jornal Ilustrado*.

The last 'present' she had given him, the previous evening, was an old bill from Laffersein's for three thousand francs, which he had placed in his wallet, quietly taking out a bill of exchange the next day on Marcenard and André, Madame Lafayette's bankers, on sixty days' notice, earning a hundred franc discount; and he had been astonished when Genoveva casually slipped the francs into an envelope and said to Mélanie with yawn:

'Put that in the post, will you, Mélanie. It's the price one pays for dishonour.'

But Dâmaso had begun to demand that their affair be more public. That happiness hidden away in the heart of São Bento, and which was costing him very dear, may have satisfied his flesh, but it did not satisfy his pride. He wanted to be seen out and about with her, to be envied in the Chiado, in the Casa Havanesa, stared at in the Teatro de São Carlos, and to hear people say: 'Dâmaso's a lucky devil, he certainly knows how to live!'

Genoveva did not put up much opposition, though she still spoke of the charm of a discreet, private affair. In fact, she was not at all keen on being seen out in public with that imbecile. She did, however, accept a first-class box at the theatre and even a Sunday at Campo Grande. Such outings became excuses for headaches, because Genoveva began to suffer from migraines, and the worst thing was they always happened at night, which was Dâmaso's time to visit.

'I'm so sorry, my love, but I feel dreadful. I'm afraid you really can't stay with me tonight. I'm going to have to put you out in the street. It's such a nuisance. If you only knew . . . I'll come to the door with you.'

And when she heard him glumly closing the street door behind him, she felt such a sense of relief that she would call Mélanie and ask her to pour her some gin and then sit up in bed until two o'clock in the morning, drinking and chatting or writing to her women friends in Paris, saying she was in Lisbon, just off the coast of Africa, causing a sensation in the streets and civilizing a savage, who was rich as a nabob and innocent as a lamb.

That morning she had already determined to have a migraine. At first, Dâmaso did not want to leave her alone and ill.

He suggested poultices. He wanted to call Dr Barbosa. But Genoveva did not trust Portuguese doctors; she was terrified of them; they might poison her or disfigure her. She longed for Dr Charmeau. And on one occasion, seeing how the obstinate return of those headaches was getting in the way of his ardent desires, a worried Dâmaso shyly suggested she take a purgative. Genoveva fixed him with a look of such cold censure and such elegant disgust at the vile suggestion, that Dâmaso never dared mention any further remedies. One day, he was on the point of mentioning magnesium, but he blushed, coughed, and changed the subject.

In the end, Dãmaso began to find those headaches, which occurred three or four times a week, somewhat exaggerated. His bourgeois suspicions were awakened, but Genoveva seemed so weary, so cast down, complained so bitterly of the Lisbon climate, that Dâmaso would leave her, feeling sad but sympathetic. He wanted to get Mélanie on his side. The first time she brought a letter to his house in Rua da Comenda, Dâmaso, thinking himself very clever indeed, gave her two *libras*. Mélanie immediately turned on the confidences like a tap: 'If you only knew, sir. She's mad about you. It gets quite boring, sometimes, always talking about you, crying, saying she doesn't want to go back to Paris because she's so jealous. You'd better be careful, because if you so much as looked at another woman, she'd kill you. She's quite capable of it. She's very impulsive.'

Delighted, Dâmaso wanted to know more about Genoveva's past. Mélanie was eager to oblige, though swearing him to secrecy. Her mistress had married the Comte de Molineux, a disgusting old man, but she had had no choice really, poor woman. Her first husband, an Englishman, had left her without a penny. But her lady had been faithful as a slave to the old man. And she had had no shortage of suitors! Dukes, princes, even the Emperor himself. But she simply wasn't interested, although, she had been very fond of one young lad with the face of an angel, his name was Paul de La Rechantraye, not that there was ever anything between them, oh no. Then Paul died in the war, and that was that. But he was a sweet person, poor lad. When her old scoundrel of a husband died, he didn't leave her anything either, and she was even obliged to pawn her jewels and then there were her debts . . . It was poverty that drove her into the arms of the Brazilian, but she couldn't stand him and he meant nothing to her, and so, one fine day, she left him, just like that. She had served her lady for ten years and this was the first time, the only time, she had known her to be in love.

'By why, why?' asked Dâmaso.

Mélanie looked at him tenderly:

'Why? Because you're such a handsome young man, Senhor Dâmaso.'

Dâmaso gave her another two *libras* and could scarcely contain himself; he put his arms around her waist, out of pure joy, and pinched her, which made Mélanie squeal.

From then on, he needed Mélanie to provide him with constant affirmations of his happiness. And Mélanie was never lost for words. She was on to a good thing; she was radiant; accustomed to the meanness of Parisians, she found the Portuguese adorable.

'If they're all like him,' she thought, 'this is Paradise.'

But Genoveva's demands for money grew and the migraines did not diminish. Dâmaso began to grow impatient; besides, he often found her odd, silent and bad-tempered, or else full of ironic remarks, and he sometimes caught her looking at him sharply, irritably. In the end, he confided in his best friend, Manuel Palma, a plump, stocky chap with a loud voice and bitten fingernails, who lived partly on Dâmaso's generosity. He told him about Genoveva's attacks of nerves, her bad moods; he was worried; could it be jealousy on her part?

'She needs a good slap,' said Palma.

That was how he always dealt with tarts (he called all women 'tarts'). He wore the same jacket winter and summer and there was always a sweat stain around the rim of his collar; he had a voracious appetite and his short, fat legs seemed always on the point of bursting out of his tight trousers. He admired Dâmaso and spent all day praising Dâmaso, his horse and his dog.

'Good God, man!' said Dâmaso. 'She's not your run-of-the-mill Portuguese woman! You can't slap a woman used to Parisian ways.'

'To hell with Paris! Give her a good slap. That's all tarts understand, a good slap!'

Sometimes, Dâmaso would enter Genoveva's house with every intention of being masterful and forthright: he was her lover and he had the right to come and go as he pleased, and to stay as late as he liked; if she couldn't agree to that, then they must say goodbye. But he had only to see the spectacle of her person, her clothes, her manner, to receive the lightest caress, and he was dumbstruck; and there was so much else too, a marvellously high degree of cultivation that cowed him and filled him with respect.

She loved to go for a ride in the morning and she looked magnificent in her riding habit. Dâmaso always took her along any streets where he might be known; he crossed the Chiado, caracoled across the Rossio, looking about him, his face alight, ready to receive admiring, envious looks. Unfortunately, the streets were entirely empty of anyone he knew, the windows empty of familiar faces. He ended up parading his glory past a few errand boys and some shop-keepers in their slippers, enjoying the sun. The experience put him in a bad humour.

He had said on several occasions that he wanted her to go out in public with him.

'You don't really expect me to go out in a hired carriage, do you? Give me a carriage, a pair of English horses and a decent groom, then we'll cause a stir.'

And Dâmaso felt almost tempted to get her a carriage. He could see her going down the Chiado in one of her extra-ordinary outfits, her two thoroughbreds trotting along; and he could already hear the envious remarks made in the Casa Havanesa, in Balthreschi's patisserie: 'It's Dâmaso, the lucky man. What class!'

Around two o'clock, he went to Genoveva's. Mélanie tiptoed in to her mistress to tell her 'that man was here'. Genoveva gestured wildly to say 'No', and then, whispering in Mélanie's ear:

'Tell him I'm asleep, that I can't receive him, but that I expect him for supper at seven, without fail.'

And when Mélanie came back from delivering the message:

'What did he say?'

'He pulled a face.'

'Well, the man can go to hell! The brute!'

And going into her room, she said:

70

'Mélanie, bring me the cards.'

Mélanie set up the card table and the cards in the bedroom. And Genoveva, with a look of intense religiosity, began to spread the cards. She shuffled them gravely and slowly, with cabbalistic care; she cut the deck with her left hand and divided the cards into sets; then, her little finger cocked, she began arranging them in symbolic semicircles, her rings glittering on her small, white hands as she did so. Mélanie, standing behind her chair, followed with interest the revelations of fate, as if reading the pages of a book. Meanwhile Genoveva was muttering:

'Chaos; an old man; a young man with a blonde woman; tears; a meeting in a public place because of a letter.'

She shuffled the cards again and reflected. Then suddenly:

'He'll come to me! He has to come to me! Three times, do you see?'

And she showed how the jack of diamonds kept reappearing alongside the queen of hearts.

'He has to come to me.'

And her beautiful, dark eyes, illuminating her pale, aquiline face, were full of wonder at the idea of that unavoidable fate.

'If I were you, madam, I'd think no more about it,' said Mélanie.

Genoveva mixed the cards up again, staring into space, her eyes wide; she bit her lower lip and shrugged.

'Otherwise,' Mélanie went on, bustling about the room, 'just ask Senhor Dâmaso to bring him along. You're getting all worked up over nothing.'

'No, I don't want Dâmaso to bring him.'

Getting to her feet and going over to the mirror to comb her hair, she said:

'I know it's ridiculous, but . . . no one has ever made such an impression on me before. Ever since I saw him at the theatre . . . Well, I barely saw him really. I was standing at the door, I turned to pick up my train and there he was quietly smoking his cigarette. And I can't get him out of here!' She tapped her head. 'He's in my thoughts day and night. Apparently, his name's Vítor and he's a lawyer.' Then with fond

71

pity, she said: 'A lawyer, poor thing. People weren't meant to sit in an office all day shuffling papers! Poor love. And those eyes . . .'

She sighed and, sitting down at the foot of the bed, stretching, her eyes suddenly liquid with lust:

'Oh, Mélanie!'

She got up again and said in a changed voice, harsh and cold:

'I swear I've never felt like this about any man. I don't even know what I want from him . . . I want to run away with him, go somewhere where no one will see us, I want to devour him, kill him, bite him. He's so handsome, so sweet. He's such a love. And yet, there's something else . . . He actually looks like me!'

She went over to the mirror to confirm the vague resemblance to him in her own features.

'Here,' she said, indicating her forehead, 'and the eyes. If I didn't dye my hair blonde . . . He must be about twenty-five.'

'Are you dressing for supper, madam?'

'Hm?'

Mélanie repeated her question.

'Yes, I'll wear black. I've got to put up with that idiot again. But I want him to find out who that old man was. I want him to demand satisfaction from him . . .'

'Are you decent, my dear?' asked Miss Sarah, at the door.

'Yes, of course. You can come in now. Would you like a drop of gin, Miss Sarah?'

The Englishwoman's face lit up: 'Just the tiniest drop, that's enough. And a little water. *Old Tom*, is it? Just a little drop more, that will do, thank you.'

She sat down to concentrate on drinking her gin, devoutly repeating that very English maxim:

'A little drink is good for the soul.'

72

IV

The next day, at around eleven o'clock, Vítor was at work, in the office of Dr Caminha, who was in court that morning. Vítor, his files open before him, his legs outstretched, was sitting at his desk smoking and staring up at the ceiling. He was filled by an enervating sense of tedium and emptiness. The certainty that Genoveva loved Dâmaso had almost made him hate her; he despised her, found her banal, simple, stupid. Fancy falling in love with that dolt! Even consoling himself with the thought that a woman of such inferior mind could not possibly deserve someone with his beauty of soul did not prevent him from desiring her with a constant and growing intensity. He despised her mind, but he adored her body, and since he was not permitted to adore it, he did his best to hate her.

He had also lost touch with his lover, Aninhas, and so, abandoning all hope of happiness in love, he had attempted to lose himself in the joys of literature. He had tried to pour all his scorn for society and life into writing odes, but, after nights spent cudgelling his brains and smoking cigarette after cigarette, despairing of finding rhymes or ideas, he had decided that in order to be an artist, he must first be happy; and since happiness did not come and art did not inspire him, he was vaguely considering a career as a libertine, getting drunk and drowning his sense of tedium in orgies. But to do that he needed money, and thus, disappointed in love, artistically sterile, with nothing but fluff in his pockets, he felt like a wanderer who finds all doors closed to him.

Suddenly, outside in the waiting room, he heard Dâmaso's voice saying urgently:

'Is Senhor Vítor da Silva in? I need to speak to him.'

The clerk lifted the curtain at the door and, thrusting in the upper half of his large body, said in a gruff voice:

'There's a posh gent here asking for you, sir.'

'Ah, you're alone,' said Dâmaso, putting on his hat again. Then, without pausing and evidently upset, he said:

73

'Your uncle's really done it this time!'

Vítor looked at him astonished, eyes wide.

'He met Madame de Molineux and insulted her!'

Dâmaso plumped himself down in Dr Caminha's special chair, only to leap up again with a terrible yell. He had sat on the point of a squat, yellow nail. Dr Caminha hated anyone else sitting on his green velvet cushion when he was out, and to avoid such a crime occurring, he always left the chair primed for revenge; whenever that powerful legal orator – as some described him – was out of the office, he would leave a small nail on the seat of the chair; it was his favourite prank.

On Vítor's advice, Dâmaso had run to the kitchen where there was a fragment of mirror near the basin. He returned feeling calmer. It was just a scratch. He was very pale, though, and described Dr Caminha as 'a vile man' and thought the prank 'worthy of an utter bounder'.

The clerk at the door, holding back the curtain with his paw of a hand, was peering at them over his spectacles, his quill behind one ear, and saying maliciously:

'You found the nail, then.'

He was pleased to see a gentleman discomfited.

Dâmaso's initial agitation had dissipated, and he recounted the previous day's 'incident' quite calmly.

'Can you imagine, he stands there on the stairs calling her names and all because of a child . . . When she told me it was a man with a wooden leg, a shock of white hair, an old-fashioned carriage, a big walking stick and a long overcoat, I knew it had to be your uncle. Didn't he say anything to you about it?'

'He did mention something at supper, but, to be honest, I didn't pay much attention. Not a day passes without him having an argument with someone over something.'

Dâmaso was now wandering about the office, embarrassed, occasionally rubbing the injured spot.

'I know, but the problem is Madame de Molineux wants me to demand satisfaction from him. Can you imagine?'

Vítor laughed out loud.

'Satisfaction?'

'Yes, man, satisfaction, that's what I said. She says she was insulted and that she has no husband here, no brother, no son, no one but me . . .' And he added rather pompously: 'So I must avenge her.'

Vítor was serious now.

'Well, it's certainly an odd situation.'

'And if I don't bring her Uncle Timóteo's apologies, she says she'll refuse to see me ever again. She was absolutely furious; she smashed two vases, snapped her whip in two and nearly killed the Englishwoman. She was in a terrible state. She wanted to challenge him herself, to shoot him. To calm her down, I swore I would talk to him. And even then she called me an imbecile. That's how I got into this situation. I've got to challenge Uncle Timóteo. Not that I'm afraid,' he added, 'I'm not, but challenging an old man, a respectable gentleman. Oh, this could only happen to me.'

Vítor was listening to him thoughtfully, watching Dâmaso pacing up and down – his plump, tremulous body, his fat cheeks, his narrow head, his lustrous hair. He could hear the dull thwack of Uncle Timóteo's stick as it struck that flesh, the way a cook might pound pork to flatten it.

But Dâmaso was genuinely upset. And Vítor could see that this business might, in some tortuous way, bring him closer to Madame de Molineux, and that hope made all his spite vanish like mist before the sun.

He spoke of intervening, of putting the case to Uncle Timóteo. Dâmaso squeezed both his hands and stammered out some almost gushing words of friendship. He was his saviour! He was extricating him from the most terrible mess!

'But you must speak to him today,' he said. 'All he has to do is write her a note, that's all. It's not much to ask.'

They decided to go and speak to him immediately. At that time of day, he would be reading *The Times*. Dâmaso had his coupé downstairs. He left the room, and the clerk, one elbow on the desk, his quill in his hand, said as he passed:

'You all right then? It's just Dr Caminha's little joke.'

Dâmaso smiled. He felt vaguely frightened of the clerk's gruff voice and large body. He had dreamed all night of dangers, riots and duels. And the clerk, continuing his slow writing, muttered:

'Rich scum!'

Uncle Timóteo was, indeed, reading *The Times*. Vítor left Dâmaso in the parlour looking at an album of views of Calcutta, while he went to explain Dâmaso's position to his uncle, to placate him and convince him.

'But what the devil has that idiot got to do with her? Is he her husband, her brother, an acquaintance, her lover?'

'I believe he's her lover, Uncle.'

Uncle Timóteo rolled his eyes.

'The sly dog!' And he slapped his thigh. 'Well, he's on to a good thing there, because she's quite a woman, oh yes, all woman!' he said, patting his own chest.

Then, standing up:

'Well, this business about "demanding satisfaction" is obviously ridiculous and it would be cruel to make him lose her, so I suppose I'd better give in.' Making a grand gesture, he declared: 'I do it for Venus' sake!' And he laughed. 'Tell the fool to come in here.'

However, Dâmaso's appearance – his plump, smug face, his yellow gloves, his fat legs, his trim little moustache – so irritated Uncle Timóteo that, without getting up, he asked abruptly:

'So you were thinking of demanding satisfaction from me, were you?'

Dâmaso turned pale and bowed his head.

'Me, sir, how could you think such a . . . please . . .'

The sheer servility of this tub of lard disgusted Uncle Timóteo. He asked him to sit down, offered him a cognac and water, and set his own glass down on the table.

'I've already told Vítor that I'm quite prepared to apologise. I don't want to spoil your little arrangement.' Then turning to Vítor: 'Go there tomorrow and leave your card and mine, and write at the bottom "With my compliments". But, as I said, I'm not doing it for her sake, because I don't like the look of her, and I'm not doing it for you, sir, either, because I don't do favours for friends. I'm doing it for Venus and for Venus alone. Anyway, you lucky so-and-so, you've certainly got yourself quite a woman!'

Dâmaso, perched on the edge of his chair, bowed, looking prosperous and proud, smoothing his moustache. Uncle Timóteo took another sip of cognac and, leaning his elbow on his knee, said:

'Do you have to pay?'

Dâmaso turned scarlet: 'Please! She's a lady, the widow of a senator . . .'

'Oh, they're the worst kind. In India, it's the colonel's widow you have to watch. There's nothing more dangerous than a colonel's widow. The only bill of exchange I ever signed in my life, at nearly three or four per cent interest a month, was because of a colonel's widow. She was the only one, though, because in my day, dammit, there was something called disinterest; people flirted, had fun, fell in love. Young women nowadays are such cold, feeble, rachitic creatures, with their secret diseases; you have to untie your purse strings just to get a little kiss. Wholesale bloodsucking it is! I've sometimes heard people say that women have changed, that they're just out for what they can get and that they make money out of what God gave them. But it's not women who have changed, it's men. In my day, men were brave, hard, bold, always ready for a fight or to play the guitar or go to a bull-fight; it was a gift to a young woman then to open her door at night to a strong lad like that. But nowdays . . . What pleasure could a woman find in one of these pale, spindly, gawping milksops, with no backbone, no wit and no muscle. The women are quite right; they should be paid to put up with pipsqueaks . . . pipsqueaks should pay! I'm on the side of the ladies, poor things!'

And he laughed, his lively face bright with memories.

'Anyway, back to the matter in hand. Is she French this woman?'

'No, she's Portuguese, sir, but she's always lived in France. She's lived there for more than twenty-five years.'

Timóteo slowly took his cigar out of his mouth and, frowning, looked hard at Dâmaso.

'What's her name?'

'Genoveva.'

And after a silence, Timóteo asked again:

'And where was she born?'

'Madeira.'

Timóteo shrugged and said:

'Well, enjoy yourself. That's what I'm always telling this goody-goody here,' and he indicated Vítor, who was sitting on the desk, gloomily tugging at his moustache. 'Some fathers and uncles preach morality. They're fools. I preach immorality. A young man should be lively and enterprising, with two or three bastard children and a couple of girls fled into convents because he broke their hearts. That's how it was in my day. It doesn't matter who it is, maid, seamstress, marchioness, it's all grist to the mill. A man's a man. But then, of course, there aren't any convents to speak of now. Have a drop more cognac and forget about it.'

Picking up *The Times* again, he said:

'What's done is done. The visiting cards will be there tomorrow.'

Dâmaso got up and thanked him.

'There's no need to thank me. I'm doing it for Venus remember.'

And he laughed and vigorously rubbed his leg.

The following Saturday, Dâmaso bustled into Vítor's office, and sitting down next to him, almost whispered:

'Just a quick word. Madame de Molineux got the visiting cards and she's asked me to invite you to go there tomorrow night . . . Nothing too formal.'

Vítor felt his heart pounding and, to disguise his agitation, said:

'Who else is going?'

Dâmaso pulled a tragic face.

'It's all her idea! Can you imagine, she says that for this first soirée she wants people there of all classes. She gave me a list: military men, journalists, poets, members of the Academy, diplomats, singers . . . I've had the devil's own job trying to

78

round these people up. And she says she doesn't want society people, she wants people who are amusing. She wanted an actor, but I haven't found one yet. Anyway, I've done my best . . . but what an idea, eh? Anyway, that's all I had to say. I'll drop in on Carvalhosa and see if he'll come, because she wants a politician there too.'

And he was just about to rush out again, when Dr Caminha emerged from his contemplation of his own moustache to say:

'Is this the gentleman who sat on the nail?'

Dâmaso spun round, furious.

'I'm terribly sorry about that,' said Dr Caminha, raising his long, thin body up a little, then sinking back again on the green velvet cushion. 'I really am terribly sorry. It's the boss' little joke. Terribly sorry, though. It's to put off intruders. My wife embroidered the cushion and here's the nail. Terribly sorry.'

He bowed and, settling back again, sticking out his lower lip, he continued his examination of his moustache, hair by hair.

Vítor pondered for a long while whether to go to Madame de Molineux's soirée in frock coat or tails. But remembering how often Uncle Timóteo had praised the English custom of wearing tails at night, even if you were just staying at home, smoking, he decided that was what he would wear.

It was a foreign custom which he felt sure would please Madame de Molineux. Should his tie be white or black? He opted for the white tie and a camellia in his buttonhole. And in the hired coupé, feeling very nervous, he experienced a similar feeling to what students describe as 'the collywobbles', a vague fear that contracts the stomach and relaxes the intestines.

What would he say to her? What delicate, spiritual things could they talk about? Would a lot of people be there? Would there be dancing? And he was shaking so much he could barely button his gloves. He imagined conversations, rehearsed maxims and compliments, and as the coupé rolled towards the house, he felt uneasy, worried lest the petals might fall from his camellia.

The carriage stopped. Vítor saw all the windows on the third floor lit up, brilliant in the dark, slighty dank night: the soirée.

A thrill ran through him as he rang the bell. A manservant with black sideburns and wearing tails and white cotton gloves, bowed nearly low enough to touch the floor and discreetly asked his name. Then, lifting a curtain, he announced in a loud voice:

'Senhor Vítor da Silva.'

In the room used as a cloakroom, there were piles of overcoats, hats on chairs, a woman's woollen shawl, and, beside them, on a table, candles burned; he heard a murmur of voices in the drawing room.

Vítor spotted her at once at the far end of the room, wearing a dress of white silk and half reclining on a sofa; her large, dark eyes, her blonde hair, her décolletage, her beautiful, pale hands glittering with jewels, made such a powerful impression on him that he felt his shoulders bow beneath the impact.

He noticed nothing around him, only that there were candles burning and reflections in the mirrors.

Dâmaso hurriedly took him over to introduce him to Madame de Molineux and said, with a bow:

'My friend, Vítor da Silva, the nephew of . . .'

He completed the sentence with a nod and a wink. She sat up slightly, smiled and elegantly bent her head, then continued talking to a bald man with a neat, black beard and gold-rimmed pince-nez. Next to her was a table on which stood a golden goblet from which she drank occasionally, sitting up to do so with a gently undulating movement and a rustle of silk.

Vítor remained awkwardly on his feet and looked about him. He knew everyone there; sitting in an armchair was an old man whose bald head, with a few sparse hairs carefully combed forward over the temples, seemed almost buried in the high velvet collar of his vast dark tailcoat; his wrinkled, closely shaven cheeks formed deep folds, and his chin was almost submerged beneath a large black silk cravat.

What was he doing here? Vítor felt almost alarmed at his presence. He was an old gentleman of nearly seventy, who had once published a translation of Aesop's fables, a book of madrigals and a few original works, and who lived off the State. He belonged to the Royal Academy of Sciences, had no teeth and was a ruin of a man.

'Delighted to see you here, Senhor Couto.'

The old man looked up, drew his hand across his face, and sniffing slightly, said:

'Hello there, how are you?

He spoke in a slurred, somewhat nasal voice, then fell silent.

'It's such a long time since I last had the pleasure of meeting you,' said Vítor, speaking loudly, because the old man was a little deaf.

The man turned to him and said softly:

'What time is tea?'

He had a very sweet tooth and was hoping there would be some foreign cakes to be had in that house. Vítor did not know and, feeling bored, was about to move on, when Dâmaso came over to him. He was studying him, and Vítor noticed a barely suppressed flicker of envy cross his face.

'You decided to wear tails I see,' Dâmaso blurted out, and then, after a pause, standing very close to Vítor. 'I very nearly did too, but I was afraid people might think I was putting on airs. It's a problem, isn't it?'

He anxiously pressed one nostril.

Vítor looked round the room.

A group of people were standing by the card table, on which candles were lit: two women and two men. One of the women was known as Pia de' Tolomei, and although he had no idea where the nickname came from, he knew her by sight. She affected a haughty demeanour and was very tall, her curly, erect coiffure making her seem even taller. Her clothes looked somewhat rumpled and grubby; the skin on the back of her neck was the dark, grimy brown of the neglected. She was separated from her husband, a second lieutenant. She had dark circles under her eyes and her whole person spoke of barrack life and the regiment.

He did not know the other woman. She was in her forties and had a spinsterish look about her; she was large, square and swarthy, with a moustache, a very hairy mole on her chin, and was wearing a strange kind of turban on her head, made out of a lot of red velvet. She spoke little and her eyes, which exuded envy, bitterness and great sensuality, never left Genoveva, except to shoot a malevolent glance at one of the other guests, like the fulgent flicker of a flame.

The effeminate, stooping figure of Senhor Reinaldo could be seen sitting down near Pia de' Tolomei, his pale fingers endlessly twirling his moustaches as he talked.

Vítor wandered into the smoking room from which the sound of voices emanated. The three men who were in there talking and smoking stared curiously at his white tie. It was a small room with curtains, a cretonne sofa, and a lamp placed on a round table covered by a scarlet velvet cloth.

One of the men held out his hand. It was Carvalhosa, a contemporary of his at University, where Carvalhosa had been known for his lack of hygiene and famous for his vices. He used to spend entire days in bed, and his room stank. Now he was a deputy and the newspapers praised his eloquence and quoted from his speeches. He had an air of superiority and spoke in mellifluous, arrogant tones.

'Ah,' he said, removing his cigar from his lips, 'here's someone who can enlighten us. Who the devil is this woman, Silva? Some kind of Venus?'

His tone of voice shocked Vítor.

'I would imagine you know better than I. This is the first time I've ever been to her house.'

'Me too.'

'And me,' exclaimed the other two men.

One of them was very gaunt and hunched; he had dull, dun-coloured hair; his face was pocked with angry spots, and he kept scratching his chin with his nails; he was a journalist. The other man was a young, handsome, vain-looking chap, wearing the uniform of the lancers.

'I'm here because Dâmaso invited me,' said Carvalhosa.

'Us too.'

'Three days ago, he told me I was invited to come to the house of a lady from the very best Parisian society.'

'He says she's the widow of a senator,' said Carvalhosa, who grew suddenly declamatory: 'But then during the Second Empire, senators were nothing but a bunch of cantankerous old debauchees.'

'With respect,' broke in the journalist, 'there were some illustrious exceptions: Sainte-Beuve and Mérimee . . .'

'Who led France into the abyss,' Carvalhosa roared. 'Please let's not talk about the Empire, my dear friend. The Empire means corruption, the law trampled underfoot, liberty in chains, orgies in the Tuileries.'

A loud voice interrupted them:

'But ahead of us stalked the dread monster, foretelling all our fates . . .'

Carvalhosa turned round, outraged, but, seeing a short, ill-shaven man in tinted glasses entering the room, he smiled and held out his hand:

'Why, here's our poet.'

'Gentlemen,' he said, bowing, then addressing Carvalhosa: 'Forgive me, I couldn't resist quoting those lines from our own dear Camões when I came in, but,' in a voice husky with emotion, 'you know that no one appreciates your enormous talent more than I do . . .'

Then, noticing the journalist, he fell silent, twitched his head slightly and, embarrassed, took out his cigarette case. Carvalhosa went on in the same sad vein:

'No, my friend, the disasters of the Empire were purely providential.'

'Oh, so you believe in Providence, do you?' said the journalist in a low, mocking voice, still furiously scratching his chin.

Carvalhosa drew himself up:

'Now don't start on religion!'

According to him, God was in everything, in the greatest historical figure and in the smallest grain of corn which, to quote Victor Hugo, the ant etc. etc . . .

But the journalist declared:

'Victor Hugo is an ass!'

He added scornfully that Victor Hugo was an old man who no longer knew what he was saying. Carvalhosa lost control; he defended Victor Hugo with wild gestures and thunderous words; he called him the prophet of the nineteenth century, the muse of Hauteville House.

'Quite, quite,' said the poet, getting to his feet and retreating.

'Victor Hugo's most recent books,' said the journalist coldly, reaching between his waistcoat and his trousers to scratch his back, 'quite frankly made me laugh.' He was smiling.

'Sir,' bellowed Carvalhosa. 'You mock the press, you mock poetry, you mock the sublime.'

'Keep your voice down,' said someone at his elbow.

It was Dâmaso, who was clearly upset. Silence fell. Dâmaso explained that everyone in the other room was afraid that some altercation had broken out, and Madame de Molineux had asked him if it was a gambling dispute, and besides, they could be heard downstairs.

'Well, if one can't have a discussion . . .'

'You do have rather a loud voice,' said the journalist, still scratching.

Provoked by the remark, Carvalhosa said haughtily:

'So loud that the whole country listens!'

'As I said, you do have rather a loud voice,' said the journalist again.

Carvalhosa stared at him, furious:

'And what do you mean by that?'

The journalist responded, feverishly scratching his chin:

'This isn't really the place . . .'

Dâmaso intervened:

'Gentlemen, please . . .' And he tried to drag Carvalhosa away. Carvalhosa was deathly pale.

'Enough of this nonsense,' said the lancer, twirling his moustache. 'It's not worth quarrelling over literature . . . and you're not at home now . . .'

Vítor left them still talking, made an excuse and sloped back into the drawing room. Madame de Molineux was standing up now, talking to Pia de' Tolomei, but when she saw him, she turned, her silk train coiling about her feet, and came over to him.

'I so wanted to meet you,' she said.

Vítor bowed and muttered a few unintelligible words; he could feel her very close to him, and something so powerful emanated from her eyes, body and hair that he instinctively drew back, as if from a blazing fire, and stood there in a slightly stooped, defeated pose.

'You uncle is certainly very quick to anger,' she said, smiling, looking down at her fan, which she was slowly opening and closing.

It was a large black fan on which two white figures were depicted in a blurred, blue forest. Vítor finally overcame the shyness that prevented him from speaking.

'He can be a bit impetuous, but . . .'

'Oh, I forgave him at once,' she said. 'Besides, I rather like people like him; he's a kind of Don Quixote riding to the rescue of widows and orphans.' And she laughed softly. 'He's a fine-looking man too. What's his name?'

'Timóteo.'

'He looks a bit like Crémier, not the one who wrote the comic operas, but the one who created the Republic,' and she laughed again.

Vítor stared at her, enchanted. The proximity of her flesh drew him the way a magnet draws iron; he felt like touching the splendid flesh of her breast, to trace its curve with one fingertip, just to know how it felt.

She was brightly lit by two lamps placed on a nearby table, which revealed the pure, soft lines of her chin and her nose, which the light caressed with adorable delicacy.

Vítor was very conscious of the slight traces of powder on her skin, of her full, red lips, delicate and soft as a rose petal; she had a warm, languid way of smiling, her smile opening slowly as if in response to a surge of warmth in her blood, and her breast rose and fell to a gentle rhythm.

'How old is your uncle?'

'Sixty, Madam.'

'Look, we can't stand here like a couple of storks . . .'

And she moved off slowly and calmly, her arms by her side, holding her half-open fan in her two hands, like someone posing for a painting or a photograph.

She sat down on the sofa, almost reclining, and indicated a nearby armchair. In that position, her close-fitting dress revealed the general lines of her body and it was very easy to imagine her naked.

'I know you're a close friend of Dâmaso's,' she said.

'Well, fairly . . .'

Vítor considered Dâmaso an imbecile and wanted to make it clear that he was far superior and only knew Dâmaso socially.

'Well, we've known each other for a while . . .'

Then, in a slightly drawling voice, and giving certain words a sing-song Parisian intonation, she spoke in praise of Dâmaso: he was a delightful companion; he had been so helpful; they went riding together; he was the one who had got her this apartment and who had brought all these people along. And lowering her voice, she said gravely:

'I'm so pleased to have a member of the Academy here.'

She looked deferentially at old Couto, who was dozing off in his armchair.

'Of course, I had hoped that . . . but then I'll be spending the whole of the winter in Lisbon.'

She spoke slowly, studying her fan; occasionally, for a lingering moment, she would look across at Vítor. Then she asked:

'Do you write poetry?'

Vítor, astonished, almost embarrassed, did not reply.

'Oh, I thought . . .,' she said, 'well, it was Dâmaso who told me.'

She uttered the name 'Dâmaso' with such familiarity.

Then she told him her views: she adored poets and other literary men. Monsieur de Molineux had always had one or two to supper; those one could receive, of course, because

86

some you simply couldn't, because they were just too, too . . .
She fumbled for the right word.

'Too grubby,' she said at last. Then, laughing: 'I don't know
if that's the most elegant way of putting it. I've forgotten so
much of my Portuguese.'

Vítor, on the contrary, was amazed she had forgotten so
little.

'Ah, now you're flattering me.'

Her eyes wrapped Vítor in a slow, languid look.

Vítor declared that if he were to live abroad, his prime
concern would be to forget all about Portugal and the Portuguese language and people; he even blushed slightly when he
said 'Portuguese'.

'Not all of them, surely,' said Madame de Molineux. And
smiling, she added: 'What if *she* were to hear you say that?'

'What "she"?'

'Well, I'm sure there is a "she", possibly more than one.'

Dâmaso came over at that point, rubbing his hands. He
bent to whisper in Madame de Molineux's ear, but she drew
back slightly, saying:

'Goodness, people will think you're whispering sweet
nothings to me. What is it, my dear?'

'It's ready. It's orange and strawberry and it's delicious, the
best sorbet I've tasted all year.'

'He'd make a very good butler, don't you think?' said
Madame de Molineux to Vítor, indicating Dâmaso with her
fan.

Dâmaso declared that he would happily serve as her lackey,
and, preparing his features to make some more subtle joke:
'Even as lord of the bedchamber . . .'

Then, putting on a grave face and speaking in a low voice:

'I'm so embarrassed. I was going to wear tails like Vítor
here, but I was afraid people might think I was putting on
airs . . . Tricky, eh?'

'Well, you were quite wrong. Men should always wear tails
in the evening. And another thing, my friend, your boots need
polishing.'

Dâmaso glanced down at his town boots and at Vítor's

87

gleaming patent leather shoes; he blushed scarlet and said angrily:

'I've got patent leather shoes too, you know. We do have them here.'

He was growing redder by the minute, but she tapped him on the arm with her fan.

'Behave,' she said with a look that quelled him. 'Have them bring in the sorbet; it's nearly eleven o'clock.'

'Right, right.' And Dâmaso scuttled off.

Turning to Vítor, she smiled and said:

'As I was saying, *she* . . .'

'But, Madam,' cried Vítor, who was losing his shyness and now had no difficulty in finding the words: 'I swear there is no "she"; I only wish there were; but more sublime than . . .'

He hesitated, he had been about to make some very literary comment about love and was afraid of appearing pedantic.

'Go on. I'm very interested in what you find sublime.'

Her voice had grown softer; she was sitting up on the sofa now, leaning towards him. Vítor was aware of her warmth, of the smell of her skin.

'Well, there are a lot of things I find sublime,' he said, adding boldly: 'Beauty, for one.'

'Beauty is relative. It's possible, for example, that many people might consider that lady in the scarlet turban . . . I can't remember her name offhand . . . to be far prettier than me.'

'Impossible,' exclaimed Vítor.

'Well, you might not think so, but . . .'

'I certainly wouldn't!'

And their eyes met. At that moment, however, Carvalhosa was coming across the room, one hand in his waistcoat pocket, looking at Madame de Molineux. Addressing her, he said:

'You are doubtless tired after your journey.'

'I arrived a month and a half ago,' she replied, laughing.

'Ah, then, you will have had time to recover,' he said, running his fingers through his hair. He drew up a chair, sat down and crossed his legs, revealing the worn elastic on his boots.

'So how are politics in Paris, then?' he asked.

'Fine,' said Madame de Molineux, feeling awkward and constrained.

'The republicans have been magnificent. That last speech of Gambetta's was pretty good . . . not to my taste though; he lacks imagery, brilliance, eloquence, flourishes. But a new dawn has come at last.'

'If you'll excuse me,' she said with a smile. And getting up, with a swish of her train, she walked lightly over to sit down by the second lieutenant's wife, who blushed, pushed back her chair, very slowly drew herself up and pursed her lips disdainfully.

Carvalhosa merely followed her with his eyes, then muttered to Vítor:

'Stupid woman, she's got no small talk.'

Raising his eyebrows and running his fingers once more through his hair, he crossed the room again and joined the pianist.

'The man's late,' said the illustrious Fonseca.

'What man?' asked Carvalhosa.

'For the surprise!'

And with a desolate air, he rolled his eyes and shrugged, saying:

'It's a secret; orders from above.'

But Dâmaso came over and linked arms with Carvalhosa.

'Carvalhosa, be a good chap, will you, and go and talk to Pascoal Pimenta.'

'Me talk to that swine?' said Carvalhosa proudly.

'He's a good enough lad, poor thing.'

'He's a brute.'

And Senhor Reinaldo – who, ever since Madame de Molineux had gone and sat next to Pia de' Tolomei, had been wandering disconsolately about the room looking for someone to talk to, incapable of being alone, always dependent on others – immediately asked:

'Who's a brute, who?'

Carvalhosa stared at Reinaldo. Dâmaso realised that they did not know each other and immediately, and with great ceremony, introduced them.

'I'm most honoured,' said Reinaldo, bowing. 'I had the pleasure of hearing you speak in the Chamber. I often go. I was there yesterday in fact.'

'Ah, so you're interested in . . .' began Carvalhosa, playing with the trinkets on his watch chain.

'No, I took a Spanish girl, she wanted to see what went on there. You probably know her. She's from . . .' and he whispered something in his ear. 'Lola,' he said out loud, '*La Magrita.*'

'Of course,' said Carvalhosa, and they went off together, arm-in-arm, chattering.

Vítor had returned to the room of blue cretonne; alone on the sofa was Pascoal Pimenta; he was chewing his nails and bouncing his legs up and down.

Vítor did not know him, but he sat down beside him and, blowing out a cloud of smoke, said:

'Things were getting a bit heated earlier on.'

'The man's an ass,' said Pimenta bluntly.

But then the lyric poet came in, lit a cigarette and sat in another corner of the room; with legs crossed and arms folded, he kept casting viperish looks at the journalist. And all three sat there, like three smoking chimneys, still and silent as idols. Then the figure of Madame de Molineux appeared at the door.

'I was afraid you'd run away!' And her eyes went straight to Vítor, but then turning back to the poet, she said: 'Your turn has come. The ladies are longing to hear you recite.'

The poet bowed low and, at a gesture from Madame de Molineux, he stubbed out his cigarette and went over to offer her his arm.

'Another ass,' muttered the journalist.

The piano began to play. Vítor returned to the drawing room.

The illustrious Fonseca, head up, gazing into space, his glasses glinting, was lightly touching the keys with his plump mercer's fingers. A slow, vague melody emerged; the two candles on the piano were burning red, and, beside them, the lyric poet was rather tremulously stroking his beard. He looked around him, adjusted his pince-nez, and coughed.

He was standing by the piano; his long, collar-length hair looked almost brown in the candlelight; and against the light, his beard seemed grubby and thin as cotton down; the smoked lenses of his pince-nez glinted black on his pale face. Then he announced:

'The title of the poem is *Contemplation-Vision*.'

He cleared his throat and began:

> All is calm and still.
> The horizon is wearing black.
> The water that flows down the hill
> Moans in the depths of the valley.
> The birds are leaving now
> For the sweet heat of the south.
> Drunk on light and azure blue
> They flee the coming storm.
> Why do you flee so far away
> Oh, sweet birds of the sky? . . .

And the poet addressed the birds, asking them the reason for their flight. What made them flee? Was it the injustices committed by those in power? Was it the sight of talent crushed? The poem was taking on a bitter, socialist turn. The voice of the poet grew cavernous, and the illustrious Fonseca, feeling anxiously for the pedal, played the deepest chords the keys could offer. Things were looking grim. But then, suddenly, the poet smiled, and, as when the sky clears in winter, his nasal voice intoned instead a cheerful verse. The season had changed; the snow had melted; the flowers were blooming.

> It is spring and all is green.
> All things smile, earth and sky,
> Weary of infernal war.
> The thick woods sing,
> As do the daisies in the field;
> Virgin girls speak of love

91

And the flower bends
To whisper a secret to the lake.

'Lovely,' commented various guests.

But then the poet grew gloomy again; his voice darkened. The illustrious Fonseca resorted once more to the pedal; an accompaniment rather like a death knell echoed about the room; the eyes of the second lieutenant's wife widened and glittered sympathetically. The poet spoke of his sorrows; in the midst of festive nature, he alone was sad; he despised the world and saw in it only bitterness; he despised potentates, armies, bronze cannon; he preferred the simple violet.

The poem again filled with joy; happiness was in every word and flowed from every line, as if from a brimming cup. What consoled him? What?

> Why do I feel this my breast
> Which once was parched and dry
> Turn into a flowering meadow . . .

And they all waited, with bated breath, to learn the reason for that happiness. Then the door opened and two men came in. Dâmaso uttered a nervous 'Sh!', his finger on his lips, and the two men froze. The one in evening dress, with a decoration pinned to his lapel, was Marinho, who leaned against the wall; the other was a tall, burly man, with skin pale as marble and a mane of glossy hair, which he kept pushing back. He was wearing a hat trimmed with satin and had a waxed moustache; everything about him bespoke a singer and a showman.

Everyone looked at him. There was a lot of whispering. The poet sensed that, with each line, he was losing his grip on their attention, like water slipping through his fingers. He tried to regain their interest. What had consoled him? SHE had!

> I saw her one sweet night,
> When the nightingale was singing,
> And all the sky was filled with stars,

A brightly lit pavilion:
Ah, Sintra! I still can hear
The sweet babbling of your fountains,
Feel the shadows cast on our faces
By the trees of Ramalhão.

The poetry was becoming indiscreet. Roma described compromising walks, he called upon the stars, upon the balconies:

Do not reveal our secret,
O sweet meadow grasses!

However, things turned sour. The illustrious Fonseca once more felt for the pedal; Roma reverted to lines of disdain:

All is over. Upon the earth
I wander, a fugitive shadow.
I hate all things; the loveliest flower
Is for me a flower of Avernus.
Let the fountains babble,
Let the earth turn green,
Let the breeze play upon the air,
For me, *all* is winter!

'*Bravíssimo poeta!*' cried the burly man. João Marinho immediately stepped forward, bowed to Madame de Molineux and introduced his friend as Sarrotini, the baritone from the Teatro de São Carlos. People clustered round, chattering. The butler came in bearing the bowl of sorbet.

Roma circulated, garnering praise; Pia de' Tolomei asked him for a copy of the poem; Senhor Reinaldo thought it lovely enough to be sung as a *fado*. They all agreed he was far better than Senhor Vidal. And Roma was still savouring his triumph as he went into the smoking room, where Pimenta was saying to the lancer:

'It's just a string of clichés like everything else Roma does.'

Roma was about to leap on him, but he restrained himself.

Dâmaso found him in the corridor, desperately pulling on a cloak.

'You're not leaving, are you? What happened?'

'No, I don't want to lose control of myself. If I stay, I'll punch that insolent lout!'

Dâmaso tried to calm him down:

'Come now,' he said, removing Roma's cloak and adding: 'We haven't had supper yet.'

With that assurance, Roma decided to stay and went back into the drawing room.

By this time, Sarrotini was standing in the middle of the room performing magic tricks. With the sleeves of his tailcoat rolled up, he produced first an egg and then a lemon. An admiring circle had formed around him. Dâmaso rushed to join them; he was smiling, radiant, and he kept muttering to Vítor:

'It's such a splendid soirée . . . if only I'd worn tails.'

Sarrotini was now imitating a fly buzzing; he pretended he was being pursued by the fly; he swatted his neck, crept round the room on tiptoe, his cupped hand outstretched, intending to catch it in mid-flight. And in the silence, the monotonous buzzing continued, now just a faint whistle, now a growl; it buzzed about, paused for a moment, then resumed its impertinent noise on the other side of the room. There was great applause. Sarrotini returned to the centre of the group. He became the showman again, speaking a mixture of Italian and Spanish, making extravagant gestures and clowning around, his tails flying out behind him; with a cheeky look in his eye, he imitated various animal noises, bent a coin with his bare hands, recounted anecdotes of the Sicilian campaign; he mimicked famous people and, since he was a supporter of Garibaldi, he improvised a dialogue between the Pope and Cardinal Antonelli in which one defended fat women and the other thin. He ended by declaring himself a republican.

Everyone was astonished.

Carvalhosa broke the silence:

'The papacy is, of course, Italy's tragedy. The Pope equates with ignorance and darkness.'

Sarrotini looked at him, asked for a translation, and recognising in Carvalhosa the soul of a patriot, went over and embraced him, clapping him on the back and confiding in a whisper that he himself was one of the Carbonari.

Then he wanted to sing the Marseillaise. He started: *'Allons enfants de la Patrie!'*

Enthusiasm spread, Roma, the poet, joined in, shouting:

'The Marseillaise, the Marseillaise!'

But Madame de Molineux intervened. Not the Marseillaise, she hated it.

A silence fell.

'Not the Marseillaise. It's a song I particularly dislike. It reminds me of the masses. Please, sing something else.'

She seemed quite alarmed, as if she had heard insurrectionary rifles being fired. She took Vítor's arm.

'Well, they've certainly livened up!'

And with her arm still linked in Vítor's, she went over to old Couto and, bestowing on him a deferential, respectful smile, she said:

'It was out of consideration for you as well that I didn't want them to sing the Marseillaise. It must bring it all back.'

'Not too bad really,' replied Couto, who had only caught the last word. 'It's much better today actually, though I've still got a touch of lumbago.'

She said nothing for a moment.

'Have you been ill, then?' asked Vítor very loudly.

'Yes, sciatica.'

Genoveva leaned towards him again:

'It's all that literary work you do, I expect.'

'Huh?' and the old man pulled a face.

'Literary work,' said Genoveva.

'Oh, he's not going to recite again, is he? What time is tea?'

Genoveva smiled and led Vítor away.

'He's a great writer, I understand. A member of the Academy.'

Vítor was about to explain to her that the Academy in Lisbon was not quite the same as the Academy in Paris, but she was leading him into the smoking room where the journalist was sitting alone. When he saw them, he stubbed out his cigarette in a candleholder and left, bowing.

'We didn't mean to frighten you off,' said Genoveva.

He mumbled something, blushed and concluded his bow.

'I've asked Senhor Dâmaso to subscribe to the newspaper you write for. It's called *The People*, isn't it?'

'Yes,' he said. He bowed again, his face even redder, and left, breathing hard.

Laughing, Genoveva said:

'Entertaining is so exhausting. Not here so much, where there's just a handful of people, but in Paris . . . oh, you can't imagine.' And striking a melancholy pose, she added: 'Society life is such a bore.'

Vítor said that surely in Paris . . .

'Oh, Paris, Paris! It probably looks alluring from a distance, but when you have to live in the midst of that whirlwind . . .'

And after a pause, she added:

'I'm thinking of burying myself here in Portugal, in some little village.' She glanced at Vítor out of the corner of her eye.

'Well, there are some lovely villages,' said Vítor, 'and if you've got a nice house . . .'

'And especially when there are two of you,' she said.

João Marinho suddenly appeared, all smiles, beating his top hat against his legs, his head bobbing:

'Sarrotini's about to sing.'

And he held out his arm to Genoveva. Vítor followed them into the next room.

Sarrotini was standing by the piano, very tall and erect, and after the illustrious Fonseca had played a few opening chords, Sarrotini's large, powerful baritone filled the room with vibrant sound. It was an aria from *Lucretia Borgia*. The guests had instinctively arranged their chairs into a semicircle, and Sarrotini, raising his arms and rolling his eyes, sang out boldly, leaning back a little to reveal his strong, white throat, which was eyed vehemently by the second lieutenant's wife and leered at by the woman in the red turban.

Everyone applauded loudly, and he immediately plunged into the aria from *Dinorah*. He was definitely 'on form'. Now he struck a serious, romantic pose; the showman had become the hero and, whenever there was a pause, he would dab at the corners of his mouth with an embroidered chambray handkerchief.

Another ovation followed, and, greatly moved, he thanked them, bowing as he did at the theatre. Then he asked Genoveva to sing. She refused: 'No, no.'

Sarrotini went down on his knees, and everyone laughed. Still on his knees, Sarrotini shuffled across the floor towards Genoveva, who was smiling and shaking her head. Sarrotini sang an old Neapolitan tune: *Preguiami la Madonna*.

To general merriment, João Marinho added his harsh, cracked voice to that musical plea.

And Dâmaso, gleefully rubbing his hands, whispered to Vítor:

'This is turning into a positive orgy!'

Genoveva finally acquiesced and went over to the piano. Dâmaso clapped and everyone followed suit. João Marinho waved his handkerchief, as people do during public ovations.

'Right,' she said.

There was an expectant silence.

'The only song I know by heart is "Ophelia" from Ambroise Thomas' opera *Hamlet*. Will that do?'

'Bravo, bravo,' they all cried.

Carvalhosa leaned towards Vítor:

'Ah, *Hamlet*! Such a profound work. "To be or not to be . . .",' he recited, closing his eyes.

Genoveva's voice rose up loud, vehement, clear as crystal, and just a little shaky on the lower notes; she sang:

> *Pâle et blonde*
> *Dort sous l'onde profonde*
> *La willis au regard du feu*
> *Que Dieu garde*
> *Celui qui s'attarde*
> *La nuit, autour du lac bleu!*

Vítor had never heard anything more delicious; that subtle

music, so full of poetic tenderness, of mythical melancholy and resignation, gave him a distant vision of a legendary land. A misty Scandinavian country, a flat land of many trees; there sleeps a lake and, caught up in that mystical exaltation, the vague shapes of water nymphs sway. The stone walls of an old Scandinavian castle can be glimpsed through the mist, and the sound of a mournful song can be heard.

It made him long to be far away in one of those Northern lands, where the women are tall and blue-eyed, or in some sad, noble park, where the fir trees cast dank shadows, a salty breeze hangs in the air and the Baltic Sea grows blue. And on the long terrace built by some old fisherman, a princess of the Swedish race, the daughter of a king, an Ophelia, hovers, light as down, silent, thoughtful, wrapped in the cold air.

In the pause before the second verse, Genoveva's eyes rested on him, and suddenly, for no reason, he felt immensely proud, glad to be alive, renewed; he almost felt like crying.

Genoveva was warmly applauded; there was near uproar; appreciative comments were heard: 'Divine!' 'Marvellous!'

'She could make her fortune with that voice!' said Marinho.

And Carvalhosa remarked with great authority:

'She's got a definite feeling for it.'

The second lieutenant agreed that she was certainly a woman to turn men's heads.

She, meanwhile, trembling slightly, as if tired, had sat down. Dâmaso came over to her and said softly:

'You sang like an angel, my love.'

'I've told you before, don't address me as "tu".'

Dâmaso was piqued.

'Well, it strikes me that . . .'

'That I sleep with you, is that it? Well, that still doesn't give you the right,' she said with a shrug.

The butler came in to announce supper was served. There was a great scraping of chairs, and Genoveva majestically went over to take the arm of Senhor Couto. The old man was asleep and they had to wake him up. Being still half-asleep, he didn't quite understand what was happening, and everyone stood around for a moment, not speaking.

Dâmaso pulled him by the arm and, after much moaning, mumbling, coughing and nodding, the old man managed to stand up on his great bunioned feet, and, grasping Genoveva's arm, he proceeded slowly and tremulously to the supper table.

The others followed. The journalist was the last; his bile had grown, he was humiliated and furious, but he did not want to miss supper; he spat on the floor and swaggered in, his hands behind his back.

By two in the morning, the supper was over, and Genoveva was immersed in a long exchange of confidences with Vítor. Vítor was telling her his worries, his interests, his opinions.

'I'm a republican,' he said.

She gently reprimanded him: he should support his king and his religion. The first duty of a well-educated man was to his religion; you could not belong to the best society, you could not be considered chic without religion. Then their talk turned to the other guests, and they analysed certain particularly ridiculous figures: the journalist, who was eating silently, stiffly and bad-temperedly, putting his knife in his mouth; the poet, who was eagerly gobbling down his food, reaching across the table and cutting his bread rather than breaking it; Senhor Reinaldo, who was chatting to the second lieutenant's wife and cleaning his nails with a toothpick. They laughed, whispered, drank. Marinho had ended up next to the woman in the turban, and he was furious; he kept casting desperate glances in Genoveva's direction. The woman did not speak so much as grunt; she had come with the second lieutenant's wife and said only four intelligible words during the whole evening. In response to Genoveva asking her if she had dined well, she declared loudly: 'I'm fit to burst.'

Couto was still eating, slumped in his chair, one arm on the table, making bread balls which turned black in contact with the grubby tips of his old, bony fingers, which emerged from capacious cuffs. And Dâmaso, always busy, getting up from the table, issuing discreet orders to the butler, went into the kitchen and returned bearing bottles under his arm. It had been established that it was he, as the second lieutenant's wife put it, who 'footed the bill'. She then engaged in a long discussion with Senhor Reinaldo about 'how much he must give her a month'.

The illustrious Fonseca was the most exuberantly happy of all the guests; Sarrotini addressed him as 'maestro', and soon everyone was calling him 'maestro'. He was quite pink with triumph. On one occasion, he said to Sarrotini:

'You with your great genius . . .'

Sarrotini replied:

'Well, speaking of genius, you have more of it than anyone here.'

The illustrious Fonseca bowed gravely. And from one side of the table to the other, they exchanged nothing but 'My genius, your genius, our genius . . .'

Someone had the idea of singing a song, accompanying themselves by banging on their plates, and Sarrotini, already in his cups, immediately launched into a solidly Garibaldian number:

> Onwards to Holy Rome,
> We'll climb up to the Capitol . . .

'No, no,' everyone cried, 'we don't want anything political.'

They wanted something light.

'Besides,' shouted Vítor, who was distinctly merry, 'the song's got it wrong. It was the Italians who marched into Rome.'

That remark inflamed Sarrotini. He got up, knocking over his chair as he did so, and went over to Vítor, his eyes ablaze. Grabbing Vítor's head in his powerful hands, he planted a kiss on his forehead, and everyone roared their approval.

'I propose that only the ladies should be kissed,' bawled Marinho. 'Although the gentleman certainly is pretty enough to kiss.'

Everyone looked for a moment at Vítor; his face was flushed and there was a voluptuous smile on his lips, his eyes shining from his proximity to Genoveva and from the quantity of Veuve Clicquot he had drunk. As Senhor Reinaldo remarked quietly:

'He'll drive the ladies wild that one!'

Genoveva looked at him too, and her eyes grew larger and darker. Her breast filled, and her eyelids flickered nervously with fleeting, piercing desire.

She said nothing, but she was smiling, a slightly crooked smile that revealed small white teeth.

Marinho was still bawling:

'I propose that only the ladies should be kissed.'

'He's afraid he might be set upon,' yelled Reinaldo, creased up with laughter.

'He should start with his neighbour,' said Dâmaso, bowing.

At these words, the woman in the red turban sprang angrily to her feet and left the room. Dâmaso ran after her; Genoveva, the second lieutenant's wife and everyone around her were saying:

'Silly woman, it was only a joke!'

'I'm a decent woman, I'm a decent woman,' the woman in the red turban kept repeating breathlessly.

They finally coaxed her back to the table and sat her down. She was apoplectic, her eyes bloodshot.

Then Dâmaso got to his feet and said something to Carvalhosa. Carvalhosa smiled his agreement. Dâmaso returned to his seat and banging his fork loudly on his plate, said:

'May I have silence, ladies and gentlemen.'

Carvalhosa rose majestically with his glass in his hand.

Everyone fell silent. The honourable member ran his fingers through his hair and wiped them carefully on his napkin, which he then threw down on the table; he fiddled with his plate and his knife, like someone shuffling through his notes at the lectern. Then he said:

'I wasn't going to make a speech, but my illustrious friend, Senhor Dâmaso, has asked me to give voice to the gratitude we all feel on this festive night to our gracious hostess.'

He paused, looked about him and raised his champagne

glass to his lips. Some listened, chewing on a toothpick, their elbows on the table; others sat with eyes downcast as if listening to a sermon; Sarrotini was looking about him, wild-eyed; Genoveva was sitting absolutely still, smiling.

'You have come to us from Paris,' he went on. 'Obviously you will not find here the splendours of the boulevards, the luxury of the Grand Hotel, the hurly-burly of the Bois de Boulogne.'

When Genoveva heard him speak of the luxury of the Grand Hotel, she had to fix her features in a look of amazement in order to suppress her laughter.

'We are poor, but glorious . . .'

'Seconded,' muttered Fonseca.

'We may not be able to compete with such lavish displays of wealth, but what we can show the rest of Europe is a lasting and continuing peace and hard, honest toil. Our glories are not small ones . . . oh, no, madam . . .'

Genoveva, finding herself referred to so directly, blushed. But Carvalhosa had not finished:

'They may not shine like beacons, but they warm like flames.'

'Oh, exquisite,' said the poet. 'Such richness of language!'

Carvalhosa, scarlet with pleasure at having conceived the phrase, repeated it:

'They may not shine like beacons, but they warm like flames.'

'Excuse me,' said Vítor, 'but I think the lady is feeling unwell.'

All eyes turned on the woman in the red turban. She seemed to be in some distress; she was breathing hard, her eyes rolled back, and she fell, head lolling, into Marinho's arms. The ladies sprang to their feet, the men rushed towards her, and Carvalhosa, pale-faced, champagne glass in hand, stood looking desolately about him, his left hand still raised and waiting.

But the room had emptied. Almost everyone had gone out into the larger salon where the piano was already playing. Only the lyric poet, slightly drunk, was still devouring a large serving of pudding. Glancing up at Carvalhosa, he said:

'What's wrong, illustrious orator, has the cat got your tongue?'

Carvalhosa, furious, cursed him roundly, put on his jacket and left.

The butler, who lit the way, remarked:

'The coffee's just about to be served, sir.'

'Well, I hope they enjoy it!' Carvalhosa said and flounced off angrily down the stairs.

Meanwhile, the woman in the red turban was busy being sick in Genoveva's boudoir. They had made her some green tea, but her unruly intestines had had enough and their contents erupted from her mouth in great spurts. In the other room, Fonseca was playing a waltz, and Sarrotini and Dâmaso were dancing together.

At last, they managed to quell the troubled viscera of the woman in the turban. Mélanie took her to Miss Sarah's room so that she could rest a little and loosen her stays. Genoveva was sitting in front of the mirror, tidying her hair, when Vítor appeared at the door; seeing her alone, he withdrew.

'I just came to find out if the lady was better . . .'

'Come in, come in,' said Genoveva. 'You're not afraid of my bedroom, are you? It's not the cave of the Bandit King!'

Vítor went slowly into the room, as if entering a church, and was immediately paralysed by the sight of the curtains round the bed, the blue satin nightdress case, the glittering bottles, the silk dressing gown and the flickering candles; they formed part of the very fabric of a life. He was so troubled that all he could say was:

'You've got a very nice room here . . .'

She laughed her musical laugh.

'Do you think so? It's just a rented room, terribly banal. I don't really know how I can bring myself to sleep in here. I had to buy new quilts and a sprung mattress, otherwise, I just couldn't sleep at all.'

These details fell upon Vítor's soul like an intoxicating draught of fine wine. He avidly studied every detail, as if hoping to discover in the furniture, in the dressing table, in a nightdress, some hint of her naked beauty or of her thoughts.

Genoveva remained at the mirror, smoothing her hair, applying more face powder, jingling her bracelets; her breast rose and fell very fast; her dark eyes shone, and her profile, lit by the light over the mirror, gleamed softly, revealing in the exquisite paleness of her skin a vivid splendour.

'If you'd care to sit down, please do,' she said. 'There are cigarettes over there. You can smoke if you like. I don't mind cigarette smoke in here. They're from Paris.'

Vítor took a cigarette and went to light it on the candle burning by the dressing table. He was very close to Genoveva; he almost brushed her with his elbow; neither of them said a word. Outside, in the other room, could be heard the noise of the piano, laughter and a driving waltz that made the old floorboards tremble.

There were some beautiful camellias in a vase. Vítor remarked on their beauty. She put down her comb, picked a red camellia from the vase and, turning round, placed it in his buttonhole.

Vítor's eyes met Genoveva's for a second, and as she adjusted the flower, her eyelids flickered slightly and, in a slightly uncertain voice, she said:

'You won't lose it, will you?'

Tremulously, weighing every word, Vítor said passionately, boldly:

'I'll keep it for ever!'

She laughed.

'Don't be silly! Ah, but I was forgetting that you're a poet.'

And having pinned the flower in his buttonhole, she stood back a little, still touching the petals of the flower.

'There you are, your decoration! My Order, the Order of the Red Camellia. You're my knight now. *Voilà!*'

A wave of passion rushed through Vítor; his head was whirling, he reached out desperate arms to her, exclaiming:

'Listen!'

She drew back, rapped him lightly over the knuckles with her fan and, as if surprised, said:

'Whatever are you doing?'

He froze, his face flushed. Then she drew nearer again.

'Let's waltz,' she said and took his arm.

At that moment, the door opened and Dâmaso's voice boomed out:

'What's all this, then?'

Genoveva, standing very erect, asked in a proud, chilly tone: 'What do you mean "all this"?'

'You talking in here . . . in private,' he stammered.

He was standing in the doorway, in front of her.

'Oh, get out of the way!' she said scornfully in English, waving her fan impatiently at him, as if shooing away a dog.

He left, his lips trembling.

'Do you speak English?' Genoveva asked Vítor calmly.

He found the perfect answer:

'I only know one phrase.'

'And what's that?' she asked, her head on one side.

'I love you.'

Genoveva walked back into the main room, fanning herself, and did not reply. She shouted:

'Maestro! The *Madame Angot* waltz!'

And they began to dance; they moved so quickly that Vítor, who was not used to dancing, felt as if the whole apartment were whirling about him; he felt her strong body bend in his arms, her hand pressing on his shoulder; she was looking down slightly, her fan in her hand, and she turned supply and gracefully, the long train of her dress sweeping behind her, and when they stopped, it wrapped around Vítor's legs, carried along by the impetus of the dance. He stood there panting, while she smiled, flushed and radiant.

Then the lancer, ramrod straight, whisked past them, turning and turning, with Pia de' Tolomei in his arms. Next, dancing or, rather, leaping by, came Sarrotini with Senhor Reinaldo.

Fonseca stepped up the tempo, and the poet Roma, propped drunkenly against the piano, was improvising lyrics to the waltz:

> Keep waltzing waltzes
> Spinning wildly on.

And in the smoking room, old Couto was slumped in one corner, snoring.

Dâmaso, meanwhile, was watching Vítor and Genoveva with furious eyes. Genoveva paused for a moment next to him.

'Don't look so gloomy! Dance! Have fun! Sulking's very ageing, you know!'

He sprang angrily to his feet.

'Oh, very funny!' he muttered and, giving her a rancorous look, stalked off.

'Idiot!' muttered Genoveva in turn.

Vítor heard the exchange and drew great hope and extra-ordinary pleasure from it. He dragged her back to the waltz, but she stopped and, instead, again took his arm and walked quickly over to Dâmaso, who was leaning in a doorway, seething. She said:

'Look, you're being ridiculous. If you're going to put on these tragic airs, then you'd better get your coat and leave.'

'But, why were you . . . ?'

'I've told you before, don't address me as "tu".'

'Right, good night, then,' he said furiously and was about to go.

'Listen, take the gentleman from the Academy with you, will you, the old chap over there snoring. Go on, off you go!'

Dâmaso, who had promised to take Couto home, went over, shook him awake and pulled him, half-asleep and pro-testing, to his feet, linked arms with him and led him to the landing. He and the butler wrapped Couto in his velvet-collared cloak, and Dâmaso then bundled him into the coupé, slammed the door and bawled at the coachman:

'Come on, don't hang around!'

Up above, the windows glowed. He could hear the piano playing and people laughing. Hunched in the dark of the coupé, Dâmaso pondered his wrath. The hussy! Flirting with another man! And her manner, her tone of voice, as if she were a real lady, when she was nothing but a vulgar prostitute, a bloodsucker. And he was fool enough to feed her money!

'Lovely party,' mumbled Couto.

'Lovely,' said Dâmaso bitterly.

V

As Vítor walked home from Genoveva's soirée, he was carried along by a profound, subtle emotion welling up from his soul and suffusing his whole being, the way wind fills a sail. The mist was lifting, the stars were shining, and a light, cold wind was stirring. As his footsteps echoed down the deserted streets, Vítor struggled to remember every detail of the soirée in order to prolong it in his mind and to experience again the feelings it had awoken in him; but everything faded into nothingness, drowned in Genoveva's brilliance.

She appeared before him either as a whole, dazzling him with her overwhelming, maddening beauty, or in fragments that gleamed in the dark night: her full shoulders where dress met flesh; her supple torso that moved with a whisper of silk; the marvellous skin of her bare forearm; or the shadows cast by her firm, round chin; he could still hear the sweet dying fall of certain tender notes in her voice, and her explosions of silvery laughter. He felt so happy that he sang softly to himself; he felt abundant life flowing through his veins, a thousand impulses driving him on, as if all the fine qualities of his soul and character, which had lain dormant for lack of stimulus, had been awoken by Genoveva's voice and eyes and were all now demanding action and movement.

His life up until then had been nothing but a slow, somnambular journey down an endless tunnel; now, suddenly, he saw unrolling before him a rich, luminous life, full of tenderness, a life whose continuous delights he would share with Genoveva in a crescendo of bliss ... for there could be no doubt that she loved him. He marshalled the evidence: the red camellia, the sweet nothings she had whispered to him, the hints, glances, allusions; he felt immensely proud.

Genoveva seemed to him almost divine, embellished by all the cities she had lived in, all the famous people she had known, all the pleasures she had enjoyed; a rich, complete, refined, powerful civilisation had created, polished, penetrated and made her perfect. And that perfect creature loved him!

She who had known so many men of captivating beauty and impressive intelligence loved him; and he felt as if he had been placed on a very tall pedestal in the midst of life.

How mean the city was, and how inferior and worthy of compassion were all those men in their dark houses, sleeping in the arms of trivial women.

He swore to be worthy of her: to wear elegant clothes, to read novels, plays, to fill his spirit with an entirely modern wit in order to be able to wield it like a foil. He would write poetry, borrow money from his uncle. When he went into his room, he looked at himself in the mirror and touched his hair; he looked serene and handsome. What had struck her about him? What had pleased her about him? Was it his curly, black hair, his large, languid eyes or his soft beard? Or his skin like pale marble?

He could not bring himself to get undressed and put on his slippers, as if taking off his tails and his patent leather shoes would destroy his own charm and that of the evening.

He woke up like a man in love, immediately feeling the memory of her filling his soul with all the sweetness of a mother's kiss; and wrapping his arms about him, he embraced the image of her and thought many tender thoughts.

The day had never seemed lovelier to him, the light more brilliant, every sound more festive; a vague languor hovered in the air. He had breakfast in bed and, leaning back against the pillows and smoking a cigarette, he lost himself in imagining various joyous scenarios. He saw them walking side by side in Sintra, beneath the murmurous trees, accompanied by the cool sound of flowing water, or he saw himself kneeling at her feet in her bedroom, coiling and uncoiling about his finger one blonde lock of hair. No lewd or impure thoughts passed through his mind; the intensity of his desire almost disappeared beneath the sweetness of love; even the vision of himself kissing her bare, white flesh with light, devout, thoughtful, ecstatic kisses was a chaste vision.

He got dressed slowly and tried to write a poem, but after

torturing his brain, all he could produce were these two lines:

> Yesterday, in the whirl of an ardent waltz
> I felt your body tremble and quake . . .

And since it was a magnificent morning, he put on his hat and went out.

He hoped vaguely that he might meet her. He did not, of course, go to the office; he had a horror of Rua do Arco da Bandeira, of Dr Caminha, or the placid figure of the magistrate. No, the last thing he needed was to shut himself up in that cave lined with legal documents. That wasn't what he had been born for. He was a man of literature, the literature of sensation, novels and poetry. To hell with official papers. He would write a book, that is what he would do, and he would dedicate it to her.

But after wandering through the Chiado, past Alves, along Rua do Alecrim and the Aterro, and back past Alves again, he had still not seen her. The day seemed to grow sad, as if, under a spell, all the colours had suddenly withdrawn.

The next day, unable to wait any longer, he made his way nervously to Rua de São Bento. Genoveva had told him that she was always at home between one and three. He trembled when he heard the bell ringing in the corridor.

Mélanie opened the door and her breathless 'Ah, it's you, sir' and the way she ran to tell Genoveva, made him think arrogantly that he was expected.

He found Genoveva lying languidly on the sofa in the living room, a book in her hand. She raised herself up on one elbow, apologised for having to receive him like this, but she had been unwell since last night; feebly letting her book fall to the floor, she indicated a chair nearby and asked:

'So, what news?'

Vítor felt deeply embarrassed. She was wearing a capacious blue robe that fell in long, loose folds about her body, emphasising her breasts and the deep curve of her waist; her small, black-stockinged feet were shod in satin slippers. She looked pale and, in contrast to the lace pillow on which she was resting her head with the white and gold of her skin and hair, her eyes, surrounded by faint brown circles, seemed even darker and gazed on him with a look that was at once sad and curious.

'What's wrong?'

She said she felt tired and vaguely unwell; her stomach was slightly upset. She asked him to call Mélanie, and when Mélanie appeared, her hands in the pockets of her starched white apron, Genoveva asked her in a faint voice to bring her some broth. Then, turning to Vítor:

'You don't mind the lack of ceremony, do you? You're a friend of Dâmaso's, so you're almost like family, really.'

The casual mention of Dâmaso's name as a justification for their intimacy, made Vítor blush angrily. He said only:

'No, no, of course not.'

And he felt everything about him grow cold, felt an immense, icy, desolate distance suddenly open up between them; and feeling the affection that had warmed him evaporate, he sat in his chair, not knowing what to do or say. What he did say was:

'If I'd known you weren't well, I would never have come . . .'

She made a gesture with her hand and smiled as if to reassure him, then, shifting slightly on the sofa, she said again:

'So, what news?'

Nothing, really. It was a lovely day, a bit chilly perhaps.

She turned to lie on her side on the sofa, facing him, attentive, curious, her cheek resting on one hand.

'What did you do yesterday?'

Her smile revealed white teeth between moist, red lips, like a rose petal in the rain. Vítor mistook her look for one of amorous invitation. He said in a low voice:

'I thought about you.'

But, at that point, Mélanie came in with the broth and, in her subtle, confidential manner, placed it on a small table next to Genoveva; she put down the silver tray, plumped up her mistress' pillow, and left with the lightness

110

of a shadow, having first shot Vítor an enquiring sideways glance.

'So, what did you do?' said Genoveva, who had again raised herself up on one elbow and was idly stirring the broth.

Vítor said again:

'I thought about you.'

And then, Genoveva, in a torrent of wounded words, asked him not to talk like that. She fell back on her pillow. It wasn't true. Would she never find anyone who spoke sincerely, who showed some common sense! Why on earth should he have thought about her? They had only met twice, and on that second occasion had dined together and danced. Was that any reason to flirt or talk of love? What sort of woman did he take her for? It wasn't right to have such thoughts about people without their permission. Surely he could see that they could never be anything more than good friends. Honestly, men were so strange! You only had to squeeze their hand or give them a flower, just for fun, with no ulterior motive, and they were immediately aflame with desire, and thinking they had the right to make demands . . .

'I'm not making any demands,' said Vítor, whose hopes were being painfully shattered by that storm of words.

'But you would start making demands if I were to listen to you and believe you. That's not a nice thing to do. You knew I had had other lovers, and so you assumed I was easy; you said to yourself: I can have her. And so you come and see me, find me ill, and tell me straight out that you spent all of yesterday thinking about me. Why? For what purpose? With what intention? So that I could become a little hobby of yours, something to boast to your friends about.'

'Madam, I beg you, you must believe . . .'

That arrant misreading of his feelings offended him, but she silenced him with a gesture.

'Listen, I'm not a young woman any more. How old do you think I am? Well, I'm thirty-two. My life has been a series of misfortunes. I'm not particularly well, I'm capricious and unbearable. I have more than ten *contos de reis* in debts. As you see, I am not a nice woman. I am not a woman that men

111

"think about",' she said emphatically. 'I like you, so come and see me and dine with me occasionally . . . I dine at seven every evening . . . we can talk, but no more than that. Anything more would be ridiculous. There, you see, I'm a good girl and I've been honest with you. You're not offended, are you?'

And when she spoke these words, there was such a mixture of tenderness and cheerful sincerity in her eyes, that he felt an urge to kneel before her and swear his respectful submission to her wishes and, in order to console her, to be merely her confidant, her brother. He wished he could pay off her debts and lightly touch the foot which, when she moved, had appeared beneath her robe; he glimpsed her ankle as well, to which the black stocking lent a piquant, romantic beauty,

'You're not angry with me, are you?' she said.

She was leaning forward now, revealing the sharp indentation of her waist, the languid curve of her hips and the outline of her leg beneath the folds of her robe; her blonde hair fell in loose curls about her brow and, with her head slightly raised like that, he could see her white throat, firm and smooth.

'How could I possibly be angry with you?' he blurted out passionately.

'Do you mean that, my friend, really? Come and sit here.'

She made room for him on the sofa and Vítor felt her feet beneath the robe touch his leg; he experienced an overwhelming desire to fall on her, embrace her and cover her with kisses.

'Why don't you wear your hair parted in the middle?' she asked, examining him closely.

Vítor touched his parting.

'I don't know. I've always worn my hair like this.'

She advised him to part his hair in the middle; that way, he would reveal more of his forehead, because he had a nice forehead . . . And she added quickly:

'Dâmaso has the forehead of a fool.'

Vítor laughed. He was just about to heap witty insults on his friend's head, when instead she began to praise Dâmaso: he was a very nice young man, very helpful; he had a good heart

112

and his teeth weren't bad either; and he rode exceptionally well. Then she suddenly asked him how old he was.

'Dâmaso? Oh, me, I'm twenty-three.'

Twenty-three, and he dared to say he had been thinking about her, her, an old, spent woman, fit only to be a grandmother.

Vítor, roused, leaned towards her and was about to tell her of his passion for her, but she, very calmly, asked him what time it was.

It was nearly three, and Dâmaso hadn't arrived. He had promised her too.

Vítor was put out and, thinking she was making fun of him, got to his feet and was about to pick up his hat.

But Genoveva seemed surprised. Why? Where was he going?

'Sit down.'

She put her hands behind her head on the pillow. The robe, drawn tight, revealed the vague outline of her legs and the curve of her breasts. She closed her eyes and her breast rose and fell. That silence made Vítor feel awkward; he did not understand and, twirling one end of his moustache, he devoured her with his eyes; that sleeping pose, in which she seemed to offer herself up, filled his heart with mad, frenetic desires, and he was on the point of speaking or of embracing her, when she opened her eyes, fixed him with an almost anguished look, then closed them again, sighing, and lay quite still, oblivious to his presence.

Vítor suddenly got up and paced around the room; his temples were throbbing. She opened her eyes again and murmured.

'No, sit down next to me. Be a good lad. I don't feel at all well.'

What was the matter? Was she in pain? And Vítor, shaking, lightly placed his fingers on her arm.

'Have I got a fever?'

And she held out her hands to him; he held her wrist between his fingers; he could feel her heart. It was beating fast and seemed to buzz inside his own head.

'No, no, you haven't.'

She laughed her strange, musical laugh.

'A fine doctor you are!'

Then, in an abrupt shift of mood, she began to say how sad life was, how alone she felt. She had never known the joy of true affection.

'All the men who have told me they loved me were mere egotists; I was young and I rewarded them with pleasure.'

But she had always realised soon afterwards that their love was not real; they were not devoted, pure, ready to sacrifice themselves for her.

'No one has ever really respected me. My husband, Monsieur de Molineux, was very, very kind to me, but he was an egotist too. No one has ever shown me any true devotion. Even Mélanie, who adores me, would leave me tomorrow if someone offered her more money. Life is so sad; everything is so illusory!'

Vítor grasped her hand.

'And if I told you that I love you, adore you, that I want to be everything to you in this world . . .'

Genoveva sat up, fixed him with her eyes, and holding his hands hard, said forcefully:

'No, it's not true, it's not true!'

There was real affliction in her voice.

'I swear it is,' said Vítor, falling at her feet.

But Genoveva stood up and said almost coolly:

'Now, my friend, don't get all worked up. You Portuguese are terrible, you catch fire so easily.'

Then she gave a brief, provocative laugh. Vítor hated her.

The door opened and the lanky figure of Miss Sarah appeared; she was about to withdraw discreetly, when Genoveva called to her:

'Come in, come in. This is a friend of Dâmaso's.'

And she introduced Vítor, saying that he spoke English. Miss Sarah curtseyed, blushing, her long arms hanging by her sides. Genoveva suddenly said:

'Ah, it's half past three!'

Vítor picked up his hat.

114

'Now do come and see the poor patient again,' said Genoveva, holding out her hand to him.

Vítor bowed to Miss Sarah, who was staring at him in amazement, her cheeks flushed.

'What have you done with the camellia?' asked Genoveva, laughing.

'I've put it in a safe place,' he said as he left.

Genoveva went over to the window, lifted the lace curtain a fraction, but immediately drew back and walked into the middle of the room, where she stretched and yawned:

'Oh, dear God!'

Miss Sarah remarked gravely that Vítor was a very handsome young man.

'He'd be a good match for you, Miss Sarah.'

The Englishwoman blushed scarlet.

Vítor got home in time for supper and found a letter from Aninhas waiting for him – four whole sheets – but the handwriting was so bad, he could not be bothered to read it, so he merely ran his eyes over it and having deciphered amongst the tangle of loops and uprights vague expressions such as: 'my wretched life', 'will adore you until I die', 'forced by necessity', 'deep regret', he threw it down, declaring:

'Oh, to hell with her!'

And he began going over his morning with Genoveva and had to admit that he did not understand her. Did she love him? To judge by certain glances, certain attitudes she struck, by her silences, by the agitation she seemed to feel when near him, she did. But sometimes she spoke to him with friendly ease, at others with cold scorn, often she seemed merely distracted or, even more extraordinary, utterly indifferent. But for those very reasons, he loved her all the more. He found her capricious, complex, enigmatic, and so, as well as loving her, he felt curious too. And in order to talk about her, out of the need which leads the weak soul to scatter and spill over others some part of its feelings, he went to spend the evening with his close friend, the painter, Camilo Cerrão. They did not see each other often, but there was great mutual respect between them.

Vítor admired the painter's eloquence and originality, and Camilo found in Vítor a patient and attentive audience for his theories and his long disquisitions, a passive repository for the superabundance of his aesthetic ramblings.

Cerrão lived in a fourth-floor apartment and had converted one low-ceilinged room into a studio, with two windows overlooking the street; the floor, which was never washed, was black with all the heels and soles that crossed it; when he needed to rest from painting or to indulge in his 'contemplative solitudes' as he called them, he would lie on a threadbare, battered old couch. That was where he did his thinking and creating. It was his Olympus. Nailed up on the walls were all kinds of engravings, as well as a few paintings acquired from a second-hand shop; there was some seventeenth-century armour purchased for a few pence from the Navy arsenal, a few plaster heads, cheap reproductions of museum pieces, a table piled high with papers, drawings and half-finished watercolours, and four old leather chairs, arranged as if in the chapterhouse of an abbey. The meagre light that seeped in through the narrow panes fell on the easel positioned by the window; another corner was occupied by pots of paint and a small dais, another by slippers, a skirt and a woman's dressing gown; there was a scattering of spent matches on the floor, and everything had a grubby, intimate air, a look of poverty, of confused, unconsidered life, and of works begun impatiently and abandoned in despair.

Wearing slippers and a scarlet double-breasted jacket over a crumpled shirt, Cerrão paced nervously about the studio, smoking furiously and spewing out words like a writer of newspaper serials. He was short, extremely thin and slightly stooped. He moved awkwardly, disjointedly; he had an enormous head, and his prominent brow was crowned by a brush of coarse, black hair; he had a gaunt face, a crooked nose, thin lips adorned by a curled moustache, and deep-set, expressive eyes that shone with life.

His days were fully occupied because, in order to live, he worked as a set designer at the Teatro de Variedades in Rua dos Condes; at night, though, at home, he 'made art'. Cerrão had talent, but because he was so entirely preoccupied by systems and theories and was so excessively talkative, always full of sayings, maxims and literary quotations, he dissipated what talent he had in that endless loquacity, and produced nothing.

He was, as he put it, in search of the one true principle of art, convinced that, as soon as he found it, he would create something remarkable; he would bring about a renaissance in Portuguese painting, win converts to his cause, fill the museums and galleries with sublime paintings and live on in posterity. To this end, he read everything written by critics and aestheticians. Since he was highly impressionable and always under the influence of the last thing he had read, he would pass from one system to another, like an errant comet, drawing light from all the opinions he passed.

At first, he had been enthused by the idea that painting, being essentially one of the plastic arts, had as its object the representation of physical beauty; to this end, he produced only pictures showing the immortal divinity of naked bodies: noble attitudes, splendid musculature, the glories of the flesh; prodigious Venuses, admirably posed gladiators. Ideas, according to him, were nothing. There should be no ideas in painting: paintings should show beautiful bodies in noble poses, paintings should be sculptures which, because they were in colour, were therefore closer to life.

To this he added a vague theory about the transformation of the modern body; he found it deplorable that people's bodies nowadays were always somehow deformed, awkward, crooked, thin, ugly or ridiculous. He attributed this to the tyranny of the idea and the abandonment of the cult of plasticity. He wanted to create a school of painters preoccupied solely with plastic beauty; soon every house would have on its walls a beautiful painting of a divine figure lit by glorious light. Pregnant wives would have these new forms ever present in the home and after the nine months gestation period would give birth, as women did in Greece, to children with perfect bodies. And soon, the Portuguese race would be the most beautiful in the world; it would rival ancient Greece; the

Chiado would be filled by seamstresses as beautiful as Venus, the ministries by clerks as noble as Apollo. The creation of beauty would become a priority for the city. Soon this influence would be seen in clothes and architecture and, in a hundred years' time, Lisbon would be a new Athens inhabited by sculptured bodies striking harmonious poses, wearing artistic clothes and strolling among splendid porticos against a backdrop as blue as the Tyrrhenian Sea.

After that, he had fallen passionately in love with the picturesque. 'What is art,' he would exclaim, 'but the idealisation of life, a means of adding idealism to the bourgeois existence. Present-day life is dull and trivial, preoccupied with matters of money, buying and selling – mean, plebeian concerns. The businessman with his packages, the lawyer with his legal documents, the banker with his lists of shares, the doctor with his poultices and the clerk with his copies of memoranda, they all live a subaltern, vulgar, plebeian, stupid life, a suffocating life. Everyone needs some noble, high ideal in their lives, something that will compensate them for their stupid jobs and distract them from their mean preoccupations. That is the purpose of art. That is why paintings are hung on walls and why people fill the museums; so that the bourgeois, the practical man, the noble soul weary of the plebeian sadness of his life, may contemplate something nobler, more beautiful, more interesting and more picturesque than casinos, the gloomy waiting rooms in law courts, the meagre light of offices and the tedium of ministries. Art, then, should be picturesque; it should show sweet, gentle landscapes, as a consolation to the man obliged to live out his life in the centre of Lisbon; paintings of grandiose skies, of festivals and triumphal cavalcades to contrast with the trivial gait of clerks or passing muleteers; paintings that show lavish clothes, velvets and jewels to people who otherwise see only frock coats and trousers. Art should be the great consoler. Imagine, then, hitherto unknown canvases with the abundance of Rubens and the splendour of Veronese; imagine a painting intended as a consoling antithesis to modern life. It would show a broad sweep of ideal landcape along the lines of a Turner. Glorious light would filter through the leaves of trees of paradisiac beauty; marvellous buildings of pale marble and transparent jasper would stand amongst the greenery; fountains would flow, filling the painting with a sweet coolness: in the foreground there would be the body of an ideal woman sitting in an arcade set in a tender landscape of exquisite colours; she would be holding a piece of lace in her hands, which would fall in full, noble folds; there would be fruit piled high in porcelain bowls, precious wines in silver jugs; couples, amorously entwined, would stroll along the avenues in the ecstatic silence of absolute happiness. Wise, serene old men with bright eyes would speak of poets and philosophers, and heroic young men would engage in athletic games, showing off their pride in their own perfect anatomy. This painting would correspond immediately to the needs of the soul. In contemplating it, people would experience the consolation of gentle landscapes, the sweetness of philosophy, the joy of fertile lands and a sense of immortal love.'

Cerrão subsequently found all this utterly idiotic and conceived instead of a kind of Venetian festival in the style of Tintoretto: on a Renaissance terrace, ladies and gentlemen would form nobly heroic groups; along the balustrades, peacocks would spread wide their resplendent tails; precious wines would be poured from golden carafes; there would be coffers filled to overflowing with gold coins, daggers telling of bloody vengeances, black-vestmented lackeys holding greyhounds on leashes; a procession of people would be reciting poems to the sound of violins; and in the background would be the flowers and trees of an artificial, symbolic landscape. All of this would feed the viewer's eyes with a luxury lacking in modern life.

But, lately, Cerrão had come to despise such ideas; he found them immoral. Art, according to him, should educate by depicting justice rather than corrupt expressions of luxury. And thus, though full of ideas and talk, images and fragments of pictures, he neglected the actual practice of painting; his drawing technique was wrong, his anatomy inaccurate, the light in his paintings clumsy, the movements of his figures unreal, mistaken; and although he had enough ideas to fill a museum, he had only actually produced one finished work of art.

Vítor found him drawing by the light of an oil lamp with a green shade that cast a crude light onto a large sheet of paper covered in a tangle of bold charcoal lines. The rest of the room lay in silent shadow, out of which emerged a few white plaster figures or the gleam of engravings, and from a room nearby came the creak of a cradle rocking.

Cerrão signalled to Vítor to say nothing, fearful that his footsteps might frighten away his inspiration (which, in his rhetoric, he compared to a subtle bird that lands for just a moment and which the slightest noise can startle), and so Vítor sat down on the cheaply upholstered couch. Cerrão was furiously covering the paper with unruly lines; he kept running his hands through his hair, leaping up from the chair, leaning forward, sighing, groaning, sniffing and fidgeting, as if in pain.

Vítor noticed the neck of a guitar sticking out from beneath the table; he picked it up and played a few chords. Cerrão jumped.

'Yes, play something as an accompaniment. That's what I need, something Brazilian or a *fado*.'

Vítor quietly strummed the guitar, and the soft, sleepy sounds created a sweet murmur that filled the veiled shadows of the room, while the charcoal skittered over the paper and, next door, a cradle creaked sadly.

'Have a look!' said Cerrão.

Vítor went over and all he could make out was the vague shape of a thickly wooded hill, above which, to one side, hung a round disc, that seemed to rise like a dot above a pointed belltower.

'Is that the moon?' he asked, pointing at the disc.

Cerrão snorted. He pushed back his chair, got out a cigarette and placing his finger on the drawing, he said:

'No, it's the Host.'

He went on to explain the drawing, developing his latest theories on art.

He had been on entirely the wrong track and had wasted ten years of his life, the best, most vigorous, most creative years of his life in pursuit of that disgusting principle: art for art's sake. What a fool, eh? But now he was in possession of the truth and, like St Paul on the road to Damascus, he saw everything clearly, thanks to the divine light guiding him. Art was a force of nature and, as such, must be used for the good of civilisation; on the other hand (he was growing excited now), art was a focus for civilisation. Humanity tended to transform great natural phenomena into things to be used. What was the wind? A movement of air about the sky. On its own, what purpose did it serve?

'What use is the wind? It's an idiot, a babbler, a brute, a telltale. I can see it now sighing in a tree like a lyric poet; there it is over there lasciviously stroking a woman's leg like a libertine; over there it's playing with someone's hat like a fool, or, like a murderer, wrecking some wretch's fishing boat. An idler, a beast! So what did we do with it? We studied, defined, explored and enslaved it. We said to it: Come over here, you layabout, turn the sails of this windmill for me and grind me some corn, fill the sails of that ship and bring me cocoa from Brazil. And so we have the miller and tugboat. What did we do with electricity? Made it into a postman, an employee of the Post Office. What did we do with steam? Made it into a horse, a puller of engines. These things come from nature and are immediately turned into something useful. Everything has a purpose, nothing exists simply for existence's sake. One must not allow any feeling, force or movement to go unused; everything must be used and put to work to create civilisation. The Sun is a portrait painter, we want no idlers in the universe; the stars are a celestial navigation chart. None of this is new, but what we do with the forces of nature we must also do with the forces of the mind. Art is a mighty phenomenon of the brain which must be channelled into some direct use, such as working for civilisation or for the revolution. Fighting the old world, old ideas, tyranny, brute force, and weighing up what is fair, balanced, right. Art should be revolutionary by its very nature. A painting should be a book, a pamphlet, a

121

newspaper article. It should attack Catholicism, the monarchy, the rotten bourgeoisie, the tyrant; it should attack all the stubborn old ogres still clinging to power. Art should be a tribune for philosophising and pamphleteering. Everything else is the art of luxury, decoration and corruption, pleasurable to the eyes, but as pointless as vanity, as vile as prostitution. That's the old art as I perceived it. I was a fool, oblivious, blind until now. Then, pop, the cork's out of the bottle, and I'm going to make the most of it. Every work I produce will be like a barricade. I'm going to take hold of the old and destroy it with brushstrokes. Here it is, this is my first picture. Look.' He held up the drawing. 'It's a picture of a mass, because the mass is also a worthy subject. Here you have the church; the worldly modern church, painted, gaslit, with organs that play music from operettas, with plush carpets up to the altar, saints dressed by top couturiers like Aline . . . with priests who are everything but priests: gamblers, pimps, composers of comic opera, flautists, everything. Here is the congregation and the celebrant in his worn shoes, pale after nights spent in the local brothel, having lunched on loin of pork; in his nicotine-stained fingers, he raises up the Host – the offering, the symbol.

That's the mass for you! Now, look at the congregation: this fat woman, her lunchtime pork still in her gullet, bursting out of her Sunday dress, scrutinising other women's outfits, criticising their hats and gossiping; the men at the side doors, looking at women's legs, making eyes, signs, passing notes, pinching girls' arms and worse. The old men who come to see which girls they could pimp for; the toadies who attend one o'clock mass in order to please their director-general; the ones who are asleep or yawning; the ones who are only there for the music; look at them get up, cross themselves, sit down and kneel. Look at their faces: one is thinking about his lover, another about the indigestion he got from eating figs at lunch, another about the interest he's going to charge on a loan, another about the 'friend at the top' who's going to get him a job as a clerk. That one's thinking about his girlfriend, that one about how he's going to get a letter to his mistress.

122

There's a feeling of constraint, an eagerness to leave; they slyly consult watches and examine their neighbours. If a dog barks, everyone turns round, whispering, sniffing, pleased that something has broken the divine monotony. And when the idiot at the top end of the church spreads wide his arms and says: *Ita missa est*, a sigh of relief leaves every chest. The dreary business is over. Watch them bowing, shaking hands, congratulating each other, pleased at a task completed. That's religion for you! What public spirit, what a painting! Give me a cigarette, will you?'

And he fell back exhausted on the couch.

'Anyway, I've found the path at last. Up here,' he said, tapping his head, 'I've got enough paintings to cause a revolution; after the mass, I'll do the funeral, then the chamber of deputies, then money-lending, and finally, elections. Off with all their heads!'

Vítor was about to say something, but Cerrão interrupted him:

'And all of this, my friend, will be done in the new style of painting. Nothing finished, mannered or polished, nothing lavish or decorative. Painting is nothing and the idea is everything. Broad strokes, shapes roughly shaded in, bold colours, so as to give a true impression of reality.' He made brushstrokes in the air. 'Expression is what counts! I can paint you a moneylender with just three strokes of my brush. You want a moneylender, here you are: greenish tones on sunken cheeks, a touch of ochre on the forehead, silvery, metallic tones on the eyes, lead black on the throat and there you have him: gaunt, cold, unbending, vile. That is great art!'

He had spoken with great excitement, pushing his hair back, swaying back and forth, making wild gestures, writhing about on the sofa in inspired awkwardness. He picked up the guitar, strummed it loudly and put it down again. Then folding his hands on his chest, he lay still, as if in a torpor, his deep-set, glinting eyes staring into space.

Vítor, who was walking about the studio, started by saying that it was undoubtedly a sublime idea, but who would buy those paintings from him? After all, if they did not suit the

123

popular taste, if they went against all preconceptions of what art is, and if they weren't even very well painted, he would be hard pressed to find buyers.

Cerrão sat up, as if someone had stuck a knife in him. That thought cut through the marvellous ramifications of his dream like an icy axe.

'Who will buy them?' he said, pacing about the studio, his head down, shoulders twitching. 'Who will buy them? Why, no one!'

And in despair, he fell back onto the couch again, uttering a bitter sigh. Perhaps he'd be better off as a seller of sausages; he himself would paint the sign, an extraordinary sign, on which all the usual grocer's goods would appear, but with human features: the white bacon fat would have the plump cheeks of a conservative; the cheeses would have the double chins of bourgeois traders; the pink pork sausages would be flushed with the wealth of usury triumphant; the tallow candles, like the columns in the Rossio, would look like constitutional monuments; the barrels of butter would have the stuffed, rancid pot bellies of the bourgeois. And underneath, in seering, radical, scarlet letters, would appear: Camilo Cerrão – Grocer to the Royal Household.'

And he rubbed his hands gleefully at the thought of his sign, thinking with excitement and joy about what people would say and the scandal it would cause! Yes, that was what he should do, become a grocer!

'Besides,' he said, 'art is impossible in a democracy. I'm sorry, but it's true. The end of the great houses saw the end of all the big collections. What the bourgeois, the parliamentarian, the constitutionalist and the liberal republican want are small things, engravings: a nice neat landscape, lambs, a stupid virgin tearing the petals off a daisy with fingers that look like melted butter. Oh, for the days of Raphael, Titian, Veronese, for the days of human painting, when the artist had stature, when he rivalled the State itself, when he had an eminent place in salons, commanded the defence of the city, bestowed immortality, and from his high estate, dictated terms to the Pope.'

It was all over, the world was eclipsed. And he returned to his idea of becoming a grocer.

'Rich people,' he said, 'might have all kinds of ideas, stupid, saucy, ludicrous, but it would simply never occur to them to commission a work of art. They would think of anything else but that: becoming a baron, setting a dancer up in her own apartment, buying a new pair of horses, getting a sailing boat for the regatta, giving a masked ball, and even more foolish things than that, but the simple, noble, useful, conciliatory, normal idea of saying: "Camilo, take up your brushes and create something sublime" would simply never occur to them.'

Then turning on Vítor, he said:

'You're rich, you've got a rich uncle, a position in society, a gold watch chain, but have you ever commissioned a painting from me?' He smiled. 'And why don't you do so? Because you're an ass.'

An idea suddenly pierced Vítor's mind: a portrait of Genoveva. He marvelled at it already, framed in his bedroom; he would lay flowers beneath it and it would become like an altar tabernacle.

'All right, I will commission a painting,' he said.

'How about the one of the mass?' replied Camilo, approaching him, his voice gruff, his eyes shining.

'No, I want a portrait.'

Camilo pulled a face and spun round on his heels.

'Oh, for heaven's sake!' he cried, opening his arms. 'Oh, of course. I suppose you want an expensively framed portrait of yourself in white tie and tails, with your idiotic dandy's face, all set against a scarlet backdrop, to get all the girls swooning.' He looked at him: 'You don't deserve it. What thought or idea could your face possibly inspire?'

He picked up the oil lamp and held it close to Vítor's face, examining it, muttering:

'Nothing unusual, nothing outstanding, nothing special; dull skin tones, anaemic white, no relief. What do you expect me to do with your phizog? A portrait can, of course, be a work of art, but you need the right model, someone with soul, ideas, energy, grandeur, but a banal bourgeois gentleman? No, photograph him.'

Vítor said:

'I don't want a portrait of me, I want one of a lady, a foreigner, a truly admirable woman.'

And he spoke of her spirit, her blonde beauty, her general superiority.

Camilo, sitting crosslegged on the couch, was furiously gnawing his nails.

He wanted to know the colour of her eyes, her hair, how tall she was. Then, striding about his studio, he began planning a remarkable work that would make his reputation: he would paint her full length, in a blue velvet dress decorated with Spanish lace and a pearl necklace round her neck, and he would portray her coming down the steps of a terrace, with, behind her, a Renaissance garden such as you might see in a Titian.

'Does she ride?' he asked suddenly.

'Very well.'

'Then why don't I paint her in a long black riding habit, long suede gloves, a Gainsborough hat, or perhaps a Fronda hat . . . and with a silk cloak lined with fur draped over her arm?'

His love of the picturesque was returning to tempt him.

'What am I saying? Art should be a civilizing force!' he exclaimed. 'It must be possible to paint a portrait that would be a condemnation of luxury and ostentation.' And gesturing as if he were sketching the broad outline of a drawing. 'One part would show a bourgeois scene – her walking beneath a pergola which, in graduating tones, leads the eye to the central point of the painting, her head, bare and silhouetted against the black of the corridor; she has a soft, kind face, serious, just eyes, straight, aquiline features, a serenity that reveals the equilibrium of her soul . . .'

A child started screaming.

'Can't you keep the wretch quiet?' he shouted, then turning back to Vítor: 'How can one be expected to work, think or even feel with a brat screaming to be fed all the time?

This narrow, bourgeois life is suffocating. Artists should live in palaces, in a civilised environment, surrounded by all the luxuries of art, alone with their ideas.'

'Is it your child?'

'Yes,' he said bluntly. 'I should have given him to the orphanage. Now what was I saying? Ah, yes, a face that would be the symbiosis of justice and reason; she'll be dressed in a chaste, sober black dress with long sleeves, and with little folds in her dress that reveal the beauty of the maternal woman, the fount of life, and holding out her hands, delicate, manicured hands . . . No, not that. What they need is bread?'

'Who?'

'Who? Why, the two frightened, weeping children, of course, snivelling, freckled, abject, shivering with cold and hunger: the people, the eternally oppressed!'

'It's not a bad idea . . .'

'What do you mean "not a bad idea"? It is quite simply the portrait as philosophy, the portrait as pamphlet, it is a socialist portrait.'

And he fixed his eyes on Vítor, as if astonished at the ambitious nature of his own plan. It would be a revelation! And punching the air with his two fists, he cried:

'There's nothing we can't do!'

'Would you like some tea?' asked a woman's voice through the half-open door.

'Yes, bring it in.'

And gripped by the fervour of his idea, he immediately asked for more information about the model: was she sensitive, what were her ideas, her political and social roots, 'because all this is vital information'.

And Vítor, seizing the opportunity to unburden himself, described both Genoveva and his passion for her.

Listening to him, Camilo's ideas changed abruptly. 'Ah, I see, a *cocotte*, a *dame aux camélias*'! He envisaged another possible interpretation: Titian's paintings of courtesans. She would be lying on a couch covered by a cloak of crimson velvet; on it the model would be half-naked; a curtain would be drawn back to reveal a garden in the background, and in the foreground, a mandolin to symbolise celebration and harmony, a dagger to evoke the avenging of some crime, and pearl necklaces overflowing from a silver goblet, the rewards of lechery. Or why not do a modern painting, in the style of Fortuny? A room lined in white satin, a fire burning in a high Renaissance fireplace, and she would be sitting on a love seat behind a great fire, with beringed hands reaching out to the golden flames?

'So you're in love, are you?' he asked suddenly, picking up a cigarette.

'Madly.'

'Very sad and very stupid.'

Vítor erupted in lyrical exclamations; what could be better than to tremble with love, what could be better than dreams, than kisses, than two entwined bodies?

Camilo shrugged and quickly set out his theory of love in a matter-of-fact voice, as if talking to himself: Passion was the worst misfortune an intelligent man could suffer. Any artist who falls in love is lost; love will introduce into his life all kinds of worries, concerns and compromises, and all work, all thought becomes impossible. Then there's jealousy, feigned emotion, the constant renewal of desire, the sloth of languor, childish dependency; a man's character becomes emasculated, the brain softens, ideas vanish, and someone who was once a force in society is no more than a bordello-keeper. The artist should shun love as the most humiliating of tyrants. To love a woman is to place all of one's vital energies at the service of . . . an organ! It's like being a glutton who only thinks, lives, works and moves in order to satisfy his stomach. The lover exists only to serve, to obey his heart, to give it its respectable name. I have set the artists of my time a great example. I have suppressed love. No woman has ever entered these doors, for woman is just a bundle of caprices, fantasies, nerves, sensibilities, tyrannies, arguments and inconstancies. But since Nature has its needs, and the brain requires to be free of those needs, I selected a female.'

The word shocked Vítor.

'I chose her for her statuesque qualities so that she could be

128

my model. At the time, I was obsessed by the most idiotic ideas. I believed in the nude. I believed in Venus. I imagined that a plastic art should concern itself only with proportions, poses, colour and musculature. Fool! I had forgotten that little thing: the idea. I chose a beautiful female, and it took me a long time to find one, because the fact is most women are hideous; there's no halfway house in women between hideousness and beauty; everything that counts in a woman – breasts, hair, buttocks – all goes to ruin eventually, if we don't turn women into goddesses. Since they are mere false additions to the true human type, which is man, as soon as they lose their beauty, their refinement, their ideal quality, that is all they are, frail additions, objects. Once her breasts drop, her bottom starts to wobble and her hair becomes thin and sparse, a woman is mere myth; she's uglier than a hippopotamus or a monkey.'

Just then, the door opened and Vítor saw the most splendid creature come in bearing a tray. She had very white skin, large, dark, ardent eyes, a mass of magnificent hair, and her small head rested nobly on a statuesque body; one could sense beneath her yellow cotton gown a singular magnificence and firmness of form. She set down the tray with her large, grubby hands, and calmly left again.

'That's her,' said Camilo bluntly, sitting down at the table and cutting himself a thick slice of bread.

'Is she from Lisbon?' asked Vítor.

'No. Lisbon couldn't produce a body like that; the breed has grown corrupt. She's from near Ovar, in the country, and she's a most unusual combination, half-Arab, half-Celt. A fine specimen.'

He walked about the studio, a slice of bread in his hand.

'She's the ideal female for an artist. She's stupid and passive. She eats, obeys, takes her clothes off. She's just a body that takes orders. She doesn't bother me or interrupt me, doesn't speak to me, she's just there. When I need a female, I call her.'

'Are you married?'

'Yes, that was the only way I could get her away from her mother. I bought her, but, instead of giving the old woman

129

gold, I gave her the sacrament of marriage. I paid her in spiritual coin. A good trick, eh? And here she is. All artists should do the same. Our loves are our creations; we give our soul, our blood and our life to love, giving away the very best of ourselves. The female is for those moments when the spirit rests and the beast inside us demands satisfaction.'

'So you're happy, then?'

'No, I'm wretched,' said Camilo.

And sitting down next to Vítor on the couch, he explained.

'I had it all so intelligently worked out, but I forgot one thing: children! I forgot the children. I was completely unprepared when nine months later, a great hefty boy arrived, a little seed of flesh, who yells, bawls, roars and generally makes the house a hell. Family life is the death of the artist. How I suffer. Did you hear the cradle creaking a little while ago, well, that's the sweetest music I hear, otherwise, in the morning, there are thunderous shouts and, in the evening, terrifying screams echoing through the house ... and of course my wife's busy, so I have to take on a maid. It's an inferno, an inferno! I must amend my maxim: what the artist needs is a sterile female. Anyway, her name's Joana. And the extraordinary thing is that pregnancy and childbirth have not changed a line of her body; there's not a fold, not a wrinkle, no slackening of a single curve. She's just perfect. A superb model ... for those fools who believe in line and form ... Joana!'

The woman came in. This time, her eyes, which she had kept lowered when she first entered, looked directly at Vítor and seemed to grow wide with astonishment; something in them flashed. Then, picking up the tea tray, she left as serenely as she had come.

'So there you have my views on love,' said Camilo, clapping him on the back.

Vítor was putting on his hat.

'What about this portrait, then?'

Vítor would have to talk to Genoveva. Camilo was thinking, one finger resting on his chin.

'I know, I'll paint her in revolutionary mode. What a

painting! Wait, I'll get someone to light you down the stairs. I won't come with you, I don't want to catch cold.' And he shouted: 'Joana, show this gentleman out, will you?'

Vítor went down the stairs, Joana followed, holding an oil lamp. But her serene footsteps, the brush of her dress on the steps, troubled Vítor. At the front door, he lit a cigarette on the flame of the oil lamp, and his eyes met Joana's eyes. It was only a moment, but Vítor's heart shuddered with desire. He took off his hat and thanked her:

'Goodnight, madam.'

She blushed and replied:

'Goodnight, sir.'

VI

The next day, Vítor went to find out how Genoveva was. In his mind, he could still see her as she had appeared to him the previous day, reclining on a sofa, her gestures languid, her words weary. He was most put out to see Dâmaso's coupé at the door. Since the coachman knew him, he resisted the temptation to withdraw discreetly and went in. On the final flight of stairs, he bumped into Dâmaso, who was coming down. They were both slightly embarrassed.

'She's gone out,' said Dâmaso brusquely.

'I thought she was ill.'

'Ill?' said Dâmaso, surprised. 'No, she's in perfect health. She's gone out. I spent the night with her.'

This was a lie, but he wanted to humiliate Vítor and make him think he was happy. The poor lad turned pale. They went down the stairs in silence.

'So, what have you been up to?' asked Dâmaso, at the front door, drawing on his gloves.

'Oh, nothing much,' said Vítor vaguely.

Dâmaso got into the coupé and, wanting to appear in command, he ordered the coachman rather sharply to drive on and slammed the carriage door shut with a satisfied air, although, he was, in fact, furious because Genoveva had gone out, having promised to wait for him.

Vítor walked slowly down the street. The brusqueness of his friend's words had set a distance between them. 'So much the better,' thought Vítor. 'The man's a fool.'

And he immediately set off on a trawl of all the places where he might meet him. He was furious with him and he wanted to meet him in order to greet him with indifference, as if his mind were on other things. He walked round the Aterro, up and down the Chiado, looked in at all the shops, ate a few cakes at Balthreschi's, but there was still no sign of Dâmaso.

At supper, he was so glum that Uncle Timóteo, who had had enough of silence, said irritably:

'Oh, for heaven's sake, say something. I'm dying for a bit of conversation.'

Vítor apologised; he was done in, under the weather. And having mumbled a few more words, as if his tongue were heavy as lead, he sank back into taciturnity. He couldn't get Dâmaso's words out of his head: 'I spent the night with her'; they sang ironically inside him; he could see her undressing, throwing her arms about Dâmaso's neck, sighing with love; he felt nothing but intense hatred and immense scorn for her. He consoled himself by thinking how superior he was to Dâmaso, but even while he despised him, he envied him.

'And how's your friend Dâmaso?' asked Uncle Timóteo.

Vítor recovered himself immediately. He didn't know, he hadn't seen him. Nor did he want do. The man was basically a fool. Vítor unleashed a torrent of remarks about the ludicrous figure Dâmaso cut, about his sheer fatuousness, his crass stupidity. He warmed to his theme, retailing some of Dâmaso's more laughable faux-pas and ridiculing his clothes. He cut rancorously into his roast veal, as if he were slicing away at Dâmaso's hated flesh.

'What did the lad do to you?'

'To me? Nothing. Honestly. If he had, I'd have split his head open, I would, as sure as two and two make four. I'd tear him limb from limb. I'd walk all over him.'

He was speaking with increasing choler, his pale skin red with passion.

Uncle Timóteo glanced at him out of the corner of his eye and smiled to himself.

'Poor chap,' he murmured.

That night, Vítor visited all the theatres. As it was growing dark, a fine drizzle began to fall. In the cab he took from Rua dos Condes to the Teatro da Trindade and from the Trindade to the Teatro de São Carlos, he was planning what attitude he would take if he should see her in a box. He would not even visit her. He would merely greet her coldly. He would flirt with other women. He would take a tip from the actors. He would speak to Dâmaso and yawn in his face, and if Dâmaso

133

so much as looked at him or made some bold remark, then he would beat him round the head with his cane.

But he did not see Genoveva, and every colour seemed dull to him, every woman hideous, every face inexpressive, and the city, wrapped in damp mist and drizzle, seemed sad as a prison, solitary as a cave. Near the Teatro Dona Maria, he met Palma Gordo, his hands in his pockets, his jacket pulled tightly around him and revealing the plump curves of his large buttocks.

'Have you seen Dâmaso?' Vítor asked him.

Palma, a cigarette between his fleshy, sweaty fingers, said drunkenly:

'He's probably with that . . .' and he used an obscene word.

Vítor almost struck him, but instead turned his back on him and stalked off home.

'Stupid vile woman! Hussy! I'm never going to think about her again!'

He went in to ask if there was a letter for him. Nothing.

That only fuelled his hatred. 'The wretch!' he thought.

And following the romantic tradition, according to which any difficulties encountered with ideal love are best remedied by a good dose of licentiousness, he went off to dine at the Malta with a Spanish woman called Mercedes, a delightful girl from Málaga, who claimed to be the daughter of a general and affected aristocratic manners, but ate with her hands and licked her fingers afterwards.

Vítor drank a whole bottle of Colares wine and two glasses of cognac, convinced that sadness made him interesting, and thinking of Alfred de Musset who also used to get drunk in order to forget his disillusion with love.

However, the next day, when he woke up, a very simple idea filled him with light and joy, like a ray of sunlight suddenly illuminating a dark room: 'It's ridiculous of me to be so angry simply because she went out for a walk.'

And at two o'clock, he was knocking on Genoveva's door. He waited for a moment in the living room and saw her come in, happy, refreshed, wearing an ample silk robe, and smiling and holding her arms out to him, amiability itself.

134

At the mere sight of her, all his anger melted like snow around a fire.

She knew he had called the previous day when she was out. It was such a lovely day for going to Belém on the ferry. And she was so sorry he hadn't gone with her; the Tagus looked absolutely gorgeous.

And then, feeling a need to unburden himself, Vítor told her that he had gone looking for her in the streets in the morning and, at night, in the theatres.

'But why, why?' she murmured, although her whole face glowed with satisfaction at his solicitude.

She declared herself to be most content.

Tormented by mordant curiosity, Vítor blushingly asked after Dâmaso.

'I don't really know. I saw him the day before yesterday in the evening, because I wasn't well during the day. He came back that night, but I wouldn't see him, and he came yesterday morning and yesterday night as well, but I didn't let him in then either.'

Vítor felt a milky sweetness running through his veins. And to make the conversation more intimate, to show how he had thought about her, he mentioned the idea of having her portrait painted. He praised Camilo Cerrão's genius: he was the only true artist in Portugal, unknown, ignored, poor, but a genius nonetheless. But Camilo's plans made Genoveva roar with laughter.

'Me giving bread to the poor? Good heavens. Why doesn't he show me boiling vegetables? What does the man take me for? He probably wants to entitle it *Rich and Poor* or *Charity*. The man's mad.'

But she didn't entirely reject the idea of a portrait; if the man had talent, then she would be interested, but only if she were wearing a low-necked, pale blue silk dress which left her arms bare, and she were holding a half-open fan and sitting on a Gothic-style chair, next to a marble vase full of roses.

She cited other famous poses: the portraits of Bonnat, of Carolus-Duran, of Mademoiselle Altheim. She spoke easily, with rapid gestures, her face lit by ever-changing expressions, all of them joyful, pleased.

And Vítor, who had seen her two days before, pale, languid, prostrate on the sofa, found a new freshness and charm in her, and, having loved her so when she was weak and ill, he adored her now in the vivacity of restored health.

'Would you like something to drink?'

She was thirsty; she had a curação and soda. She was very happy at the moment and saw everything through rose-coloured spectacles.

'Don't you ever have times like that?'

'I used to,' he said, and they launched into a long conversation about their shared sympathies and their many affinities.

'We're very alike in a lot of ways, aren't we?' she said.

And she gave him a long look, as if utterly charmed with him. Then she sprang to her feet and went over to the piano; she wanted him to play.

He regretted not being able to oblige, because there were times when the piano could be so companionable! There were certain states of mind that only music could express. Sometimes, at dusk, for example, he longed to set to music all the vague emotions filling his soul.

'You poet!' she said, laughing.

She seemed to listen to him avidly, to thrill to each new confidence he made about his feelings, ideas and habits, always drawing him out. She wanted to know what time he got up, what books he read, which were his favourite operas, as if pushing open the closed doors of his soul, just a crack, but wanting to be shown the whole house; and her eyes never stopped scrutinising and studying him.

'And how's Miss Sarah?' he asked.

She clapped her hands, laughing out loud.

'You'll never imagine, she's in love with you.'

'No!'

'It's true. She speaks only of you. She says she finds you handsome, interesting, romantic. And I don't think she's right,' she said, her eyes wide and shining, fixed on his.

She got up and placed her hands on his shoulders, examining him closely.

'No, I don't think she is,' she said. 'You're very sweet, but that's all.'

Vítor almost blushed. She seemed to him to be taking the provocative role of the man, and he seemed more like the woman, receiving those incitements to love with feminine passivity.

Genoveva tidied his hair with the tips of her fingers and straightened his cravat, but she wouldn't let him hold her hands; she drew back, saying:

'That's what we agreed. We'll always be friends, but no more than that.'

She made him an old-fashioned curtsey, and her shining eyes blazed a challenge.

She went and sat down at the piano and began to play her favourite song:

> *Chaque femme a sa toquade,*
> *Sa marotte et son dada.*

She sang out boldly, giving to certain words the charming, saucy inflection which the singers at the Teatro do Bulevar used when they wanted to be provocative or lewd.

> *Voyez ce beau garçon-là,*
> *C'est l'amant d'A . . .*
> *C'est l'amant d'A . . .*

And she looked at him in a way that made him tremble with desire.

> *Voyez ce beau garçon-là . . .*

Her eyes seemed to indicate him, confirming her feelings, surrendering herself:

> *C'est l'amant d'A . . .*
> *C'est l'amant d'A . . .*
> *C'est l'amant d'Amanda.*

Then she stopped singing and remained sitting on the piano stool, her face suddenly serious; and she said to him with an almost disdainful smile:

'Like Aninhas, eh?'

Vítor froze.

'There's nothing to be ashamed about. They say she's very pretty. She was a cook, I understand, and gets an allowance from a shopkeeper in the Chiado of fifteen thousand *mil réis* a month; she's learning French, and can already conjugate the verbs. You see how well informed I am. So how is this interesting young woman?'

'It's a lie,' said Vítor.

'No, it's not,' said Genoveva, standing up. 'Dâmaso told me. He knows her.'

Vítor swore to himself that he would give Dâmaso a good beating, and then began justifying himself, explaining away his relationship with Aninhas. It was true, he had been with her; she was a poor uneducated creature, terribly stupid; she was more like a friend, really; he had never given her his heart . . .

'A man with my tastes and feelings is hardly likely to attach himself to a woman who can barely read. Besides, I haven't seen her for a month. She bores me, so I left her. She wrote to me the day before yesterday, and I didn't even read the letter.'

'Really?' she said.

'I swear.'

'Not that anyone has any rights over you.' And she walked about the room, her silk robe dragging behind her. Then, looking directly at him: 'I knew you weren't getting on actually. She met Dâmaso and told him all about it. Poor thing! Make it up with her and don't break her poor heart.'

'You're making fun of me,' said Vítor, hurt.

'No, it's just the advice of a good friend. She, naturally, can console herself with a fine length of cashmere from her lover . . . or with one of his assistants.' She laughed. 'You used to write poems for Aninhas.'

'Right, that's it, I'm going,' he said angrily.

She took his hat out of his hands.

'I'm sorry to have spoken disrespectfully of your beloved.'

Then, seeing his angry face. 'I'm only joking,' she said, stroking his silk hat. 'Will you write poems for me?'

'Of course.'

'I want you to write me a sonnet a day. That would be so chic!' Holding out his hat to him, she added: 'And now, my dear friend, goodbye. It's three o'clock.'

'You're sending me away!'

'I have to.'

'You're expecting Dâmaso,' he said with a rancorous smile. She placed a finger on her lips.

'Shh! Be good now and off you go.'

Vítor was filled by jealous, despairing rage.

'All right, I'll go, but I won't be back.'

'Fine,' she said, shrugging her shoulders.

They looked at each other for a moment.

'Why do you make me suffer?' he asked disconsolately.

She gave a forced laugh.

'Suffer? What an extraordinary young man you are. You've been to see me twice, you barely know me and yet you think I'm making you suffer simply because I have to be alone at three o'clock. That's most unfair.'

'It's because I adore you,' he said.

She placed her hand over his mouth.

'No grandiose words. It's not right.' Then she curtseyed and smiled: 'If you want me, come and ask my mother for my hand.'

She laughed out loud and ran into her bedroom, from which she returned bearing a posy of violets.

'Now, be a good boy,' she said, placing them in the button-hole of his frock coat. 'You see what care I've taken over them, so no complaints. *La voilà*! Bonapartist violets.'

He leaned beseechingly towards her, his lips humbly begging a kiss.

Genoveva looked suddenly troubled and, lowering her head, she received his kiss on her hair.

He was so moved, he let out a heartfelt sigh and stood there in the middle of the room like an idiot, looking at her, trembling, not moving.

'*Addio!*' she said gravely.

He left, feeling the ground moving beneath his feet.

When she heard him shut the door behind him, she called Mélanie.

'As soon as Dâmaso arrives, show him in. I need to talk to him. I've run out of money.'

She sighed and sat down hard on the sofa, leaning back with her hands behind her head.

'Mélanie, this is not going well.'

'The poor lad looked so fed up,' said Mélanie.

'Poor love! Oh, Mélanie, where does this absurd, sudden passion come from? Who would have thought it?'

'These things happen, Madam.'

Genoveva shook her head sadly, her eyes fixed on the floor.

'No, this is serious. My heart tells me it will end badly.'

Vítor did not forget Genoveva's request: 'I want you to write me a sonnet a day.' He remembered the hero of the novel *Don Juan de Pasini*, who, every evening after supper, would sit quietly smoking a cigar on the terrace of his castle by the edge of a wood and write a sonnet to his current lover. Italian gentlemen of the Renaissance, whom Titian had painted and who had dined with Cesare Borgia, used to do the same. And he thought it very elegant to write a sonnet each morning and send it to her like a bouquet of flowers. Later, he would publish the poems as a collection and entitle it *Caresses;* the book would gain great notoriety and he would become famous, but a prospect had only to open up before him and his imagination would gallop away into it like a racehorse, only to lie down after a few jumps, its flanks heaving, like an exhausted nag.

And the following morning, after breakfast, he shut himself up in his room and sat down in his slippers, with a packet of cigarettes on the table and a glass of water to clarify his ideas, and prepared himself to write. For hours he paced the floor and, by supper time, he had produced the first eight lines.

When Clorinda came to call him for supper, he appeared at the table with the wild eyes and animated face of a man newly emerged from the world of ideas.

'Have you been asleep?' asked Uncle Timóteo.

'No, I've been writing,' he said with all the reserve of an initiate speaking to the uninitiated.

After supper, he shut himself up in his room again until nine o'clock, when he at last finished the final two tercets and went out to get some air.

It was a windy, rather gloomy night, with large clouds wandering the sky, occasionally revealing the pale moon. The gusts howling about him made him shudder to his very soul; the houses were all shut up, the gaslights sputtered fearfully, and as he roamed the streets, he was filled by premonitions of terrible misfortunes and mysterious murders. He walked along the Aterro; the water beat sadly against the quays, and over the glittering expanse flickered the narrow lights of boats whose masts, lit by a sudden, icy light, stood out like spectres against the sky.

But that backdrop did not coincide with his luminous state of mind, and so he returned home to make a fair copy of his sonnet with almost paternal delight.

He went to bed with a book by Alfred de Musset, feeling that life was good; at last he felt that ideal, noble, picturesque passion he had read about in books and poems and which had so enchanted him. And fortune had favoured him by giving that passion a dazzlingly glamorous wrapping, which seduced both his mind and his imagination. What other woman in Lisbon could compare to Genoveva? Who else had such clothes, such admirable ideas, such experience of love, so much knowledge of the world and of society?

Of course she had had lovers, but that simply made him appreciate her love all the more. It's so easy to please a poor bourgeois woman who sees only her husband's slippers and her ill-tempered children; it's so easy to seduce a girl of eighteen with her schoolgirl imagination and ideas about motherhood derived from playing with dolls. But what a glorious thing to be able to interest a woman who knows men so profoundly, a woman whom repeated disappointments have made sceptical, who has grown weary of sensation. It must be akin to the austere pleasure an atheist might feel on becoming

141

a Catholic. One would possess not merely a beautiful body, but a whole complex being. Each of her lovers, each of her relationships, had shaped her, leaving in her spirit or her sense of remorse some part of their personality; holding her in one's arms, possessing her, would be like possessing the refinement of all the elegant people she had known, the wit of dramatists, the polished manners of diplomats, and all the civilisations of which they are the flower, the essence, the delicious, artificial epitome.

How his life had changed. Only a month ago, his existence had been as stupid and banal as the macadam surface of the road, traipsing from the tedium of Dr Caminha's office to the vulgar pleasures of Aninhas' bedroom: he had been a dullard, a nonentity!

Now, though, Genoveva's love had idealised him, ennobled him, lined his soul with sweetness inside and clothed it with glory outside. And he stretched out proudly on the bed, listening to the wind moaning and brushing against the walls of the house.

How she would admire his sonnet, how pleased she would be that he had obeyed her; how could she resist giving him a kiss; and that hope filled his soul with a fierce languor.

The next day, with his sonnet in his wallet, he went to Rua de São Bento. Mélanie opened the door and said:

'She's not in. She went off to Queluz this morning with Senhor Dâmaso. But Miss Sarah's here . . . do come in.'

She opened the door and called Miss Sarah. Vítor went in, like a man fallen from a great height. Saddened, a vague smile on his lips, his heart cold, he entered the salon. He heard the swish of stiff silk over the carpet and Miss Sarah was by his side, red-faced and erect; she too told him that Madame and Mr Dâmaso had left very early for Queluz.

And sitting down, opening and closing the book she had in her hands, she gazed admiringly at Vítor, fixing him with her bluish eyes, with their murky, yellowish whites.

Vítor, holding his hat on his knees, was so embarrassed he didn't know what to say.

The Englishwoman remarked that it was a lovely day. Vítor looked very grave and, after serious reflection, said: 'Yes, it is.' Then Miss Sarah told him that Madame and Mr Dâmaso had gone off in an open carriage and taken their lunch with them. They seemed very happy. She added a few words of praise about Mr Dâmaso. He was charming, a perfect gentleman.

Vítor, downcast, muttered:

'Absolutely.'

'And when will they be back?' he asked. Miss Sarah said that they might well spend the night in Queluz; she hadn't actually heard them say so, but it seemed the logical thing to do. She asked if Queluz was very pretty.

'Oh, yes,' said Vítor, getting up.

But Miss Sarah did not want to lose him so soon. She started talking about Portugal and the Portuguese – such charming people. 'It was paradise here. They treated women with such respect. The English could learn a thing or two from them.'

She spoke, gesturing awkwardly, bending her neck this way and that, bestowing the widest of smiles on Vítor, then glancing away as if dazzled, only to look back at him, fascinated, revealing all her spinsterish hopes to him.

But Vítor was standing up, tapping his hat impatiently against his leg. Miss Sarah then declared that she mustn't keep him, that she, of course, lacked Genoveva's charms.

Vítor, embarrassed, protested: 'No, it's just that I have such a lot to do.'

Miss Sarah recovered herself: 'You're probably off to see some lady love. Oh, I know what you fickle young men are like, so easily taken in by appearances.'

Her crisp, singsong tones, her dull English eyes, seemed to paralyse Vítor; finally, with an effort, he broke through his inertia, said goodbye to Miss Sarah and left. She curtseyed deeply and placed in one last glance a fulsome declaration of her desires.

Once Vítor was out in the street again, he vented all his rage against Genoveva in one thought: 'She's nothing but a vulgar prostitute.' That calmed him down. And like a candle extinguished by a puff of wind, his love disappeared. Clutching his cane, he strode off down the street; his hatred kept pace with his dissatisfaction with her, with home and with life in general; it spread like a gas, embracing everyone and everything; he wanted to pick a quarrel, to round on someone with his walking stick, to write an article in the newspaper saying vile things about women, to see her poor and begging for alms! He felt no hatred for Dâmaso; he hardly gave him a thought: he was what she deserved, a dumb brute. He thought sarcastically: 'I hope they have lots of children and all go to hell together.' It was a splendidly sunny day, but everything seemed to him blurred by a sad mist; and the voices drifting up from the river seemed to him but an importunate buzz. Back home, he flung his hat down on the floor and was suddenly overwhelmed by a sense of abandonment, solitude and emptiness. It was as if all the things he cared about, his friends, his home, his relationships, had retreated and left him alone, a martyred, solitary figure in a vast, dark, empty space; he felt weak, unhappy, unfitted for life, and he sat down on his bed and wept.

In order to avoid Uncle Timóteo's questions and conversation, he went to dine at Silva's in a private room. And when the waiter offered him a menu and asked him what he wanted, Vítor replied in desolate, woebegone tones:

'Poison, if there is any.'

The joke consoled him. He even read the newspaper that the waiter brought him; but he always remembered to strike a sad pose whenever the waiter returned, for nothing consoles effeminate temperaments more than letting others know of their pain.

He walked slowly through the Chiado, with the weary abandon of an adolescent and he gazed calmly about him with the bruised lassitude that follows tears, and yet he did not mind suffering for love, because at least he could console himself with the thought that his sorrow had a noble origin.

He went into the Teatro de Dona Maria, bought a box in order to lend elegance to his grief and, leaning his elbows on the worn leather balcony, he glanced distractedly about the theatre, occasionally watched the play, and out of habit and to pass the time, made eyes at a good-looking woman in a box near the stalls, who stared furiously back. But he really was suffering; sometimes, just the thought of Genoveva troubled him; and when he saw that it was half past ten and imagined that, at that hour, *they* would be going to bed in Queluz, he was gripped by despair and by such intense anger, that he flung open the door of his box, left the theatre and again aimlessly wandered the streets. His footsteps took him as far as Rua das Janelas Verdes, for his thoughts were so agitated that he was trying, through sheer physical exhaustion, to restore calm to his soul. A clock struck one o'clock, and he returned home.

When he reached his front door, he was just taking his key from his pocket when out of a dark doorway nearby emerged the figure of a woman, who ran towards him and clung to him, crying softly:

'Vítor!'

It was Aninhas.

'What do you want?'

'Please, don't turn away. Listen. Just say a few words, please. I'm going mad. If you don't hear what I have to say, I'm going to throw myself in the river. Vítor, I swear I will . . .'

Her voice was choked with tears and she was speaking loudly now.

To avoid a scandal, for people were still coming out of the Writers' Guild, he walked with her as far as the Academy, in darkness at that hour, opposite the arcade of the Museum of Fine Arts.

Aninhas clung anxiously to his arm, sobbing softly and murmuring:

'I've been like a madwoman . . . I didn't care about anything any more . . . I simply wanted to die.'

'But what do you want from me?'

The words poured out of Aninhas, who walked, then stopped, gesturing wildly, as she tried to explain what had happened 'the other day': No, it wasn't Policarpo who had been with her. That was true. It was another man. But he

145

wasn't her lover; he was an old man, a devil, an animal, a Senhor Lopes who lived in Travessa da Palha. Necessity had driven her to it. Policarpo was so mean, he barely gave her enough to pay the rent. She had two bracelets in pawn, as well as the diamond pendant. She just hadn't known where to turn. The old devil had been after her for ages, and she had to get those things out of pawn. In the end, she had agreed. But she cursed him now. She hated him.

'That's the truth. I swear on my mother's life. May I die if it's not true. Ask Rosa. I wrote to you explaining everything. And if I hadn't found you today, I would have done away with myself.'

She grasped his hands and squeezed them tight. In the darkness of the square, he could see only her dark eyes gleaming in her pale face shadowed by the black lace shawl she wore over her head. A sweet sensation softened him; that passionate declaration was compensation for Genoveva's disdain for him, and with his vanity thus consoled, he was filled by a desire to forgive. In a gentle voice, he said:

'But if you were in difficulties with money, why didn't you say? I could have given you the money.'

'No, no, I wouldn't take a penny from you. I love you and from you I want only love. I'll get whatever I can from the other man, but not from you. Let's make it up. I haven't slept. I've been ill. Ask Rosa. Today, I just couldn't stand it any longer and so I came to wait for you. Please, say yes.'

But the pain he had suffered at Genoveva's hands gave Vítor a desire to avenge himself on Aninhas. He brushed her harshly aside.

'Oh, no,' he said. 'This isn't the first time you've done this to me, and I've had enough. Goodbye.'

And he addressed the sinner in a low voice tinged only with melancholy:

'Be happy, Aninhas.'

The girl was crying softly, and still Vítor did not leave. Feeling weak, and annoyed with his own weakness, he took out on her his feelings of irritation, saying that she wasn't to be trusted; he wasn't prepared to put up with her games any longer; he had plenty of other women; and just to make her cry all the more, he said that he loved her, that he had always loved her, but that, on reflection, he had decided it was over.

'Goodbye.'

'Are you going, then?' she said blankly, holding back her tears.

'Yes, goodbye.'

'Goodbye, Vítor.'

That easy acceptance of their separation infuriated Vítor. He did not leave, but kept walking, his hands in his pockets, saying horrible things to her, repeating his litany of tedious complaints, his words oozing a rancorous, misanthropic, desperate bile.

'Don't be angry, Vítor,' she was saying, resigned and tearful. 'I don't want to force you to do anything. I did what I could. I only came to ask your forgiveness. Now, goodbye.'

Then Vítor insulted her and listed the names of all her lovers: Alves, Guerra, Teira Vesgo, João Patriota.

Aninhas grew angry too then.

'Why throw those names in my face now? Yes, I've been with them, but they weren't deceiving you; I was deceiving them with you. Have I ever asked you for anything? Tell me, have I ever asked you for so much as a penny?'

She was speaking loudly, standing on the tips of her toes.

'Be quiet, the watchman will hear you,' said Vítor furiously.

She shrugged impatiently. 'It's best if we finish it,' she said. 'That's what happens when a woman makes sacrifices for a man.'

'What sacrifices?' exclaimed Vítor proudly.

'Several times I came close to losing Policarpo because of you. And then what would become of me? The house is rented in his name; the furniture is in his name. He's quite capable of putting me out in the street with just the clothes I stand up in. And then what would I do? Go on the streets and give my name to the police? And all for you! If my poor mother were alive today . . .'

Her tears redoubled.

Vítor felt profoundly humiliated; that argument was placing him in the infamous position of a pimp, and yet he had to recognise the truth of what she said. He felt an instinctive animal vanity because her words were proof of her disinterested love for him.

He walked on in silence. His life with Aninhas reappeared before him: he was tempted by the memory of voluptuous nights during which they had loved and laughed and played, eaten supper in bed. He compared that loving girl with Genoveva, so scornful and stubborn; he remembered the graceful, vigorous perfection of her body, her voluptuous sighs, the firmness of her skin; the thought troubled him. Besides, it was his duty not to be ungrateful, and so heavily does such a duty weigh on the conscience that even the least convincing accusation seeks shelter beneath that sublime justification. He stopped and asked:

'What is it you want?'

Sensing from his voice that he was softening, she said urgently:

'Come back home with me now!'

Vítor made a resigned gesture and asked:

'But what about Policarpo?'

'He's gone to Almada. Anyway, I don't care. Say you'll come. We'll be so happy!' She clung to him with renewed passion.

'Stop it. People might see.'

'What do I care. The whole world could see and I wouldn't care. Come back with me, Vítor.'

'And you won't deceive me again?' he said, giving in.

'Never. If I ever deceive you again, you can kill me. I'll leave a note to say it was me; there'll be no need for you to go to court over it.'

She was utterly sincere; she had read that oath of love in *The King of the Mountain* and was determined to carry it out.

And so Vítor went with her. Aninhas clung tightly to his arm and they almost ran along the street. They reached her apartment breathless and, while Vítor lit a match, she hitched up her skirts and bounded up the stairs; she was laughing

148

nervously, impatiently. She rang the bell so loudly that the startled maid came running to open the door.

'He's here, Rosa, he's here! I've brought him, look!'

And she dragged Vítor along the corridor and into the room. She threw off her shawl and her cloak and hurled herself on him, covering him in kisses. She clapped her hands; her excitement only increased the charm of her wild, furious affection for him; her lovely grey eyes glinted with passion. 'I can read you like a book,' he used to say.

'Ask Rosa. It's true, isn't it, Rosa, how I cried and cried!'

'Oh, she was in a terrible state,' said the maid glumly.

'You see, you see!'

And she asked Rosa to prepare the supper at once. They dined in bed. She put her arms around him; she pushed him onto the sofa, climbed on top of him and devoured him with kisses, examining him with wide, voracious eyes, as if she had never seen him before; his white forehead, his sparse beard, his curly hair, his effeminate beauty drove her mad; she smothered him in abrupt kisses, her eyes closed; she bit his lips; then she knelt before him, overcome with emotion, and burst into tears.

Touched by such passion, Vítor swore to himself that he would always love her, that he would forget the other hussy.

He lifted her up, sat her on his knee, kissed away her tears and said:

'I love you, Aninhas, really I do. But don't deceive me again, all right?'

She stood up, her tears dry now and shining; she held out her hand.

'No, never, not even if I were dying of hunger. I'm yours alone.'

Impelled by a great wave of passion, she fell, half-fainting, into his arms and planted wet, urgent, drunken kisses on his neck.

The next day, Vítor did not leave Aninhas' room until one o'clock in the afternoon, and Dâmaso's coupé happened to pass just as he was coming out of the street door.

As soon as Dâmaso saw him, he had the carriage stop and he called to Vítor, who approached with the greatest reluctance.

'So you've made it up, have you?' said Dâmaso knowingly. 'I met the poor girl the other day and she was so upset. You did the right thing.'

Vítor tried to deny it. He had only come to see her because he had heard she was ill.

'Now, now,' said Dâmaso, beaming, still half-asleep, his collar all crumpled. 'You can't conceal the truth from me. Enjoy yourself. We went to Queluz yesterday.'

'Have you just got back?' asked Vítor, terribly pale.

'No, we got back last night. We had a lovely trip.'

He seemed full of healthy joy; he was rubbing his hands, fidgeting in his seat, overflowing with a superabundance of happiness; he shouted to his coachman to drive on.

'Enjoy yourself. And come and see us.'

Vítor returned home, furious. Dâmaso was sure to tell Genoveva that he had seen him leaving Aninhas' house. It was too much! But, then, what did it really matter? Genoveva had made fun of him; this was his revenge; he would show her that he wasn't dying of love for her. It was over. It was better like this. After all, Aninhas was younger, fresher, more loving. And if Genoveva was jealous, so much the better. Let her suffer!

He did not go back to Genoveva's house. Policarpo stayed on in Almada and Vítor more or less lived with Aninhas; it was their honeymoon. They would get up at two in the afternoon, they dined several times at Silva's and, one night, they went to the Teatro de Variedades to see a magician. It was the first time Aninhas had been to the theatre with Vítor and she spent all afternoon getting dressed. Vítor had advised her on her clothes, trying to emulate Genoveva's elegance. She no longer wore her hair piled high or in ringlets; she dabbed opoponax on her handkerchief and wore pearl-grey gloves with eight buttons; that night, in her close-fitting, wine-red silk dress, a lace cravat, and with her pretty face, she looked so graceful and simple that Vítor felt quite proud.

When he sat down in the box with her, however, he turned pale as wax. In another box sat Dâmaso, in white tie and tails, looking prosperous, pleased, plump and victorious; and he was talking to Genoveva. Vítor was about to withdraw to the back of the box, when Dâmaso's friendly waves pinned him to his chair; Genoveva merely nodded. She was looking splendid in a black silk dress decorated with embroidered velvet; she wore her hair in the plain English style that showed off her small, adorable head to best advantage. Her ears were adorned by black pearls and around her neck she wore a pearl-grey ribbon to match her gloves and, on it, a pendant made out of turquoise.

And like a wave bursting through dykes and sweeping all before it, the love Vítor used to feel once again filled his heart, overwhelming him. At first, he just stared like an idiot; and the stage, the dim lights and the moss-green walls of the boxes, all blurred into one; but Genoveva's manner, the way she was laughing with Dâmaso, so enraged him that he leaned towards Aninhas, whispering sweet nothings, laughing loudly and dragging his chair closer.

Aninhas could not take her eyes off Genoveva; she wanted to know who she was; she studied her through her opera glasses, instinctively imitating certain of Genoveva's poses. Vítor continued to affect an attitude of expansive intimacy with Aninhas, but Genoveva, grave-faced, did not look at him again. Vítor was desperate. Her indifference made him grow embittered. He began to be somewhat abrupt with Aninhas. He did not hear the actors' amusing barbs and, sitting in the back of the box, he could not take his eyes off Genoveva. Even Aninhas noticed; she turned pale and asked him why he was staring at that woman?

'Me? What possible importance could she have for me? I can look at whoever I want, can't I?'

Aninhas' eyes glittered; she already hated Genoveva.

But Genoveva did not look their way once. Dâmaso, on the other hand, took every opportunity to show Vítor how close he and Genoveva were, how happy; he struck triumphant poses, proudly twirled his moustaches and shrugged his

151

shoulders pityingly whenever one of the actors muffed his lines.

At the end of the second act, Vítor noticed Genoveva get up and saw Dâmaso help her on with her cloak; it was the same cloak he had seen her in at the Teatro da Trindade; a thousand memories bore down on him. He felt like throwing himself at her feet, begging her to speak to him or look at him; and he picked up his hat and rushed out into the corridor. He got to the door just in time to see Genoveva entering the coupé, with a movement that revealed layers of white petticoat. Dâmaso smugly banged the door shut and gave him a pitying wave.

Vítor went back to the box with anger in his heart. He wanted the whole theatre to be burned to the ground, for the world to shatter into pieces. Sitting down again next to Aninhas, he did not take his eyes off the empty box opposite, where she had sat, where her perfume must still linger. The accumulated tears he could not shed flooded his heart.

VII

Vítor did not go back to Genoveva's house and, instead, resumed his old way of life; he became more assiduous about going to the office and was a frequent visitor to Aninhas' apartment; he went for his usual walks through the Chiado, occasionally pausing sadly at the door of the Casa Havanesa. But all his actions, all his words, even the way he walked had the sad, weary indifference of mechanical movement. The image of Genoveva had become embedded in his brain and nothing that life had to offer could erase it. As soon as he woke or glanced up from the book he was reading or concluded a conversation, that idea would immediately rise up in his spirit. He would invent monologues, imagine what he would say to her if they met, create painful dialogues, witty turns of phrase . . . and all that cerebral labour had but one end: to possess her.

Sometimes, he would be seized by a sudden desire to run to her house and see her, but he was held back by pride, shyness and fear of her indifference. And yet, life seemed unacceptable without the demonstrations of affection she had shown him, which were the sweetest thing he had ever known, an affirmation of his self-worth.

He almost despaired of his inability to excise that idea from the circumvolutions of his brain, where it had installed itself, like a parasite, in the deepest, most inaccessible folds, whence it directed his soul, his body.

Her indifference seemed to him a crime; not a word, not a single invitation, nothing! It was as if she had died. And he did not see her again in the street or at the theatre. He had twice walked past her house; the windows were open and the place seemed inhabited. What would she be doing, how would she be passing the time, what would she be thinking about?

One morning, he was just getting dressed to go to the office, when his bedroom door flew open and Camilo Cerrão came in. He tossed his hat onto a chair, sat down on Vítor's bed and launched into a discussion of his plans for the portrait of Genoveva.

'You've been thinking about it again, then?' said Vítor.

'Of course, I've thought of nothing else!'

He began striding about the room, expounding his latest theory. Portraiture was the noblest, most profound, most useful art. He was going to abandon set design, which was, anyway, repellent to his temperament (he considered painting landscapes to be a puerile pursuit), and devote himself to portrait painting.

'In modern art, there's nothing to compare with it. After all, what are the two main branches of painting, the two noblest, most elevated and necessary branches? Historical painting and portraiture. But what could be more absurd than historical painting? Even the greatest artist can make nothing of it but a display of costumes and weapons; he can't paint a man, a hero, a philosopher, because physiognomy isn't everything; you would need to know the person. Let us suppose I wanted to paint Charlemagne. What do I know about Charlemagne, about his ideas, his sorrows, his nerves . . . if he had any . . . his passions, his terrors, in short, about all the things that consti- tute a man? I know some of the historical facts of the time: that he had a white beard, that he played chess with Arch- bishop Turpin, and that he could spend hour on enchanted hour watching the lake at Aix-la-Chapelle. Lovely. But could I use those facts to paint Charlemagne? No. I could paint a vast old man, with great exactitude of technique when it came to the armour and the weapons, but he would be a man- nequin, the figure of a knight, not Charlemagne. That is why historical painting is so absurd; it can never be anything more than an archaeological exhibition of costumes, weapons or torches. The soul of the person, whom we did not know, with whom we have nothing in common, from whom we are separated by centuries, eludes us: it is all conjecture.

Now look at the portrait. What do we paint? Men like us, with similar ideas and feelings, who eat what we eat, belong to the same race as us; we have only to question them in order to find out about them; we know about their lives, their works, their family history, their vices; it is all there before us, revealing to us what they feel: their eyes, their smile, their gestures, their skin tone.

Now note the importance of this work in painting: through the portrait, the artist bequeaths his contemporaries to the historians of the future, complete with physiognomy and character. To paint a portrait is to write history, the most useful, authoritative history there is.

What do great men bequeath to the future? Their books, their speeches and their actions, but man does not reveal himself fully in deeds and words; he always adopts some affectation, some convention, some reserve and a great deal of reticence. A man never reveals himself entirely through his work. Then along come we artists armed with our brushes and we take the physiognomy of the famous man and put it on canvas; and that picture, which describes in brush-strokes the man's temperament, character and defects, provides the historians of the future with a commentary on and an explanation of that man.

Think then of all the important people who did not leave books or speeches behind them, and who, nevertheless, make up the personal or social history of a century: kings, bankers, courtesans, criminals and revolutionaries.

These people would be incomprehensible without their portraits, as would the age they lived in. Portraits provide a contemporary gallery in which future historians can find in physiognomy an explanation for men's actions. Look at Michelet. What makes his history so important, why does it have that sense of something living, animate, felt, resuscitated, something that speaks to us directly? It is because he explains men through their portraits: he studies them and, in their features, he finds their soul, their intentions, their feelings. It is almost impossible to understand the sixteenth century, the Italian Renaissance, without Raphael's portraits of those pagan Popes, without Titian's robust, haughty subjects, or without Tintoretto's portraits of wilfully sensual virgins. How could we understand fat, sensible, hardworking Flanders if it were not for those paintings of portly burgermeisters or of the good bourgeoisie of Antwerp? Velázquez is the finest historian of Spain and of its proud, mystical, etiquette-bound court. What better explanation of the graceful, frivolous, impertinent, philosophical eighteenth century than Watteau's portraits? So what should modern painting set out to explain? Would not portraits of our contemporaries with their troubled, tormented faces, tortured by doubt and their love of creation, provide a portrait of this age of renewal? I know what I think. I am going to paint the history of nineteenth-century Portugal. When I have done fifty canvases of men and women, with their plump, empty faces, their frightened, turbid eyes, demoralised and weak, I will have explained far better than any memoir or chronicle the sterility of Portuguese constitutionalism.'

While Camilo was talking, Vítor was thinking only one thing: the portrait would be a way of seeing Genoveva again. And as soon as Camilo paused for breath, he said:

'So you think the portrait of Genoveva might . . .'

'I demand that portrait. I need it. I want to begin my series of portraits immediately. Is she a *cocotte*, an adventuress, a sentimentalist, a voluptuary? Well then, she's important. I will use her to personify this time of universal prostitution and lechery in which pleasures can be bought and sold and emotions gambled with. I will show her as the personification of the great fact of modern-day life: prostitution. My idea the other day was absurd, absolutely ridiculous . . .'

He went on to describe exactly how he would pose Genoveva: she would be lying on a sofa in a boudoir, surrounded by all the artefacts of luxury and frivolity, a summary of everything that breeds, feeds and provokes the modern sensibility: on the piano, music by Offenbach; scattered about the floor, books by Dumas *fils* and Baudelaire; beneath a jasper goblet, a pile of British banknotes; on a chair a pile of Court Gazettes, showing details of judicial debates; and there she would be on a sofa, lit by a harsh, honest light, with the exalted look in her eye of a bacchante and, on her lips, the egotism of the usurer.

'It will be my greatest work. It's all in here!' he said, tapping his head. 'Painting is my glorious destiny. But I must start now. When does she want to begin?'

Vítor said that he would have to speak to her, to arrange a time and a place.

'The light in my studio isn't that good, as you know. But it's not a question of light. On the contrary, I want a false, degraded, civilised, domesticated, modern light, the light of slums and crowded houses. I will have to invent a light in order to find the right tone to illuminate this modern phenomenon. It is the light of the century. In my studio, then.'

He picked up his hat.

'Wait, where are you going?'

'I need to walk, to move, so that I can mull over this idea of mine. When will you talk to her?'

'Well, I'm not sure . . .'

'You must do it today! We're talking about a truly great idea here, about the renewal of art in Portugal, about the public interest. We have no time to lose.'

Vítor hesitated; he was delighted, but he needed to be given more reasons to go to Genoveva's house.

'I need to go to the office.'

'Forget about the office! Lawyers, huh, don't start me on lawyers . . . The lawyer with his disorderly rhetoric is the true scourge of this verbose, astute century! Those jaundiced, wise, ambitious, empty men, full of clichés, are the essence of constitutionalism. To hell with the office today . . . Go and see that woman!'

He was about to leave, but seeing, at the foot of Vítor's bed, an engraving of *The Judas Kiss* by Ary Scheffer, he stopped and, with immense disdain, said:

'How ludicrous: *The Judas Kiss*! The conventional image of Christ with a carefully combed beard, his hair neatly parted; anyone would think the Redeemer had come straight from the barber's. One day, I'll paint a Christ as the terrifying, wretched figure he must have been, wearing a Syrian turban on his head and a yellow camel skin; he'll be unshaven, with the wild eyes of the visionary, seared by the sands of the desert, his face gaunt, tanned, blackened, scorched.'

And after silently shaking his fist at the engraving, he added:

'There are no ideas behind it, no symbolism. Let's suppose the Catholic view of Christ is correct. How should we depict him?'

'Well, full of idealism and grace.'

'No,' boomed Camilo. 'Anyone who had taken upon himself all the ills of man and the degradations of life would have cut a frightening and repellent figure. Yes, one day, I'll paint a Christ. We must combat the traditional Christian view of him. Now go and see that woman!'

And he left.

Vítor was in a state of high excitement. He now had a plausible, justifiable, urgent reason to return to Genoveva's house. But his pride or, perhaps, his timidity, held him back; then it occurred to him that the portrait could make Camilo's fortune; he remembered how little money Camilo had, how the poor man was obliged to paint stage sets for a living. How could he refuse to contribute to his potential wealth and fame? As an intelligent man, did he have the right to hold back such a great artistic project? Should he not go and persuade Genoveva to have her portrait painted?

And while declaring to himself that he was making this sacrifice for Camilo's sake, inside he was thrilled to be given this excuse to see Genoveva again.

He dressed carefully, dropped in at the Casa Havanesa, and at one o'clock, he was knocking at Genoveva's door. He could hear someone playing the piano and was much put out to see Dâmaso maritally installed in an armchair, smoking. Genoveva was singing a popular song, accompanied by Miss Sarah on the piano, and the scene was one of happy families and conjugal ease. Genoveva did not at first get up; she finished the song but did not turn round.

Then, the piano fell silent, and she came over to shake Vítor's hand, for Dâmaso, as if he were the master of the house, remained seated on the sofa.

'We thought you'd died. The least they could have done,

we said, was to send us an invitation to the funeral. Anyway, we've missed you.'

And that 'we', in which she conjugally included Dâmaso, was uttered in a bright, easy, musical tone that tortured Vítor.

He muttered something about having been very busy.

'I do hope,' said Genoveva, 'that it's not that young lady.' She turned to Dâmaso: 'What was her name, my dear?'

'Aninhas Tendeira,' said Dâmaso, smirking.

Genoveva put two fingers to her lips to suppress a laugh.

'Ah, yes, Aninhas the Shopkeeper. I assume, as her name suggests, that she is open all hours for love. I hope she leaves you at least a couple of hours a day free; too much love can be very dangerous; you're certainly less talkative than you used to be; all that love must be wearing you out.'

Dâmaso was bouncing one leg up and down, looking very superior. This display of wit on his lover's part aimed at Aninhas Tendeira's lover filled him with delight.

Then, leaning back and yawning slightly, Genoveva said:

'Though I must say she's very pretty your Aninhas. But, my friend, you really must tell her not to wear her hair like that, she looked as if she had a melon on her head.'

Dâmaso laughed out loud.

'And that scarlet cape she was wearing, really, it was so garish. And she does fidget so; anyone would think she had fleas!'

Dâmaso was now writhing about with laughter.

Vítor felt the blood rush to his head; his hands were trembling. He said in a cutting tone:

'The poor girl has never been out of Lisbon. Not everyone can travel the world having "adventures".'

Genoveva turned pale.

'Oh, so she's always clung to her little rock, has she? Perhaps we should call her Aninhas the Barnacle.'

'Rather a barnacle than a bird of passage.'

Dâmaso immediately adopted a serious, offended air, and turning to Genoveva with a stiff, stupid smile on his face, he said:

'Our friend appears to be in a rather insolent mood today.'

Vítor smiled and gave the reason for his visit; he told them about the portrait. As soon as Dâmaso heard that the artist in question was Camilo Cerrão, he declared authoritatively that he was 'useless'.

Vítor grew heated; he spoke of Camilo's genius, described his ambitious plans, the studies he had done. Everyone in Lisbon had great hopes for him. Only someone who knew absolutely nothing about the things of the mind could fail to understand the place Camilo occupied in Portuguese art; he was a great critic, a great painter and had a great heart.

'The man's a mere dauber,' spluttered Dâmaso, humbled.

'And what would you know about that?' asked Vítor scornfully. Then, turning to Genoveva:

'The man's a genius. He has the passionate temperament of the great artist, much as Delacroix did. His portrait of you will be a sublime work, a searing criticism of Catholicism.'

He philosophised on, citing Camilo's various admirers, quoting Senhor Fernando's words of praise; he made things up, mentioned Constable, Ary Scheffer, Decamps, Meissonnier, Carolus-Duran, crushing Dâmaso beneath a weight of literary verbiage, in order to embarrass and humiliate him.

'What do you think of his painting *The Tavern*? Everyone agrees it constitutes a revolution in art.'

This was a canvas Camilo had exhibited and which a few friends had written about in a pamphlet. But Dâmaso, who had never seen *The Tavern*, said irritably:

'Well, frankly, I didn't like it.'

'But why? What about the idea behind it? The work is full of delicately observed physiognomy. And the draughtsmanship is masterly. And what about the light, the wonderful transparent light in which the characters live? And the clear, brilliant, confident colours.' And for good measure he threw in: 'Colours worthy of the Flemish, of the old masters.'

Dâmaso fell into a humiliated silence. Genoveva had followed Vítor's words avidly. She kept nodding, her eyes fixed on him. His words fell on her soul, bringing with them a tumult of sensations. At last, she said:

'Well, if he really is as fine an artist as you say, it's a compliment to me that he should want to paint my portrait.'

Vítor immediately told her Camilo's plan, suppressing certain aspects and concentrating instead on the silk boudoir, the sofa, the tunic, her bare shoulders . . .

'Exactly what I had in mind,' said Genoveva.

Dâmaso broke in:

'Dear lady, if you want your portrait painted, let me introduce you to a Spaniard who has done all the well-known people in Lisbon; it only takes him two weeks, and the likeness is quite extraordinary.'

Vítor got to his feet and, spreading his arms wide, said to Genoveva:

'If that's your view, I have nothing more to say. Tell the Spaniard to come.'

Genoveva got up too and said:

'No, no, it's a stupid idea!'

Dâmaso was about to speak, but Genoveva loftily stopped him:

'Who do you take me for? Do you imagine I would want to be painted by some peripatetic artist who sells paintings by the dozen?'

'He's really awfully good!' protested Dâmaso. 'And very cheap.'

Vítor said with a triumphant air:

'Oh well, if it's a matter of money, there's no need to worry. Camilo doesn't even mention money. He wants to create a work of art. He had been unable to find a worthy enough model in Lisbon until he saw Genoveva and was so struck by her beauty and her presence that he immediately wanted to paint her. He hopes to produce something truly remarkable. But he's not interested in money at all.'

Genoveva's chest was rising and falling.

'Bring him to see me tomorrow, so that we can meet.'

'Here?' said Dâmaso, scandalised.

Genoveva fixed him with a look as sharp as a fencing foil.

'What's the matter with that?'

Vítor savoured his triumph; sangfroid, confidence and his

facility with words had come to his rescue. He remarked ironically:

'I wouldn't want my idea to mar your happiness in any way. Let's say no more about it.'

Genoveva, however, was trembling with agitation.

'No, I want to meet him. Bring the man here tomorrow at two.'

And she bowed her head.

Vítor left, saying to Dâmaso.

'See you tomorrow then.'

Dâmaso waved to him limply, then walked about the room, puffing out his cheeks, his hands in his pockets. As soon as he heard the front door close, he turned to Genoveva.

'What do you mean by treating me like that, Genoveva?'

She replied bluntly:

'Look, don't upset me, my nerves are bad.'

Her abruptness and her sudden pallor alarmed Dâmaso.

'But what did I do wrong?'

She leapt to her feet.

'How could you let that man get away with calling me a "bird of passage"? How could you allow him, in my presence, to treat you like a fool? Why come out with a string of imbecilic, ridiculous remarks? I can put up with all kinds of things in a man – old age, wickedness, violence, drink, cynicism, cruelty – but the one thing I cannot tolerate in a man is stupidity!'

Dâmaso froze. He stood perfectly still, looking very pale and blinking like someone who has just woken up. He felt a buzzing in his ears and could think of nothing, not a single idea, word or remark.

'Goodbye,' she said, growing weary of his immobility.

'Are you sending me away?'

Genoveva made a grimly impatient gesture.

'Yes, I am. I'm sick of your face, your figure, your rough voice . . . of you. Goodbye.'

She clapped her hands once.

'What a fool I've been!'

He picked up his hat and left, almost apoplectic with rage.

For two hours, Genoveva paced about her bedroom, in a state of high agitation. She hated Dâmaso, Vítor, herself, Lisbon, life! And in that whole jumble of ideas, what annoyed her most was Vítor's indifference, his calm, his quick wit, his air of superiority. Yes, she hated him most of all. She considered leaving Lisbon and going back to Paris. But only debts awaited her there, and she had no money. Worse, in a fit of pique, she had offended Dâmaso. But she really could not bear him, his plump, prosperous manner, his short, fat legs. All her vague irritations ultimately centred around him.

For days she had been living in a state of permanent agitation; her situation was fraught with difficulties and problems. She adored Vítor with a frenetic, servile, fanatical, overwhelming passion. She was thirty-nine years old and found herself madly in love with a boy of twenty-three. This passion was unlike anything else she had ever felt; she realised that up until then, she had known only caprices, crushes, obsessions, illusions, sensual desires, impulses. And suddenly, on the brink of old age, she was possessed by a fervent love that was complete and irresistible. She loved him with all the vehemence her soul could muster and with every desire in her body; she felt herself capable of serving him as devotedly as a sister of charity or as unstintingly as a mother, but she also wanted to devour him with caresses, as wildly as a bacchante and as shamelessly as a whore.

She had known men who were more handsome or more intelligent, and yet no male beauty had made her tremble so, no human words had so captivated her. He lived inside her brain like some aberrant, tyrannical presence; like a virus that passion penetrated her flesh, the very depths of her being, the circumvolutions of her brain, until she had only one thought, only one desire circulating in her blood – him. And what could she do?

She wanted to live with him, and once she had given herself to him, she could not bear the idea of belonging to another man. Like all courtesans, she made a very precise distinction between 'man' and 'lover'; between the man who pays the bills and the rent, and to whom one gives only mercenary love and a polite affection, and the lover, who pays nothing, who, indeed, receives presents, and to whom one gives all one's sublimest feelings, all one's most ardent sensuality. Yet she could not even bear to think of Vítor as being merely her lover.

If she gave herself to him, she would never give herself to anyone else. She wanted to live with him, absolutely alone, but neither of them had enough money for that. She could sell her jewellery, rent a small house, give up all her luxuries and live a mediocre, straitened life. He would perhaps accept that. But for how long?

She was thirty-nine; she might still be beautiful in ten years' time, but after that? After that he would come to hate her, he would fall in love with someone else, marry. And then what would become of her? She would be left alone and poor, too old to start again, possibly too wretched even to live.

She had even considered accepting that possibility, and when she first began to notice in him the coolness of satiety, she would enter a convent, or else she would kill herself. She would at least have enjoyed a few years of infinite happiness, before it all ended. She would devote the rest of her life to God, her final lover, who, in his forgiveness, accepted all those wounded by love . . . otherwise, there was always the Devil. She knew, though, that this was all pure fantasy. She knew herself well. She wasn't the kind of woman who could accept refectory food or confinement behind a convent grille. And she could certainly never kill herself. She wept hysterically if she had so much as a headache; she so worshipped her own pampered flesh that she had made of herself a personal cult. Destroy herself? Never.

She knew what her future would be. If she ever lived with him, the first indication of coldness or lack of affection would signal the beginning of a life of struggle, jealousy, anger; she would take to the gin bottle and would end up in a mental asylum, old, poor and useless.

That passion had come at the most delicate moment in her life. Love was her only means of becoming rich; as long as she was beautiful, and with her knowledge of love, her talent for

164

intrigues, she could still find a man who could provide for her later on, who might even marry her; or with different men, a hundred *libras* here, a hundred *libras* there, she could save up enough to get her through a rheumaticky old age. If she could not forget Vítor, she would have to go back to Paris in order to keep a cool head, sharp wits and a steady hand. Was she capable of doing that?

'No, no,' she murmured, reaching up her arms and stretching, full of love and desire.

She would accept anything; difficulties, poverty, sadness, but she would not leave him. Up until then, she had lived in a kind of limbo, adoring him, but not yet ready to make the final sacrifice; she was busily 'fleecing' Dâmaso as quickly as she could, and lately, every day, by means of loud, exalted displays of love, she had managed to extract considerable sums of money from him. She had begun to see Dâmaso as a real goldmine and was exploiting him with wily enthusiasm. However, when Vítor did not visit her for a whole week after her trip with Dâmaso to Queluz, her passion for him had grown. She had thought it wise not to write to Vítor, choosing instead to irritate him by an appearance of utter indifference, but Dâmaso's presence grated on her more and more with each day that passed. There were days when the clatter of the doorbell set her nerves on edge.

'I immediately imagine Dâmaso's pudgy hand tugging on the bell cord,' she said to Mélanie.

Then, when she saw Vítor with Aninhas at the Teatro Variedades, she realised she was hopelessly in love. When she saw him with another woman, a kind of mist appeared before her eyes, a kind of vertigo gripped her. The long habit of dissembling, however, saved her, and she managed to acknowledge him, then look at the stage, study the actors, smile at Dâmaso and converse. Only when she got home, having told Dâmaso not to come in, that she wasn't well, did she explode in anger, alone in her bedroom with Mélanie. She literally rent her clothes, wept, smashed two crystal glasses; she even wanted to go to Aninhas' house and kill the woman; all kinds of mad, absurd ideas boiled in her head. She drank half a bottle of gin

165

and, after a wild, alcohol-induced fit of rage, during which Mélanie could barely control her, she fell asleep, drunk. The next day, she looked much older and felt ashamed of herself; but her jealousy was still there and seemed to be growing.

After that, she waited each day for Vítor to return. She made plans, only to abandon them, wrote letters which she tore up, weeping; but all these emotions were hidden, because, at the risk of compromising the interests of her heart, she needed to safeguard the interests of her pocket; and so she had appeared before Dâmaso smiling, pleasant and utterly calm, but pale and ablaze with hatred.

VIII

Vítor left Genoveva's house like a general joyfully leaving the battlefield at nightfall after a victory. All kinds of emotions crowded in on him, offering him sweet consolation: he had been witty and eloquent; he had demonstrated to Genoveva that he could return her scorn in rather gentler kind; he had humiliated Dâmaso, crushed him and confounded him . . . and he had secured both the portrait and a reason for future visits. He had avenged himself, he had shown his strength and had gained a strategic advantage. 'I'm another Bismarck!' he thought, scything through the air with his stick.

Life had never seemed so good, and he felt he was intelligent and strong enough to devise further intrigues, to triumph at parties, to succeed by sheer talent. Waves of ambition swept over him. He rather fancied himself as a poltician. After all, why should he make himself wretched and tie himself to such a woman? He must work, concentrate on his career, become a deputy, a minister; and he could imagine himself walking through the Chiado clutching a document case or treading the carpeted corridors of a ministry with a minister's portfolio under one arm, the sleeve of which would be embroidered with gold.

He was walking so fast that, outside the post office, he collided with a man whose overcoat was pulled tightly around him.

'Senhor João Marinho!'

'Silva, my friend!'

And withdrawing into the shelter of the post office doorway, their talk immediately turned to Genoveva. Marinho had not been back to her house since the soirée; he was embarrassed about it really, but he hadn't had a moment to himself; then he uttered his usual formulaic words of praise: She was a most distinguished person, none too virtuous, but who cares! If everyone were virtuous, what a dull place the world would be! And he laughed at his own wickedness.

'Don't you agree, Silva?' Then he went on: She was, of course, out of place in Lisbon. She should be in Paris. She's got spirit and refinement and she's a marvellous hostess. And her clothes, what could one say? And she knows about carriages too! He had even heard Cora Tear say . . . good old Cora . . . the 'Mary Magdalene of the Debauch'. That's what he used to call her. He was the one who gave her that name. Once, he even said it to the Prince of Orange. And his Highness actually laughed.

And he himself burst out laughing, stamping his foot. Then he calmed down again and rolled his eyes. He had completely forgotten what he was saying; he did sometimes suffer these lapses of memory.

'It was something about Cora.'

'Ah, yes,' he almost yelled. 'Cora. Cora said of her: *Elle est trés futée, cette petite Portugaise!* I knew her well. And Monsieur de Molineux was a funny old chap . . . But what suppers! That's all over with now though . . . Paris without an empire isn't worth a thing.' And he shook his head sadly, as if he could see laid out before him the ruins of France.

But Vítor, seized by a sudden idea, said familiarly:

'Marinho, do you fancy having supper with me at the Central?'

'My dear chap, I'd love to. We can have a private room; they've got a delicious Mouton-Rothschild, and very cheap; we can order a couple of bottles . . . Would six o'clock suit you?'

'Six at the Casa Havanesa.'

'*Au revoir!*'

And for no apparent reason, Marinho's whole face convulsed with laughter. He moved off, his overcoat flapping in the wind.

Vítor thought the supper an excellent idea. A well-fed, well-oiled Marinho was bound to tell him everything he knew about Genoveva. Vítor would thus clear up certain obscure points; he would at last have a proper idea as to the identity of that 'adventuress'. He wanted to know about her past, about her lovers, about wild Paris nights; he would beat

Marinho's memories like someone beating woods to drive out a hare.

He went straight to Camilo Cerrão's fourth-floor apartment to warn him that Genoveva was expecting them the following day at two o'clock.

Camilo's beautiful wife, his 'female', came to open the door. She blushed slightly when she saw him and said that Camilo wasn't in.

'Could I leave him a note then?'

Joana showed him into the studio, and Vítor observed her while she was looking for pen and ink. It was winter, and yet either out of habit or poverty, or because she disdained comfort, she was wearing a grubby, faded dressing gown over her nightdress, revealing every movement of her magnificent body; she was clearly wearing no under-bodice, and her breasts were worthy of Praxiteles' Aphrodite. Shut up in that fourth-floor apartment, she had lost her fresh village complexion; her hands, though, were rough and red from plebeian work; there was a statuesque beauty about her shoulders, hips and arms; one sensed the warm blood circulating beneath soft, milky skin. What most troubled Vítor, though, was that faded dressing gown, which clung to her body and, when she moved, revealed her almost as if she were naked. She seemed taller in the low-ceilinged room; amidst the artistic debris of paintings, sketches and plaster statues, she looked like a living statue dressed as a cook, with her angular profile, solid Roman head, round, firm chin, and dark, startled eyes, velvety and thick-lashed.

'Don't worry if there's no pen,' said Vítor, 'I'll use a pencil.'

She walked over to the window, and when he turned round, Vítor saw that she was staring at him with her superb, dark eyes. His heart beat faster; he was shaken by a gust of pagan sensuality. The silence in the studio, the battered chaise, aroused in him a brutish desire, and his hand trembled as he wrote.

'Right,' he said when he had finished. 'I'll leave the note here for him.'

169

She looked down. Vítor did not leave; he slowly drew on his gloves; he was slightly pale and felt embarrassed, troubled, fumbling for something to say.

'It's a lovely day,' he said at last.

'Yes, it is.'

She had a soft, musical voice. Vítor began studying the walls, as if interested in the sketches. He went over to the easel on which stood a painting of a sunset, the paint thickly and clumsily applied; in it a tree trunk lay fallen near a hut.

'This is nice,' he said, turning to her and indicating the canvas.

She remained by the window, where her magnificent breasts were outlined against the rather dim, murky light. She had her hands clasped in front of her.

Vítor had to force himself not to touch her, not to lay his hands on her, such was the magnetic attraction of her splendid body.

'You won't forget to give him the note, will you?'

'No, sir.'

Vítor looked for his notebook; he had dropped it on the chaise, but couldn't find it, and was looking all around him. She helped him look, and they both saw it, caught between the chaise and the wall. As they stooped to pick it up, his chest brushed her shoulder. He felt a delicious, animal warmth on his skin, like a firm caress. When Joana stood up, her face was scarlet; she looked timid, frightened, and her eyes now seemed more sombre.

Vítor held out his hand to her:

'Good afternoon, madam.'

'Goodbye.'

Her hand grasped Vítor's and lay, soft, dead and rough as a washerwoman's in his hand.

Out in the street again, Vítor took a deep breath. He felt as if he had just escaped from an oven charged with an unhealthy, heavily sensual atmosphere. That woman made him uneasy, the way sultry, stormy weather did. He swore never to be left alone with her again, because, if he did, he couldn't answer for his behaviour.

170

But he couldn't forget her strong, robust, pagan beauty and, above all, how the touch of that body had filled him with a sense of melting, delicious, intoxicating warmth.

'God, what a terrifying creature!'

By six o'clock, however, he had forgotten all about her and was walking spryly down Rua do Alecrim with Marinho, on their way to the Hotel Central for supper. As soon as they arrived, Marinho summoned the maître d'hotel, with whom he had a discreet, thoughtful discussion, then joined Vítor in the library, where Vítor was leafing through a book of caricatures by Gavarni.

'The supper menu looks delicious, but we have to wait half an hour.' Then, seeing what Vítor was reading, he exclaimed: 'Oh, I love Gavarni, he's so amusing!' To pass the half hour before supper, he suggested they go upstairs to see a special friend of his, the Baron de Markstein, a diplomat, who was rather poorly. And when Vítor hesitated, he added:

'Don't worry, I'll introduce you. He's an excellent person, a good client of mine. A real gentleman.'

Out of indolence and inertia, Vítor let himself be dragged up to the diplomat's blue silk-lined room. The Baron came mincing in, wearing a floral dressing gown which he held wrapped about him with his left hand, while, with his right hand, he kept doffing a Turkish fez and bowing repeatedly. He had a black silk scarf about his neck and wore a vague expression of foolish melancholy on his pale, thin face. He shook Marinho's hand warmly, invited Vítor to sit down, offered them cigars in a faint voice, and apologised, explaining that he had caught a cold last Sunday coming home from the Marquis' house. He had even had to have a tooth out.

Marinho expressed his deepest regrets. The Baron gave a sad, resigned shrug, and they both smiled and made comforting noises to each other. Marinho then mentioned the imminent departure – so people said – of the Spanish ambassador. The Baron grew heated and, getting to his feet, declared that nothing had been decided, nothing at all; that something of the sort might well happen, but they were still only at the discussion stage; he could confirm nothing, that would be too dangerous; it was a possibility, but he must abstain from giving any firm opinion; it was an extremely delicate matter, and they must draw no false conclusions from anything he said, for he knew no more than anyone else; he knew only that it was a possibility, but that didn't mean he knew anything or had been told anything, not at all. He was always very cautious about such things. He raised one hand to his chin and pulled a grim face that dissolved into a smile.

Then, wanting to show Marinho the latest photograph he had had taken of himself, he minced back into his bedroom.

Marinho turned to Vítor and rolled his eyes as if to say: 'A great man and so deep!'

The Baron returned with his collection of photographs of himself. They showed him in morning clothes, in uniform, dressed for a ball, leaning against a truncated column, in hunting gear, and, lastly, in philosophical pose, studying a map, his cheek resting on his hand. He stood there, his fingers on his chin, awaiting Marinho's reaction.

'Admirable!' said Marinho.

The Baron confided that he had offered one to His Majesty the King. He had hesitated about doing so – it was, after all, a very delicate matter, and he had given it great thought. But since the King had once asked him jokingly if he could have a photograph of him, he had felt that he could . . . His Majesty, as everyone knew, was kindness itself. Indeed, the King not only deigned to accept his portrait, he reciprocated with one of himself. A great man. He couldn't have been more pleased than if he had presented him with the Grand Cross. Not that he had ambitions in that direction, he wouldn't want his words to be misinterpreted . . . Oh, but the King was so friendly, one couldn't imagine a kinder, simpler, more affable monarch. He had immediately informed his own government about the honour the King had done him. He hadn't received a response yet, but he was sure it would make a good impression, oh yes, a very good impression.

Then, turning to Vítor, he said how much he liked Portugal; the climate was divine, the society perfect and the people so extraordinarily kind . . .

He then offered Marinho one of his photographs, slipped it into an envelope, licked it energetically and with bureaucratic thoroughness, despite his poorly condition, and handed it to him with a bow. And when they made to leave, he came with them to the door, still insisting that he knew nothing about the Spanish ambassador's withdrawal, that he had merely expressed a personal opinion, that 'it was a very delicate matter'.

He asked where Vítor lived. He declared that he had rarely met such a knowledgeable young man; he asked if he would see him on Thursday at the Prime Minister's house and proffered a few words about the Prime Minister's reputation throughout the rest of Europe; then he stood at the door, bent into an F, muttering words of farewell into his moustache.

'A very deep man,' Marinho said, carrying the photograph as carefully as if it were a holy sacrament.

They enjoyed a long, delicious, copious supper. The Mouton-Rothschild was excellent.

Naturally, they spoke about Genoveva, but Marinho who seemed to have caught the Baron's infectious diplomatic caution, confined himself to vague generalities. He spoke more about Monsieur de Molineux, described his political views, the beautiful mansion he owned on Rue de Lord Byron, his voracious appetite at table, his repellently aged body, his vices . . .

'So did she have any lovers during that time?' asked Vítor. 'She couldn't have been contented just with the old man . . .'

'Oh, he may have been old,' said Marinho, chuckling, 'but he had a lot of experience and great abilities . . .' By which he implied that the old man's knowledge of debauchery made up for his lack of youth.

He almost wept when the waiter came in bearing a *perdreau au choux*. He checked to see that the little slice of Roquefort he had specified was there, and when he saw it was, his eyes welled up and he looked at the waiter and at Vítor with tender gratitude.

He served himself generously, filled his glass, made sure he had the right knife and enough bread, that the window was properly closed, that the gaslight was working, and then, at peace with the world, he attacked the partridge, saying to Vítor:

'I'm not one to speak ill of anyone. I'm no gossip, as you know. I see, I hear, I say nothing. That's my philosophy.'

He wriggled about in his seat, as if someone were tickling him, and said again:

'That's my philosophy. But the fact is that, while poor old Molineux was still alive, there was one very good-looking lad, La Rechantraye was his name, who was a frequent visitor to the house. Not that I saw anything myself, you understand . . .'

But under the influence of the partridge and the Mouton-Rothschild, he admitted that he had seen something.

He didn't want to speak ill of anyone, but he was there one day, and he did see . . . something. It was at a soirée in poor Molineux's house; there was a conservatory next to the dining room; everyone else was in the gaming room, and he just happened to go into the rather dimly lit conservatory . . . not that he wished to speak ill of anyone, but . . . he leaned towards Vítor, he saw Genoveva lying in the young man's arms, running her fingers through his hair. 'That's what I saw!'

Vítor pushed his glass away from him so brusquely that it tipped over, spilling the wine. Marinho immediately dabbed two fingers on the drenched tablecloth and made a mark on his forehead. For good luck, he said.

'And what happened to the young man?'

'He's dead, dead!' And Marinho's voice took on a lugubrious tone. 'He died in the war.'

Vítor felt pleased and rather grateful to the victorious Germans.

Marinho gave a careless shrug, then, spotting a bottle of champagne, he blurted out:

'The woman has no heart! Just between you and me, not that I'm a gossip, of course, but just between you and me, I think she's an adventuress.'

And he added:

'Of the very worst kind.'

He tried the champagne, found it excellent and, leaning

174

back in his chair, declared that he had always had his suspicions about Genoveva.

'But why?'

'There's some mystery there,' said Marinho, looking very solemn and adding in sepulchral tones: 'Some hidden tragedy.'

Vítor's curiosity knew no bounds. He leaned on the table, devouring Marinho with his eyes. But the excellent chap spoke only intermittently, occupied as he now was with his roast beef, eating methodically, smacking his lips and savouring every mouthful. It was only when the waiter brought in the charlotte russe that Marinho drew one hand across his brow, as if to bring clarity and order to his thoughts, and revealed everything:

'What made me distrust her was this. I knew she was Portuguese. Well, that was easy enough; she had the most diabolical French accent. Not so much now, but then she did. Such open e's and o's – awful. Awful! I'm not the suspicious sort, you know that, but I was curious to find out the truth. I wanted to know where she came from, from Lisbon or the provinces. She told me she was from Madeira. What was her family name, I asked. Gomes, she said. Gomes? I said to myself . . . I just didn't believe she was from Madeira, not for a moment. I've got a good nose for these things.' And he sniffed his way across the table. 'I said to myself "You're not from Madeira, and your name's not Gomes!" But, what did it matter, one dined superbly at her house and she was very charming. What did I care who she was? None of the other Portuguese in Paris knew her. And then, she's not young. She must be thirty-nine or forty now, but very well preserved. Have you seen her in a low-cut dress? Oh!' Marinho threw his arms up in the air. 'Such a throat, such breasts! It's enough to drive a man wild.' And his pupils grew extraordinarily dilated. 'Well, one day, a Brazilian by the name of Couceiro appears at their house, a friend of . . . of . . . oh, I can't remember now. This memory of mine, really! A vulgar man, who looked like a . . .' He searched for the right word, but then announced resolutely: 'Oh, what the devil, we're amongst friends . . . He looked like a thug. And he was!' He added in

175

sombre tones: 'No one knew much about him, but there was talk of a murder. He had married the widow of a very wealthy man for whom he worked as a cashier, and he later went bankrupt. He lived in Paris, though, in the most extraordinary luxury. That's all talk, of course, and in the worst possible taste. Genoveva knew perfectly well what everyone was saying about the Brazilian, but she still received him in her house; after all, what did it matter to her? He was a millionaire, he had gambled and lost; who cared if he had or hadn't killed someone; such things are of no importance in Paris. Did he have money? Fine, then, "Come here, my dear!" One evening, at supper, Couceiro said in Portuguese to Genoveva: "Do you know Guarda at all?" I was looking straight at her and I saw her . . .'

The door opened and the waiter came in, saying that the Baron de Markstein had asked if they would mind if he joined them for coffee.

'Certainly not,' said Vítor, glancing at Marinho. 'I mean, certainly he can.'

'So kind, so kind,' said Marinho, looking radiant.

'Go on, Marinho. You were saying . . . You saw her . . .'

'Saw what?'

'Saw Genoveva when the Brazilian said . . .'

But the door opened again, and the Baron entered, repeatedly doffing his fez. He begged reassurance that he wasn't being a nuisance; but he had felt so alone in his room and he knew how kind the Portuguese were, well, it had been proved to him time and again . . . and he had thought . . . But they were sure it wasn't inconvenient. He wasn't interrupting anything?

And only when they had both said: 'No, no, of course not' did he sit down, gesturing and bowing, begging them not to go to any trouble, simply to pretend he wasn't there; then, stirring his coffee, he asked, as a favour, for any society news. He had been shut in his room for days and he knew nothing about what was going on. Who had gone to the Brazilian minister's house? Had the King's reception been well attended? Had so-and-so been there, and so-and-so? How was His Majesty? What was on at the opera? He knew nothing, he felt positively ashamed.

But Marinho knew everything and reported in detail. Vítor, furiously peeling a tangerine, incensed at being interrupted, listened to that conversation about people he did not know, feeling rather humiliated, afraid that, if the Baron were to ask him, he would have to admit his complete lack of aristocratic connections.

To avoid that possibility, he threw in a few comments about the Far East – did they think there would be a war?

The Baron sank his chin into his silk scarf and shrugged: It was hard to say; one couldn't really venture an opinion; everything was so very complex; but it was a grave situation; not that they should give much weight to his words just because he was a diplomat, he was merely expressing a personal opinion. But the situation was indeed very grave. That is all he could venture to say. Would there or would there not be war, that was the question. Things were looking very serious indeed.

Gazing into his cup, absorbed in thought, his eyebrows raised, he slowly stirred his coffee.

Vítor was talking about the Chancellor of the Empire, Prince Gucharof . . .

'A very deep-thinking man,' the Baron remarked at once.

Vítor mentioned Bismarck.

'Extremely worried,' said the Baron, and added that 'it was all very grave, very grave indeed.'

And he invited them to spend the rest of the evening with him. The minister from France was coming and the Italian attaché; they could have a game of whist. Marinho accepted with alacrity and joy, as long as the stakes were not too high, because otherwise . . . amongst friends, one didn't want to lose too much.

The Baron said: 'Absolutely!' and expressed his regret that Vítor could not stay.

'I can't, I'm afraid. We have visitors at home.'

The Baron bowed and suggested they go up to his room; he had some excellent cognac and cigars . . . But Vítor, unable to speak privately to Marinho and extract the rest of Genoveva's story from him, said his goodbyes in the corridor:

'I'll come and see you, Marinho.'

'Oh, yes, do, dear friend, do. An excellent supper, delicious.'

And Marinho contentedly followed the Baron, who turned on the stairs and waved to Vítor, doffing his fez again and again.

Vítor left feeling thwarted. He had a profound need to know the end of the story. He decided that the next day he would go to see Marinho at the Hotel Universal, but then, wandering aimlessly about, he found himself going down Rua do Correio towards São Bento. It had not occurred to him that this would lead him straight past Genoveva's house. Dâmaso's coupé was at the door; the lights were on in the living room and in her bedroom. That only upset him more and, feeling sorry for that poor fool Dâmaso for being embroiled with such an adventuress, he strode furiously down the street, his angry thoughts in turmoil, wanting both to beat Genoveva and to bite that marvellous neck of hers, of which Marinho had spoken, filling Vítor's blood with tremulous, glittering desires.

That evening, Genoveva had, in fact, sent Dâmaso this note:

'Forgive me, my dear; I was upset; I didn't know what I was saying today. Please come; I've done nothing but cry since you left.'

And Dâmaso, thrilled, had arrived at the gallop.

Genoveva had calmed down since the morning and had reflected upon the inconvenience of quarrelling with Dâmaso; after all, he had the money; whatever she might feel or subsequently decide to do, she must not offend him; if her passion and her self-interest demanded it, she could get rid of him later, but until that time, it was best to seduce him, dazzle him, enslave him, and, note by note, squeeze the last drops of generosity from him. She dressed somewhat provocatively and thus 'armed' (as she put it), she awaited the beast.

The moment he came in, breathless, she held out her two hands to him in a gesture full of loving humility, saying:

'Forgive me. My nerves were bad today.'

She was surprised, however, to find that Dâmaso's brow remained furrowed; she contained her anger and, placing her hands on his shoulders, murmured:

'But what can I do? All women suffer with their nerves. I just lost control.'

Still frowning, Dâmaso mumbled:

'You went too far. You sent me away. I like things clear-cut and I don't like scenes.'

She curtseyed and moved away.

'Fine,' she said icily. 'Let's shake hands and let that be an end to it. Our relationship is over. We will be just good friends.' She affected a slight tremor in her voice. 'It's rather cold today, isn't it?'

Dâmaso was devouring her with sensual eyes; he burst out:

'You don't love me, Genoveva!'

She smiled sadly and cast her eyes heavenward as if to ask heaven, her confidante, to bear witness.

'I don't love him!' she said angrily. 'Who do you take me for? What kind of woman do you think I am? I wouldn't lie about loving you. But, let's not talk about this any more. It's over. What's on at the Teatro de São Carlos tonight?'

She was sitting in a way that emphasised her delicious curves.

He dropped down on the sofa beside her, almost crushing her feet.

'Ouch, you're hurting me!' she said in heartfelt tones.

'Sorry, I didn't mean to.' And he sat nearer the edge of the sofa. He took her hand in his plump hands. 'Just tell me that you love me.'

She sat up, put her arms about his neck and, in a warm voice, her amorous breath brushing his cheek, said:

'Why else am I in Lisbon? Why? I have friends and acquaintances in Paris who would give anything, money, possessions, their life, to be sitting here with me on this sofa as you are. But why am I here in Lisbon?' Her voice became passionate and intense. 'Because of you!'

And she kissed his earlobe. Dâmaso shivered with delight; he put his arms about her and stammered:

179

'Do you swear?'

'I swear, my kitten!' And she drew him close, touched him, aroused him, kissed him, with caresses that burned and words that intoxicated. 'I love you so much, you and your chubby cheeks; I can't resist you. And you know it perfectly well, you rascal; that's why you take advantage of me. Say you love your little Genoveva. Go on, say it. But say it properly; whisper in my ear; tell me with your mouth . . .'

Dâmaso was panting, sighing, he had fire in his blood.

'Mélanie!' shouted Genoveva in a harsh, resonant voice.

Mélanie came running in and smiled when she saw Dâmaso there; she greeted him, expressing the household's general delight to have him back, the beloved, the master, the lord.

'Bring us something to drink, Mélanie.' Then, turning to Dâmaso: 'What would you like, my love? Make him something special, Mélanie. Would you like some Turkish coffee?'

Dâmaso hesitated; his face was red and congested. And Genoveva impulsively grasped his head in her hands.

'Oh, that big head of yours! What have you done to me? Why do I love you so? You're not particularly handsome or very intelligent . . . What have you done to me?' Then in a low voice: 'Make him a Turkish coffee, Mélanie.'

She next ran to the piano and said in a light, cheery voice:

'You see? I'm a new woman. You just have to appear, and I'm a new woman.' And she sang:

> *Chaque femme a sa toquade,*
> *Sa marotte et son dada!*

She broke off and went over to him:

'You're my *toquade*, my *marotte*, my *dada*.'

Dâmaso, however, with a look of very bourgeois distrust, muttered:

'Then why were you making eyes at that idiot, Vítor?'

'Making eyes?' asked Genoveva, and she burst out laughing and asked again: 'Making eyes? At that poppinjay? Why? Well, because he's handsome.' Then smiling: 'But I've seen plenty of handsome men, my dear! Who cares about Vítor? Forget about him.'

And Dâmaso said to her:

'All right, but do one thing for me: let's go and spend a fortnight in Sintra together.'

That sudden proposal took Genoveva by surprise. She turned round and looked down, the way she did when she wanted to hide her feelings. She asked:

'To Sintra? But why?'

'Just for a couple of weeks. It's fun there. The weather's beautiful. We can go to my house, if you like; otherwise we can go to the Hotel Lawrence.'

'I don't know what to say,' said Genoveva.

'You see, you don't want to leave Lisbon, that's what it is. Do you think I don't understand? I can see what's going on.'

Genoveva shot him a fierce, revealing look. At that moment, she felt nothing but intense hatred for Dâmaso. Instead, she opened her arms wide, and with a sad look, said:

'There you are, you see. I was so happy and then you go and make a scene with your nonsensical ideas and . . . No, it's too much. It's over. It's best to finish now.'

And she walked across the room, her handkerchief pressed to her lips, her silk train rustling on the floor.

Dâmaso put an arm about her waist and spoke to her over her shoulder:

'But why are you so against going to Sintra? I'm only asking you this one thing. We would spend two weeks there in the lap of luxury; we could take the caleche, we could eat and drink . . .'

While he was talking, Genoveva suddenly saw the great advantage in their being alone together; it was an opportunity to 'fleece' him thoroughly.

She turned to look at him, her eyes still blazing.

'All right, my love, if that's what you want. I'm happy wherever you're happy. Are there fireplaces in your house?'

'No, but you can stay at the Lawrence. I'll expect you

181

tomorrow. I've prepared everything in grand style; it's lovely in Sintra. It'll be our honeymoon, eh? Am I right?'

'You're a saint . . . and you're all mine.'

That night, they agreed to leave Rua de São Bento. Dâmaso had rented a furnished apartment in Rua das Flores; he would buy some new furniture too, as well as a carriage, and install her officially as 'Dâmaso's mistress'.

The next day, Vítor was impatiently waiting for Camilo Cerrão in order to go to Genoveva's house. The meeting had been arranged for two o'clock, but it was already a quarter to and Camilo had still not appeared. Vítor was waiting in the living room, nervously putting on his gloves only to take them off again, pacing up and down, constantly going over to the window to look out.

At two o'clock, he sent a messenger to Cerrão's house. The gentleman was not in. At half past two, in a state of fury, he himself went. A small, tousled boy opened the door and said that Senhor Cerrão had not been seen since the morning. Vítor went down the stairs, cursing Camilo, and went back to his own house to find out if Camilo had arrived in his absence or sent a note. Nothing. He went to the Teatro de Variedades where Camilo worked. He went upstairs to ask if he was there, but he wasn't. It was three o'clock; they had missed the appointment. He decided that Camilo was a scoundrel unworthy of interest; he would make sure he did not get the commission for the portrait; Camilo would perish in obscurity and poverty. 'The fool!' he said, walking back through the Chiado in despair.

He began writing a note to Genoveva and, after tearing up his first few attempts, he decided to adopt a lighter tone.

'With the absentmindedness of all men of genius, the great artist entirely forgot you had honoured him with an invitation to your house. Artists are like children, whom one must forgive often because they feel things so deeply. However, as soon as I locate him, I will lead him, bound hand and foot, so that he may ask your pardon and contemplate his model.'

The satisfaction he gained from composing the note

slightly dissipated his irritation at having missed the appointment. And to distract himself, he went to see Aninhas, where Rosa told him:

'My mistress is in a terrible state!'

He found Aninhas lying on her bed, her faced bathed in tears. With red eyes and a look of terror on her face, she begged him, for the love of God, not to stay. She was lost. Policarpo had received an anonymous letter informing him of her affair with Vítor; Policarpo was furious; he wanted to leave her and take away her monthly allowance. 'What will I do, what will I do?'

'But what did you tell him?' asked Vítor, frightened.

'I denied it, of course. I flatly denied it, but the brute wouldn't believe me. He said he was going to consult a friend and then he left. I'm expecting him any moment.'

She rolled about on the bed, uttering tormented cries.

Vítor was horrified; honour demanded that if Policarpo abandoned her, then he would have to protect her. Looming before him he saw only embarrassment, expense, restriction, dullness. He was touched by her tears, though; he was on the point of consoling her by saying that he would 'make her happy'. However, he feared making such a positive commitment and said instead:

'I'd better go then, in case he should arrive.'

Aninhas flung her arms about his neck.

'What will become of me? I've lit a candle to Our Lady of Joy, but who knows? He said he would be back at four o'clock, the brute. Oh, Vítor, if I'm left with nothing, will you help me, my love?'

'What a question, my dear. Everything will be all right.'

'Off you go, then. I'll write and tell you what happens.'

Someone rang the door bell.

Aninhas stared at him, petrified.

'It's him! May Our Lady help me! Vítor, I'm lost.'

She was pale and trembling, clinging on to Vítor, who was looking desperately around for some hiding place, some hole, some way out.

Aninhas breathed a sigh of relief; she had recognised the

voice of the woman selling fruit. Pressing her hands to her heart, she said:

'Oh, what a fright! I nearly died. The things I suffer for you, my love.'

Vítor was touched and kissed her tenderly; she accompanied him to the door, calling out to Rosa to be sure to keep the little lamp to Our Lady of Joy filled with oil.

IX

The next day, Vítor looked everywhere for Camilo Cerrão, without success. At the theatre, a young lad in a blue shirt was smoking a cigarette and strolling about on a 'forest' painted on a backdrop laid out on the floor. He said that when there was no great pressure at work, Camilo would often disappear for a few days. You never could tell with Camilo, but he was probably to be found at Botelho's, a tavern in Rua dos Retroseiros.

Vítor went there. The smell of fried fish and another unidentifiable odour filled the tavern; the black floor was more like earth; a single gas jet emitted a harsh, crude light; the loud voices of the customers emerged from inside a thin-walled cubicle, separated off by faded cotton curtains.

Cerrão was sitting in one corner, his elbows resting on a stained tablecloth, eating the speciality of the house, chicken with peas, alongside a large sallow-skinned young man whose small, sad face was covered in angry red pimples; he was wearing a blue scarf.

Camilo introduced him as 'my friend Tadeu'. He listened to Vítor's complaints about the missed appointment, about letting him down, and immediately inveighed against the constraints of punctuality.

'Pff . . . an artist cannot be expected to be punctual, like a notary. Isn't that so, friend Tadeu?'

Tadeu coughed, snuggled down further into his scarf, took a sip of wine and said:

'Pff!'

'Have you never met my friend Tadeu?'

Vítor had not had that 'honour'.

'Show him, Tadeu!' Camilo said.

Tadeu picked up a roll of paper from beside him on the bench and spread it out on the table. It was a confused, rather smudged composition, in which one could just make out beneath some trees a few figures wearing tall boots and musketeers' hats; they were standing outside a tavern, drinking and gesturing vehemently; they seemed to be soldiers or gentlemen; they were all heavily built and apoplectic-looking, brimming with Herculean strength and a kind of brutish joviality; their fists could have killed bulls with one blow; their burly chests were so puffed up, their very breaths must have been hurricanes and their words as thunderous as mortars. Sitting on the knee of one of them was an ample young woman, built on an equally colossal scale, with plump cheeks, enormous breasts and arms as thick as columns; another woman, similarly proportioned, was laughing out loud, revealing a horribly bestial broad back, thighs and muscles. The drawing was entitled *The Strong Race*, and the sheer opulence of the work was in comical contrast to the scrawny artist.

When asked for an opinion, Vítor declared it 'magnificent, magnificent!'

'There's real strength there, don't you think, real power!' exclaimed Camilo. 'It shows the brutal, blazing poetry of the flesh! All of those figures have monstrous appetites, thunderously jovial temperaments, colossal musculature, abundant flesh, the very epitome of all that is strong, material and animal. It is vast, rich, opulent, strong, fat, brutal and healthy. It's the poetry of the flesh! Tadeu is another Rubens! His work is all on an equally gigantic scale. It's a salutary lesson for the modern race, which is thin, pale, anaemic, alcoholic, malnourished, breathing the foul air of tavern rooms and existing on cakes and *horchata*. There is no substitute for strength!'

Tadeu glumly rolled the drawing up again and said, stroking his gaunt, sallow face:

'Strength is everything. We must paint strength!'

Camilo then lamented modern civilisation, especially what he called the 'national depression'.

Painting was impossible in the presence of the Portuguese race, where there are no men or women; there are little bisque statuettes, debilitated, sluggish creatures, like characters out of a novel, with hospital-sallow complexions. They don't walk, laugh, move or think; they slither, they smile faintly, they slump, their arms are flabby as gelatine; they are a cachectic,

186

withered, desiccated, limp race of people with skin the colour of chicken flesh.

And he harked back to a heroic age when men were colossi and women were living statues, when war was a diversion and massacres were national feastdays, when people drank down whole wineskins and consumed an entire wild boar served on a golden platter, when blood ran thick and scarlet. What blood they had then!

'What blood!' murmured Tadeu weakly.

'Love was purely animal. A man would take a woman to the brothel and their moans would be a frank, heroic expression of sensuality. One night,' he exclaimed, 'Knight Ernalton of Spain went into the Conde de Fox's house and noticed that there wasn't much wood on the fire, only one branch of a tree. He immediately went out into the courtyard where some donkeys had just come from the forest, bearing bundles of wood; he picked up one of the donkeys complete with its load, put it on his back, went up the twenty-four steps leading into the gallery and hurled the wood and the donkey onto the flames. What a man!'

'What a man!' said Tadeu, rolling his eyes.

'Paint that scene for me, you who understand about strength. Can't you see it already?'

'I can,' said Tadeu, his mouth full of chicken.

'The high-ceilinged room with thick stone walls, a fireplace large enough to contain the spoils of a whole forest; the casks of wine that they drink in one draught; swords and broadswords weighing thirty kilos thrown down in one corner; the gigantic men, barbarous and primitive, with bloodshot eyes, with hair the colour of iron on their chests, talking about battles and lootings; minstrels playing the harp and singing of the deeds spoken of by the magician Virgil, women with their heavy breasts exposed, with virile arms that could kill a Turk, and sensual nostrils, which, after drinking mead laced with spices from Taprobana, send out a warm breeze, as if from the embers of a lubricious pyre. What a painting! Do you see what I mean, Tadeu?'

'I do! Strength! The age of barbarism!'

And he rearranged his blue scarf.

Vítor felt vaguely embarrassed; they were like two mad-men, and he could not take his eyes off Tadeu, who coughed incessantly as he ate his peas one by one with his fork and who had the sallow, greasy complexion of one who suffers with his digestion. Vítor merely said timidly:

'So when shall we meet, Camilo?'

'Tomorrow at two.'

Before Vítor left, however, Camilo insisted that he drink some white wine and eat some toasted almonds; he acted as if he owned the tavern and even summoned, as an object of curiosity, one Fabião. Fabião came. He was a Galician with a long face, who wore his shirtsleeves rolled up. Camilo asked him to recite the menu. Drawing himself up to his full height, Fabião put his hands on his hips, closed his eyes and said in one uninterrupted flow:

'Chicken soup with rice, vegetable soup, seafood risotto, dried cod and onions, fried fish, chicken and peas, sausages and cabbage, pig's trotters, calf's foot jelly, veal stew, roast veal, loin of pork, veal cooked with beans, duck stuffed with olives, pig's ears, kidneys, steaks, ready to serve, one price only, table wine and toasted almonds included. Do not miss this bargain now, we'll even throw in our very own Fabião!'

The two painters writhed about laughing.

'Go on, show us your biceps!'

Fabião rolled his sleeve up to his shoulder and revealed a huge, bulging muscle.

They poured him a glass of wine. He drained the cup and wiped his mouth with the back of his hand.

'Bring us two classically beautiful naked nymphs,' said Camilo, spluttering with laughter.

Tadeu was laughing too.

'Bring me a barbarian woman covered in precious stones, who can kill a snake with her bare hands.'

From the room next door came the sounds of an argument. Harsh voices, the thud of fists crashing down on tables and insults being exchanged. Fabião went calmly in to observe the 'party'. Tadeu, terrified, reached for his hat. But the argument ended in laughter and voices calling for red wine to celebrate the reconciliation.

Bored, Vítor got up and, having exacted a promise from Camilo to be punctual, he departed, leaving the two once more immersed in their mutual worship of strength and animality.

In the end, it was only two days later that he managed to persuade Camilo to go with him to Genoveva's house. He was most upset when Camilo turned up in his worn jacket and broad-brimmed hat. What would Genoveva make of that ugly, dishevelled artist with his mass of curly hair and his scuffed boots? He was too timid, though, to comment and they set off in a cab.

Just as they were entering Rua de São Bento, Vítor saw Miss Sarah, looking her usual thin, grave self, all dressed in black and gazing straight ahead as she walked neatly along with her elbows tight in to her body.

Vítor got out and ran over to ask if Genoveva was at home.

Miss Sarah blushed to see him and gave a broad, carnivorous smile. Did he not know? They had left for Sintra three days ago.

Vítor felt dashed.

Yes, the two lovebirds had gone off to Sintra, and she had stayed behind with Mélanie to get things ready for the move.

'What move?'

They were going to move house, explained Miss Sarah. They were going to move to a splendid new apartment.

Very erect, firmly planted on her two large feet, she was devouring Vítor with her eyes; she mentioned the weather, in an attempt to keep him with her a little longer, but Vítor, too stunned to speak, bade her good afternoon, ran back to the cab and said to Camilo:

'She's gone.' He punched his own knee and launched into a series of bitter accusations aimed at Camilo. It was all his fault; she had got fed up with waiting and had left. Now, of course, she wouldn't even want to have her portrait painted. Camilo had let the opportunity slip. He would always be the same, careless and unreliable. He would never get anywhere as a painter. He would die poor and in obscurity, a ruin, a wretch, with only a horde of children to show for it!

'Stop, my friend, stop!' shouted Camilo, wanting to call a halt to that flow of angry eloquence.

'It's all your fault!'

'*Mea culpa, mea culpa, mea maxima culpa*,' said Camilo, laughing.

But Vítor was desperate. He vented on Camilo all the anger overwhelming him.

'It's not decent to keep a lady waiting. It's just bad manners.'

Camilo, in turn, grew heated:

'Artists aren't at the beck and call of the bourgeoisie! Pope Julian would humble himself before Raphael. Francis I used to put away Titian's brushes for him.'

'Oh, go to hell!' exclaimed Vítor, jumping down from the cab and paying the driver.

Camilo got down after him, citing Rubens whom princesses would kneel to, begging him to paint their portrait, and Charles I of England, who would stand up when Van Dyck entered the room.

'Art creates its own royalty.'

Vítor hurled a curse at him and stalked off.

'So you're leaving me here,' yelled Camilo, 'alone and shipwrecked in this inhospitable street, prey to wild beasts, with no model and no cab.'

'Oh, go to hell!' said Vítor, already some way down the road.

He went straight to Genoveva's house; he wanted to talk to Mélanie, to question her and find out what it all meant – the trip to Sintra and the move.

Upstairs, he found the front door open; he knocked on the door and went into the house; he peered into the living room where he saw Mélanie standing before him and the broad back of a man in a jacket disappearing into Genoveva's bedroom. Mélanie, quite unperturbed and with the familiar air of a lady of the house and the manner of a confidante, invited him in and asked why he hadn't been to see them.

There were two large trunks in the room, which Mélanie was filling; on the chairs were dresses, various packages and hatboxes; on the floor were piles of underclothes and the occasional sachet of aromatic herbs; there was lace, ribbons on nightdresses, a whole intimate feminine world that gave Vítor a troubling sense of half-glimpsed nakedness.

'So, where are you moving to?'

'To Rua das Flores, a third-floor apartment, on the corner. It's a lovely house and all newly fitted out.' And she praised the house, but that only irritated Vítor.

'And where are they staying in Sintra?'

'At the Lawrence. I'm not going until tomorrow, because I had to do the packing. They're in Sintra for a fortnight.'

'I see,' said Vítor, preparing to light a cigarette.

Mélanie ran off to find a match for Vítor, and Vítor strolled about the room. 'So she was permanently installed with that fool Dâmaso!' Vítor felt neither jealous nor sad; he simply hated her, found her vulgar and stupid. 'How I despise her!' he thought. 'If the silly woman came to me now on bended knee, I wouldn't touch her even with tongs!' His foot touched a hat and he gave it a kick that sent it flying against the wall. And all that linen, all those petticoats, even the smell of them irritated him; Dâmaso would have touched them. That beast had lounged on those sheets. It was comical really. Dâmaso! If only he were there now; he would like to hear Dâmaso make one of his facetious comments. And he laughed to himself. What a punch he'd land him. He would, with pleasure, tear him limb from limb. Not out of jealousy, mind, but because he had always disliked him; he was a bourgeois, a conformist and a dandy. He hated him.

Mélanie came back bearing a box of matches.

'So, they're off for a honeymoon in Sintra, are they?'

Mélanie made a slight gesture with her head, smiled faintly and shrugged; then she bent down and went back to packing the trunks, saying:

'Well, when you can't have what you want, you have to make do with what you have.'

'Oh, like in the *The Grand Duchess of Gerolstein*,' said Vítor, sitting down nonchalantly. 'I'm glad to see you're so *au fait* with the classics.'

Mélanie giggled and said again with her eyes fixed on him:

'As I said, when you can't have what you want . . .'

Vítor sprang to his feet and went over to Mélanie:

'What do you mean, Mélanie . . . tell me.'

His voice sounded harsh, his eyes were shining; Mélanie's words were all it took for his scorn for Genoveva to disappear and for him to be filled with immense hope. He insisted:

'Tell me.'

Mélanie drew back modestly, shielding her face with her hands, as if to ward off a kiss.

'I don't know anything. I'm just doing my job. Nobody tells me anything.'

'Tell me, Mélanie, there's a good girl,' Vítor said. 'Has she spoken to you about me?'

He had grasped her hands, slender hands with large fingers, and Mélanie shrank back, trying to free herself, 'she didn't know anything, honestly', and she kept glancing up at Vítor with a mixture of flirtatiousness and lubricity.

She got free of him at last, ran over to a small table and picked up an ivory box which bore Genoveva's monogram in silver. Still saying that Genoveva never talked to her about anything, she went very quiet and polished the box, stroking it, opening and closing it. Vítor, suddenly curious, said:

'Let me see the box, Mélanie.'

She clutched it to her and ran to the other side of the room, pretending to be afraid, as if wanting to keep something from him, pulling faces and laughing loudly.

Vítor chased her and tried to catch her. She was laughing hysterically by then, as if someone were tickling her; she leapt away and her thin body was light as a deer's, languid as a panther's.

'Mélanie, I'll give you two *libras* if you let me see the box.'

That was all he had, and it was a lot, but hopeful curiosity made him boldly prodigal.

'Two *libras*, Mélanie.'

He clinked the coins in his hand.

Mélanie, with the box behind her back, her chest thrust forward, came over to examine the coins with a greedy eye.

'And you won't say anything to Madame?'

'I swear.'

'What else will you give me?'

'Good grief, I haven't got anything else. Two *libras* and a kiss.'

'Do you give me your word of honour?'

'The word of a gentleman.'

Then with great solemnity, Mélanie opened the box, holding it up to him; inside was a bunch of faded violets and two crumpled gloves.

Vítor was furious.

'You robbed me, Mélanie!'

But Mélanie, looking very serious, showed him the withered flowers. Didn't he remember? It was a bunch he had brought with him when he came to see her and she was ill. He'd left his gloves behind. That was one of them.

It was indeed his glove and each finger of his glove was tied in a knot to a finger of a glove belonging to Genoveva.

A blush of pleasure suffused Vítor's face.

Mélanie proffered her hand and her cheek.

'Listen, Mélanie,' he said, very agitated. 'Do you think she likes me?'

'Madame?' She raised her arms to heaven, then said in low, rapid tones: 'I shouldn't say this, and, if she found out, she would kill me, but I can't bear to see Madame suffering like this. And her friendship with Dâmaso gets on my nerves. Madame is mad about you, she's passionately in love.'

Vítor's heart started beating fast.

'Do you know what she did when she found those gloves? No, I'd better not say . . . yes, I will. She covered them in kisses, then took one of her own gloves and knotted them together like that; she said she was binding your soul to hers. Silly, eh? I say to her sometimes: "You're stupid to get so upset over a man. There's no shortage of other men!" But, no, she won't have anyone else.'

'Is that true, Mélanie?' said Vítor, looking wildly at her.

'Of course it is.'

She held out her hand and Vítor gladly gave her the two *libras*. He would have liked to give her more. The whole house seemed transfigured: the trunks full of linen and underclothes opened up like the hollow in a warm bed of love; he found the lace on the nightdresses profoundly touching; all the perfumes seemed to him like Genoveva's own breath. An immense, deep love filled him and beat inside his chest, like the growing waves of a flood tide. A sudden, mad idea had pierced his mind, leaving a vague, sweet, luminous trail behind it, like a meteor. He would go and see her.

'So they're staying at the Lawrence?'

'Yes, at the Lawrence. Now, what about that kiss?'

Vítor laughed, grabbed her round the waist and kissed her full on the mouth. Mélanie turned slightly pale and her eyes glazed over.

'I think Madame may be right,' she said demurely.

Vítor had picked up his hat and, indicating the bedroom into which the man in the jacket had disappeared, said:

'Enjoy yourself!'

'Pff!' she said with a shrug.

As Vítor went down the road, he had his plan already drawn up: he would go to Sintra. He did not consider that she might not want to be pursued, that Dâmaso might go mad with jealousy. He wanted to see her; two weeks without her seemed impossible; now that he knew she loved him, it seemed to him that she had taken with her all the breathable air, all the necessary light. He would go there via Cascais, so that it would seem like a chance encounter.

Mélanie's words had restored hope to him, but they had not given him certainty, and he wanted that certainty. All the thoughts and doubts, all the torment he had gone through in the past week now seemed unbearable and, now that Mélanie had allowed him a glimpse of Genoveva's love for him, he wanted to see it for himself, intense and complete, rather like a man who stands resigned before a locked door, but hurls himself through it if he finds it ajar.

And if it wasn't true, then she could say so, she could

despise him, turn her back on him. That at least would make his mind up for him. He could then forget her and seek consolation elsewhere.

And now he attributed all Genoveva's indifference entirely to himself; he had not shown himself to be sufficiently loving or sufficiently tenacious. Love requires, above all, patience. He had demanded passion from her too quickly, on only the second occasion they had met, like an impatient creditor; and then when he had drawn back, she had felt a woman's natural doubts, the instinctive reticence of the object of desire; he, like a fool, had got angry and distanced himself. What had he expected? That she would take him straight to her bedroom, like some prostitute, the moment he looked at her? How stupid he had been!

His visit to Sintra was a way of making reparation for that gross impatience. He would show all the persistence, humility and tender sympathy of a dog; he would show her how dependent on her he was, a satellite, like the moon. Yes, he would definitely go to Sintra.

Alas, he had no money, and that banal little difficulty blocking the passionate onward march of his desires irritated him: Oh hell, he would have to go and ask Uncle Timóteo. Timóteo gave him a monthly allowance. Vítor had never asked for any other money from his uncle, except on odd occasions. He was, therefore, somewhat nervous. He went to the study door and listened; if his uncle was whistling, that indicated he was in a good mood; a profound silence reigned, but desire made him resolute. He went in and found his uncle asleep in his armchair. At a movement from the dog, his uncle opened his eyes, his head on one side, like a bird, and grunted.

Oh, no, he was in a foul mood! Vítor could tell. He stroked Dick and played with him, kissing his snout.

'How are you, Dick?'

'What do you want?' muttered Uncle Timóteo.

'Nothing, Uncle.'

He went over and opened the window, and stood in front of it.

'Having a nap, eh?'

Uncle Timóteo yawned, like a bored lion.

Then, sitting up in his chair, he said:

'I bumped into Dr Caminha. He says you've hardly set foot in the office lately.'

Vítor swore mentally to give Dr Caminha a sound beating.

'That's ridiculous. I have been there, not much perhaps, but I have.'

His uncle, now fully awake, added vehemently:

'And why haven't you been to the office? So that you can stroll through the Chiado and down Pote das Almas, like a fool. What pleasure can there be in wandering around Lisbon! Now wandering around India or Calcutta, that I can understand. But Lisbon? What is there worth seeing?'

Vítor said:

'I've not been very well, actually.' And he coughed piti-fully. 'I was even thinking of going to spend a few days in Sintra. I really don't feel at all well.' He felt his own forehead, then, taking courage: 'I was wondering if you could give me some money.'

His uncle started in his chair.

'To Sintra? Whatever for?'

Sintra was one of his pet hates; he could not stand all the classical praise heaped on the place; it seemed to him the ignorant admiration of one who had never seen the marvellous woods and landscapes of India.

Vítor mentioned a change of air.

'It's your life you need to change. The air's fine, it's your life that's bad. Go to bed early, eat regularly, stop writing poetry, go punctually to the office, and you'll be amazed how much your health improves. Sintra! An outing fit for a shopkeeper.'

'No, I really do need . . .,' began Vítor pathetically.

'I smell a woman,' said Timóteo menacingly.

And Vítor, knowing his uncle's weakness for libertine adventures, confessed with a fatuous smile that, yes, there was a woman involved.

'Who is she?' Uncle Timóteo asked bluntly, taking a large pinch from his snuff box.

Vítor hesitated. He felt an urge to tell him everything; he so needed to talk about her; Timóteo would give him the money if it was to advance a love affair; and wasn't he, after all, his dear, old friend?

He flung wide his arms in frank, confessional mode:

'All right, I'll tell you, Uncle. It's Dâmaso's mistress.'

'Dâmaso's, eh? Has she encouraged you?'

'We have an understanding.'

'How much do you want?' cried Uncle Timóteo, delighted, sitting down at his writing desk and opening a drawer. 'Dâmaso's mistress! Well, it's always worth spending money on a good cause. This has taken years off me! That fool pays, and you . . . Excellent. Off you go, my lad. How long are you going to Sintra for? Three days? Well, you'll need some money, then.'

And he placed a little pile of fifteen *libras* on the table. He got up, his eyes shining.

'And it's love, is it? Wonderful! That's what I like to hear. Ha, that fool Dâmaso. And when are you off?'

'After supper.'

'Clorinda!' yelled Timóteo. 'Hurry up with supper.'

He was beaming and rubbing his hands together.

'You must tell me all about it later. I want to know everything!'

And he gazed at Vítor lovingly, proudly.

At six o'clock, Vítor, with one small suitcase at his feet, and feeling very nervous, was rolling along the Benfica road in a coupé driven by one Toirão, a driver of public hire carriages. How would she react, what would she be doing? What would he say to her?

He could already imagine different dialogues. They would probably just be finishing supper. He could see her in the hotel dining room, he could see the two oil lamps, the two windows that looked out on to the small terrace. He would pretend astonishment, exclaiming: 'What a surprise!' And what excuse would he invent? He would say he was there to sort out a lawsuit, to see some land, something vague, couched

197

in abstruse legal jargon. They would spend the night in the salon; they would perhaps play cards and, if it was a warm night, they could go for a stroll beneath the trees. Would he have a chance to speak to her? Would he be able to slip a note into her hand? Should he mention the intertwined gloves?

As he puffed on his cigarette, he wrote a note, laconic, profound and poetic:

'Do to my soul as you did to my glove; entwine it with yours.'

It struck him as mediocre. He preferred it in French:

'*Que les deux gants soyent le symbole de nos existences.*'

But then, fearful of Dâmaso and because it seemed more chic, he decided to write it in English:

'I saw the gloves. Might our souls be joined together so closely.'

He had a suspicion that the English wasn't quite right, but he liked its brevity.

In Porcalhota, while the horses were resting and Toirão was drinking a glass of brandy, he went for a walk. It was already getting dark, and in the cold night air, two stars were shining; there was silence, apart from the occasional barking of a dog in the distance. The road ran between low stone walls and, beyond, the black fields stretched out into the diffuse dark, with a few bare trees casting a still darker shadow.

As Vítor walked slowly along, he was thinking of her. In keeping with the place, the love filling him had something of the vagueness of the night and the solemnity of the silence. He thought how sweet it would be to live with her in the country, in a remote village. On winter nights, they would sit by the fire, looking at each other and talking quietly; the cold wind would moan outside; the dogs on the farm would bark, and anyone coming down the road would turn and glance curiously at their happy house and, sensing family, love, higher interests, would continue on their way through the desolate night. In certain temperaments, the envy that happiness arouses in others only makes it seem all the sweeter.

He could see the two lamps on the coupé coming down the road. He stopped and jumped inside.

'Off we go, Toirão.'

His little affair made him happy because it was like some piquant episode out of a novel or an adventure story; alone, in one corner of the carriage, he felt a kind of pride spread through him, knowing that he was being carried along at a gallop down an empty road towards a new chapter of love. He would occasionally lower the window and look out; the dark, monotonous landscape rolled past on either side in the darkness; a chill wind undulated slowly over the smooth earth; and the bright clouds in the sky seemed to tremble with cold. Verses from popular songs and fragments of arias came into his mind, but the mournful *fado* best expressed the slightly sad sentimentalism of his spirit; he closed his eyes and started singing, filled by a sense of infinite longing and an overwhelming tenderness.

The road was passing between two high parallel walls, where the branches sobbed and murmured. It was Ramalhão. The air seemed thinner, as if cooled by the abundance of water; the parks and the trees exhaled a sweet serenity, an atmosphere of gentle elegance; the silence there was one of delicate repose and indolence. Ramalhão.

The shops in the square dimly lit the provincial night; there was no noise and it was not long before the coupé was drawing up outside the Lawrence. A servant ran out to open the carriage door for him and show him up the terrace steps to the dining room. The table had not been cleared; there were plates, bottles of wine and only two places set, doubtless theirs; and it seemed to him that the perfume of her clothes wafted in the air.

'Senhor Dâmaso is staying here, isn't he?'

'He's downstairs in the salon,' said the servant.

Vítor went up to his room to comb his hair and wash his hands. Through the window he could see the night and hear the vague murmur of trees all along the valley – the somnolent beauty of the mountains.

And ignoring the servant, who was asking him if he wanted anything to eat or drink, he went downstairs. The door of the salon was ajar; he went over to it. She was alone, sitting by the fire. The light from the fire lent her skin a rosy glow; she was wearing black and was lounging back in her chair, staring into the flames. There were clothes draped over the chairs; on the table, between two candles, was a magnificent bunch of camellias.

When Vítor pushed open the door, she slowly raised her beautiful eyes and uttered a cry.

'I couldn't bear not being able to see you and so I came.'

A passionate sound, half-sigh, half-sob, escaped her; her arms fell to her side and Vítor pressed her to him, and they kissed.

'Oh, my love!' she murmured, resting her sad, happy head on Vítor's shoulder.

The floorboards along the corridor creaked, and Dâmaso suddenly appeared at the door and stood there, petrified.

However, once Vítor had explained that he was there investigating a lawsuit, dressing up his excuse with a complicated legal name, Dâmaso took a deep breath and, clapping him on the back, said:

'Good for you, man! We're off to Peninha tomorrow.'

Then he ordered a cognac, suggested a game of cards and seemed entirely unaffected by Vítor's presence, either because he believed what Vítor had said about the lawsuit, or because he had no doubts now about Genoveva's love. He fidgeted on his chair, talked loudly and pompously, and his fat little figure seemed so entirely odious to Vítor that he felt deeply happy to be deceiving the fool.

Genoveva remained seated by the fire, as if fascinated by the flames; she made the occasional comment, but a sad air of lassitude hung about her.

'She's been like that ever since we arrived in Sintra,' Dâmaso remarked.

'Sintra makes me sad.'

And she waved her hand in the direction of the valley, the surrounding mountains, the melancholy emanating from that tangle of dark green vegetation, the melancholy of artifice.

'It's quite different in summer. There are picnics, all the

200

hotels are full, there are outings to Cascais, plays . . . It's tremendous fun.'

'Thank God it's winter,' muttered Genoveva.

She got up, saying that it was such a pleasant night, she would like to go for a walk.

They all went. Genoveva took Vítor's arm and they strolled along beneath the trees, without speaking, as far as Seteais. The night was very dark, but calm; a slight chill dampness filled the air and there was something almost sad about the great sea of greenery, the deep valley down below and the lonely silence of the gardens and the empty houses; melancholy dropped from the trees and, beyond, everything was drowning in murky shadows broken here and there by the pale, sweet light of some small dwelling.

Vítor and Genoveva kept very close, holding each other's arm tightly, ardently, ecstatically; they did not speak, gripped by the intense silence that comes with a superabundance of tender feelings. Genoveva's long dress brushed the ground, occasionally dragging with it a dry twig or a stalk.

Beside them, Dâmaso was softly whistling the march from *Faust*. A quarter of an hour passed thus, then Dâmaso said:

'We're all silent as tombs! And it's cold too.'

He sneezed.

'Go back to the hotel; you don't want to catch a cold.'

'No, you certainly don't,' seconded Vítor.

'Go in!' said Genoveva.

Dâmaso replied, half-amused, half put out:

'It's like that scene from *The Barber of Seville*: *buona sera, buona sera*! I won't go in, I don't want to.'

Genoveva laughed, as did Vítor, just to flatter Dâmaso, who, pleased at his own joke, confessed that he too hated Sintra out of season.

'You need warm weather and plenty of people. In the summer, it's wonderful.'

Vítor disagreed: he enjoyed the isolation of winter there. Everything, the trees, the air, the light, was touched with such intense melancholy. He proffered some rather literary phrases. The worst thing about Sintra were the bourgeois, the banker and the dandy, the carriages full of Spanish women, the English in their dark glasses, all those fine clothes obscuring the view of the trees; the mountains became a mere annexe of the Chiado. There was nothing like solitude; he mentioned the monks in Peninha, praised the tranquillity of the monasteries, quoted Lord Byron.

Dâmaso broke in impatiently.

'Well, I'm no poet, of course.'

Genoveva sighed. And Dâmaso, touching her arm and addressing her as *tu*, said:

'You're not going to take up poetry as well, are you?'

Genoveva stopped and said in a sweet, resigned voice:

'Really, my friend, I just can't get used to that horrible, familiar use of *tu*!'

Dâmaso, cut short, did not reply. Vítor, fearing a scene, said apprehensively:

'Don't these silent trees and this darkness make one think of legends and ghosts?'

'They do,' said Genoveva, and, as she spoke, she pressed close to Vítor, as if overcome by amorous languor.

'Do you believe in ghosts, then?' asked Vítor, laughing.

No, she didn't, but when she was a little girl, she had heard of some very strange incidents; she had had a nursemaid from Trás-os-Montes, who used to recount such tales; Genoveva could still remember them; her nursemaid had known all kinds of tales and stories in verse.

'I can still remember some. Wait . . .' And she sang:

> The Lord High Admiral came sailing by
> On his ship with sails so full
> And so many men below the decks
> Too many by far to tell.

'It's lovely, don't you think? Then there was a princess who saw him and fell in love . . . but I can't quite remember. But there was another even lovelier one which I still sometimes recite to myself; it has a special something about it:

> Whoever will come and be my maid,
> Whoever will take my money,
> Must carry this letter to my true love,
> Dom Clarim Across-the-Water.

It's about a princess who lives in a tower . . . or some such thing. It's odd how sometimes these childhood memories stay with us, stories about journeys and countries that we never forget . . .'

'Yes, that's true. I can still remember a song my nursemaid used to sing to me; it's a very slow, sad tune.' Vítor sang:

> Go to sleep, go to sleep, my little man,
> Your mother has gone to the fountain . . .

It's sad, don't you think?'

Genoveva did not reply. Vítor felt her arm tremble slightly and a soft sigh left her lips.

They walked along in silence again. The earth, grown insubstantial in the mist, muffled the sound of their footsteps. Then Genoveva spoke again:

'Yes, nursemaids often used to sing that song. Your mother died a long time ago, didn't she?'

'Yes, I was only about one or two; I've never even seen a picture of her; she didn't leave a portrait, not even the sort people used to have painted at the time. But I think she must have been very pretty.'

'And what about your father?'

'He died in Africa.'

Dâmaso was becoming irritated by this conversation and was whistling the quartet from *Rigoletto*. They were near the Penha Verde. A light breeze had got up, and from the ancient trees came a soft, sad whispering.

'So many things happen in a lifetime,' murmured Genoveva, as if thinking out loud.

The night was almost pitchblack, and Vítor took her hand and held it tight in ecstatic tenderness; he had never loved her so much. The dark, dumb melancholy of the night, the shifting shadows, the silence of the trees, the occasional ripple of running water encouraged a sentimental, almost mystical mood. Genevova had never seemed more adorable; he found a tenderness in her voice he had never known before, and in her words a delicate spirit open to the poetry of legend and the influence of nature; he seemed to have uncovered in her a poetic soul; having desired her so much for her resplendent, bounteous beauty, he loved her now for the refinement of her feelings.

'This is better by far than the boulevards of Paris,' she said.

Dâmaso stopped whistling to protest. No, no! He loved Sintra in the summer when there were plenty of people and good company to be had, but the boulevards of Paris, that he wouldn't change for anything, what with all those willing women dressed up to the nines, walking up and down at nine or ten o'clock at night, and the cafés full to bursting . . .

'Oh, yes,' he said to Genoveva, 'the boulevard's the thing, all right.'

Genoveva responded in the same sweet, resigned tone (the tone one uses when speaking to harmless idiots):

'Yes, my love, of course. Not that I ever walked up and down the boulevards of course.'

Dâmaso was about to add something, when she said:

'And another thing, I can sense that you're about to start whistling *Rigoletto* again. Well, I beg you, please don't. Shall we go back?'

They did so in silence.

When they returned to the room, bright flames from the coals were leaping up, filling the dark room with flickering, rosy reflections. Dâmaso lit a candle and sat down wearily, yawning ostentatiously.

Genoveva lifted her dress slightly and held out her small foot to the fire; she was wearing patent leather shoes and silk stockings with black and yellow stripes. Vítor was leafing through a book that was on the table, but when he heard Dâmaso yawn noisily for the second time, he said:

'Well, time for bed.'

Genoveva turned and gave him a long, meaningful look, as caressing as a kiss and as solemn as an oath:

'Goodnight.'

'Goodnight.'

Vítor went into his room drunk with happiness, placed the candle in the candlestick, reached his arms heavenwards and, closing his eyes, said, smiling:

'Oh, my love!'

He slumped down in a chair, and sat there, his eyes fixed on the floor. Happiness had the same enervating effect on him as over-exposure to the intense August sun; his mind was empty and his soul inert, as if it lay in a bath of milk; he saw her dark eyes shining before him and could see her body too, as bright as a gold coin on a black cloth.

Just then, the door opened, and Dâmaso appeared, bearing a candlestick; he was followed by the sleepy, shivering servant.

Since there was a spare bed in Vítor's room, he had come to sleep in there, and, so that the servant would not understand, he explained in slow, mangled French that Madame was 'indisposed'. He was in a bad mood, though, and was gloomily smoking a large cigar.

As soon as the sleepy servant had mumbled a goodnight, Dâmaso said he was heartily sorry they had ever come to Sintra.

He gave immediate vent to his feelings: Genoveva had been in a foul mood from the moment they arrived. He couldn't get a word out of her at table. In Lisbon she was jolly, she sang, but here . . . ! And then there were her nerves, her moods . . . She hadn't moved from the fireside for three days and, if there was one thing he couldn't stand, it was seeing a woman sitting by a fire.

'Today was the first time we've been out . . . and that was only because you were here.'

Then, fearing that he might have revealed his vague feelings of jealousy, he added:

205

'Not that she doesn't like me, no, she's mad about me! And in bed, well . . .' He went into some detail, recounting the oaths of love she swore to him, the pet names she gave him. Oh, she was in love, all right, but she was so moody.

He got undressed and described the apartment he was setting her up in and the carriage he was going to buy her, all the while smoking his cigar and describing her intoxicating beauty, her sumptuous body.

Vítor affected indifference, but his heart was pounding, and Dâmaso, like someone relating his 'conquests' to the company in an inn, talked on and on about Genoveva's many attractions.

Vítor did not feel jealous and, for some reason unknown to himself, he kept comparing Dâmaso to Aninhas' protector, Policarpo.

Before turning out the light, Dâmaso turned his back for a moment, and Vítor saw that he was making the sign of the cross.

'What superstitious nonsense is that?' asked Vítor from his bed.

Dâmaso turned round at once, ashamed of his devotion, and lied.

'It's just a childhood habit. I don't believe in it. It's just habit.'

And he lay down, expressing a few obscene opinions on the subject.

The following day was cloudy; there was thick mist on the mountains and in the valley. When they all met for breakfast, the weather had closed in further and a fine drizzle was falling; the only trees they could see appeared hunched and cold.

As they sat down at the table, Genoveva suddenly said to Dâmaso, in the most affectionate tones:

'*Caro mio*, I forgot my scarf. Would you mind fetching it for me?' She looked at him tenderly. 'I do so need Mélanie.'

Dâmaso left the room and Genoveva immediately held out her arms to Vítor. He went over to her; she put her hands about his neck and placed on his lips a long, avid kiss that made him tremble, as if he had touched an electric spark. She gave him a letter.

'Leave this morning. Go back to Lisbon. Read this.'

She drew him to her again and, with a sob, kissed him once more, murmuring:

'Oh, my love, my love!'

They heard Dâmaso come bounding up the stairs, and when he came in, Genoveva, who was unfolding her napkin, said calmly:

'Thank you, kind sir!'

Dâmaso sat down noisily and yelled:

'Bring on the veal steak!'

'I dreamed of witches,' said Genoveva. 'It was probably that conversation we had last night.'

'I had a lot of dreams too,' said Dâmaso. 'I was dreaming all night; it was that loin of pork we ate, too indigestible. It was so confusing . . . first I was at a bullfight and then I dreamed the Castelo da Pena was on fire . . . Terrible.'

'You ungrateful thing,' said Genoveva. 'Didn't you dream of me?'

'Yes, I think I did actually.'

'I dreamed about my father,' said Vítor. 'It was very strange. I dreamed I was by the side of a river and, suddenly, I saw a boat coming towards me . . . I saw two people standing up, a man and a woman all in white. I recognised you at once,' he said, turning to Genoveva, 'and I only recognised my father from a particular gesture he made when he bent down. I dived into the water and began to swim, but my father picked up a pole and tried to push me away from the boat. I held on to the edge and tried to climb in, but he kept driving me back, pushing me down under the water. In the end the boat moved off.'

'And what happened to me?' asked Genoveva, interested.

'My father had his arms about your waist, he seemed quite desperate, trying to hold you back from the edge of the boat; but I saw you reach out your bare arms to me and in a very sweet, light voice I heard you say:

207

Whoever will come and be my maid,
Whoever will take my money,
Must carry this letter to my true love
Dom Clarim Across-the-Water.'

Everyone laughed. It was too absurd and clearly the fault of the conversation they had had last night.

'That and a touch of indigestion,' added Dâmaso, leaning back.

Immediately after lunch, Vítor ordered a carriage. Dâmaso, who was in jovial mood, insisted that he stay. Genoveva made some vague invitation to go with them up to the castle. But Vítor said he had to meet up with his colleague; he would go on to Lisbon from there.

Genoveva and Dâmaso watched him from the dining room as he got into the carriage; Dâmaso even jokingly waved to him with a white handkerchief. As soon as the carriage moved off, Vítor opened the letter. A few violets fell out; he picked them up, kissed them and placed them in his waistcoat pocket, then read Genoveva's letter.

My dearest love,

I had to put off that idiot with a decent ... and monthly ... excuse, and the moment he had turned his back, I sat down to write to you, to tell you that I love you, adore you, desire you, but you know that anyway, or, rather, you don't. Men never really know these things, because their love is all of a piece: they love and that's that: *rien de plus*. But our love, the love of women, the poor female gender, is made up of so many things, of so many tiny things. Saying that I love you is merely telling you about the feeling, nothing more; but if you knew what lay behind those words. There's admiration for you, for your adorable eyes, for your divine eyes, which illuminate me, which I love and which I would pray to if I knew how to pray; it's desire for your love, your kisses, your arms, to feel you close to me, as if you were a little child; perhaps I feel that because of the difference in age between us: you with your twenty-three years and me, poor me, an old, ugly, withered creature, with my thirty-two years; I'm the experienced one, the mother. If you only knew what I felt when you said that your mother had died. I'll be your mother. That is partly how I feel towards you, dear, adored Vítor. Do you know what I would do if I were rich? I would carry you off with me to Paris and make of you the most elegant, most handsome, most captivating *jeune homme de ton temps*; I would have you learn fencing and riding; I would counsel you and direct you, I would educate you, my adored one, and how proud I would feel of you. I would be your Mama, but a Mama deliriously in love with her baby, who would devour him with kisses and spend nights of wild, unrestrained passion with him. As I write to you, my head is burning. Why did I see you that night? Why did I come to Portugal? And there are even moments when I don't love you, when all I feel for you is friendship. But I'm talking nonsense. I feel for you only mad, vehement, absurd love. Tell me what I can do for you? Invent something: some demand, some sacrifice, anything; I promise I will carry it out, without complaint. How fortunate men are! When they love a woman, they can ruin themselves for her, cover her with flowers, adorn her like an idol. It must be truly delicious to do that, don't you think? To heap upon a woman everything that art, luxury and fantasy have created; to give her all your money, your health, your honour. Well, that is how I love you. I cannot give you bracelets or diamond *rivières*, but my health, my life, my blood, my soul are yours. And is there just the teensiest bit of love in your heart for this poor old woman sitting here at one o'clock in the morning, with the fire almost out and thinking of her adored baby? Tell me, do you love me? If you knew what I felt when I saw you at the theatre with that coquette . . . How could you appear with such a creature in public? The woman's indecent! Women like her should be publicly whipped! She's ugly, she's stupid.

But that's all over, isn't it? By the way, do you remember you called me a 'bird of passage'? My poor love, I knew you said that because you felt hurt by me and that your scorn was really love. And I was very provoking too. But here I am prattling on, instead of talking about what's important. The important thing is that I will be staying on here in Sintra for as long as it takes to finish some business. What business do I have in Sintra? Very important business, which my lover and slave, Dom Vítor, need know nothing about. I can't deal with it while you are here, but I'll be back in Lisbon within the next three or four days. I want you to write to me, though, today, and give the letter to Mélanie and tell her to send it on to me. Mélanie the Maneater knows everything. And when I get back to Lisbon, we can talk about it all in a leisurely fashion. Goodbye, my love. It's late. The fire is out and I'm tired. Do you know what I'd like to do? I would like to creep into your room without waking you and place the softest of kisses on your adored mouth and then creep out again. Just one kiss. Would I be brave enough to do that? Could I resist whispering in your ear: it's me, Genoveva, your slave; take me, be my lord and master. My love, how I love you! Sometimes, I even think you make me a better person. You're a purifying influence on me; I'm filled by nobler feelings, by more serene thoughts. How love changes us! Goodbye, my love. I wish I could stay here writing to you all my life, but my poor little hand, *pauvre petite menotte*, is tired. If only I could rest my head on your shoulder! Wasn't that a lovely walk beneath the trees? Did you feel the warmth of my arm? Did it pierce you to the heart? My dear angel, I'm going to pray; I never pray, I hardly know what it means, but I want to ask God to make you happy, to make you very much in love with me, to give you everything that glorifies men and captivates women. Not that it's necessary; I'm already under your spell. But you really have finished with that woman, haven't you? Promise. I must tell you something: this letter is false; it doesn't represent what I feel or think; I don't love you in this light, frivolous way, I love you profoundly. But I don't want to reveal too much; I want to keep a corner of my heart a secret from you. To keep you guessing, to keep you interested, so that gradually, day by day, you take possession of a soul that has always belonged to you from the very first day. I love you, Vítor, I swear it. I have never loved, never felt, never, I should say, suffered for anyone but you. My life is only just beginning. There is no before, just sensations, like the life of an animal or a tree. Now I am alive, because I love you. Goodbye: I kiss your very soul. I fall on my knees and kiss you, adoring you, loving you, my own sweet baby. Goodbye. Here on these dots . . . . I place my lips. Goodbye. You left your overcoat here. I'm going to put it under my pillow or else fall asleep with my cheek resting on it. Goodbye.

Your
G.

When Vítor arrived back in Lisbon, Uncle Timóteo immediately asked him:

'Back already? Did things not work out, then?'

Vítor smiled and he looked so radiant, so happy, so in love, that Timóteo said:

'Ah, so the cat got the cream!'

And when Vítor denied this, he added:

'Well, discretion is a virtue. It's not in the catechism, but it's a virtue nonetheless.'

Vítor replied to Genoveva that very afternoon, a long, carefully rehearsed letter in which, here and there, a few sincere outbursts of instinctive passion peeped through the literary prose, like very plain plants in a cultivated garden. At the end, he added an infinity of kisses and slipped some dried violets in the folds of the letter; he also enclosed a small poem, a sonnet, and so eager was he to give expression to his feelings that, had he known music, he would doubtless have included a melody or a musical meditation.

211

Then he awaited a response. It was not long in coming – ardent, wild, full of foolishly sentimental jokes and passionate interjections. He wrote again, enclosed more verses and spent his life longing for a letter from her and for her to come back to Lisbon.

He had now abandoned the office altogether, as being incompatible with his romantic preoccupations. He still made the occasional visit to Aninhas; the ideal exaltations of his correspondence with Genoveva created in him a physical need for love. He thought himself a scoundrel, but he was proud of it. His excuse was that he could not possibly break off with the poor girl after all the sacrifices she had made for him. However, he felt less and less attached to her. Aninhas had vulgar manners; he hated the old man who lived in the house; he detested the constant toing and froing of things being pawned, bought and resold; he could not bear her pro-saic nature and he did not feel she understood him . . . for he longed for a soulmate who would raise him up to a more refined and idealistic state, who would understand poetry, who would love the silences of the night, feel for the char-acters in a novel, weep with emotion over music and know what true elegance meant.

He found all these excellent virtues in Genoveva and, ever since that sad, poetic conversation in the shadows of Penha Verde, he had attributed to her an exceptional delicacy of feeling, comparing her to certain Renaissance women: to Madame de Champvallon in *Monsieur de Camors*, to the sweet heroine of *The Lily of the Valley*, to other of Balzac's female characters, finding in her strange, tenuous echoes of *La Dame aux Camélias*.

The life he led was, he felt, different and in keeping with his sensibilities; he would go to the Teatro de São Carlos to listen with intense melancholy to the most romantic of operas. He no longer saw Cerrão, because his aesthetic theories seemed overly scientific; in the evenings, he went to see a musician friend, Serafim Galvão and, lounging in an armchair, a cigar-ette in his mouth, he would ask him to play feverish melodies by Chopin or songs by Schubert in which he sensed mystical impulses, or music by Mendelssohn, who provoked in him vague, dreamy thoughts, or Mozart, who drowned him in subtle sweetness, or Gounod, who exemplified for him the elegant extremes of modern love.

Otherwise, he would walk the streets, rather despising his friends and acquaintances, whom he imagined to be mired in the cares of everyday life, while he lived in the splendid world of a shared passion.

Genoveva, meanwhile, still did not return. In her letters, all she said, referring to Sintra was: 'I'm still sorting out my business affairs: Sintra is my office; *ce que j'y fais d'affaires!*'

And this had been going on for three weeks. Mélanie had made the move to Rua das Flores and had left for Sintra, as had Miss Sarah. Sometimes Vítor felt impatient and jealous with Genoveva so far away in the company of Dâmaso, who was, after all, her lover. But with Aninhas he had grown used to the subaltern role of 'true lover'. He took a certain pride in it: the other man was the cashier, the payer, the purse; he was the beloved. He felt such profound scorn for Dâmaso that he did not even feel jealous of him. Genoveva could not possibly love Dâmaso; she merely put up with him. Just as Dâmaso, if he did not have money, would have to put up with some wealthy but unpleasant bourgeois woman.

She gave Dâmaso her body, but what did that matter? All her soul, her desires, her devotion were his, Vítor's. He made the distinction, so common amongst men who live with debauched women, between feigned pleasure and genuine pleasure. Genoveva doubtless pretended with Dâmaso, but with him she would not. It was the same with Aninhas and Policarpo. He found points of contact between him and the low trivial character of Armand in *La Dame aux Camélias*, except that he did not believe himself to be ignoble . . . he considered himself highly poetic!

One night, when Vítor was walking up Rua do Alecrim, by the light of a streetlamp he saw and recognised Palma Gordo.

Palma was brandishing a huge walking stick and had his hat pushed back on his head, revealing his broad, flaccid face. Swaying his hips suggestively, he said:

'So Dâmaso's still in Sintra with that . . .' and he said an obscene word.

Vítor went pale and replied with trembling lips:

'I am a friend of the lady and I find that word offensive.'

Palma gave a lewd laugh.

'Well, too bad!'

Vítor gave his fat face a resounding slap.

Palma, furious, raised his walking stick. Vítor, to whom anger gave a kind of convulsive energy, wrenched it out of his hand and threatened him with it, saying through gritted teeth:

'You scoundrel!'

'Give me back my stick,' hissed Palma. 'Give me back my stick, or I'll call the police!'

A man passing by on the other side of the road ran over and calmly separated them.

'Come on now, you're not going to fight in a public place, are you? What is this, a matter of honour?'

'Tell him to give me back my stick,' roared Palma.

Vítor scornfully threw it to him, saying:

'There you are, you coward!'

Still very worked up, he walked away with the other man, who happened to be Carvalhosa. Vítor told him what had happened.

Carvalhosa gave his opinion; he had been quite right to slap him; the duel was a barbaric tradition. Landing a good, hard punch on a fat face was both consolation and sufficient revenge.

'One should respond to the brutality of a verbal offence with the brutality of the fist,' he declared eloquently. 'Where are you off to?'

'Nowhere in particular.'

'Well, I'm off to see Marinho, who's ill, poor thing.'

'What's wrong with him?'

And suddenly remembering the story Marinho had failed to finish during their supper at the Hotel Central, Vítor expressed an urgent desire to go and see Marinho, 'the poor thing'.

They found him in his room in the Hotel Universal, in Rua

214

de Camões; he was tucked up in bed, wearing a nightcap; his bedside table was crammed with various medicaments and the windows were tightly sealed. The room smelled of camphor and was meticulously tidy, from the highly polished boots lined up like a batallion, to the clothes carefully folded and draped over the chair. Not a scrap of paper on the floor, not a cigar butt to be seen. One sensed the extreme caution of a wise and prudent spirit.

He silently shook hands with both of them; with a sad smile, he briefly, and again silently, indicated a person wearing a magnificent, fur-trimmed overcoat and mauve trousers. But they had recognised him at once: it was Sarrotini.

The famous singer got solemnly to his feet and sombrely shook hands; then opening his arms wide as if to hit a high note, he looked at Marinho and muttered:

'*Il poveretto!*'

And he sat down again, gazing at him compassionately.

'What's wrong?' asked Carvalhosa, dropping heavily onto the bed.

Marinho pointed to his throat and conveyed the diagnosis with eyes and lips – very bad.

'You've got a sore throat? Well, try belladonna.'

'*La donna é mobile . . .*,' muttered Sarrotini, reminded of *Rigoletto*. And he gave a soft nasal laugh and explained quietly to Vítor in a mixture of Portuguese and Italian:

'*Per o distraire! Il povero!*'

Then he folded his arms on his terrifying chest and resumed his solemn pose.

Then Carvalhosa got up, his hands in his pockets, and declared that, as an orator, he was very interested in throat ailments; turning to Sarrotini, he asked pleasantly:

'What do you gentlemen use to clear your voice?'

In Italian sprinkled with French and diluted by Spanish, Sarrotini explained that he drank chicken soup with a beaten egg in it. Patti, on the other hand, swore by a glass of sherry and soda water.

'I, like José Estevão, rely entirely on sugar water. We orators tend to use emollients: Thiers, for example, drank *horchata*;

215

Garrett drank sweet *sangría*. We have to keep our intellects clear.' And raising himself up, he addressed Sarrotini again: 'For you sing notes and we sing ideas. I cannot recommend sugar water highly enough.'

Then he added that he found quite ridiculous all the guidelines laid down in the old compendia of rhetoric that the orator should be a naturally imposing figure, with a full chest and a resonant voice. Rubbish! Garrett was a bit of a dandy and Thiers is almost a dwarf and has a harsh, reedy voice. What matter are the images, the poetry, the inspiration.

'What matters is art, genius!' And he tapped his forehead with one finger.

'*Il genio!*' said Sarrotini approvingly. And he got up and leaned over Marinho, calling him tender names: '*Carinho figlio mio, amato Marinho!*'

He advised rest, quiet and patience.

'*No parlare, no parlare!*'

And leaning nearer still, he kissed him on the forehead.

He picked up his floppy-brimmed hat, shook Vítor's hand with an almost equally loving look on his face, and bowed to Carvalhosa:

'*Salute a voi egregio oratore!*'

'*Salute cantore!*' said Carvalhosa contentedly.

And the moment Sarrotini had left, he said smugly:

'Poor chap!'

Marinho rolled his eyes in an expression of mute surprise.

But Carvalhosa had a meeting to go to and, clapping Marinho on the shoulder, he bade farewell with these words:

'The weakness of nature must be conquered by the power of the will! And belladonna of course!'

And he left, saying to Vítor:

'Farewell, heroic Vítor!'

Almost immediately, the door opened and in came a man wearing a dressing gown and carrying a candlestick. He was in the next room to Marinho; it was the Brazilian, Prudêncio. He glided across the carpet in his embroidered slippers, swaying his hips; he had a fringe of grey beard and two bright, penetrating eyes which shone out from his long, dark face.

He wanted to know if the doctor had been and if Marinho had taken his medicine. And he responded to Marinho's slow gestures with:

'Quite, quite!'

And whenever he said this, he raised his hands to his face and screwed up his eyes.

With one limp hand, withdrawn cautiously from under the bedclothes, Marinho introduced Vítor. And Prudêncio immediately remarked in a very odd high voice:

'Illness is a great misfortune.'

'It certainly is,' said Vítor.

'Quite,' said Prudêncio.

And he explained that he had problems with his liver. Vítor suggested he try the waters at Vidago.

'Quite,' said Prudêncio; he had been there already, but it had done no good, no good at all.

Then he fell silent, staring at the carpet, slowly scratching his stiff beard.

'Are you in business?' he suddenly asked Vítor.

'No, I'm not.'

'A civil servant?'

'No, sir, I'm a lawyer.'

'Quite!' And he resumed his study of the carpet; then his face lit up and, resting his piercing little eyes on Vítor again, he said: 'The defence of orphans and widows.'

Vítor agreed, politely bowing.

'Quite!' He was sorry Marinho had missed supper. 'A delicious meal, delicious! And such philosophical conversation!'

He addressed Vítor again:

'I enjoy philosophical conversation.'

'It's always interesting.'

'Quite.'

He seemed to be searching for a word or for ideas in the carpet, but unable to find any, he made as if to withdraw with his candlestick, saying to Marinho:

'I do hope you get better soon.'

He shook Vítor's hand.

217

'Sir, at your service. I would be most honoured if you would dine with me. Room number 20. Quite.'

And he glided out on the light soles of his slippers.

When he was alone with Marinho, Vítor, sat down on the bed and said:

'You never finished telling me that story the other night. You'd got as far as the Brazilian asking Madame de Molineux if she was from Guarda.'

Marinho indicated his throat, placed one finger on his lips, and shook his head vigorously, expressing via this comic pantomime that he would not utter a sound. And he lay there, his eyes very wide, red-faced, dumb, muffled up, terrified and glum.

'Well, goodbye, Marinho. Get well soon.'

Outside, in the corridor, he met Sarrotini again, who seemed to have regained his cheerfulness and joviality, and to have lost the lugubrious face he had worn in Marinho's room.

'*E la signora, la signora Ginoveva?*'

'She's very well, thank you.'

'*L'altra notte*, the dance . . . Lovely! *Havemi fatto una buona seratta . . . Beaucoup!*'

And he laughed and tickled Vítor.

'We had a good time, no? *Addio!*'

Then he ran after him and said in confidential tones:

'I'm your friend. I have not forgotten *lo que lei me a ditto*; that you are a republican. *Anch'io, uno republicano. Tutto per la libertà!*'

'*Tutto!*'

Poised at the top of the stairs, Sarrotini raised his hand and repeated, this time more loudly:

'*Tutto per la libertà!*'

When Vítor wrote to Genoveva that night, he told her he had been obliged to strike a friend of Dâmaso's who had spoken disrespectfully of her. A few days later, Genoveva replied:

If you love me, what does it matter what others say about me? Dâmaso's friends are bound to be as

218

imbecilic as him. Now, my love, great news, which might make you happy: I arrive in Lisbon tomorrow night. Come and see me on Wednesday morning. *À toi, ma vie, mes rêves, mes pensées, mes désirs, mes ardeurs et le petit coeur* of your, for ever,

G.

X

Vítor woke up on Wednesday in a state of high excitement. It was the most important day of his life, for he was certain that this was the morning that would see his happiness made perfect. She loved him, she was at last in Lisbon again, and free (that fool Dâmaso didn't count); with the first kiss, she would surely abandon herself to him, and his heart beat faster at that joyous thought. He dressed himself with almost devout care; he bought a flower for his buttonhole and, smoking an expensive cigar, set off for Rua das Flores. He took a voluptuous pleasure in not hurrying, but savouring everything slowly, the air, the sun, the bright façades, and, under the influence of his overflowing heart, everything seemed to beam back at him.

Genoveva lived on the third floor; the house had been restored and newly painted, and Genoveva had added a few touches of elegance to the otherwise bourgeois building – an electric bell and two bushes in pots on the landing.

When he arrived, Genoveva was still in her bedroom, and Vítor waited nervously in the living room. He could not have been more agitated than if he had come all the way from India.

The furniture was upholstered in a brightly-coloured, oriental-style fabric; there were two flower paintings, which he had seen in Dâmaso's house; and the polished wood and the new carpet gave the apartment a new, uninhabited air. Two imitation Majolica vases adorned a marble console table, which stood beneath an oval mirror with an ornate imitation eighteenth-century frame. Everything had been done quickly, superficially and cheaply; one could sense bourgeois thrift and caution.

'Do come in,' Mélanie said.

And as he went into a small boudoir, Genoveva drew back the curtain to her bedroom and ran to him, her dressing gown unfastened, and put her arms about his neck; they met with a long, eager kiss. Still with her arms about him, she led him into her bedroom, made him sit in an armchair, where she knelt at his feet; then, looking long into his eyes, as if to penetrate into the very depths of his soul, she asked him all kinds of questions: Did he love her, had he thought about her, what had he done, had he seen other women, where had he spent the nights? Her questions and more kisses followed so fast one upon another that she barely listened to his answers, but clutched his hands convulsively, frenetically, and studied his face with such luminous, passionate insistence, it was as if she wanted to take possession of his hair, his skin, his lips.

'Why had she stayed so long in Sintra? What had taken so much time?' Vítor's voice was full of loving reprimand.

Genoveva immediately stood up and, going over to the dressing table, she rearranged first a comb and then a glass bottle.

'Business, my love. I told you so in my letters. Didn't you read them? I couldn't come earlier, but I came now because I couldn't bear to be without you any longer. Who knows, my haste may have been unwise.'

Vítor put his arms about her waist and said in a soft voice:

'But you're here now and you love me, don't you? Say you do . . . you look so lovely. I adore you so.'

Genoveva's eyes closed and she grew pale.

He kissed her slowly on her ear.

Genoveva's breast lifted with a sigh of love and pleasure.

She said almost mournfully:

'You're making me feel sleepy.'

Taking this as a sign of complete abandon, he led her over to the bed, but was astonished when Genoveva pulled away, drew back, saying almost angrily:

'No, Vítor, no!'

'Why not?' he asked, confused.

'Not as long as there is another man here.' And taking his hands in hers, she murmured in tender supplication: 'I want to be yours alone!'

'Well, get rid of the fool, then!' exclaimed Vítor with all the impatience of frustrated desire.

Genoveva frowned and looked away.

'No, I can't do that, not yet.'

'But, why, why?'

'Because I can't.'

There was a silence. Vítor felt a painful desolation chilling his blood, but she again squeezed his hands and said:

'Listen . . . I just can't. You won't understand . . . I don't even want to tell you. Don't ask me any questions. But it can't be. It's for your own good. I have a plan. We only need suffer for another twenty days, my love, but after that . . .' And her eyes shone. 'Do you promise to obey me?'

'But . . .'

'No. Say it, do you promise?'

And he loved her so much that, though humiliated and unhappy, he agreed.

'Fine,' she said, 'you can come and see me every day at the hours I specify; when I cannot meet you here, we will meet elsewhere. But leave me free to act, don't ask any questions, and obey me in everything. Do you swear?'

'But . . .'

She got impatiently to her feet.

'All right, you don't want to. So much for your love and your promises.'

'I swear, I swear,' he said, surrendering everything to her, his will, his purpose in life, his time, making himself his own executioner and her slave.

'All right, and when I tell you that I'm yours, it will be forever.'

Pressing her face to his, she said with all the solemnity of a sacred oath:

'There will never be anyone else.'

Vítor became a regular visitor at Rua das Flores. He usually went to see Genoveva at midday. At first, he would occasionally find her still in bed, but looking so fresh, with her hair so beautifully coiffed, it was as if she had dressed herself the night before and spent the night in chaste and solitary sleep. However, he found everything – the disorder in the room, the piles of clothes, Genoveva's bare arms – so troubling that he did not even have the strength to speak; he would look at her, kiss her

222

hands, almost dizzy with painful desire. In the end, Genoveva said:

'No, my love, no. I won't receive you in my bedroom any more.'

And she would appear before him dressed and corseted as if she were about to go out; she seemed to fear provoking him, even by wearing one of her loose morning gowns.

Vítor would tell her of his love for her, but Genoveva always seemed to turn the conversation to more general subjects. She would play, sing some song that he liked; sometimes she would even call in Miss Sarah.

The Englishwoman would immediately appear and the conversation, made awkward by her presence, would falter. Vítor spoke English badly and his preoccupation with Genoveva's presence in the room made him even more tongue-tied; he did not have enough vocabulary and, sometimes, he could respond to Miss Sarah with only ohs and ahs and a foolish smile. The Englishwoman, however, almost always spoke directly to him; she dressed with great care, dusted her face with rather too much face powder, struck romantic attitudes, ogled him shamelessly and even got angry one day when Genoveva said to him:

'You know, poor Miss Sarah is terribly in love with you.'

Genoveva seemed to enjoy that desperate passion, either because it served as a further humiliation to the Englishwoman, or because it was yet further proof of Vítor's perfection.

At other times, he would find Genoveva embroidering, and she would not pause in her work. If, when she occasionally glanced up at him, she found his adoring, devouring eyes fixed on her, she would say:

'Stop looking at me like that! You know it's impossible.'

It was a torment! Vítor's presence was like a daily recrimination. One day, Genoveva herself remarked rather angrily:

'I know you think my life is easy, but I've given my word of honour to myself. When I'm free, then I will be your slave and your servant; then you can kill me if you like, but only then!'

But they also spent sweet, tranquil mornings together, with

no allusions to love. Genoveva delighted him with talk of Paris and London. She was intelligent, she sang well, she could capture someone's face and character in a sketch. She had picked up the strong, colourful language of the witty men and artists with whom she had once kept company; she could retail anecdotes about famous men, repeat their epigrams and their more original opinions.

Vítor never tired of hearing her talk; it was like a personal chronicle, a contemporary memoir from which he gleaned intimate, human details about the lives of people in the world of art or learning who, otherwise, he had known only from the solemn, conventional view of established fame. He loved to hear anecdotes about the libidinous Prince of Wales' sentimental attachments; it was like having someone suddenly fling open the bedroom doors of duchesses and court adulterers.

What fascinated him most, however, was Paris and its politics, its artists, its courtesans. He savoured every morsel of information about Dumas *fils*, Gustave Doré and about the masked balls held by Arsène Houssaye. It was as if he were being introduced to whole new worlds. He was fascinated by her account of Napoleon III's private life, how the Emperor would shut himself up for hours on end with an agent from the secret police, feeding his appetite for intrigue and his morbid love of gossip; at night, when the Emperor withdrew to his chamber, and everyone assumed he must be pondering the fate of France, he was, in fact, skilfully cutting out little figures which he would stick onto a sheet of paper to create fantastic scenes; and on other nights, he would shut himself up with four women at a time and indulge in excesses that would leave him inert, mute, stupefied, plunged in dark thoughts, one moment longing for the excitement of war, the next for the peace of a monastery. Vítor was equally fascinated by the world of the Jockey Club and the courtesans and notorious gamblers who frequented it. Genoveva painted vivid pictures of the eccentric members of the royal household, of suppers costing thousands of francs, of their petulant and often eccentric ripostes; then she would talk about the extravagant behaviour of certain famous ladies: there was one woman with a historic name, whose maid kept a list of names and the portraits of all Paris's handsomest men, her task being to entice them, one by one, into her mistress' bedchamber; another, in a moment of madness, left the palace, ran to a tiny ground-floor apartment in the Champs-Elysées, where she declared to her lover that she was prepared to run away with him and abandon the throne! Vítor was thus initiated into the refined, elegant world of dramatic love affairs and delicious mysteries. Genoveva's reminiscences seduced Vítor even more than the jewellery and the dresses that she wore.

She educated him too; she gave him advice on how to dress, counselled him on which colour to choose for cravats and silk socks, introduced him to sober English dandyism. She wanted him to learn to fence; she taught him whist and *bouillotte*; with all the wisdom of a lover and the solicitude of a mother she told him which books to read, endowing him with the qualities she believed to be important.

Whenever he had spent the morning quietly listening to her, she would reward his loving submission with a kiss, a passionate word, a sweet look.

Occasionally, Vítor also went to supper there, but since Dâmaso was always present, he found the experience most disagreeable. Dâmaso was unbearable, with his noisy self-importance, his amorous declarations to Genoveva, his protective, insolently happy air; he had a way of leaning back in his chair, a cigar in his mouth, which filled Vítor with homicidal longings; and he would affect the tone of an elegant, noble wastrel — Dâmaso of all people! And he found Genoveva's cook appalling; he would read the supper menu out loud in mangled French and shrug his shoulders dismissively.

'Well, it's hardly the Café Anglais,' he would mutter.

And yet Vítor had seen him greedily gobble down veal steaks at the Hotel Pelicano and praise them to the heavens! Dâmaso was changing, he was becoming chic. He wore blue shirtfronts and had a shirtpin in the form of a silver riding boot and an enormous golden spur; he was quite the sportsman. He would sometimes remark as if it were a matter of deep, long-pondered concern to him:

'I wonder who will win the Derby this year.'

And he even pretended to care about the 'big race' in Paris.

After supper, he would, inevitably, have Genoveva sing songs from the Paris music halls and would go into ecstasies over them, opining that 'France was the finest country in the world for bawdy songs'; now he could even sing:

> *Chaque femme a sa toquade,*
> *Sa marotte et son dada!*

He would bawl out the refrain, his voice thundering round the room, and every night, he would turn up wearing white tie and tails. He found Portugal vulgar and spoke of moving to Paris, which, he said, was 'one long orgy'.

Vítor always left with his nerves in tatters and he begged Genoveva not to make him come to supper. He was beginning to feel jealous of Dâmaso now; the weeks passed and there he still was, in firm possession of Genoveva, and so involved in the general household arrangements that he had become a permanent fixture blocking Vítor's happiness.

When Vítor complained to Genoveva, she would smile and try to calm him by saying:

'It won't be for much longer, my love.'

Vítor, however, grew sad. When he was with her, he resigned himself to his fate, as if his desires found a calming contentment in the mere contemplation of Genoveva; the certainty that she loved him filled his soul with delight; he felt so happy watching her talk, embroider, smile, that he almost forgot his impatient hopes for a more absolute happiness.

When he was far from her, though, he burned with furious desires; he grew gloomy, nervous, irritable; the slightest effort exhausted him. He had abandoned both the office and his friends; he no longer went to the theatre; he would spend whole nights in his bedroom re-reading her letters, re-constructing in his mind everything she had said to him during the morning, however slight. At table, he tried to talk, to hide his sadness from Uncle Timóteo. But he spoke with the lassitude of one bowed under a heavy weight. What made matters worse was that Uncle Timóteo did not mention Genoveva either and he too was often plunged into long silences during which he would frown terribly.

Uncle Timóteo was perfectly aware that Vítor went to see Genoveva every day, that he had abandoned the office, along with all his other interests and former habits. As an old libertine and one-time duellist, he was eager for Vítor to have a mistress, but to be so absorbed by a passion, to be so tied to a woman's skirts, to lose all joy and appetite, that was too much.

He had found out what he could about Genoveva; he had heard that she was a cold, rapacious adventuress, bent on ruining Dâmaso. And Uncle Timóteo thought it wrong that Vítor should sacrifice his career, his future, his decent feelings, possibly his dignity, for that intimate relationship with a shameless concubine. He also felt the natural fear of illegitimate love affairs felt by all aged parents. For him Genoveva was the siren, the *femme fatale*, who ruins men and forces them into drawing up bills of exchange and making unsuitable marriages – the bugbear of nervous mothers and devoted grandmothers. He thought: 'There's nothing wrong with having fun, that's only natural, but to prejudice his career, his health, his freedom, his honour for the petticoats of a hussy . . . I'd rather break his bones one by one.'

Out of the passionate friendship he felt for his Vítor, though, he did not dare speak to him seriously about the matter. Vítor was all the family he had in the world; he had never crossed him, never told him off, and now that the moment had come to do so and to place an obstacle in the path of passion, Timóteo, normally so quick to anger and quick to strike, felt as shy and inhibited as a weak mother.

But he would torment himself with worry and be unable to sleep if he noticed that Vítor was more than usually self-absorbed or if he barely touched his food; he heard him pacing up and down in his room for hours on end; he wracked his brains to imagine the cause of that melancholy; he thought that Genoveva must know Vítor would inherit his

227

money when he died and was 'keeping him dangling' in order to lure him into marriage. But if she wanted a rich husband, she could have Dâmaso. Had she taken a fancy to Vítor, then grown bored and sent him away, leaving him in love and in despair? Perhaps a trip abroad would distract him. One day, he had even blurted out:

'What do you think to a trip to Paris? A man ought to see a bit of the world.'

But Vítor had roundly declined the offer, declaring himself to be perfectly happy in Lisbon, and Uncle Timóteo attributed his foolishness to the stupefying effects of happy passion and consoled himself with this thought:

'The poor wretch has his father's stubborn heart and his mother's impetuous spirit.'

After that, he felt too angry to ask Vítor any direct questions. Sometimes, when he wasn't eyeing him secretly with tear-filled eyes, he would shoot him a sideways glance, full of despair and anger.

And Vítor's melancholy continued to grow. Sometimes, he felt like not going to see her, but as the hour approached, an irresistible force would carry him to Rua das Flores. He found Genoveva nervous and irritable now; she would sit in silence for long periods, then dart a devouring look at him.

'What is the point of this torment?' Vítor asked her one day.

She did not reply, and he, interpreting her silence as the consent of a now defunct resistance, clasped her wildly in his arms. She covered him with almost painful kisses, full of passionate fury. Then she sat up:

'No, what's said is said. But, listen, in two weeks' time I will be yours.'

Vítor found her extraordinary, almost fantastical. Occasionally, he would be shaken, as if by a shudder, by the thought that she might be toying with him. 'I'd kill her if she was!' Because now his love was becoming mingled with a vague feeling of hatred. He almost hoped she was deceiving him, mocking him: 'Then I'd cause some scandal or commit a crime!' he thought. And in the hope of vengeance he found some respite from his passion.

On the occasions when Genoveva had aroused him beyond endurance, simply by wearing a close-fitting dress, or by squeezing his hand more tightly than usual, he would have to resort to visiting Aninhas to calm that excitement, to dissipate and expend it. But he detested Aninhas now; her trivial manner, her vulgar way of speaking, the smell of fried vegetables in the corridor, all filled him with boredom and irritation.

It was so different being with Genoveva! And yet he enjoyed going to see Aninhas too in a way, because there he was master; he gave orders, talked loudly, tormented her, making up for the abstinence imposed on him by Genoveva. He always found something to criticise in Aninhas; she was either ill-dressed, ill-coiffed or ill-shod, or else the room was untidy, or the towels unwashed.

'Why are you so rude to me?' asked Aninhas. 'What's wrong? Don't you like it here?'

Her sweetness exasperated him and her caresses humiliated him; that vulgar young girl, whom he despised, overwhelmed him with exuberant love, while the other, whom he adored fanatically, frenetically, would barely even let him hold her hand.

Sometimes, he would push Aninhas away:

'Leave me alone, will you!'

The poor girl racked her small, soft brain to find some way to hold him, to captivate him, but, alas, her efforts at seducing Vítor were so clumsy they drove Vítor to despair. If, in order to seduce him, she struck a romantic pose, Vítor would inevitably find her ridiculous; if she tried to draw him into literary conversation, she would talk to him about the books she was reading, *The Bandit King*, *The Revenge of Calabria*, *The Black Tailcoats* and other such horrors; if she tried to behave like some bright libertine, Vítor would find her crude attempts at abandonment as ridiculous as the feigned ecstasies of a professional whore. Poor Aninhas only managed to increase Vítor's gloom. She truly loved Vítor, though, and sometimes he would allow himself to be swept along by her passion. Then, through a commonplace trick of the imagination, he would bestow on her the words and kisses he wished he could bestow on Genoveva.

Aninhas could not understand why Vítor should want the lights out in the room, but, seeing him so aroused, so mad with desire, she was quite happy. Vítor would evoke the image of Genoveva and visit upon Aninhas the most exalted words of love, the most voracious of caresses, the mad rebirth of his insatiable desire. Vítor would emerge from those excesses feeling even more distant from her, and Aninhas, the poor fool, would emerge even more besotted.

Under the influence of his love for Genoveva, Vítor became almost femininely susceptible to changes in the weather: his nerves could be set on edge by a cloudy sky or a harsh wind; certain arias or pieces of music could move him to tears; he began to have religious yearnings; one day, he went into a church; they were holding a sung mass, and the high voices and the sound of the organ provoked in him almost mystical feelings, so much so that he knelt down and decided to flee to the peace of a monastery.

It was in one such mood that he said to Genoveva:

'Look, I've been waiting for nearly two months; if you're not serious about me, then I won't come here again.'

'Don't then,' she retorted, for she was in an equally nervous state.

Vítor was so shocked and saddened that he burst into tears.

Genoveva fell at his feet, caressed him wildly, kissed his hands, clung to his arms, and, sobbing, said:

'You said you understood. I love you as I have never loved anyone. But I want to live only for you. That is why I hold on to you. When I am yours, I want to be yours alone.' And in a heartrending voice, she added: 'But I'm not rich, my love. I have debts and I have to pay them. Let me get everything I can out of that fool . . . and then . . .'

She sat back on her heels, opened her arms and with a sad smile said:

'Let me earn my dowry.'

That sacrifice, so sincerely expressed, seemed sublime to

Vítor. He begged forgiveness, promised to be more resigned, and he left, still in the grip of that obsessive desire, which prevented him from seeing the ignominy of the situation, and thinking all the while:

'Her dowry, poor love, poor angel!'

Genoveva was telling the truth; she worshipped Vítor. And beneath her apparent resistance, she suffered, even more than he did, the pangs of desire and the torments of impatience. Sometimes, as soon as he had left, she would kiss the back of the sofa where he had rested his head or the edge of the table where he had leaned his arm. She combined that physical passion with other idealistic feelings: she could not bear the idea of having to share her bed with another man. When she belonged to him, she wanted their love to be absolute, perfect, uninterrupted, with no obstacles, no holding back, no suspicions, no trickery; she did not want to have to hide from anyone or be disturbed by anyone; she did not want to suffer any loss of prestige either; she wanted to have the same dresses, the same jewels, a carriage, a nice apartment; however, since all that could take a long time, with a consequent diminution of her beauty, she would need to supplement her beauty by adorning her person. To do that she required money. He, poor love, had no money. Neither did she. In Paris she had only debts. She had to pay them off and accumulate some capital for the first few years before she could be Vítor's lover, with no worries, no financial problems, no creditors. At first, Dâmaso, in the 'sensible' Portuguese tradition, had been unwilling to give her money, and she had never viewed him as bottomless source of cash; she had made no secret to him of her liking for Vítor, and had been quite ready to show Dâmaso the door and to send him away. Later, though, Dâmaso – madly in love, infatuated and enslaved – had become more generous and revealed the true extent of his fortune, and she had developed for him the respect every prostitute has for a rich client. He was a man worthy of consideration. She played out for him the resigned comedy of physical love. She told him that she loved him, not perhaps with her heart, but with her senses, knowing that nothing sways a fool so much as the thought of the pleasures he imagines he brings. In Sintra, feigning abject passion for him and falling at his feet, her eyes rolled back, she had put on a skilful act of rapt delirium; she had bound him to her so subtly, had so enslaved him, that she had begun to remove bundles of money from him as easily as from a cash till. One day, Dâmaso had even paid off her debts, a mere ten *contos de réis* and had given her three *contos'* worth of bonds. That encouraged her. Together with a usurer in Paris and with the intervention of a friend, she had drawn up a bill of exchange, signed by her, for five *contos de réis*. She told Dâmaso that, if he could not pay the bill, she would have to go back to Paris and sell her furniture and her two horses (which she did not have); she wept at the thought of leaving him, her love, her Dâmaso; she showed him a letter in which a certain Sauvières (whom she claimed was a very rich young man in Paris, an agent for the Oppenheimers, and who had declared his love for her) had made her a very generous offer if she would go with him to Frankfurt. Dâmaso, moved by her tears, afraid of losing her and glad to get the better of an agent to the Oppenheimers, paid the bill. Such imbecility encouraged her still more. She now had a small capital of eight *contos*. She would go to Paris with Vítor and then see what happened next! However, since Dâmaso continued to 'give out', she wanted to hang on to him for as long as possible. The more money she extracted from him, the easier her life with Vítor would be. She would sell everything she had in Paris and go and live with him in Auteuil or in Neuilly, and since he had a small allowance from his Uncle Timóteo and a fortune to inherit, the arrangement seemed to her an excellent one, full of future happinesses brimming with love. Lately, though, passion had weighed more heavily than prudence and she would have dismissed Dâmaso sooner if her birthday were not approaching. She hoped to receive from him a generous present; at first, he had suggested jewellery, but she, showing a good bourgeois sense that pleased Dâmaso, said she did not want jewellery – she had so much already! She would rather he helped her build up a small amount of capital; if he did, she would no longer allow him to pay the household expenses.

'I love you so much that I really hate having to take money from you. You can give me presents, but no money. I need a small income. We can live perfectly well in Lisbon on thirty *libras* a day. Give me enough money to achieve that and forget about jewels. I want our love to be an entirely disinterested affair.'

An ecstatic Dâmaso promised to give her a nice surprise along those lines. And Genoveva calculated that he would give her about three or four *contos de réis*. The following day, she would shut her door to him for ever. It was 10th March and her birthday was on 1st April.

Vítor still went to supper at Genoveva's house, though only rarely because, he said, he found Dâmaso's presence so 'stupefying'. However, at about this time, when he did turn up at the house one evening at eight o'clock, he was surprised to be greeted by Miss Sarah. She showed him into the living room, explaining that Madame had gone out with Dâmaso in the afternoon, that they had dined at a restaurant and gone on to the theatre, and that Mélanie had disappeared off somewhere to amuse herself. She spoke in an overly vivacious manner, her eyes glittered, and she kept laughing for no apparent reason; Vítor understood why when he saw the bottle of gin; Miss Sarah was tipsy. He found this rather comical and, accepting a small gin himself, he lit a cigarette and settled down to enjoy the show.

Miss Sarah was in loquacious mood and she immediately launched into a series of complaints about Genoveva. She was, according to Miss Sarah, a very nasty person; hardly surprising in a woman with no education; it was tragic that she, Sarah, well-educated and from a respectable family, should have to depend on such a creature. She sighed and consoled herself with another glass of gin. Besides, Madame had no principles; she had never once seen her go to church. She, of course, did not approve of these awful Catholic practices, but if one had a religion and one was a lady, one owed it to one's dignity to go to church and hear the sermon. She poured herself another gin.

'She's getting thoroughly soused,' thought Vítor, highly amused by it all.

Miss Sarah then sat down next to him on the sofa and began trying to persuade him to pay less attention to Genoveva. The woman was mad about Dâmaso; her behaviour was positively indecent sometimes; she was always kissing him and caressing him; they even shut themselves up in her bedroom during the day, quite shamelessly. It was disgusting, quite disgusting!

Vítor felt a sudden urgent interest in what she was saying and asked for more details. Miss Sarah gave them: Last Sunday, they did not get up until three o'clock in the afternoon! She had been so outraged that she had left the house so as not to have to breathe that air of corruption and iniquity.

As she continued to talk and drink, she kept moving closer to Vítor; he was sitting at one end of the sofa and he watched her red, blotchy face, inflamed with talk and gin, gradually coming closer.

Then she bemoaned her own existence. There she was in a foreign land, with no friends, no family, with no one who cared about her in the whole wide world. No one.

She folded her hands in her lap and looked at Vítor. He mentioned Genoveva and she said:

'Oh, please don't talk about her. I hate the woman!'

Was it right that someone like Madame de Molineux, a woman with no principles, no religion and no morality, should have all the good things in life, beautiful clothes, a comfortable home, people who loved her, while she, a normal, well-educated woman was obliged to live like a mere dependant? Madame de Molineux was not even a lady.

She pushed out her chest and repeated emphatically:

'No, she's certainly no lady!'

Placing one hand on Vítor's arm, she asked him tenderly why he loved a creature who could never make him happy, who did not love him in return, and who was interested only in money.

Vítor, feeling slightly embarrassed, though mildly diverted by Miss Sarah's alcoholic loquacity, said that he did not love Genoveva, he merely found her amusing.

'Really?' asked Miss Sarah excitedly.

'Of course,' he said, making himself more comfortable on the sofa. But why was Miss Sarah so interested to know?

Miss Sarah, who was pouring herself more gin, suddenly threw her arms around Vítor's neck and declared that she loved him.

Vítor leaped to his feet, as if a skeleton had touched him, and exclaimed:

'No, no, please don't! Please, Madam, no!'

But Miss Sarah seized hold of him again and called him all kinds of affectionate names, like 'darling' and 'pet'. She said she could not live without him, it was a feeling she could not fight, she was mad about him . . .

Vítor could feel her smooth, bony fingers on his shoulders and neck. Her scarlet face was tremulous with desire; her words stumbled over her own large teeth. Vítor was furious; he felt ridiculous and, at the same time, the sensual arousal of that long, thin woman, drunk on gin, provoked in him a certain brutal, absurd desire. There was something stirring about that English puritan burning with the furies of the flesh; but if he gave in to her, how would he ever get rid of her afterwards?

That idea crossed his mind like lightning; he pushed her roughly away and hurled one word at her in his very limited English:

'Shocking!' he said, and tried to tell her to calm down, to recollect herself and to go to bed.

Miss Sarah made one last attempt to embrace him, but, by then, he had picked up his hat. As he retreated, he said:

'No, please, don't. It's not decent!'

Miss Sarah, humiliated, gazed at him angrily and said:

'You blackguard!'

And, as he went out, Vítor heard her saying that she would have her revenge.

He reached home feeling thoroughly annoyed. He could

not help but be flattered by that sudden explosion of passion on the part of a devout Englishwoman, but he nevertheless felt slightly ridiculous; it reminded him of the story of Joseph and his cloak. He was afraid Miss Sarah might plot against him.

He said nothing about it to Genoveva the next day. Genoveva would dismiss the Englishwoman and that would spell ruin for the poor creature, alone in a foreign country. Two days later, however, he was surprised to receive a note from Genoveva, saying:

> My love,
> It is vital that you do not visit me or write to me for the next five or six days. Don't come until you get a letter from me. Much of our future happiness depends now on your discretion. I know this is truly horrible, but it is necessary.

'This is the doing of the Englishwoman,' Vítor thought.

What had she said? What had she done? She had doubtless spoken to Dâmaso. Would she have invented lies about him? The uncertainty drove Vítor almost to despair, and yet he was forbidden to visit Genoveva or to write. He hoped to see her in the street, in the Aterro, at the theatre, but without luck. At night, he would walk past her house and see the windows lit. He would have given anything to know what was happening. What was she doing? Who was she with? What dress would she be wearing?

Sometimes, he saw Dâmaso's coupé at the door, and that exasperated him and filled him with jealous rage. He tried then to remember and to ponder all the proofs of love she had given him, the letters she had written, her kisses, her evident anxieties, so that he might gain the courage to wait and to live. Sometimes, her words would come back to him: 'I have to earn my dowry.' And looking up at the brightly lit windows, he would imagine her sitting on Dâmaso's knee, her arms about him, selling herself in order to 'fleece' Dâmaso.

He was overwhelmed then by a kind of disgust for that

passion which he perceived suddenly as besmirched and stained. And who was that dowry for? For him, of course. And was that not vile and unworthy? He really was a blackguard. To plot with a woman to 'fleece' a poor fool and then share the spoils between them. And while the fool was in her bedroom, he prowled about, waiting, his heart in anguish, tormented by that ignoble love, his eyes fixed on those bright third-floor windows. Is that not what pimps did?

He resolved then to leave her and forget her. But could he? His body, blood, conscience and judgement belonged entirely to that woman. He swore then never to live with her as man and wife, to keep their interests wholly separate, so that only she would benefit from that 'dowry'.

One rainy night, Vítor, wretched and consumed by jealousy, walked past Genoveva's door and saw a hired cab stopped outside. The two horses stood with their heads down, indifferent to the rain falling on them; he saw the glow of a cigarette inside the carriage where the coachman had taken shelter. There was a light on in Genoveva's bedroom. The suspicion came to Vítor that it might not be Dâmaso up there, and his heart was immediately flooded with all kinds of other doubts. Could it be another man? She was so beautiful, so elegant, she must be desired by many men. In order to complete her dowry, could she have taken another lover? Was that why she had told him not to visit her, so that he would not encounter another man apart from Dâmaso? He approached the carriage, as if to hire it.

'I'm taken,' said the coachman.

'By Senhor Dâmaso?'

'A customer, I don't know who he is. It might be Senhor Dâmaso, but I don't know him.'

'A short, fat fellow.'

'I don't know,' said the coachman brusquely. 'I'm not a policeman.'

Vítor resolved to wait. The rain continued to fall and, shamed by the coachman, he had taken refuge on the corner, in Calçada do Pimenta; he did not take his eyes off the window for a second, but no female silhouette appeared; the

237

rather dim light seemed to come from the candles on her dressing table.

He swore to himself that if he found out there was another man, he would break off his relationship with her; he had already composed the cold, desperate, violent letter he would write to her. What if it was another candidate for that dowry? What if it was another lover, a caprice, a fancy? What if she wanted to rid herself of him?

The rain still fell, his feet were cold, his knees soaked; the street was deserted; the wet paving stones gleamed beneath the gaslamp; rain spouted from the gutters and the light in the bedroom was still on; in the misty rain, the lamps on the carriage shone like two dull, reddish eyes.

Suddenly, a harsh voice next to him said:

'Could you spare a moment, sir?'

Before him stood a tall, thin figure, wearing a broad-brimmed hat, a threadbare tailcoat, all creased about the collar, and a pair of ragged trousers. In the shadow cast by the hat he could make out two shining eyes set in a gaunt face with a day's growth of beard.

'It's you Silva!' said the man.

But Vítor did not recognise him. He was looking in horror at that young man dressed in the rags of poverty and vice.

The man raised the brim of his hat and murmured:

'My friends don't recognise me any more . . .'

Vítor froze; it was an old friend of his from university, who had left in his second year; he was the son of a well-known family, but gambling, wine and debauchery had gradually transformed the handsome young man who used to ride along the streets of Coimbra from dandy to good-for-nothing, from good-for-nothing to nonentity, from nonentity to this hollow-cheeked wretch who had to shelter at night in doorways and scrounge money off old acquaintances.

The man had held out his hand to him, but Vítor felt reluctant to give him his.

'You can touch me, I haven't got mange,' said the other man solemnly.

Vítor felt ashamed, gave him his hand and said vaguely:

'What are you doing here?'

'I'm sheltering over there and I need a bit of money.'

Vítor pressed a few coins into his hand. The other man put them in his pocket and said brightly:

'Things are bad at the moment, you don't get much return on property these days ... And everything's so expensive. What are you doing here?'

'I'm waiting ...'

'A woman, eh? And your belly's good and full too. I bet you had soup, roast beef and dessert for supper!' He laughed and snorted: 'What a life, eh? Give me another couple of coins, will you?'

There was something at once menacing and pathetic about his outstretched hand, and he swayed about, tottering like a drunk, shifty as a pimp.

'How are your friends? How's your aunt? Have you got a cigarette?'

Vítor gave him a cigar.

'So you smoke cigars, eh? Nice frock coat too.'

He indicated his own ragged clothes and said:

'The tailor let me down this week. You couldn't spare a bit more change, could you?'

'Listen,' said Vítor, 'did you see who got out of that carriage?'

'No, I was waiting for whoever it is to come out. I didn't see him. I was waiting for him so as to borrow a bit of money off him. I've got a three-month bill of exchange to pay off ... at low interest, mind ... Damn them! Do you want to know who the fellow is?'

'Yes, I do.' An idea came to Vítor. 'Could you do something for me? Could you wait here and see who comes out and then meet me somewhere else afterwards? Have a good look at the chap. You know Dâmaso, don't you, well, see if it's him.'

The other man was scratching himself as if he had fleas.

'And what would you pay for this little service? A *libra*?'

'All right, a *libra* it is.'

The other man threw his hat on the ground.

'Your servant, sir! Go and wait for me at the café in Rua do Norte. Do you want me to give the fellow a beating too? I can knife him if you want. I'll do anything for a friend.'

Vítor glanced up again at the window, then walked off to the café in Rua do Norte. It was nearly empty. The grimy, yellow, smoke-stained walls seemed to absorb the light from the gaslamp; there was a fug of smoke in the room, and behind a glass pane at the rear glowed the yellows and reds of dormant bottles of liqueurs unopened for years. At one table, where she was drinking with three men, sat a dark woman with black hair, a pockmarked skin and wearing a full white petticoat. One of the men was asleep with his head on his arms on the table; another, his pipe stuck in the corner of his mouth, his dull eyes blinking, white spittle foaming on his lips, was so drunk he could not even hold his head upright; the third man, a gaunt young fellow wearing a red cravat and his hat pushed back was leaning on the table, talking in a low voice to the woman and sipping coffee from a glass.

Vítor sat down in one corner, ordered a coffee and waited. The younger man had noticed him at once and the woman immediately straightened her headscarf and fluffed her petticoats, striking a languid pose.

Outside, the rain was now falling in torrents; there was the brief sound of a carriage moving off in the distance; and behind the glass compartment, a kettle was boiling.

A sense of disgust and sadness filled him, and he lost himself in imagining the calm existence that could be his. Why did he love that unworthy woman who betrayed him, dishonoured him and who would doubtless lead him into idleness and dishonesty? There he was at two o'clock in the morning in a café for pimps, waiting to receive information from a scoundrel about the behaviour of a prostitute; because he was sure the man in the apartment was not Dâmaso; Dâmaso would not go out on a rainy night like that; or if he did, he would have his coupé drawn by the white horse he used in the winter. It was obviously someone else. She was deceiving him. How different it would be if he were married to some decent girl! At that hour, he would be at home, sitting by a good fire, just closing an interesting book and hearing his wife's sweet voice saying: 'Come to bed, Vítor, it's late!' And she would love him. Why was his life so disorderly, so full of doubts and torments?

Perhaps it was hereditary. His uncle had been married only briefly and had had all kinds of strange adventures; his father had died young in Africa; his mother had died somewhere abroad. What would she or her soul do, assuming there was a heaven and she had a soul, if she were to see him there in that ignoble moment of his sentimental life? He wondered what his mother had been like. Why were there no pictures of her?

The door was flung open and, dripping water, out of breath from running, the wretch came in; he sat down next to Vítor. He smelled of wet clothes, stables and debauchery. Vítor could see now his begrimed hands, his long nails, his patched and faded tailcoat, pinned at the neck, the pockets long since torn off, the ragged shirt and the unspeakable trousers.

'I saw the fellow. A young, bearded chap. Can I have the money now?'

'It wasn't Dâmaso, then?'

'What do you mean 'Dâmaso'? The chap had a big beard. So, can I have the money?'

'Was he alone?'

'He got into the carriage, the coachman drove off, and I left. He had a heavy black beard, top hat and tails. João, give us a coffee, will you?' he yelled.

Vítor gave him the money and, as he got up to leave, the other man grabbed his arm.

'Damn it! Stay and have a coffee. You're not embarrassed, are you? Don't be such a fool. Sit down, go on. Oh, well, go to hell, then, and give my regards to your Aunty. And give us another cigar, will you? Go on, damn you. And if you ever need any help, you know where to find me. I'll do anything, I'm not a gentleman now, and if you don't work, you don't eat, and I want to eat, you bet I do. In fact, it's the only thing I do want. It's good to eat, don't you think? Of course it is, man!'

'Goodbye.'

'Oh, to hell with you, and thanks for nothing!'

Vítor almost ran down the Chiado. He was sure now. It was another man, a man with a big black beard. He went through all the people he knew with black beards. Could it be so-and-so or such-and-such? But some were too poor for her to get any money out of them, others too ugly for her to love. He hated her; he wanted revenge and he was determined to break with her once and for all; but his overriding desire, stronger than his own jealousy, was to make her jealous of him or to make her regret having deceived him.

He wished he had a fortune so that he could live in Lisbon in luxurious fashion, with a magnificent house and carriage, then she would be sorry she had scorned him; or else he would take a lover, a countess or a marchioness, as ostentatious proof of his sentimental superiority. Since these triumphs were rather hard to achieve, he prepared another; he would write a great book, he would be famous; his name would come to torment her when he was extravagantly famous and popular; it would be a book of poems, and when she read those passionate, sublime pages, she would see what a great heart she had spurned.

He spent part of the night writing her a letter, only to tear it up; one moment, he wanted to write a fiery letter, full of angry statements and scornful addresses, the next, he preferred a brief, cold note, very correct, like the gleaming blade of a scalpel cutting into her heart. Then he decided that scornful silence was the best option, as if she did not even exist or were of such little worth she did not even merit disdain.

Sometimes, as he paced about his bedroom in his slippers, he felt almost glad to have ended the affair; a contented serenity filled his soul, as if all the different elements of his life had come suddenly into balance again. Where could such a passion lead him? She was a prostitute, a calculating, middle-aged woman; during her difficult life, she had lost all freshness of heart, all ability to feel ingenuous passion. What could such a relationship hold for him? A life of humiliating jealousies and distrust? He would abandon his career, lose all interest in working and live an obscure life, known to others only as the lover of Dâmaso's mistress. It was fortunate his eyes had been opened in time; it was lucky he had gone to her house that night. It was a shame he did not know the identity of the man with the black beard. He would go to him, shake his hand and say: 'I'm in your debt, my friend, you did me an enormous favour.' But then he suddenly imagined her, Genoveva, sitting on the knee of the bearded man and embracing him; he saw the soft, captivating undulations of her body, imagined her abandoning herself to pleasure, and then he felt rage and a desire for vengeance, death and blood; unable to do anything, feeling too weak to cope with the difficulties life brought him, he threw himself down on the bed, tore at his hair and wept.

A remnant of pride restored his calm. He said out loud: 'Oh, to hell with her, she's nothing but a whore!'

He lay down and slept deeply.

The following day, in order to resume a dignified life, he went to the office. He had not been there for a month and he found Dr Caminha sitting comfortably in his chair as always, clutching one foot with one hand, while with the other hand he smoothed, one by one, the long hairs of his blond moustache.

'Ah, the idler returns!' he said to Vítor.

Vítor made some excuse about problems with his health, difficulties at home . . .

'This job isn't obligatory you know . . . you just come and go as you please.'

He laughed at his own irony and, leaning back in his armchair, he resumed his study of his moustache.

Shortly afterwards, a man came gingerly into the office and, having carefully put down on a chair a hat with an Indian silk handkerchief tucked in the lining, he began explaining his business in a dull voice, making slow gestures, forming an O with his thumb and forefinger. It was some case involving the restitution of pension rights.

The man spoke very softly, addressing Dr Caminha as 'sir' or 'my dear Caminha'; he riffled through bundles of papers, and now and then, he went over, picked up the yellow hand-kerchief, blew his nose and tucked the handkerchief back into

243

the lining of the hat. He seemed to be enjoying the meeting and savouring all the legal terminology.

Vítor, leafing sadly through some files, heard the gentle buzz of his voice saying:

'But can the usurpee sue the usurper?

'He can.'

'What if the usurper has died?'

'Then he can sue the relevant heirs.'

'Is that all?'

'Or he can sue any third parties to whom the usurper may have transferred the rights. It's in article 5.4 of the Civil Code.'

'The act of usurpation took place only recently,' said the man with a smile.

'It would lapse after a year.'

'What if the usurpation had been carried out secretly?'

'When did the injured party find out about it?'

'Six months ago.'

'Then he has six months, my friend; article 5.4 is absolutely clear on that point . . . it has to be within a year of usurpation taking place, or, if it was carried out secretly, within a year of the interested party finding out.'

'So we have the usurper where we want him, then?'

'If the injured party so chooses . . .'

Then the attorney Gorjão came in. Although it was still winter, out of habit, he removed his hat and mopped at the few grizzled hairs on his head with his handkerchief. Then he sat down quietly and waited. Suddenly, he put on his glasses, crossed his feet under the chair, and sticking out his large stomach, started reading, meanwhile stroking his smooth chin with his short, fat fingers. After a while, he went over to Vítor and, peering at him over the top of his glasses, said gently:

'If a mortgage has been registered at more than one registry office, should action be taken in the judicial district in which the taxable property is to be found and where most of the direct contributions have been paid or in the judicial district that covers the registered party's home address?'

Vítor looked at him in horror. He had not understood a

word Gorjão had said. He asked him to repeat the question. He tugged at his moustache, his eyes wide with panic.

'Don't you remember?' Gorjão consulted some notes. 'It's Chapter 10, Section 4, Subsection 7, Division 4 of the Code . . . It must be there. Don't you remember?'

'I can't at the moment . . .'

'I think it can be in either place if the home address of the registered party is part of the relevant property.' Then he whispered in his ear: 'It's Taveira's bankruptcy case . . .'

The other man had got up and left the office, so Gorjão went over to discuss the matter with Dr Caminha.

In the waiting room outside, a dull, smug, monotonous voice was saying to the clerk:

'It was a little crop-tailed mare, just minding her own business. Anyway, near Golegã . . .'

'It can be in either place,' said Dr Caminha, turning to Vítor.

'I'm sorry?' said Vítor.

'The action can be taken in the judicial district covering the registered party's home address or the one covering the area where the taxable property is to be found.'

'Ah,' said Vítor.

And the voice in the waiting room:

'I didn't say a word. I got off the mare and tethered her to a tree . . .'

The voice broke off. A man in an overcoat had arrived, and the loud, harsh voice of the clerk could be heard saying:

'You'll have to talk to Dr Caminha.'

The man in the overcoat came in. He had a greasy, sallow, gaunt face and a day's growth of beard; his lustrine trousers were shiny with wear, and he was carrying a black bag; he explained that Senhor Albuquerque, of the Second Precinct, wanted the papers immediately and had told him not to leave there without them.

Dr Caminha got to his feet and thumped the desk.

'Well, you can tell Senhor Albuquerque that if he wants slaves, he'll have to send to Brazil for them. Tell him to go . . .'

245

He sat down again, dipped his pen violently in the inkwell and threw it down.

'He's got a cheek. If it's not ready, it's not ready! Honestly!' He thumped the desk again. 'If Senhor Alburquerque thinks I'm going to kill myself in order to please him, he can think again. I can't work with a knife at my throat. I can't and there's an end to it. Tell that to Senhor Albuquerque.'

And the great barrister sat down again, furious.

The man in the overcoat left, bowing, and from behind, you could see that his ears stuck out so much from the sides of his head that they looked like the handles on a vase.

There was a silence. Overcome by a profound feeling of melancholy, Vítor gave a deep sigh. Outside, the sun was shining brightly; carts rolled by; sometimes a street crier shouted his wares. A warm, sad tedium seemed to be filling the office like smoke; the sight of the legal papers before him made him feel sick; the spines of the folios on the shelves exuded a calm, lugubrious sadness. The voice outside continued:

'When I got to Golegã, I went straight to the administrator . . .'

And Dr Caminha, still consulting with the attorney, was saying in a monotonous voice:

'Any charges registered prior to the mortgage, which result from the expropriation . . .'

Vítor could stand it no longer; he got to his feet, picked up his hat and said he would be back soon.

' . . . or those from the transfer mentioned in the preceding article . . .' Dr Caminha was saying.

As he went through the waiting room, Vítor heard the man – a heavily built man, his face brick red, and wearing huge spurs on his boots – declaring roundly:

'If he doesn't put that boundary ditch on the other side of the valley, there's going to be trouble.'

Vítor left, slammed the waiting room door, and went down the stairs. Out in the street, he took a deep breath. He resolved never to go back to the office. The boredom of the work was more than he could bear. He only had to go into the office for all his faculties to grow dim. He couldn't understand all the legal jargon; it was a strange, barbarous language that filled him with melancholy. The attorney, the administrator, the lawsuits, the tedious explanations of the different parties, all created a heavy atmosphere in which he could barely breathe and which made his head spin. And that was his profession!

What else was left to him? He had lost Genoveva, and his life was in ruins; he hated his profession and had been deceived in love; socially and sentimentally, it seemed to him that everything was over. He hated Lisbon. Suddenly, he remembered Uncle Timóteo's offer to send him to Paris.

He felt a rush of enthusiasm; his mind filled with plans and hopes; he would travel via Madrid. He could already see himself on the boulevards of Paris, dining in historic cafés, applauding famous plays, seeing geniuses pass by in the street. He might find some woman who would love him . . . Why not? After all, Genoveva had said a man with his looks would be popular in London. London! He would go to the races, reverently visit Shakespeare's tomb or stroll in the parks, where the peacocks show off their brilliant plumage and the deer raise their noble necks.

That same evening, at supper, he exaggerated his sadness; he hardly spoke, but sighed so deeply and seemed so utterly desolate that Uncle Timóteo finally said:

'Look, if I were you, I think I'd just shoot myself.'

'Why?'

'Because here you are, twenty-three years of age, and you're all sighs and melancholy, as if you were some mystical friar. Kill yourself, man. I can lend you my gun if you like. Only don't miss. It makes you look a complete fool and you'll just end up disfigured.'

Vítor asked him then if he was still minded to let him go on a trip.

'Ah, so you want to go now, do you?' said Uncle Timóteo, removing his pipe from his mouth and looking at him hard. He shook his head. 'Well, what's said is said. I'm getting a bit old to be left all on my own, like a dog . . . but you go if you want to.'

'Just for three or four months,' said Vítor.

'What's said is said. When do you want to leave?'

Vítor said he would like to leave that week, straight away.

'What's said is said,' grunted Uncle Timóteo. 'Or *Quod scripsi, scripsi*, as our friend Pilate would have it.'

He coughed, tutted and said no more, but he looked furious.

That night in his room, Vítor was already savouring the joy of departure. He seemed to have forgotten all about Genoveva; he now thought himself a fool to have wasted months of his life on that passion. But, then, if because of her he was now going off to Paris . . . The best part was that it gave him the opportunity to avenge himself on Genoveva, by going to see her, sitting coolly down and saying, with his hat in his hand: 'I'm leaving for Paris.' 'You're leaving?' 'Yes, just for a year or two; I'm so bored with Lisbon!'

And he hoped she would be horribly jealous. She might even want to come with him.

At that thought, his blood raced. Travelling with her, visiting museums together, dining in restaurants, spending delicious nights in a hotel bedroom, caught up in a great adventure and in the ecstasy of passion!

No, if she wanted to go with him, he would refuse. He despised her now. Let the man with the black beard have the scarecrow, the whore!

Clorinda opened the door and said:

'A coachman's here. He says there's a person downstairs who wants to speak to you.'

'What person?'

'He didn't say. He says they're waiting downstairs.'

Vítor went down, feeling very agitated. He saw a hired carriage. He opened the door and Genoveva's voice said:

'Vítor, get in,' and she grabbed his arm.

He found himself sitting next to her. The coachman immediately drove off.

'My love,' Genoveva said breathlessly and threw her arms about his neck, covering him with frenetic kisses, murmuring ardent words of love.

'I couldn't bear to be away from you any longer. It's almost driven me mad. But it had to be. If you only knew. Someone wrote to Dâmaso. Tell me you've thought about me. Do you love me? Speak.'

Her embrace was so sudden and Vítor so surprised that he responded to her kisses out of pure instinct. The carriage was travelling down Rua do Alecrim. In the light, he could see the great circle of her white skirt around his feet; she was wearing a fur-trimmed jacket and some black lace on her head; she was all rustling silks and penetrating perfume.

'I didn't bother to change. I just had to slip out for a minute. We're free, completely free now . . . But what's wrong?'

Vítor had withdrawn to the other end of the carriage.

'I'm sorry, but there can be nothing between us now. Who was the bearded man who was at your house until two o'clock in the morning?'

Genoveva did not reply at first, then she said:

'What man, when?'

'He left your house at two o'clock yesterday morning.'

'It must have been a friend of Dâmaso's.' She hesitated, then seemed to remember. 'They had supper and were playing cards until late; there were two men: the Viscount of Tovar and another man whose name I can't remember; he had a blond beard.'

'No, no, this man had a black beard and he left alone.'

'How should I know who he was? He may not even have come from my apartment. There are other apartments; he could have come from the first, second or third floor. What a ridiculous question!'

He could have come from another floor! Why had he not thought of that before? He had been so convinced that he must be another of Genoveva's lovers. But what persuaded him was her voice, the warmth of her caresses, the perfume from her skirts; he wanted to devour her with kisses, but, out of a remnant of proud stubbornness, he said:

'There were no lights on in the other apartments.'

'What are you insinuating?' She banged on the windows angrily. 'Stop, coachman, stop!'

'What's wrong?'

'I want you to get out now, to leave.' Genoveva's voice trembled with anger and scorn. 'At great risk, mad with love, I come to see you, and you receive me with insolence. Stop the coach!'

The coachman stopped. Genoveva furiously flung open the carriage door, drew in her skirts and said coldly:

'Goodbye, you may leave.'

'Genoveva . . .'

'So you think I receive men, bearded or otherwise, at two o'clock in the morning? Maybe you're confusing me with Aninhas. Now get out, get out!'

'Drive on, coachman,' shouted Vítor, slamming the door shut again.

'I don't want you here,' she said.

But he took her in his arms, covered her in kisses and said:

'Forgive me! I was so jealous. I walked past your house and I saw the carriage stopped outside; there was a light on in your window. Genoveva, swear to me there was no one there.'

'No, I won't swear anything,' she said forcefully. 'What right have you to insult me?'

'Forgive me.'

'You've known me for two months; I do everything for you; sacrifice myself for you; you know the repellent things I have to do . . . and just because you see some man leaving my building, you accuse me of receiving other men.'

'I didn't say that!'

'You did!'

'I swear . . .'

'If we're going to start with suspicions, ridiculous questions and sulks, then we'd better finish the whole thing now.'

'No, never, never. Tell me you forgive me. I was mad. I was all set to go to Paris. I was going to come and see you tomorrow and say goodbye, to ask you coldly if you wanted me to send you anything from Paris.'

'You,' she said, placing her hand on his shoulder, 'you go to Paris and leave me?' She put her face very close to his. 'I would kill you first.'

She clasped him to her; she kissed his eyes, his lips, his

250

forehead; her straying hands seemed to want to take full possession of him.

'My adored Vítor, my love! Tell me you're mine, my only love, my life, my lover, my husband! Oh, my love!'

She lay in his embrace, as if in a faint, then suddenly, looking up, she said:

'I can't stay any longer. I have to be at home by ten o'clock. Tell him to go back to the house. You can get out at the top of the road.'

Vítor broke in:

'But tell me what's going on. Why this separation?'

'You can't imagine . . . Someone sent Dâmaso an anonymous letter saying that you visited me when he wasn't there, that you were my lover . . . It came at the moment when I most needed to keep him, and so I had to remove all suspicion. These days of separation have earned me two *contos* . . .'

'It was the Englishwoman,' said Vítor. And he described his encounter with Miss Sarah. It was her revenge.

Genoveva was horrified.

'I'll put her out on the street the day after tomorrow. But don't say a word to her, the traitor. Women like her should be whipped. And did you resist?'

'Like Joseph of Egypt!'

They laughed and she kissed him again.

'Who could help but adore you with those eyes of yours? Listen, that fool Dâmaso will probably come and invite you to supper tomorrow. Be sure and come, my love.' In his ear, she said: 'It will be our wedding feast. Tomorrow I'll be free.'

The carriage stopped at the top of Rua do Alecrim. Vítor jumped down. She still had hold of his hand and she kissed it. Vítor was so deeply touched by that kiss that his eyes filled with tears. He watched the carriage move off as devoutly as he might follow the bright trail of an angel across the heavens. He looked about him. He wanted to talk to someone, to embrace someone, to help someone. A poor woman wearing a veil approached him. Vítor gave her all the money he had: fifteen *tostões*!

'Tomorrow, tomorrow,' he repeated to himself as he walked up Rua do Alecrim.

He seemed to be walking on air, borne up by his light, volatile soul, and in a joyous impulse, he started singing the *Marseillaise*.

XI

When Vítor arrived at Genoveva's house at seven o'clock in the evening on 1ˢᵗ April, he was amazed: he didn't recognise anyone.

Genoveva had told Dâmaso:

'I don't want anyone who was at that first soirée; no tetchy academicians, no argumentative poets and no old ladies in turbans. I want people who are clean, well-dressed and amusing.'

After complicated negotiations, Dâmaso had submitted a list to Genoveva; she knew some of the people, others seemed acceptable either because of their sonorous names or because of certain biographical eccentricities. A radiant Dâmaso gathered together what he described later as 'a really chic group of people'.

The room was brilliantly lit by a gas chandelier; on the table large numbers of tallow candles glowed in golden candelabra; there were vases of camellias and violets; the piano stood open; the women's colourful dresses and the men's white ties stood out against the rather dark furnishings, lending a dash of opulence that complemented the discreet murmur of conversation and the whisper of fans.

Genoveva immediately came forward to greet Vítor. She looked marvellously beautiful; she was wearing a corn-coloured dress in faille, trimmed with magnificent lace; the low-cut, square neckline revealed her splendid shoulders and the delicate flesh of her bosom; the sleeves were elbow length, ending in a foam of lace; her blonde hair was arranged simply *à l'anglaise* and slightly waved, with only a simple pin in the shape of an ear of corn as decoration; her skin was milk-white, and that combination of pale skin and golden dress lent her an imposing, aristocratic, elegant beauty; she wore no jewels, but, on her bodice, between the curve of her breasts, she wore a superb magenta rose, a single point of bold, vigorous colour.

The passionate squeeze she gave his hand filled Vítor with a delicious sense of pride and mystery. Vítor bowed and kissed her hand. Genoveva introduced him to the lady he was to lead into dinner, Madame Sivalli, who played minor roles at the Teatro de São Carlos; she was a tall, powerful woman, with a Bourbon nose, jet-black hair and splendid teeth; she had spent most of her acting career in the theatres of South America; she knew Mexico, Peru and Chile well and Brazil slightly; she had performed for many years at Covent Garden and spoke every language well, even a little Portuguese; her many journeys and adventures made her a lively and original conversationalist, with her store of picturesque anecdotes and her masculine boldness; she dressed in the somewhat ostentatious, explosive style of Havana or Valparaíso, and combined an easy theatrical manner with a Venetian sense of ceremony.

Dâmaso then introduced him to two men. Vítor knew them both by sight: one was the Count de Val-Moral, who was standing motionless, a model of courtly correctness; he had been to Genoveva's house once before and she had said then that 'while he was unbearably stupid, purely as a figure he was indispensable'; he was one of those silent, impassive people, much appreciated in London and Paris, who cut a beautiful, decorative figure, the human equivalent of a rare vase or a modern painting. He was blond too, which made him even more useful, since the furniture and the upholstery were all rather dark. Genoveva had said: 'The imbecile could make a living in Paris by renting himself out for twenty *libras* a night at formal suppers.' He was tall, well-proportioned, always exquisitely dressed and had slightly patrician features and a beautiful blond beard; he had been educated abroad, and his manners, his cravat patterned with a tiny check and his black silk socks were all perfection; he was considered 'the most elegant person in Lisbon'; he always struck conventional, formal attitudes and his shirt-front was always stiff and gleaming; he had the imbecilic opinions of a mannequin, but he expressed them with majestic certainty; he was a great player of whist and was married to a noble lady whose lover was in commerce. Were it not for his corns, he would have been an entirely happy man.

'Do you know Dom João da Maia?' Dâmaso asked Vítor.

'Only by sight.'

João da Maia was the son of one of the oldest houses in Portugal. He had a terrifying old aunt, whose first question about anyone would be: 'Is he or she a plebeian?' or 'Is he or she a commoner?' and who would make frequent mention of the fact that they were descended from Egas Moniz, who had served King Afonso Henriques. João da Maia, however, was a republican, though he hesitated to reveal his revolutionary sympathies because he was convinced that republicans did not wash. He got on well with ordinary people and liked ordinary food: potato and cabbage soup, salt cod, etc. He was often to be found in taverns, where he enjoyed the conversation of pimps; his manners, however, were delicate in the extreme, and he was a man of scrupulous habits and literary tastes. Although his family was very devout, he was an atheist. He did not believe in God and he hated priests, but he found church music very moving and nurtured a refined, elegant, rather bookish respect for the poetic image of the blond Christ telling parables in a long white tunic and surrounded by young men on the shores of the sweet lakes of Galilee. He adored art and worshipped Alfred de Musset. He was always in flight from boredom and in search of amusement. He was witty and would occasionally come out with sharp little comments that would make people open their eyes wide, but he was far too charming for anyone to take offence.

He was tall and handsome and had curly hair and a somewhat languid air about him; he was affectionate and friendly towards women and had a winning smile; he was as generous as a nabob, but poor as Job. His creditors were not, for the moment, pursuing him, for he knew how to get round them. He had been educated in England, received by the aristocracy of St James's Square and been a member of clubs in Pall Mall; he had preferred, however, to go dancing at the Argyle or to one of the boxing clubs at the London docks.

People called him a bohemian, though no one said it to his face because he was very quick to lash out or to punch someone; he would also be the first to wash any wound he had

255

caused or to have stitches put in at the nearest pharmacy, and then usher his victim into a carriage and carry him back to his family. He was always in trouble over either money or women; but he would laugh about his problems with friends and he always found someone prepared to lend him money or to give him the benefit of their financial advice. He lived in hotels, spending lavishly, and often had to pawn his watch; he gave generously to others and, when he had no money, he would simply stay in bed with a novel, a science book and a bottle of champagne.

He felt at ease everywhere; he was every inch the Prince Charming. Genoveva greatly admired him. She said: 'One couldn't possibly fall in love with him, but it's hard not to have a small crush on him!' He was one of the most delightful people in Lisbon, and stood out in sharp contrast against the banal backdrop of Lisbon's bourgeoisie. That was why people said he was mad.

But one of the people who most impressed Vítor was a woman sitting on the sofa talking to Genoveva. He had heard others address her as Dona Joana Coutinho. She was extremely tall, thin, ethereal and frail; she was wearing a dress made of floating tulle and gauze in soft, pale blues; her dark eyes were tender and kind; the gestures she made with hands and arms had the impatient eloquence of wings; she was half-sitting, half-lying on the sofa, and with her weightless appearance, in her tulles and gauzes, she looked as if she were about to fly off and disappear.

'Who is she?' he asked João da Maia.

'A soul!' he replied.

'And what about the other woman?' He indicated a strong-looking woman in a tight, scarlet dress, with butter-yellow hair, a slightly turned-up nose and lips thin as a crack.

'That's Madalena Gordon, but no relation of the Duke of Richmond and Gordon. She's a German dancer and she's with the Baron de Means, the old man with the wig. He's not here tonight. The young lady came on her own. She's a useful person to know; she gives good suppers and doesn't bore people. But she's very virtuous, too virtuous really; she has a horror of men and a penchant for women.'

The clock struck seven and Genoveva immediately took the Count de Val-Moral's arm; Dâmaso, plump and jubilant, rushed over to grab his partner, Dona Joana Coutinho, and they all proceeded solemnly down the carpeted corridor with a swish of silk trains.

'Such an elegant apartment,' remarked Madame Sivalli to Vítor.

The table gleamed beneath the gas chandelier; the new knives glittered beside the plates of oysters; the fruit for dessert had been arranged around the two vases of flowers; the wine glasses glinted softly and the air was filled by the delicate smell of lemons; above the sideboard, a tall oil lamp set bright points of light on the curved edges of plates and serving dishes. Two of Dâmaso's servants were at the table, along with a waiter from the Hotel Central.

The table was square and each of the couples occupied one of the sides. Genoveva, who had the Count de Val-Moral on her left, immediately placed her foot on Vítor's and pressed it passionately. Inside each napkin was a small bunch of violets.

'This is clearly a Bonapartist household,' remarked João da Maia to his neighbour, the German dancer Madalena Gordon, and to the ethereal Dona Joana Coutinho.

'It's my favourite flower,' replied Dona Joana. 'There is none more poetic.'

And she put her head on one side, as if in a swoon. João quickly turned back to Madalena and asked after the excellent Baron. Had his luck at the baccarat table changed at all? He had won eight *libras* from him last time he had dined at the Baron's house, which only proved the truth of the proverb: lucky at cards, unlucky in love. The German replied in monosyllables; she could not take her cold, blue, pale-lashed eyes off Genoveva.

'She's lovely, isn't she?' said João following the direction of her lubricious gaze.

'Perfect,' said the German.

João then asked what her idea of the perfect woman was

and, when she hesitated and drew back, pursing her thin lips, João threw the question open to the whole table, as if they were a council of cardinals.

Dona Joana Coutinho believed the perfect woman was one with soul, 'a noble soul, of course'.

Dâmaso craned his neck and, with a saucy glance at Genoveva, said authoritatively:

'The perfect woman is right here at this table.'

'No, that doesn't count, we're talking in general terms,' everyone said.

When Vítor was asked, he replied:

'The woman one loves,' and with his foot he indicated to Genoveva that she was the woman he was thinking of.

Then they asked the Count. Sitting very erect, adorning the table with the beautiful solemnity of his person, he had remained silent, his elbows tight in to his body, wielding his knife and fork with a scrupulous delicacy and a cocking of fingers that set his rings glittering; he smiled, considered and then said in a sonorous voice:

'Her Majesty, for example.'

'No, that doesn't count,' exclaimed João da Maia. 'We're talking in general and, besides, you're wounding my republican sensibilities.'

'And mine!' cried Vítor.

'You're spoiling our soup!' added João.

The Count, startled, placed his hand on his heart and said:

'I'm so sorry if . . .'

They calmed him down and assured him it was all a joke.

'My respect for others' opinions . . .,' spluttered the Count.

'No, no, it's all right!' everyone said. 'They're just pretending. They're not really republicans.'

Then João da Maia, to amuse the ladies, described a republican conspiracy in which he had taken part. The meeting place had been a fourth-floor apartment in Rua dos Capelistas; the password was: *Sic itur ad astra*, This is the road to the stars, which, according to João, seemed extremely appropriate as one toiled up to the fourth floor.

'It was such fun,' he said, 'we were never bored for a

moment. The plan was simple: we would recruit six thousand workers, who would buy weapons, storm the Castelo de São Jorge and then march on the centre of Lisbon, declaring: 'Give us a republic now, or we open fire.' Naturally, all the shop-keepers and property owners with stores and buildings in the centre would vote for a republic; then we would institute a revolutionary tribunal. We already had our list of victims drawn up: at the top, the royal family, then you, Dâmaso, and about two or three thousand other people. Every night, we would each take a list of people to be sacrificed. Father Melo had given us the names of all the bishops, and I gave the names of all my creditors. The thing failed because we didn't have any money for the weapons; we never managed to get together more than seven thousand two hundred *réis*, and one *libra* of that was mine. In the end, Father Melo ran off with the money, and order prevailed. I'll have the Chablis,' he said to the waiter, who was behind him, proffering a bottle.

Dâmaso immediately asked the Count's opinion of the Chablis.

The Count tasted it, reflected, concentrated for a moment with his eyes closed, then said in profound tones:

'It's a Chablis.'

'Yes, but what do you think of it?' insisted Dâmaso with the urgent interest of a host.

He looked round at the servants, smiled, leaned back and gazed at Genoveva.

'What do you think?'

The Count, who was still considering, said:

'A good Chablis.'

Dona Joana Coutinho was saying to João da Maia:

'My favourite wine is lachryma Christi!'

Besides, she thought it absurd to drink wine and eat at the same time; one should never eat in public; it was most unbecoming in a lady.

'I've always thought that people of real delicacy should get together to drink milk and eat strawberries.'

'And afterwards, I suppose, behind closed doors in one's

259

bedroom,' said João, 'one could get stuck into a good side of beef.'

'Oh, how awful!' she said, disgusted.

But she did eat; she picked at crumbs of bread with her fingertips. The way she shifted about on her chair was reminiscent of a frightened bird, and there was always a bit of gauze or lace or tulle floating about her, surrounding her with ethereal transparencies and a vague suggestion of wings.

João da Maia had asked Vítor opposite him:

'Don't you agree? I was just saying to this lady that I find it quite wrong to affect a horror of good, solid food. I don't mean Dona Joana, of course, but, for example, it's the same with Platonic love. There are women who talk only of the soul, who say to their admirer: "Ah, my friend, carnal desires are just so disgusting." And they appear to live in a state of ideal purity; when the fact is that these same women are married to healthy husbands, who make sure they get . . .'

Dona Joana protested, horrified: 'What a topic for conversation!' Even Genoveva pulled a serious face; the German pursed her lips in scornful disapproval; and Dâmaso, leaning towards João, rebuked him almost sadly:

'Really, my boy . . .'

João fell silent, smiled and said to Dâmaso in bad schoolboy German:

'Is this some kind of monastery?'

'No, it's someone's dining room,' retorted the Baron's concubine.

'Shameless hypocrite,' thought João.

The excellent Madame Sivalli had taken up the matter with Vítor and was saying:

'I've never believed in Platonic love; well, we all know what that means in men.' And she laughed mischievously, covering her face with her napkin. 'In women, it's desire that's the driving force.'

'Really,' said Genoveva, frowning.

'Can't we have a bit of fun?' said Madame Sivalli. 'Allow us at least to talk; there's nothing like talking about sins, as long as they're not real ones.'

João wanted to join in, and he raised his glass of Bordeaux to her from afar, to show that he shared her love of loose talk.

Dona Joana Coutinho brought the conversation round to pilgrimages to Lourdes and the miraculous water there.

The women all went into ecstasies over the sublime virtue of the spring water.

'Have you got any?' Dona Joana asked Genoveva.

Alas, she did not; she had some in Paris, though, given to her by Abbot Beauvet de Madeleine.

'I have,' said the German.

And she blushed with smug, devout enthusiasm. Dona Joana, raising her glass to her lips and taking a sip, said:

'It's a balm from heaven.'

Dâmaso, who thought she was praising his Bordeaux, said:

'Oh, I'm so glad. It's Chateau-Léonville. I much prefer it to the Margaux.'

'No impiety, please,' said Dona Joana, outraged.

'That was in the worst possible taste,' said Genoveva imperiously.

'But my love,' exclaimed Dâmaso, terrified. 'I thought . . .'

Genoveva cut him off.

'That's enough.'

Dâmaso turned scarlet. There was a brief silence. Then João da Maia quietly asked:

'One can, of course, drink the water of Our Lady of Lourdes with wine.' And seeing the scandalised faces around him, he went on. 'Oh, I know what I'm talking about. It's an opinion I've heard expressed by the highest ecclesiastical authorities. Last year in Rome, at the house of the Princess de Barbaccini,' João said in a pompous, formal voice, 'there was Cardinal Cazabianca, Monsignor Bassorchi, two bishops from the House of Lords, His Grace the Duke of Norfolk, and . . .' he struggled to recall other devout and famous men.

The women were listening to him now, intent, interested; in their bent heads and their sympathetic silence lay an elegant reverence for that Catholic litany of names.

'Anyway, the cream of Rome was there, and I heard that saint of a man, Abbé de La Chermaye, say that, in case of illness, it was perfectly acceptable to take the water of Our Lady of Lourdes with a little Spanish wine.'

'Well, I've never heard that before!' said Dona Joana, astonished.

'I'm citing the opinion of Rome, Madam.'

There was a discreet silence; everyone seemed to be savouring the revelation of that holy truth, and João da Maia was thinking: 'What fools! What ridiculous women they are!'

Then Dâmaso, who always grew relaxed and loquacious at supper, revealed his views on Our Lady of Lourdes:

'It's just religious fanaticism.'

Dona Joana Coutinho seemed very shocked, and Genoveva declared that she found that brand of facetious atheism excessively bourgeois.

'Besides,' said Vítor, who wanted to bury that fool Dâmaso, 'such beliefs are a great consolation to many poor, sick, crippled people who have no other hope – for them Our Lady of Lourdes is all they have.'

That seemed extremely well said, elegant and aristocratic. Even the Count nodded approvingly. Genoveva said:

'Spoken from the heart.'

And her eyes kissed him gratefully.

Meanwhile, the Count was torturing his intellect to find something to say to Genoveva. At last, after great internal preparations, he asked her if she was planning to go to the races in Belém.

Genoveva said that she thought not. She had heard it was a frightful bore.

Dâmaso objected; he spoke of the stands, the horses, the English jockeys who would be there . . .

Vítor broke in:

'Genoveva is quite right. The races here are enough to send one to sleep. They lack everything that makes the races exciting: elegant women, four-in-hands, champagne drunk sitting atop your carriage, the thrill of betting . . .'

His scornful remarks so incensed Dâmaso that he felt obliged to riposte, red-faced:

'And what would you know about that?'

'Or you for that matter?'

Genoveva declared at once that Vítor was right. The true national sport was bullfighting; there wasn't the right public for racing in Portugal, there weren't the horses, the jockeys or the money.

João da Maia added:

'It's a joke really! They're like the jumps in Campo Grande: a few chaps on hired horses stumbling over an artificial hedge made out of branches held there by two lackeys. It's grotesque.'

'But . . .' said Dâmaso.

'Enough, my friend,' said Genoveva. 'I have no faith in you as a sporting man.'

Dâmaso, flushed and humiliated, could not think what to say and instead downed a large glass of wine.

Dona Joana Coutinho found all these amusements brutal and suitable only for vulgar people. Bullfighting, horseracing, sports, wrestling, croquet . . . what did it all mean? It was a ridiculous waste of energy and involved so little delicacy of soul. A man should occupy himself with other things.

'Like what?' asked João.

'Noble things, lofty feelings, grand deeds.'

'But a man can't spend all day doing grand deeds.'

'Well, they should read the poets, cultivate themselves by reading the great authors,' and turning to Dâmaso, she asked: 'Who is your favourite poet?'

Dâmaso pulled a face and stammered:

'Well, I can't quite think offhand . . .'

'Oh, don't ask him,' said Genoveva. 'He has a horror of the printed word.'

'I beg your pardon,' said Dâmaso.

'An incurable horror of the printed word and of cold water,' she added and leaned back in her chair, laughing.

Everyone else laughed too. Dâmaso was furious. Why was she attacking him? That very morning he had signed over to her three *contos de réis*, and her hostility seemed shockingly ungrateful and gave the unsettling impression of a rupture between them. Desperate because he could not think of some vengeful riposte, he took refuge in the Bordeaux and the *salmis* of partridge.

Dona Joana Coutinho, who was still on the theme of literature – 'the only proper employment for a noble soul' – and who admired Vítor because he was handsome and because of his devotion to Our Lady of Lourdes, said to him with an affectionate smile:

'I understand you write poetry.'

Everyone congratulated him and asked him to recite something after supper.

Vítor said modestly that he was merely an amateur, not a professional lyric poet; indeed, it seemed to him rather a ridiculous profession; there were, however, certain sensations, certain enthusiasms, certain confessions that need to find expression in verse or in music and, since he did not know music, how else but in verse could one tell a woman one had dreamed of her? How else could one express all the delicate feelings her love arouses? Prose won't do. We should speak to women either on our knees or in verse.

Everyone applauded. The sentiment seemed particularly delightful in the mouth of a handsome young man. Dona Joana Coutinho struck various poses indicative of a melancholy ecstasy. Even Madame Sivalli, for all her ironic vivacity, found his words terribly 'artistic'. And Vítor, enlivened and encouraged by the warmth and sympathy surrounding him, and somewhat surprised to discover that he had such a facility for literary speeches, said to Dâmaso:

'I'm sure that's what you do! Being an elegant chap, how could you not send the person you love a bouquet of flowers and a sonnet each morning. That's the only proper thing to do. What was today's sonnet?'

'Mind your own business!'

'Oh, sorry.'

Genoveva had turned pale and she nervously bit her lip; and everyone seemed surprised by this sudden lapse in manners. João da Maia, who was enjoying himself, said:

'Our friend Dâmaso is quite right to keep silent. One should not ask a lover to confess his feelings.'

'He only has one way of expressing his,' said Genoveva coldly.

People were beginning to feel uneasy. They all saw that Genoveva was intent on humiliating Dâmaso, but why?

'The honeymoon is obviously over for those two,' João said in a low voice to the German woman.

'I find him most disagreeable,' she replied, looking at Dâmaso.

'Oh, he's a fool all right, but he has some very good wine.' Then raising his voice: 'For a poet, Senhor Silva, you're not very peace-loving. The other day, I saw you in Rua do Alecrim, wielding a walking stick with remarkable skill.'

Everyone looked at him, surprised.

'Oh,' said Genoveva, 'he was just dealing with a friend of Dâmaso's.'

'My friends would never allow themselves to be beaten like that.'

'No,' said Vítor. 'I only had to raise the walking stick as if I were about to hit him, and he called for the police.'

From that moment on, as João da Maia said to the German woman, the supper was 'ruined'. It really was absurd to invite people to supper without warning them they were in for a family spat.

Everyone was convinced that Vítor was Genoveva's lover and that a grim little comedy of terrible jealousies was being played out before them. The growing embarrassment made conversation awkward and slow. Dâmaso ate his food glumly and said nothing. The Count, who found it all most indecorous, maintained a dignified silence. The German woman gazed admiringly at Genoveva, and João da Maia watched Vítor; the others kept up desultory dialogues.

João da Maia and Vítor discussed duels; Genoveva and Madame Sivalli talked about Paris and various mutual friends.

'Don't you think Senhor Silva looks like Genoveva?' the German woman asked João quietly.

'Not really, although there is something. If she didn't dye her hair, there really would be a striking resemblance.'

The champagne had been served and when, once dessert

was over, Genoveva slowly drew on her gloves and rose to her feet, there was a general sense of relief because, as João da Maia put it, 'the supper had been a frightful bore'.

Dâmaso, who hung back a little, said to Vítor with a bitter little laugh:

'You were most amusing, my friend.'

'And you were not.'

Dâmaso could think of nothing to say in response and so went into the salon, chewing rancorously on his cigar.

The Count had sat down at the piano, and Madame Sivalli was standing beside him; she was humming softly, beating time with her fan on the piano, kicking back her long train; she stood behind the Count, opened her lips, and her contralto voice sang out, grave and solemn. It was a song from Campagna; the melody sometimes swayed, languid, expansive and voluptuous, then rose to an amorous crescendo of high, passionate notes that had all the ardent insistence of a lover's plea; at those moments, Madame Sivalli leaned her head back, revealing her beautiful plump, white throat.

A few more people arrived: Senhor Elisiano Macedo, who brought his cello, Sarrotini, jovial and talkative, filling the room with the noisy spectacle of himself, and Marinho, all discreet smiles and affectionate handshakes.

Genoveva received them with ceremonious grace and warm words, smiling and showing her small white teeth. She seemed to have recovered from the nervous irritation she had shown at supper, and her dress, her bare throat, her graceful white neck, the beauty of her figure all filled Vítor with almost painful excitement. The Burgundy too made his blood flow through his veins with amorous vigour, and he roamed the room, hoping for a moment when he could quietly pour out to her his heartfelt admiration. When, at last, he saw a free space on the sofa next to her, he rushed over and whispered:

'Genoveva, you're wonderful. I must see you alone. Please, don't send me away tonight.'

She slowly opened her fan and, leaning back on the sofa, said slowly:

'Listen, at eleven o'clock, leave the room, put on your

jacket and wait downstairs in the porter's lodge. Mélanie will come for you and take you to her room. And don't talk to me too much tonight or seem too happy.'

Then she bowed to Sarrotini, who was standing before her, asking if they would be having the honour of hearing her divine voice.

Vítor moved away, so troubled that he could not reply to Elisiano's enquiry after Camilo Cerrão. He was aware only of his heart beating wildly and a feeling of immense pride flooding through him. The lights, the women's dresses, the men's white ties and the music were all further incitements to his love, further fuel for the furnace. And the extraordinary certainty that he would possess Genoveva, and the mysterious charm of knowing that he would, were almost too much to bear. He went into the smoking room off to one side, dropped down on a sofa, his arms hanging loose, and gave a deep sigh; he sat there motionless, his eyes closed in a spasm of joy.

He heard boots creaking over the carpet. Marinho had sat down next to him on the sofa and immediately launched into a speech praising Genoveva. He had never seen her so lovely! As regards time, she was definitely walking backwards, like a crab. No one would think she was more than twenty-five. What a woman! Lucky Dâmaso, eh? He was ruining himself, of course, but he was certainly getting his money's worth!

He giggled and was about to continue, when they heard the plangent sounds of the cello. It was Elisiano playing a composition based on Gounod's *Ave Maria*. They slowly approached the door.

Elisiano, his blond hair slightly dishevelled, held the cello in his arms, his body bent, and tenderly, languorously caressed the strings with the bow. Vítor thought the music utterly divine; the sounds bore the soul up to vague worlds of feeling where it swooned with mystical, elegant love. Everyone was still and silent; the tailcoats and white ties lent a touch of aristocratic life to the room, embellished further by the vase of camellias glowing in the candlelight; here and there, a fan fluttered, and Genoveva's corn-yellow dress and her blonde hair, contrasting with the dark tones of the room, seemed possessed of a natural luminosity, as if made of some finer substance.

Vítor occasionally caught her eye and, as if borne up on the subtle notes of the cello, his soul rushed towards her, driven by impulses so strong and movements so eager, that the effort of having to remain standing where he was in the doorway made his hands tremble like leaves in the wind.

The last chord sounded, there were cries of 'Bravo!', and Elisiano, wiping the sweat from his brow, slowly got to his feet; the buzz of conversation filled the room with festive murmurings. Vítor suddenly remembered Marinho's still unfinished story and he was just about to go and ask him how it ended, when he noticed that Marinho was deep in conversation with Madame Sivalli. Sarrotini came over and took his arm; the excellent fellow was slightly bored. The first soirée he had spent there had been wonderful, such fun, but today everyone was more serious, everyone was putting on airs; he didn't like that; he liked to enjoy himself with friends, he liked to laugh. But Genoveva was looking stunning, absolutely dazzling!

Everyone said the same, and she was his lover; in two hours' time, he would be in her bedroom.

He looked at the clock and turned pale; it was eleven o'clock!

He went to say goodbye to Genoveva and was standing in the corridor putting on his overcoat, when Dámaso came out to him:

'You're not leaving already, are you?'

'Yes, I'm not feeling very well.'

'Sorry about that business at supper.'

'Oh, that's all right!'

'Lovely party, eh?' said Dâmaso. He seemed perfectly contented now. He helped Vítor on with his overcoat and called for Mélanie to light his way. From the top of the stairs, he shouted:

'Be sure to come and see us!'

He went back into the salon, beaming.

Genoveva beckoned him over.

'Who was it who left?'

'Vítor.'

'Ah . . . now just come and sit here for a moment.'

She began speaking slowly, complaining about his ill humour at the supper table.

'But why were you so unpleasant to me? You seemed to want to give everyone the impression that you couldn't stand the sight of me.'

'Why were you so irreverent? You know I hate jokes about religion.'

'But you know, sometimes, my girl . . .'

'It's all right when we're alone, in the bedroom, although even then . . . But in company, in the salon, religion is a matter of politeness.'

He was about to get up.

'Sit down. Anyone would think you didn't want to talk to me. Apart from all that, I want my lover to be able to converse, to be witty, to shine . . . You were so awkward.'

'I'm afraid I'm not one of the literati,' he said scornfully.

'Maybe not, but you could still be an entertaining conversationalist. Anyway, I've got a headache,' she added, 'and I'm not sure I want you to stay tonight.'

Dâmaso became angry. Tonight of all nights, on her birthday, tonight when she was looking so lovely, when he loved her so much . . .

'At least leave when the others do.'

'But I'll come back afterwards.'

Genoveva did not reply.

'I'll come back at midnight or one o'clock.'

Genoveva was opening and closing her fan, as if distracted.

'I'll come back, shall I?'

She gave a hesitant smile and, getting up, said:

'All right.'

She took a turn about the room, with a word here, a smile there, and then, crossing the smoking room, she went swiftly into her bedroom; she rang the bell; she glanced quickly round: a jar full of opoponax, the sheets drawn back. She looked at herself in the mirror and sighed deeply. 'The die is cast,' she said out loud. Mélanie had come into the room.

'Is everything ready?'

'Yes, madam. He's locked in my room,' said Mélanie, laughing.

'Poor love! Take him a bottle of champagne, a cake or something. And you know what else you have to do, don't you? As soon as everyone leaves, wrap some cotton wool around the doorbell or cut the wire. Then, if Dâmaso does come back and he does kick up a fuss, we won't hear a thing.'

Mélanie said:

'It would be best if he didn't make a fuss.'

'If the fool wants to come back at one o'clock, well, let him. Sometimes, it's best to make a clean break; it avoids complications.'

She smoothed her hair, turned round, gave one more glance about the room, then went back into the salon.

'These gentlemen,' João da Maia informed her, 'want to waltz.'

'And why not?' she said with a happy smile.

Sarrotini and Elisiano had moved the table. They were talking loudly and laughing. The Count, sitting gravely at the piano, played the opening chords of the *Blue Danube*.

At around one o'clock, Dâmaso, well wrapped up, was walking across the Largo do Barão de Quintela. Darkness had closed in. It was starting to rain. He opened the street door with his key and, lighting a match, went up the stairs. On the second floor, a brilliant flash lit up the stairs with pale light, followed by a loud roll of thunder overhead.

When he reached Genoveva's floor, he gave a sharp tug on the bell pull. Nothing. He waited, then gave the string another violent tug. Not a sound.

'The bell's not working!' he thought angrily.

He crouched down and put his ear to the door; inside was a dark, sleeping silence.

'Now what!'

In despair, he tried the bell pull again. Nothing. He rapped impatiently with his knuckles. In the silence, he could hear his heart beating. Flashes of lightning lit the stairs; thunder crashed above the rooftops. He pounded on the door with his fist; the bolt trembled in response to his frenetic pounding. Inside, an impassive silence. He thought perhaps the thunder was drowning him out. In a moment of quiet, when he could hear raindrops falling on the skylight, he actually kicked the door hard. It made such a noise it startled him and, in his cowardice, he feared causing a scandal. He called for the maid:

'Mélanie! Mélanie!'

A huge thunderclap broke, reverberating about the sky.

Dâmaso was cold. He felt vaguely frightened, desperate and suspicious.

'There's something odd going on here.' And in the grip of blind rage, he battered the door with his heel. Nothing.

'The whore!' he thought, frantically shaking the door, then kicking it; he could feel beads of sweat forming on his forehead and he flinched every time there was a flash of lightning, and the subsequent boom of thunder shook his body.

Then, losing all self-control, he hurled himself against the door, kicking with his heels. Suddenly, on the second floor, a door opened and a person yelled:

'Who's that making that row upstairs?'

Terrified, Dâmaso replied:

'I was just knocking at the door.'

'But why, sir?' roared the harsh voice. 'A lady lives there alone. What do you mean by hammering on someone's door at this time of night, in a respectable building?'

Rage gave Dâmaso courage:

'And what's it got to do with you?'

'What's it got to do with me?' bellowed the voice. 'I'll show you what it's got to do with me with my stick.'

And the man went back into his apartment, still bellowing.

Dâmaso had a real horror of scandal and violence and so, grabbing the bannister, he raced down the stairs, pursued only by the brilliant lightning.

Out in the street, he looked up at the windows. The whole house was closed, dark and silent.

Rain was falling in torrents now. Dâmaso had no umbrella. His patent leather shoes splashed through the puddles. He had

271

a fierce desire to throw stones at the windows, but he feared the police, the inevitable uproar, the man with the walking stick.

'Whore!' he snarled, prowling absurdly round the house in the darkness, not knowing what else to do.

In the limpid, blazing clarity of the occasional lightning flash, he would see the house, the stains on the façade, the window frames, the wrought-iron balcony railings, even the white shutters behind the window panes, the lace curtains half drawn. The yellow light would become tinged with red, followed by an intense glow that lit up everything as if with white fire . . . then the thick darkness would close in again, and through it rumbled the thunder.

'The whore!'

He started running through the drenching rain as far as the Largo de Camões – not a single carriage to be had. Furious, half-mad with rage, he walked to Rua de São Francisco; the Writers' Guild was closed; 'Everything's conspiring against me!' he muttered wildly.

He went down to the Rossio. Not a cab in sight. The rain was torrential now; the water hissed on the paving stones and the lights from the streetlamps could be seen through a thick mist of luminous, watery threads. He was almost crying. He set off towards his house on foot; his silk socks were sodden; the brim of his satin top hat had become distorted in the rain and was funnelling water down his neck; he was panting, weary and sweating despite the cold, his fury reaching ever murkier depths as he crossed the market place; he could feel his trousers wet against his shins. Choking on tears, cursing Genoveva, calling her the most obscene names possible, imagining his revenge, in a state of near hysteria, he arrived at his house, where he had to bang on his own front door for half an hour. When the servant, woken from sleep, came to open the door, Dâmaso ran up the stairs, hurling out further curses and obscenities.

XII

The following day, at eleven o'clock, Dâmaso went to Genoveva's house. The bell had recovered its voice, but Mélanie said through the grille that her mistress was still in her room.

'Why the devil didn't you open the door last night. I was banging for nearly an hour!'

Mélanie shrugged and opened her eyes very wide. All she had heard was the thunder.

'Open the door.'

'Madam doesn't receive visitors before three o'clock,' she said and closed the grille.

Dâmaso controlled his anger and flounced down the stairs, thinking: 'There's something odd going on here!'

He returned at three o'clock. He was profoundly worried; he could sense some treachery against him. He was deeply in love with Genoveva, and, apart from that, the money he had given her and the expense he had incurred installing her in the apartment made her still more precious to him. His vanity trembled at the thought of losing her, of being supplanted; he was filled by an emotion stronger than any he had felt in the whole of his bourgeois life and he was terrified.

Mélanie opened the door to him and said:

'Madam has gone out and left you this note.'

He read it while still in the corridor and stood, transfixed.

I could not receive you yesterday for the simple reason that I was not alone. In the light of this confession, our relationship is, I take it, at an end. I thank you for all your kindnesses to me and I remain your friend. An overcoat of yours and some handkerchiefs will be returned to you immediately. I hope you will have the delicacy not to insist on seeing me again. That would only cause unpleasantness.

273

Mechanically, Dâmaso walked into the salon with the piece of paper in his hand; not a single word, idea or decision came into his head.

Mélanie waited with eyes cast down, her hands in her apron pockets. Dâmaso, looking very pale, took a few steps about the room, re-read the note, convulsively ran his fingers through his hair and, dropping on to the sofa, said:

'This could only happen to me!' Then turning on Mélanie: 'Who was here with her? Who was the scoundrel?'

Mélanie shrugged; she didn't know anything; she had been busy working and had seen no one.

Dâmaso gave her a rancorous look; he hated her faded, corrupt little face, her narrow waist, her laced slipper, the way she stood with one foot forward.

'You're no better than she is, the filthy whore!'

Mélanie said she was not prepared to hear him call her mistress names; he was not in his own home; she would not allow . . .

'When I gave you money, there were no complaints then!' roared Dâmaso, whey-faced. 'And when I gave her a few hundred *mil réis* . . . the thief! God, I've been a fool! I'd like to smash all this to pieces.' And he looked round at the mirrors and the drapes.

Mélanie giggled.

'You'd only have to pay for it all again.'

Dâmaso glared at her, but Mélanie's bold, imperturbable eye, her scornful laughter, frightened him. If he hadn't been afraid of the police, of scandal, he would have beaten her. He picked up his hat.

'You haven't seen the end of this. I'll be back!'

'Madam only receives . . .'

'Oh, to hell with your thief of a mistress!' But at the door, he stopped, mad with curiosity. 'Listen, Mélanie, I'll give you two *libras*, if you tell me who she was with.' And he took the money out. 'Here you are.'

She held out her hand, slipped them into her apron pocket, patted them to make them jingle, and said in a low voice:

'It's no secret. It was Senhor Vítor.'

274

'The scoundrel!'

And he went down the stairs, trembling with rage.

At five o'clock, he returned. Mélanie said that her mistress was in, but was not receiving guests. And she shut the door.

In a frenzy, Dâmaso desperately jangled the bell. Mélanie returned, looking annoyed, to tell him that her mistress would call the police if he continued to make so much noise.

'Thief!' bawled Dâmaso when Mélanie slammed the door in his face.

Thrown out! Threatened with the police! And to think he had spent more than twelve *contos de réis* on her! Only the evening before, he had given her three *contos'* worth of bonds. And he had furnished the entire apartment! The thief!

Panting and sweating, he crossed the Largo do Quintela; his little brain was boiling; he was planning to expose her in the newspapers; he would arrange for someone to beat up Vítor. He felt an intense, mean, complex hatred for them both, mingled with the despair of passion betrayed, the anger of the rejected, humiliated lover, the fury of the despoiled capitalist. She was a thief! Surely there were laws against it! There must be!

He spent the day and part of the night pacing his room, cursing, uttering obscenities and thumping his fist down on tables.

He wanted to write her a letter, but could not find the words. He did not dare tell anyone of his defeat. He feared the ironic smiles, the humiliating consolations. How demeaning! He had been deceived, mocked and scorned; they had treated him as if he were a sack of money, and once they had removed all the money, they had tossed the sack in with the dirty laundry. They had done that to him, Dâmaso! This bout of grotesque despair was immediately followed by a deep sleep, and, the following morning, he went straight to see his lawyer, Torres.

The old rogue listened to his tale and, taking a pinch of snuff, said:

'There's nothing you can do. That's what happens when

you get involved with French women. It's hopeless, I'm afraid. Something much worse happened to me, much worse!'

And he gave a detailed account of his affair with a bareback rider from the old Salitre circus. An utterly heartless woman!

'I'm sorry, but there's nothing I can do.'

Dâmaso walked up the Chiado, trembling with rage. 'What will happen when word gets out? To think of those twelve *contos* just wasted. Oh, this could only happen to me!'

His vanity provided a different explanation: perhaps it was jealousy. Perhaps someone had plotted against him and told Genoveva he had another lover. He immediately wrote her a letter in which he said that he realised this was the only possible explanation for her ending their relationship; he swore that he had been faithful to her, that 'never, never . . .' and he gave a long list of proofs of his fidelity, he spoke of the hours they had spent together, of his personal honour, and, in his sprawling hand, added a whole string of further ineptitudes.

He told the errand boy to wait for a reply. Dâmaso sat on a bench in the Casa Havanesa, nervously smoking a cigar.

Carvalhosa came in and joined him.

'So, how's that woman of yours?'

'Fine,' said Dâmaso, turning scarlet.

'Does the honeymoon continue?'

'Of course!' said Dâmaso, trying to look smug.

The errand boy returned, bent beneath the weight of his sack, a letter in his hand. Dâmaso could not believe it; she had returned his letter; on the back, in pencil, was written:

> Your letter made me laugh so much I was nearly sick. No, my dear friend, no one went to the trouble of plotting against you; I have simply decided not to bore myself with your presence any longer. I would be grateful if you would not bother me with any further correspondence of any kind.

'Is that your beloved summoning you?' asked Carvalhosa, who was buying cigars at the counter.

'Yes, I've got to go and see her now,' spluttered Dâmaso.

'Well, enjoy yourself, Romeo!' cried Carvalhosa, swaggering out of the shop.

Dâmaso went to the door to get some air. Everything seemed as if wrapped in a mist and the noises from the street came to him like a distant hum. He was searching urgently for some means of revenge; he didn't care how base it was; he could set fire to the house or report her to the police; he thought of vengeful acts committed in more violent times by jilted lovers; he could organise an ambush and arrange for her to be violated by lackeys or pimps. These thoughts brought with them fears of the police, of being beaten up himself, and, being a coward, he quickly recoiled from the idea of revenge.

Suddenly, a shudder ran through him. Vítor had just walked into the Casa Havanesa. When he saw Dâmaso, he hesitated and turned pale, but, with sudden resolve, he bowed and said simply:

'Hello.'

'I don't speak to scoundrels,' said Dâmaso in a loud, uncertain voice, shaking his head and raising himself up on the tips of his toes.

Vítor raised his walking stick, and Dâmaso instinctively flinched. A large man, who was lighting a cigarette, rushed towards them, grabbed Vítor and said:

'Now, now gentlemen, be sensible! Believe me, I know what I'm talking about.'

Looking dreadfully pale, Vítor clenched his fists and, his lips curled in a sneer, said:

'I'll be sending you my seconds, you coward,' and with that he left.

Dâmaso was deathly white; the cashiers were staring at him in astonishment; a man in gold-rimmed spectacles, who was licking a stamp, approached him with a look of amazement on his face; and the large man said in professional tones, shaking his head:

'A matter of honour . . .'

'The man's a scoundrel! If he really thinks I'm going to fight a duel, he's very much mistaken. But just let him come near me again and I'll break every bone in his body.'

277

'Now, now!'

Dâmaso was breathing hard and his eyes were red. Two tears rolled down his cheeks; he turned even paler and swayed on his feet.

'Give him a glass of water,' said the large man.

One of the cashiers ran over with some water. They made him drink it.

'Come on, man! You'll feel better soon.'

'Thank you, thank you,' said Dâmaso, reviving. 'I'm not afraid. He just took me by surprise. The scoundrel! He used to be a friend; the number of times I've lent him money. I'll break his bones . . .'

Hearing raised voices, a couple of passers-by stopped to look – a small boy carrying parcels and an army sergeant; seeing these strange, gaping faces, Dâmaso felt suddenly embarrassed and called a carriage. His audience dispersed, laughing.

'It'll be about some woman,' said the well-built chap.

The man who had been licking the stamp said in a reedy voice, his eyes bright with desire:

'Do you think they'll have a duel, then?'

The large man shrugged dismissively:

'A duel? In Lisbon? It'll be a complete farce!'

'You mean, there'll be some sort of conciliation?' said the other man, opening his mouth and licking another stamp, standing on tiptoe, eyes wide.

The robust fellow made an obscene comment on the subject of conciliation and moved off, twirling his cane.

Vítor's first concern was to find seconds. He liked the idea of a duel with Dâmaso; it would be some compensation for all the little humiliations he had suffered; he would acquire an aura of courage which Genoveva would find attractive; it was somewhat indelicate to have supplanted Dâmaso and to have taken advantage of everything he had done for Genoveva, but that would all be wiped clean if he beat him in a duel, like a blemish beneath a powerful light. He would teach that fool a lesson!

278

But who would be his second? Camilo Cerrão couldn't be relied on and Carvalhosa was too theatrical. He tried Marinho; he found him in his dressing gown in his bedroom, rearranging his brushes. When Vítor explained what he wanted, Marinho recoiled, turned pale and exclaimed:

'But I'm an old friend of Dâmaso's. We're close friends.'

He stared at Vítor with horrified eyes and, hurrying over to close the door of his room, said:

'Couldn't we sort something out?' And when Vítor shook his head: 'Let's see, let's see . . . We must be sensible. We don't want a scandal. Your uncle would be terribly upset. Poor Dâmaso. Wouldn't you rather I dealt with it all? Believe me, I know about these matters.'

Vítor, however, seemed immovable.

'But, Vítor, surely you don't want the blood of poor Dâmaso!'

'I want satisfaction: I need two friends to go and see him and get a letter of apology from him. If he won't write one, then we fight.'

Such ferocity amazed Marinho. He looked at Vítor with something akin to terror.

'Good heavens!' he said, rubbing his hands together and wrapping his dressing gown more tightly about him.

And as Vítor was about to leave, he added:

'Look, I'm sorry, my friend, but I can't. I've been a close friend of Dâmaso's for years. I knew his mother – a devout, saintly lady! And now a duel of all things . . .'

As he left Marinho's hotel, Vítor suddenly thought of João da Maia. The very man he needed! He went immediately to the Hotel Central; it was four o'clock in the afternoon, and he found him in bed, smoking, with a jug of lemonade on his bedside table and a novel lying on the floor; he was chatting to a Herculean young man with close-cropped hair and a kindly, rather ingenuous face.

He introduced him to Vítor as his cousin, Gonçalo Cabral.

Normally Gonçalo lived in the provinces; he was the eldest son of a wealthy family and a graduate in law. He always spent part of the winter in Lisbon, which he thought was as corrupt

279

as Babylon and as seductive as Paradise itself. He was, unfortunately, cripplingly shy and found the Lisbon ladies rather too refined. He imagined they were all making fun of him, and in the street, at the theatre or in someone's house, he was always very reserved and suspicious, ever ready to crush with his great peasant fists anyone who made fun of him. He was, however, extremely charitable, the soul of honesty and in his giant's chest beat the heart of a girl. He had one weakness: his ambition was to become famous in Lisbon and his secret desire was to take a Spanish girl back to the provinces with him, because he considered Spanish girls to be the acme of libertine luxury and human beauty.

At first, Vítor hesitated to put his case, but João da Maia said:

'I keep nothing from Gonçalo!'

Vítor made his request. João stubbed out his cigarette, rang the bell violently and, perched on the edge of the bed, said:

'I'll go at once, my friend!'

As he was dressing, he declared himself delighted. It was like a gift from heaven; he had nothing to do and was mortally bored! And who was the other second?

That was precisely what Vítor lacked.

'Gonçalo,' called João da Maia. 'Go and put on a black frock coat, quickly!'

The noble giant was off like a bullet, thrilled at the idea that his name would appear in the newspapers in connection with a duel.

Vítor and João agreed that Dâmaso should be asked to write a grovelling letter of apology; otherwise, he should choose two seconds and be prepared to fight with swords, at Cruz Quebrada, at eight o'clock in the morning, with the first person to draw blood being the winner. Vítor would go to the hotel at six to receive 'that fool Dâmaso's' reply.

'Can you fence?' asked João as Vítor was leaving.

'A bit, though . . .'

'That's all you need. We'll tell Dâmaso that you fence like Petit. *Addio!*'

Vítor left and started walking slowly along the Aterro. He

was going to fight in a duel! The thought of it made him feel proud and virile.

He would, after all, be fighting for her. That struck him as a very noble, almost heroic idea. He was already savouring how he would appear before her after the duel, looking pale and interesting, his arm in a sling. Then he recalled reading of a duel in which, by some fateful accident, two people who had never fenced or fired a gun were both killed. And he saw himself lying on the grass, the blood gushing out of him. That made his heart beat faster, and he was filled by the certainty that life was something very precious. He looked up at the sky, which seemed utterly delightful, as did the city, wrapped in the soft, bright tones of winter. He saw clouds tinged with red near the horizon; again he thought of blood, of the red lips of wounds. Was he afraid? The blood drained from his heart. To steady himself he went into the Taverna Inglesa and drank two glasses of sherry. The wine warmed and restored him and he left the tavern, wishing he was already out in the country-side, in shirtsleeves, wielding a sword, fierce as a lion. It would be in all the newspapers; he would become famous for his bravery; women would look at him, men would fear him. He was almost afraid now that Dâmaso might not agree to fight. And yet, he also felt vaguely envious of the people walking quietly by, who would doubtless not be fighting a duel at eight o'clock in the morning.

At that moment, João da Maia and Gonçalo Cabral were drawing up in a hired carriage at Dâmaso's door. João felt that such a carriage was necessary to achieve 'the effect of normality'. They were shown into a room full of furniture upholstered in green. They sat down with great solemnity. Dâmaso soon appeared, looking pale, red-eyed and alarmed.

As soon as João da Maia had gravely explained the 'object of that regrettable visit', Dâmaso stood up, his lips white.

'So Vítor really intends issuing a challenge? Surely you gentlemen don't think that I . . . that I'll fight? It's positively immoral!'

João da Maia, remaining seated, observed coolly:

'My dear sir, those words constitute an offence both to my friend and to us.'

'Oh, João, João!' said Dâmaso in a voice full of deep sorrow. 'I don't want to offend you or this other gentleman. I apologise and to you too, sir. It's so unfair. You know, I was the one who introduced him to the hussy; I was a good friend to him; I used to invite him to supper, take him about in my coupé, and it was always Vítor this and Vítor that, whatever he wanted. And now he does this to me! To me, a person known in society and respected by everyone! He steals my woman and challenges me to a duel . . .'

He was rambling now, gesturing wildly, his eyes wet with tears.

'I'm sorry,' said João da Maia, 'let's not stray from the matter in hand. Did you or did you not call my friend a scoundrel?'

'And I would again!' shouted Dâmaso, beside himself. 'He is a scoundrel. That woman cost me a fortune! And the number of times I've lent him money too.'

He stood in the middle of the room, folded his arms and raised himself up onto his toes.

'I'm sorry,' said João da Maia roughly, 'but that is quite another matter. Are there unsettled money matters between you? Does he owe you money?'

Dâmaso hesitated, blushed and muttered:

'No, he always paid me back.'

'Well, that's a very serious allegation you were making. And I warn you that I too . . .'

Dâmaso cried out desperately:

'Oh, my friends, I give you my word of honour. I swear,' and he conscientiously placed his hand on his heart, 'you have no better friend than me, João. And I respect this gentleman too, but, devil take it, put yourself in my place!'

João da Maia slowly wiped his forehead with his handkerchief and, speaking in grave tones, said:

'Are you prepared to issue a categorical apology?'

'But for what? What did I do wrong? What the devil did I do? He was the one who threatened me with his walking stick. A man with a moustache in the Casa Havanesa had to restrain him . . .'

'Then fight him,' said Gonçalo, who was bored by all this grotesque verbiage.

Dâmaso opened his eyes wide with terror. Then, resolutely, he said:

'No, I won't fight, I won't! That's all I need. And why, just so that people can make fun of me? And whoever heard of a duel in Lisbon? I don't want to lose my friends. I have family. What would my aunt say? It's not that I'm afraid. I'm ready to face him, tell him to come here.'

The two friends got up.

'Fine. Since you refuse to apologise or to fight, we will have to issue a statement. You may do as you please, my friend,' and João da Maia's voice dropped a note, 'but I warn you that Vítor is resolved to humiliate you in public.'

'Humiliate me?' Dâmaso stared at them like an imbecile. 'Oh, this could only happen to me!' He raised his hands to his head. 'What am I to do then? You're my friend, João, tell me what I should do.'

'We've already told you: write a categorical apology.'

'I'll write anything.'

'Fine, you write it and then we'll see. Do you want to consult anyone else?'

'No,' said Dâmaso, 'I would rather we kept this between you and me. I just want to avoid any scandal. Oh, this could only happen to me!'

He went in search of paper and ink; he went through the wrong door and had to come back; his eyes were wild, he was sweating; he sat down and the pen trembled in his hand; he stared at the paper, terrified.

'I'm sorry, I can't think. You write it, João.'

João smoothed his moustache, strode about the room a little, considered, then went over to the table and said gently:

'This is a very difficult situation, because, since you did actually call Vítor a scoundrel, you're going to have to ask his forgiveness.'

And he stood there, his eyes fixed on Dâmaso.

Dâmaso bleakly scratched his head.

'Ask his forgiveness?' Then he added in a melancholy voice. 'You don't think that will make it seem as if I'm afraid?'

João gave an ambiguous smile:

'You could give some sort of excuse, but what?'

'Yes, what?'

Dâmaso looked anxiously from one to the other.

'Why don't you say you were drunk?' said João. 'What do you think, Gonçalo?'

'Yes, say you were drunk.'

Dâmaso said:

'All right, I'll say I was drunk. But this won't be made public, will it?'

'I'm afraid it will, it'll be in all the newspapers.'

Dâmaso leaped to his feet.

'Do you want to make me a laughing stock? Does the wretch want to discredit me entirely?'

'Well, then, you'll have to fight,' said João with a shrug. 'The injured party chooses to fight with a sword. Your seconds will arrange . . .'

Dâmaso threw his arms in the air and exclaimed:

'This is the work of scoundrels!'

João da Maia grew angry. He picked up his hat and said sternly:

'Fine, we await a visit from your seconds. I should tell you that the word "scoundrel" still constitutes an insult to us too and that, after the duel with Vítor, we will have the honour of challenging you ourselves.'

As they were about to leave, Dâmaso grabbed João's arm, with tears in his eyes.

'Oh, please, my friends, I didn't mean to offend you. I'm sorry! Oh, dear God, you know me, João, you know I could never . . . I'll do anything. You write the statement and I'll sign it.'

He dropped down on the sofa and wept.

João sat calmly writing, occasionally consulting Gonçalo in a low voice. Then he read what he had written to Dâmaso.

'Do you agree?'

'What can I do? If I'm to avoid scandal . . .'

He sat down and signed.

As he accompanied them to the door, he said in a still tearful voice:

'And to think I called that man "my close friend"! Thank you, my friends, thank you!'

The following day, Vítor and Genoveva were having lunch. She was wearing a loose robe of dark blue silk, her hair still slightly dishevelled from the pleasures of the night, and she was looking even more sensual than usual, her graceful neck as white and firm as ever. Her whole person exuded an air of sublime sweetness; a sense of abandoned lassitude lent her movements a languid grace; the happiness of passion satisfied bestowed a new tenderness on her gaze, a new softness and freshness on her splendid flesh. Her body gave off a sweet perfume, and Vítor gazed on her in humble ecstasy. They spoke little; occasionally, they would clasp each other's hands over the table. The loose sleeves of her robe revealed her bare arms, and when they talked, Vítor would cover her arms with kisses and his eyes would fill with desire.

'How do you feel? Are you happy?' he asked.

She sighed and inclined her head to one side:

'I'm so happy it almost frightens me!'

Mélanie came in; she brought the newspaper that Vítor had asked her to buy. He opened it immediately and rapidly scanned it; then, proudly, he said:

'Listen to this. It's Dâmaso's statement:

Senhor Vítor da Silva: Charged by you to ask Senhor Dâmaso to provide some explanation and apology for a word which you judged to be offensive to yourself, I proceeded to the house of the said gentleman who, immediately and spontaneously and in a spirit of conciliation, provided me with the following statement:

To Senhor Vítor da Silva:

Sir,

   I understand that you were offended by a particularly

285

coarse word I addressed to you in the Casa Havanesa. I have great pleasure in declaring that no insult was intended by that word, that, indeed, I was unaware of what words I was using because I was, on that occasion, completely drunk. I sincerely hope you will continue to honour me with your esteemed friendship.

    I remain,
        Yours respectfully,
          Dâmaso de V.

    In view of this categorical apology, we judge our mission to be at an end.
We remain,
Yours respectfully,
Dom João da Maia
Gonçalo Cabral

Genoveva tossed the newspaper to one side.

'I'm surprised anyone is still willing to shake the man's hand,' she said loftily.

'Who, Dâmaso?' said Vítor. 'Why he's greatly respected in society. He's one of society's ornaments our Senhor Dâmaso!'

Genoveva went and sat on Vítor's knee.

'And were you really going to fight him? What if you had been hurt? What if he had marked your lovely face?'

'What do you mean?' He struck a valiant pose. 'Why, if we had fought, I would have cut off his ear and that would have been an end to it!'

She let herself slide down to the floor and knelt before him; she picked up his hands and kissed them.

'Oh, Vítor, my love, I'm so happy I could die!'

Her eyes were filled with a kind of tender ecstasy; she slowly reached out her arms to him with the lascivious submissiveness of an enamoured slave. Then, moments later, she said:

'Let's go and see how the renovations are getting on.'

'Ah, the renovations!'

The 'renovations' were now one of Genoveva's main

distractions; she wanted to enclose the balcony outside one of the living room windows and have flowers in one half and caged birds in the other.

The carpenters had been working on this for days and had now removed the railings from the balcony.

They went into the living room, arm in arm.

'So, Senhor Tomás, how are things progressing?' asked Vítor.

The sturdy old man removed his hat and said:

'It'll be ready in less than two weeks.'

Vítor stepped onto the balcony, stood right on the edge where the railings had been and looked down into the street. Genoveva grabbed his arm.

'Be careful, my love. Without the railings there, you might fall.'

'And it's a fair old drop too,' said the carpenter, laughing.

XIII

A few days later, Vítor met Camilo Cerrão in the Rossio. He did not seem his usual animated self; he looked tired and melancholy and, casting angry glances about him, his face contorted, as if dissatisfied with the city, its inhabitants, the colours, the light and the entire universe, he launched immediately into a litany of complaints.

Things were going badly. He had quarrelled with the people at the theatre and wasn't earning a penny. He blamed it all on constitutionalism and the law of primogeniture. With the great families gone, all the famous collections had gone too. The moneylenders who had taken over from the nobility only bought lithographs. The only client was the State, but the State was a fool. His one hope was a revolution. But it would have to happen tomorrow, because one more week and there would be no bread in the house.

Vítor was shocked: 'That's ridiculous. Have you no money?'

'No, no. But I've been thinking again about that portrait of the foreign lady.'

Vítor promised to talk to Genoveva at once. He was sure, he said, that she was still very keen to have the portrait painted.

They walked round the Rossio a few times. Camilo, soured by life's vicissitudes, described the city as 'horribly dull and bourgeois' and as having 'the inexpressive physiognomy of the modern Portuguese man, the idiotic façade of the Teatro Dona Maria', it was, he said 'the vile tallow candle which had as its wick the immortal Constitution'. Consoled by his own jibes, he declared that he 'was going to rethink the portrait; he now envisaged her dressed all in black, with, as a backdrop, a curtain of brilliant yellow damask'.

'Imagine the impact! Because, we are, after all, trying to attract the attention of the bourgeoisie! And how do we do that? By confronting them with loud colours. So, yellow it is, then!'

Genoveva did, indeed, like the idea. The portrait would be for Vítor to hang in his room, with fresh flowers beneath it, like a votive offering at an altar. But could the artist do the portrait in her room? It was such a bore having to go to a studio every week! Especially if it was on the fourth floor!

Camilo, however, reacted ambiguously to this proposal. What about the light? The light was what mattered. Besides, artists received, they did not procure clients. Art was like religion: it waited for the faithful to come to them, it did not go looking for them. An artist's studio is his temple! He again mentioned Francis I picking up Titian's paintbrushes and declared that, no, he would only work in his studio.

One morning, in order to study the light, to meet Genoveva and to agree on what dress she should wear, Vítor took Camilo to Rua das Flores.

'How's your wife?' he asked him as they went up the stairs.

Camilo shrugged.

'She's turned melancholy and she sighs all the time, yes, sighs! I think she misses her village and the maize bread and the gossip round the fountain. She's fading away in that fourth-floor apartment of ours. She needs green fields, the countryside, cattle; she's like a cow shut up in a room. Like all exiled creatures, she's pining for her natural milieu.'

Vítor said nothing. He was thinking about the woman's splendid 'animal' forms and her yellow cotton gown.

Camilo seemed very impressed by Genoveva. For a moment, he even seemed shy; with his broad-brimmed hat clutched in his hands, his feet crossed under his chair, he had the uncomfortable look of an awestruck plebeian. Genoveva spoke to him kindly of his genius and his work; she mentioned famous painters she had known: Carolus-Duran, Bonnat, Regnault; she talked about exhibitions; she even had something to say about chiaroscuro, and Camilo, like a fish put back in the water, recovered his usual expansive gestures and his facility for discursive speech.

He was soon on his feet, his jacket pushed back, his hair dishevelled, talking with his usual picturesque fluency. He began by criticising the colour of the upholstery and the furnishings in the room: That backdrop of chocolate brown and yellow really wasn't suitable for her type of beauty: a stately blonde with an aquiline profile and majestic forms should be set off by a very severe décor: a rich, sober combination of dark oak and cherry-red candles; a few paintings by Spanish masters, blackened by time, from which the pale, mystical face of a saint shone forth out of the gloom; oh, and a large divan.

Genoveva agreed, but thought that what he was describing was perhaps a décor more suited to a bedroom: 'It would give to love a profound, religious character, a dash of mysticism and sensuality.'

Camilo looked at her, surprised.

She was right, of course; it was an idea worthy of an Italian beauty of the sixteenth century. Yes, he would paint her dressed in black velvet, lying on a divan, *a la Veneziana*, in the style of Titian.

Then they discussed clothes. Camilo wanted to see some of her dresses. Mélanie gradually brought Genoveva's entire wardrobe into the living room; she draped the dresses over the chairs. Camilo rearranged the folds artistically, and this exhibition of silks and velvets and faille gave the room the opulent air of a seamstress's shop; the dresses lay limply over the chairs, sleeves drooping, like dead arms, the bodices flat, flaccid, revealing the padding and the boning; the carpet was awash with sumptuous trains and fabrics; the pale failles set off the fresh brightness of the silks; the velvets revealed their heavy, ceremonious nature in soft, supple pleats; the filigree lace stood out against the more sombre colours; and Camilo, deep in thought, his hand on his chin, his lips pursed, walked amongst the clothes, crumpling some silk here, a velvet train there, studying the different tones, the play of light on folds of fabric, the bluish shadows, the sheen of smooth surfaces.

He was much taken with a dress in dark blue velvet; he would stand before it, thinking, then cast a studious eye over Genoveva.

He combined the meditations of a philosopher and the ceremony of a priest: How the deuce was he going to capture all that on canvas?

Yes, it would have to be the blue dress against a backdrop of dark magenta velvet, with her skin and her blonde hair set off by that severe colour, absorbing the light, monopolizing the viewer's gaze and taking from the grave tonalities of the backdrop (here he made the broad gestures of someone painting) a generally softening, veiling effect from the interposing of harder, smoother planes . . .

'Did you get that?' asked Vítor, smiling at Genoveva.

'It will be a superb work,' said Camilo.

Carried away by his own enthusiasm, he wanted to start the next day, but Genoveva had promised to visit the Baron's German mistress. 'When then?' They agreed that Vítor would go and tell Camilo when they had fixed on a day.

'Meanwhile, I will prepare my paintbrushes.'

Three days later, Vítor was going up the stairs to Camilo's apartment to warn him that Genoveva would come for the first sitting in two days' time.

When he went into the studio, he saw at once that Camilo had begun making preparations; the floor had been washed and the pictures and plaster casts dusted; on a low dais covered with an old green carpet, stood a leather chair with yellow studs, and hanging behind it, as in a photographer's studio, was an old velvet curtain in dark magenta; there was a clean canvas on the easel and on the table, a vase of flowers, a plate of apples and a kind of glass jug full of white wine.

Vítor laughed; he recognised in that arrangement Camilo's desire to imitate Rubens' studio, familiar from the engraving that shows fruit piled high in silver dishes, vases overflowing with flowers and all the accoutrements of aristocratic life.

The door opened at that point and the lovely Joana walked in. As soon as she saw Vítor, the blood rushed to her pale face. She curtseyed and said that Camilo had gone out and would not be back until the evening.

Hearing that Camilo would not be back filled Vítor with a troubling sense of pleasure, though quite why he did not know. Joana was wearing the same dangerous yellow robe, but Vítor noticed that her hair was neater and she had on lace cuffs.

'I came to say that I'll be here the day after tomorrow at one o'clock. You won't forget to tell him, will you?'

'The day after tomorrow, at one o'clock,' she repeated.

She had remained standing, the tips of her fingers resting on the table. She was standing almost in profile to Vítor, who could not take his eyes off her beautiful shoulders, the marvellous curve of her breasts and throat, firm as marble and white as milk. But what troubled him most was the yellow dress that seemed to cling to every curve of her body, and was more provoking than nakedness itself; even the colour seemed strangely arousing.

He struggled for something to say and, looking around, he remarked:

'Has that lazy husband of yours still done nothing new?'

She shrugged.

It was pure ignorance, but Vítor thought he saw in it some intelligent disdain for Camilo's contradictory fantasies.

'And how's your little boy?'

'Very well, thank you,' she replied.

She did not move from the table, but her eyes were fixed on Vítor with all the spontaneous frankness of an animal. That bothered him; he felt a kind of languorous peace taking hold of him. He got up, looked at a grubby, mediocre portrait of a beggar, entitled: *Estremadura: A Victim of Society*.

'This is a lovely head!'

She came over and looked at it and said:

'Hm.'

'Has Camilo never painted you?'

'No, sir.'

And she sat down on the divan; the dressing gown clung to her body as if she had no petticoat on underneath; those clinging folds seemed to reveal a whole marvellous world. Vítor said:

'That's a pity.'

But she got up again, walked over to the window and came back. They were sitting next to each other on the divan now. Vítor thought he could feel a glow coming from her as if from a distant fire; he saw her breast rise and fall, the magnificent roundness of her arms beneath the tight sleeves; he felt like touching them, as if to feel their suppleness. He said again:

'That's a pity.'

'Do you think so?' she said.

And her voice was so warm that Vítor turned to her, trembling slightly. Joana's eyes shone and she leaned bodily forwards in an attitude of surrender and passivity.

Almost instinctively, he placed one hand on her shoulder; she closed her eyes, threw her head back and moaned softly.

Half an hour later, Vítor was going back down the stairs, feeling very annoyed with himself. How ridiculous. It was clearly the act of a scoundrel; Camilo was, after all, his friend. He did not even love that beautiful peasant; it was that yellow dressing gown of hers! The bestial impulse of a moment! And her last words to him: 'I want to live with you' were simply intolerable! Live with her – she was a magnificent creature, yes, but she was stupid and passive . . . a mere female!

He was wondering how he could avoid meeting her when he returned there with Genoveva. Fortunately, she never went into the studio when Camilo was working, and besides, even if she saw Genoveva and were jealous, she was so passive, such a nonentity, that he need fear no recriminations from her, no scenes.

Genoveva, of course, must never know. He had not, after all, done anything so very wrong. He had been stupid and he felt angry with himself, but he still could not think without a tremor of Joana's extraordinary beauty and her profound, silent way of loving.

But what about Camilo? The thought of Camilo terrified him. He would advise Genoveva to pay him sixty rather than forty *libras*. Satisfied that those twenty *libras* made up for his betrayal, he hurried off to see Genoveva, contented with himself and with life.

He was certainly popular with the ladies!

Two days later, Camilo was there to greet them. The plate of apples was still on the table, along with the jug of wine; Camilo, wearing a stained velvet jacket and a sort of scarlet cap, said jovially to Genoveva:

'We're going to make a great work of art and I say "we", because it will be a collaboration between model and artist.'

He immediately had her sit down on the chair on the dais. It was May, but it was a cold, overcast day, with a hint of approaching rain. Genoveva was wearing a loose, dark overcoat edged with fur and carrying a huge muff; against the fur collar her face seemed even whiter and more delicate, giving her an appearance of gentleness and vulnerability to the cold; on her head she wore a hat of dark brown velvet, turned up at the front and decorated with a rose. Suppressing a desire to laugh and shivering slightly in the cold studio, she looked adorable.

Camilo considered painting her exactly as she was, against a yellow background. He pondered, tried out a few sketches on the canvas, then burst out:

'No, no, you'd look much better in the blue dress and with some pearls in your hair. These street dresses are unworthy of appearing in a work of art.'

At that moment, Joana came into the studio, but on seeing Vítor standing next to Genoveva, she opened her large, dark eyes very wide, turned first crimson, then very pale and stood there motionless, her hands trembling. Camilo noticed her and said:

'What is it? What's wrong? I'm working. Off you go.'

She bowed her head slightly and left.

When Genoveva found out that Joana was his wife, she congratulated him: 'She's remarkably beautiful.' Then she glanced at Vítor, who was leaning on the windowsill, trying to conceal his blushes.

On that first day, Camilo worked on her hands and, as he worked, he discoursed at length about art. Lately, he had felt a great desire to devote himself to religious art. For what is the root cause of the decadence of modern society? The lack of spirituality. And what better way to raise souls up from

294

their baseness and distract them from their prosaic lives than to paint the great figures and characters of the saints and martyrs? He felt, however, that he lacked sufficient faith. In order to paint St Sebastian you had to believe in him. He didn't. In order to paint holy pictures one had to be a saint oneself. And then, he said, he envied the withdrawn lives of ascetic artists such as Fra Bartolomeo and Fra Angelico who, in the seraphic peace of the cloister, possessed by divine love, had had such a clear vision of heaven that they could paint a person's soul as easily as someone nowadays might paint a tree . . .

He stepped back from his easel, looked at the canvas and grew angry. There was nothing more ridiculous or more dangerous than trying to paint the modern, whilst thinking of the ancient. One instinctively began to draw like some ghastly ascetic!

'Let's talk about the Renaissance instead, about the Borgias, about lascivious prelates, about Catholic pomp and artistic deeds . . .'

And he talked on and on about Renaissance artists, until Genoveva finally declared that she was tired.

And Camilo, still caught up in thoughts of Renaissance artists and their kingly ways, offered Genoveva the apples and the wine, as if he were Titian offering pomegranates from Tivoli and a glass of lachryma Christi.

On their way home in the carriage, Genoveva kept asking Vítor about the beautiful creature who had come into the studio. Did he know her? Where was she from? Had he seen much of her before?

Vítor replied reluctantly and as if distracted.

Did he often go to Camilo's house? Did she have children?

'Why so many questions?' he asked, laughing.

'I don't like you to have such acquaintances.'

'Don't tell me you're jealous of a woman like that.'

'Some men like such women.'

'Not me, not with my artistic tastes, my delicate sensibility . . .'

Genoveva giggled.

'And that extraordinary yellow thing she was wearing,' she said. 'She's certainly got a good figure.'

'Hm,' said Vítor.

'Hm what?'

'Well, yes, she's all right.'

Genoveva fell silent, casting him angry sideways glances.

'It really is a terrible bore having to go all the way up to the fourth floor,' she said.

Dâmaso had sensed that the published statement did not perhaps show him in a very honourable light, but it was only when he actually saw it in print that he felt the full impact. That same day, a relative of his came to see him, Senhor Casimiro Valadares; he was a serious man with bushy eyebrows, of whom people said: 'Valadares is not a man to be trifled with.' Fifteen years before, he had fought a duel with a Spanish emigré, during which he had received a small cut to his finger and, ever since then, he had considered himself and was considered by others to be an authority on matters of honour between gentlemen. Now, he swept into Dâmaso's room, flung a copy of the *Diario Popular* down on the table and said:

'That is the most shameful thing I have ever read!'

Dâmaso turned scarlet and babbled on about how he had wanted to avoid a scandal, that he was really the injured party, that Vítor was a close friend of his, that it wasn't proper to fight over a prostitute, that it wasn't that he was afraid, he was ready to fight with whatever came to hand, knives, fists if necessary.

'Words, words, words,' said Senhor Casimiro. 'What Silva's seconds persuaded you to do is downright shameful and, in my opinion, you should fight João da Maia and that other fellow, Gonçalo . . . what was it, Gonçalo something or other . . . ah, yes, Gonçalo Cabral. You should send them your seconds now. If you had been advised by me, things would have turned out very differently; Vítor would have been the one called on to give satisfaction. But, in my opinion, this is positively indecent.'

Dâmaso protested that they had been most helpful to him and had got him out of a mess and, besides, he still intended to fight Vítor man to man.

He was about to expand on this, when Valadares stopped him with these words:

'If I were you, I would, for decency's sake, go and spend a few months abroad.'

Dâmaso was horrorstruck. But why? Was what he had done so discreditable?

'You have, in my opinion, declared yourself to be a coward and a drunkard.'

Dâmaso then heaped blame on João da Maia. He had no experience of such matters; he had simply done what João da Maia had told him to do; he had trusted him; João da Maia had even sworn that it wouldn't be published.

'Then, in my opinion, you should challenge João. Would you like me to go and see him?'

Dâmaso was adamant. He had suffered enough. He was fed up with complications. He hadn't slept for two nights.

So Valadares left, saying wearily:

'In my opinion, you might as well carry a distaff on your belt.'

Dâmaso began to wonder if people really would cut him in the street.

For a few days he only went out in the coupé, keeping well out of sight, and he avoided the theatre; then, one night, he risked going to the Writers' Guild, walking quickly from room to room. He received two very friendly cries of: 'Hello there, Dâmaso!'

Encouraged, he appeared later on at the Casa Havanesa; he was received, as always, with the usual warm handshakes that his wealth merited. He went to the Teatro de São Carlos and when he visited various boxes, the ladies were their usual amiable, smiling selves. He thought: 'Either no one read it, or else they find it all quite normal.' He considered Valadares antiquated and belligerent. And one night at the Writers' Guild he spoke angrily of Genoveva and Vítor. As far as he could see, that shameless lout Vítor was living off the whore;

297

he himself had grown tired of her, he declared. Only a few days before he had told her to find someone else; he had better things to do; and she hadn't cost him a sou; besides, she was all show; without her clothes on she was nothing; that fool Vítor was quite likely to end up marrying her; she was just after his uncle's eighty *contos*.

The generally held view (each man believing in his own vanity) was that there was no such thing as disinterested love.

Around this time, a small newspaper was being published in Lisbon entitled *The Devil's Trumpet*. Editor and newspaper bore a close physical resemblance; the man's physiognomy and the paper used for the gazette were both equally cheap and vulgar; the paragraphs were as wretchedly irregular as the editor's habits; and the typeface used was, like the man himself, small and paltry.

The aim of the newspaper was quite simply to earn enough money to buy the editor a few litres of wine, a few rounds with 'knaves' and 'queens' and the occasional visit to a prostitute. Otherwise, he did not need money. He had a little swindle worked out. The method was simple: he either extorted money from people by threatening to publish defamatory articles about them or else took money from cowards who wanted to publish calumnies about other people; the 'injured party' brought him the article and gave him a fee; the editor punctuated the article and pocketed the fee. He shook off any consequent beatings like a dog shaking off water, and to restore himself, he would drink two litres of wine rather than one; his response to the forgiveness or indifference of those he libelled was always the same, he would puff out his chest, push back his hair and declare at the card table or in the bordello: 'He was afraid of me! Just let me at him!'

He carried out his profession in a third-floor apartment in an alleyway in the Bairro Alto, furnished with a bed and a table; in the filthy bed, the editor drank his wine and sweated through the fevers of a second-degree tubercular infection; at the table, he composed his articles, and spat on the floor; he lived a wretched life amongst all that squalor, in constant fear that the police might come for him.

One morning, Vítor received an issue of *The Devil's Trumpet* through the post; a paragraph in a section entitled 'The Trumpeter' was marked with ink. Vítor read it:

'So, Senhor Vítor, you've left the office of the illustrious Dr C. Do you no longer need to exploit widows and orphans? This question was put to a certain Vítor, Vítor the Fair, in the Chiado. One Pai Paulino, who just happened to be passing, heard the following trumpet blast: Senhor Vítor, it seems, has found better paid employment and, instead of exploiting widows, he's now exploiting foreign ladies. And meanwhile his Dulcinea exploits a certain cloth merchant. If this is true, Senhor Vítor, the Devil has his trumpet ready to trumpet to the world your many lucrative conquests!

Vítor finished reading the paragraph with tears of rage in his eyes. His first thought was to go and give Dâmaso a good thrashing, because he was convinced he was behind this; he recognised Alípio's style, but the revenge was Dâmaso's. Doing so, however, would only cause a scandal; he didn't want to attract more publicity. The Devil's words, which otherwise only very few people would have read, would come to the notice of many. A lot of people would say: 'How disgraceful!' But others would say: 'He obviously touched a nerve!' because calumnies are like certain oily stains, they always leave a mark when you try to remove them.

With luck, Genoveva would not have read it, and even if she had, she would laugh. But what about Uncle Timóteo? He quaked at the thought that someone might have sent him a copy of the newspaper. He went down to the dining room, his heart quivering. There, folded up on top of the sideboard, was a copy of *The Devil's Trumpet*.

Uncle Timóteo was sitting in his armchair, waiting for supper, with *The Times* draped over his knee.

Vítor saw at once that he should be the first to broach the

subject and so, in an indifferent tone, as if giving the matter no importance, he said:

'Oh, so they sent you a copy of that rag too, did they?'

Uncle Timóteo nodded. His silence somewhat shook Vítor's confidence, and with a forced laugh, he said:

'It's just Dâmaso getting his revenge . . .'

Uncle Timóteo carefully folded up his *Times*. Feeling uncomfortable now, Vítor walked round the table.

'Not that I care of course! After all, who pays any attention to what *The Devil's Trumpet* has to say about anything? Luckily, people know me and . . .'

Uncle Timóteo got up and stared at Vítor. He looked worried; he blinked, as if embarrassed, cleared his throat and said:

'Tell Clorinda to bring the supper in.'

He sat down, unfolded his napkin and spoke about the likelihood of war in the Far East. '*The Times* has got a long article about it . . . but England's policy has, up until now, been so selfish, so head-in-the-sand and, yes, cowardly. Everyone thinks so. Both Lord Beaconsfield and the Queen know that the general view of it is just that: cowardly!'

Vítor was so delighted to see that his uncle's concerns were so remote, far beyond the Danube and the Dardanelles, that he encouraged him and carried him even farther off, to the Americas and to India, occasionally dropping a few vague words into the conversation, like logs on a fire, so as not to let it go out. He declared himself angry with the Turks. 'Utter madness. I've thought about it a lot,' just to give the impression he was interested in generalities, 'and frankly Turkey is finished.'

'And then there's Russia.'

And Uncle Timóteo duly laid into Russia, the Czar, the partition of Poland, the exiles in Siberia and the enslavement of the workers. He even translated an article from *The Times* for Vítor, thumped the table and spoke at length on the subject.

'Either he hasn't read *The Devil's Trumpet* or I've driven it out of his mind,' thought Vítor.

And after coffee, he was about to leave the table, when Uncle Timóteo, who was filling his pipe, said in a slow, grave voice:

'I read that "rag" as you call it.'

Vítor sat down again, blushing.

'I read it,' went on Uncle Timóteo, 'and I'm sure it's untrue because I cannot believe that a member of my family could ever live off a woman.'

'Uncle Timóteo!' said Vítor, looking suitably shocked.

'I don't believe it, of course, but I still don't like the fact that you're ruining yourself for her sake.'

'What do you mean 'ruining myself'?' said Vítor angrily.

'Sit down. I'm talking quietly, so listen to me quietly. By "ruining yourself" I don't mean financially, because you haven't got any money of your own.'

He lit his pipe and puffed on it calmly, pressing in the tobacco with his finger.

Vítor kept his eyes fixed on him.

'As I say, you haven't got any money of your own, but a man is not made of money alone. There are other things that can be ruined: one's health, one's reputation, one's intelligence, one's character, one's profession . . .'

'But . . .,' began Vítor.

'Sh!' Uncle Timóteo closed his eyes and raised his hand. 'My friend I call "ruining yourself" abandoning your friends, your career, your office, your ambitions, your plans, in order to live tied to a woman's skirts like some kind of paid companion.'

'Uncle Timóteo, let me . . .'

'Be patient. I am of the opinion, and I've said so many times, that a man should have a lover; for any young man of twenty to be neither married nor have a lover is simply unhealthy.' He had spoken quietly, but suddenly rousing himself, he banged on the table with his fist. 'But it's one thing to have a lover and to visit her occasionally, or even every day, every hour or every moment, if that gives both parties pleasure, but it's quite another matter to send everything to the devil, family, home, profession, career, and to spend every

301

hour of every day and night clinging to the woman like a leech! It's not decent.'

'But . . .'

'You have breakfast there, spend the morning there, occasionally do me the honour of dining here with me, only to go back and spend the night there; you go for walks with her, go to the theatre with her; you have no other thought or idea or aim in life! Now I find that pathetic. A man who is sound in brain and limb really should have something better to do than live tied to a woman's skirts. I'm not telling you off. I've never done that. I'm simply telling you the truth. Think about it. If you decide that your one talent lies in cooling a woman's ardour, then fine, but if you've got any intelligence and strength in those arms, use them to do something else! Am I right?'

'Yes, Uncle, you're absolutely right,' spluttered Vítor, his face crimson.

'Right, end of conversation.'

He got up and went and sat in his armchair with his *Times*.

Vítor did not move from his chair, his face still ablaze; he kept nervously twisting his moustache and knocking the ash off his cigarette on the edge of his saucer.

Vítor told Genoveva about the conversation with Uncle Timóteo.

'Tell the old fool to go the devil!' she exclaimed. Then, as if repentant, she put her arms around his neck and said: 'I'm sorry, I shouldn't speak like that about our dear Uncle Timóteo. I rather like him. But what does he expect you to do? A man like you wasn't born to vegetate in a lawyer's office. What do I care, anyway? Your obligation, your occupation, your principle of life is to love me. Isn't that so?'

There was such passion in her eyes, her face was so sweet and pale, her body weighed in his arms with such amorous abandon, that Vítor could only murmur:

'Yes, of course.'

'Tell him to go to the devil, then!'

She made the gesture of someone insolently closing a

particularly dull file of papers. The following day, at lunch, however, she spoke more seriously. She did not in any way want Uncle Timóteo to take against her, to imagine she was perverting his little boy; Vítor could do as he pleased; he could go to the office every day from one to three; his return would then be all the sweeter; a man really should have some occupation and being a lawyer did seem rather nice really: speaking at a trial, defending political causes or crimes of passion; and he would look very handsome in a robe, and she loved to hear him speak.

'Can you arrange it so that you defend a murderer and I can come and watch?'

On another day, she seemed even more enthusiastic about the law as a profession. How wonderful to save a man trembling with fear, to save him from death or exile! And the law was also a way into politics; he could be a deputy, an orator, and how proud she would be to see him at those tumultuous parliamentary sessions, standing on the tribune boldly addressing a frightened, astonished minister!

Vítor began to think she was right. Now that she found it interesting, the life of the lawyer seemed less bourgeois to him, less monotonous; he even began to find in it a certain hidden poetry. He began going to the office again, but when the more exciting elements of the law did not immediately show themselves, when he was not given a murderer to save or a crime of passion to defend, he soon wearied of papers and consultations with clients. He would begin to yawn and to feel sad and sleepy. Then he would pick up his hat and rush off to Rua das Flores, where he would find Genoveva getting dressed or reading or smoking a cigarette.

She would tell him off at first: he shouldn't leave the office, he must work; but he would swear that thoughts of her prevented him from working, that he could not bear to spend a moment away from her . . . And then, pleased, she would give him a kiss.

'All right then!'

One day, she said:

'Don't go to the office any more. I have another plan.'

And when he questioned her, she responded with laughs and kisses and a kind of affectionate circumspection: She was madly in love with a poor young man and she was not rich herself, but she could never take another lover, she would rather live in a garret, or take in sewing or beg on street corners.

This was Genoveva's plan: her debts were paid, she had a capital of twenty *contos* at six per cent interest; if she sold her jewels and the carriage and the furniture she had in Paris, that would bring in between four and five *contos de réis*. That gave an income of one thousand five hundred, sufficient for two people to live on. They would go to France and rent a charming little house on the outskirts of Paris, on the banks of the Seine, with a bit of lawn and a few old trees; they would travel about Paris on the omnibus and live the delicious, cheerful life of two students in love. She had already written to Paris ordering everything to be sold; and so as not to eat into the capital she had in Lisbon, she would cut back on certain expenditures.

They were together in the living room one night after supper. Vítor was lying on the sofa, smoking a cigarette. Genoveva was sitting at the piano playing the score of *La Petite mariée* and occasionally singing some of the words. Vítor thought her utterly delicious; the music made him feel bold and amorous; he watched her fine profile silhouetted against the light and the camellia-white firmness of her neck caught in the glow of the candles; as he sipped his cognac, he felt happy, and life seemed to offer itself to him like a bright selection of coloured sweets.

'Did I tell you I've got rid of the carriage?' she said suddenly.

And when Vítor asked why, she said:

'Because I'm not rich, my child, and I need to economize.'

Vítor blushed. He knew she was giving up her luxuries for him and he hated being unable to provide her with them himself. Genoveva joined him on the sofa and, lost in thought, she too began to smoke a cigarette. Then she said:

'I have to economize in order to carry out my plan.'

Vítor moved closer to her and, slowly stroking her hand, he asked her what the plan was; all she ever talked about was 'her plan'. What was it? Was she going to declare herself Queen of Iberia?

She was silent for a moment, blowing out a cloud of white cigarette smoke; then she got to her feet, played a few bright tunes on the piano, turned brusquely and came and knelt down before him.

'We're going away!'

Seeing the surprise on his face, she told him about her idea of leaving Lisbon and finding a house near Paris; they would live meagrely, like two students; they would live the selfish life of the young.

'But what about poor Uncle Timóteo?'

'What about him?

Vítor began pacing about the room; he explained that he really couldn't leave Uncle Timóteo; he owed him everything; his uncle had brought him up; he was heir to his uncle's fortune; the poor man had no other family but him; he was old now, and it seemed ungrateful simply to abandon him.

'Well, don't leave him then; you stay and enjoy yourself with him, sleep with him if you must!' exclaimed Genoveva.

Vítor thought that outburst cruel and egotistical, but, fearful of displeasing her and seeing in her anger merely the passion of love, he said almost pleadingly:

'But, my love . . .'

She firmly folded her arms.

'Here am I ready to make all kinds of sacrifices, to abandon my house, my habits, my friends, and go and bury myself like a retired shopkeeper in some horrible cottage in the country all year, and you won't even give up your Uncle Timóteo.'

She paused and looked at him hard. Vítor was sitting with his elbows on his knees, staring at the floor, his head bowed in the presence of her greater verbal power.

'If he were a woman,' she went on, 'if he were your mother or your sister, who depended on you, then I could understand it; if he were a poor old cripple, fine! But a man in the prime of life, with plenty of money, with whom you spend, at most, half an hour a day . . . in what sense is your company necessary to him? What would he lose with your departure?'

Her reasons, the warmth with which she spoke, and the power of her beauty were beginning to convince him. He said in timid, adoring tones:

'But couldn't we live like that in Lisbon?'

That was impossible. Lisbon was so monotonous, so dull, that the only way one could make up for having to live there was by living a life of luxury, having a fine chef, a lot of servants, sumptuous décor, lavish meals, a carriage and horses, etc. etc. Only in Paris could one live happily on little money, she said.

Vítor saw there was some truth in that. He even imagined the temptations of a happy existence in Paris with her – visiting museums, seeing celebrities, having a box at the theatre, enjoying intimate suppers in restaurants and a bohemian life of love, but he said nothing, he merely sat twisting his moustache and blowing out the smoke from his cigar.

'Well, say something,' she said.

He sighed and frowned as if struggling with a difficult decision.

'But, my love, I don't have enough money to go to Paris.'

She was about to speak, but he stopped her:

'I know what you're going to say, that you have money, but Genoveva, I can't live off you!'

There was a brief silence. Genoveva was now walking about the room, leaving behind her a rustle of silk.

'I had no idea you were so proud,' she said, rearranging some books on the table, not looking at him.

He went over to her and put his arm about her shoulder.

'It isn't pride, it's a matter of decency. Do you really think it right that I should live off you?'

She looked at him with her lovely, luminous eyes.

'But when a poor man marries a rich woman, isn't he living off her?'

'Ah, but they're married.'

They both fell silent, the same thought doubtless buzzing

306

inside them. Genoveva went over to the piano, impatiently leafed through the music, played a few chords, then sang:

> The nightingale was singing
> So tenderly . . .

Turning back to him, she said:

'And this is not a serious relationship, is that what you mean?'

He went to the piano.

'It is serious, Genoveva, but I can't . . . What would people say? Everyone knows I live off a monthly allowance from my Uncle Timóteo. How could I possibly afford to go to Paris? It would be shameful . . . My dignity . . .'

'Don't talk to me about your dignity!' she exclaimed angrily, getting to her feet. 'Goodnight!'

'Genoveva!'

'What? I said "Goodnight". As long as your dignity does not allow you to love me, to sacrifice yourself for me, to devote yourself to being with me, to living with me, then we had better say goodbye. We'll just shake hands and forget all about it. Goodnight!'

She held out her hand. Vítor, who had turned very pale, stared at her hand.

'You don't think I'm serious, do you?' she said. 'Well, you clearly don't know me very well.'

She stalked out of the room. Vítor heard her call Mélanie and then the sound of her bedroom door slamming.

Vítor did not know what to do. It did not even occur to him to break off their relationship, but could he really accept the subaltern position of going to Paris with a woman who would buy his train tickets, his supper at the station, any books he might need, even his cigarettes? Uncle Timóteo might quite understandably cut off his monthly allowance if he went to Paris with Genoveva. And even if, out of sentiment and generosity, he did not, what would ten *libras* buy in Paris? All he could do there was accumulate debts!

Did he trust her? What if she fell out of love with him one

day, or took a fancy to someone else? Could he continue to live off a woman who betrayed him? He would have to return to Portugal – to what? Utter dishonour. No one would want to shake his hand; he would always be Vítor, the kept man of 'Dâmaso's mistress'. These reasons fell upon his resolve like hammer blows, nailing it in place.

One thing consoled him: the knowledge that Genoveva loved him and that, once she had got over her resentment at having her idea turned down, she would resign herself to living in Lisbon or postponing her departure indefinitely.

He drank another glass of cognac and then went to her room. The door was locked from inside; he knocked, he called: Genoveva!

Mélanie ran into the corridor, clearly embarrassed and carrying his overcoat and hat.

'Madam says she is unwell and that she will write to you tomorrow.'

She held out his coat to him.

'Is this some kind of joke?' he said.

'Madam is very angry. She's locked herself in her room and gone to bed.'

She offered him his hat. Vítor ran to the door and pounded on it, saying:

'Genoveva, are you mad?'

The impassive silence made him even angrier; he pushed against the door and rattled the handle. Mélanie, looking very pale, tried to pull him away. What was he doing? Please, don't make such a noise. Her mistress was very upset!

'Genoveva!' roared Vítor, furiously shaking the door.

He did not have to wait long. The door suddenly opened, and he almost sprang back. Before him stood Genoveva. She was wearing a long petticoat and a silk chemise cut very low, half undone, revealing her neck, her shoulders, her breasts; her golden hair, pushed back, lent her beauty a remote, voluptuous air; the candles were lit on the dressing table; the unmade bed drew him ineluctably on. Vítor rushed towards her, but Genoveva, who still had the key in her hand, said very clearly:

'I swear that you will not set foot in this room until you say that you will come to Paris with me.'

And she fixed him with piercing, ardent eyes, and then in a low voice, urgent with desire, said:

'Will you come?'

'I swear I will,' he said.

She uttered a proud sigh, and Vítor fell into her arms.

XIV

The next day, their departure for Paris was fixed; they would leave in September, and they would travel overland, spending two weeks in Madrid and possibly a few days in the Pyrenees. Genoveva laughed eagerly and excitedly to think of the pleasures of that journey. Vítor was no less enchanted with the idea; Genoveva's kisses and embraces had dissolved what remained of his character and will. He felt like soft wax when he was with her, incapable of resisting her. A single word could reduce him to a state of despicable weakness, and certain kisses seemed to suck up his very soul, enfolding him in such ardent pleasure that he would, if she had asked him, have become a thief; Genoveva's zealous, egotistical love had extinguished in him everything that did not satisfy or serve that love; it had extinguished his will, his dignity, his desire to work and all thought for the future; it had preserved in him only furious desire and one talent, a talent for writing verse. His sole occupations were to love her and to write lyric poetry. All that remained of him was rhyme, metre and his poetic temperament. The idea of the journey corresponded to his deepest desires, it was an idea he had always nurtured: the classic dream of the sentimental, to go on a journey with the woman one loved, and now he was about to see that dream fulfilled. How could he even think of resisting? Besides, it was childish to worry about money; if they loved each other, then what was hers was his; love should be prepared to sacrifice everything, and since love was of a divine nature, why would it not have the same validating effects as marriage, given that marriage was merely an administrative affair? And if his conscience could live with it, why should he care what others thought? Who were those others anyway? Dâmasos and Marinhos and Carvalhosas. He, after all, was a man of pure ideals, the bourgeois laws governing trivial morality were not made for him.

And as for Uncle Timóteo . . . That thought made him feel uncomfortable; he did not dare to tell him he was leaving with Genoveva; he respected and feared him and, being of a naturally loving disposition, he had grown fond of the good old man during the many years he had lived with him. What should he do? His effeminate nature immediately suggested this feminine idea: he would pack his bags in secret, run away and leave his uncle a letter.

With all difficulties smoothed away, he abandoned himself to the delightful prospect of that great romantic adventure; but there were still things to be bought, shirts, a velvet smoking jacket, patent leather shoes, a new tailcoat . . . because in their new life such things would be as essential as his uniform is to a soldier.

Meanwhile, he noticed that Genoveva seemed, at times, preoccupied; he would look up and find her staring at him, as if studying him, as if about to say something very serious. At other times, she seemed sad; he was occasionally surprised by things she said, which seemed to reveal a fear that their love was over. He became worried and asked her:

'Aren't you happy? Isn't it enough that I've agreed to come with you?'

'No, it's not enough, not yet,' she replied.

What did she want then? But when he asked her, Genoveva would smile and say secretively:

'I'll tell you in Paris.'

One day, it suddenly occurred to Vítor that she might be pregnant. He knelt at her feet and whispered the question in her ear. She laughed loudly.

'No, no, don't be silly!' And then she sighed: 'If only I were.'

She was thinking about marriage. She had been thinking about it from the moment she had fallen in love, but now that she knew Vítor's weak, loving, submissive nature, the possibility of marriage only increased her desire for it. She had at last found the great passion for which she had longed all her life and which, like some marvellous bird, had always seemed far away, flying across some distant sky. And now that she had it,

311

she wanted to use every means at her disposal to preserve that love and not let it escape.

Vítor fulfilled all her desires; he was beautiful as an angel, according to her, and she adored him; he was submissive and malleable enough always to obey her; he was intelligent and elegant enough to satisfy her pride; and, of course, he was the heir to Uncle Timóteo's eighty *contos*. Where would she find another man like him, especially now that her youth was past and her skin was beginning to show the first signs of ageing?

If she did not bind him to her with something stronger than lust or love, he might, after a year or two, leave her. And if she did not gain his consent now, while she could dominate him by vanity, concupiscence, pleasure and beauty, it would be too late afterwards. With her fortune and his they could live happily in Paris, but she did not want to speak to him directly of marriage, she wanted the idea to surface first in his own mind; if he were to throw himself into her arms in joyful acceptance as soon as she mentioned it, it was vital that he should have secretly desired it all along.

She began, therefore, by doing everything she could to nurture that idea, to develop and embellish it. She skilfully disguised her ambitions beneath the solicitude of love.

One Saturday night, she said suddenly:

'Would you come with me to mass tomorrow morning? Very early, at seven o'clock . . . so as not to compromise you. It would bring good fortune on our love . . .'

Vítor went with her and thought she looked wonderful, all dressed in black, bent over her prayer book, in an attitude of elegant devotion.

During the following week, she often spoke to him of the church, of religion and repentance, and was always quick to add that it was love which had brought her back to morality; he could not imagine how much she regretted her past errors; her martyrdom was to have belonged to another man, but her soul and her heart were still virginal, and they belonged to him alone. She had said to him:

'You are the husband of my heart; in my heart you are my first and only lover.'

Such eloquent refinement thrilled Vítor. She took other pains with him as well. Who starched his clothes? she wanted to know. His shirts were never properly starched. It wasn't his fault, poor love, he didn't have a wife to look after his things. In Paris, he would see what care she took of everything. She started embroidering him handkerchiefs. She changed her manners, her clothes, her expressions. She affected charitable attitudes, a lofty morality. One day, she heard him humming her favourite song:

Chaque femme a sa toquade,
Sa marotte et son dada . . .

She asked him not to sing 'that dreadful song'.

'It reminds me of people from the past,' she said sadly.

She dressed more soberly, choosing severe colours. He voiced his regret that she no longer wore the very outfits that made her so exciting and captivating.

'They're the kind of clothes a *cocotte* would wear, and I'm a married lady now. I've done with being chic.'

She even crossed herself before going to bed.

One day, seeing her dressed in those dark clothes, sewing at the window, her sweet profile silhouetted against the light, Vítor thought:

'What an adorable woman! What a wife! What a shame we met so late!'

In the midst of all those concerns, he had somewhat neglected the portrait and, one morning, he received a letter from Camilo Cerrão, which said:

I demand the return of my model, who has not appeared now for two whole weeks. What does this mean? Has she changed her mind? That would be unforgivable! I was counting on this portrait to launch my career; surely you want me to have within my grasp glory, fortune and a remarkable piece of work? All this is vanishing like a soap bubble. Genoveva will be responsible to Art and to God (if such a hypothesis is

313

acceptable) of failing to make use of an artist. Bring her here, my boy, for her to be immortalised in oils.

Yours etc. Camilo

Genoveva found the joke about God in bad taste, but Vítor convinced her that it would a terrible disappointment for poor Camilo: 'Who knows, the portrait might make him his fortune?'

'I don't like his wife.'

'Oh, honestly,' said Vítor, shrugging, but feeling the colour rise in his cheeks. 'Will you go there today at two o'clock? Say you will.'

'Only because you want me to, my little husband,' she said, looking at him tenderly and humbly.

And Vítor went ahead to forewarn Camilo. He found the door open; it was half past one; he went into the studio; instead of Camilo he saw Joana sitting at the window, sewing. She got up, her face flushed. She said that Camilo would be back at two. They both stood there, embarrassed, until Vítor, out of politeness, took her hands, glanced around him and kissed her coldly. She put her arms about his neck, lay her head on his shoulder and Vítor heard her sobbing softly.

'Look, someone might come in,' he said, trying to push her away.

'What do I care?' she said tearfully.

'Well, I do!' he said. He immediately regretted such brutality; her tears flattered his pride and, despite himself, Joana's beauty sapped his strength and reawoke his desire. He slowly disentangled himself from her, and said gently:

'There now, don't be silly, calm down.'

'Is that woman your lover?' she asked, her arms hanging by her side, the tears rolling down her face.

'You know she is.'

She dropped down onto the divan and her magnificent breasts shook with her sobs. Vítor was desperate. What if Camilo should arrive and find her bathed in tears. It would be dreadfully embarrassing. In a moment of cowardice, he picked up his hat.

But she grasped his arms, took his hat from him and said pleadingly:

'Just one moment longer. I won't cry any more.'

And she wiped away her tears, controlled her sobs and remained sitting on the divan, her eyes fixed on him in dumb despair. Vítor sat down next to her, saying:

'You must be sensible.'

But a wave of desire filled her and, with a sob, she put her arms about Vítor and kissed his face, his lips, his eyes. He felt himself weakening, but a rustle of silk in the corridor alerted him, and he just had time to push Joana away and see Genoveva, looking very pale, standing in the doorway.

He got to his feet as Genoveva, her hands trembling, her lips drained of colour, came slowly into the studio, her cold, angry eyes fixed on Joana and on him.

'You do know,' she said to Joana, 'that this man is my lover.'

Joana, looking deathly pale, said nothing. Genoveva shot her a cruel, piercing look.

'Well, if you forget again, I will find some other way of reminding you.'

Then turning imperiously to Vítor:

'Shall we go?'

Vítor silently followed. A carriage was waiting at the door and they rode all the way to Rua das Flores without saying a word, without even looking at each other. Vítor paid the driver and went up the stairs behind Genoveva. They went into the living room and Genoveva hurriedly removed her hat, threw it down on a chair and looked at herself in a mirror. Then, pale as wax, she turned brusquely round:

'What more do you want from me?'

'Listen, Genoveva . . .'

'What? I've sacrificed everything for you, wealth, amusements, pleasures, luxuries, everything, and you deceive me with a servant, a cook, a nothing . . .'

In his distress, almost weeping, his voice trembling, Vítor tried to embrace her, crying:

'Please, for God's sake, listen to me!'

And he gave her a hurried account of how he had met the

woman before he had ever been with her, that he had never flirted with her or tempted her, that it had been she who . . . That he had been alone with her once in the studio, that it had been a moment of madness, of stupidity . . . It had only happened that once.

'You're lying!'

'I swear on my mother's soul!' he said suddenly.

There was a silence. She was shaking her head sadly.

'No, Vítor. Listen, I love you as much as it is possible to love another person in this world. I adore you. I was prepared to give you my whole life, to be your slave, your mistress, whatever you wanted, my love.'

Those words provoked in Vítor a delirious exaltation. He murmured:

'Oh, Genoveva, Genoveva!'

'But my trust has been destroyed,' she said sadly. 'I can never trust you again.' Rocking her clasped hands back and forth, she cried: 'Oh, my God, my God!'

Two tears ran down her cheeks, and she fell onto the sofa, sobbing.

He threw himself at her feet and said wildly:

'Ask me anything you like as a proof of my love. I want to give you my life, everything . . .'

'No,' she said, sobbing. 'I'm going away, I'm going to leave, where I don't know. Oh, my God, my God!'

'If you leave, I'll kill myself!'

He had got to his feet. At that moment, he spoke with the utter sincerity of passion. Seeing their love ebbing away, his life seemed to him in ruins.

She walked towards him; her eyes held him; he had never seen her look so beautiful; her tears lent a new purity to her face; he found her noble, dignified, perfect. He said again:

'Tell me what you want me to do, because I adore you and I ask only your forgiveness.'

She slowly placed her hands on his shoulders and in a low, tense voice said:

'Marry me.'

Vítor turned pale and recoiled slightly. Genoveva kept her eyes fixed on him. She gave an infinitely sad smile and murmured:

'Don't you want to?'

And she placed her hands on her heart and closed her eyes, as if she were about to faint.

He quickly took her in his arms.

'I do, I do,' he cried. 'I do want to marry you, Genoveva, I do.'

She put her arms about his neck.

'You'll marry me?'

'I swear by all that's sacred. In a week's time, here or in Paris, wherever you want.'

The rest of that afternoon was spent deliciously making plans. They would marry quietly in Lisbon, in the morning; she would wear black and he a frock coat. That same night, they would set off on their honeymoon. They would leave all the furniture in the apartment, and she would write to Dâmaso telling him to do with them as he wished. That generous gesture delighted Vítor.

'You're a good woman.'

'As you will see,' she said, with a smile that promised infinite joys.

Vítor could not stop looking at her and kissing her. There was something so sweet, so dignified, so noble about her face; tenderness shone in her eyes and a serene happiness showed in her every move.

And what a life they would live in Paris, hidden away in their cosy nest. It would be best not to sell the furniture at first, it would save them the expense of staying at a hotel, and the apartment was rented until December. They would have no carriage, of course, but there was nothing wrong with a hired cab.

Genoveva was radiant; she seemed to have acquired a veneer of girlishness; she blushed when he looked at her, as if she had been overtaken by a sudden virginity; she knelt at his feet, shyly submissive as a weary dove; she never wearied of

317

calling him 'my little husband', and even when they went to the bedroom and Vítor took her in his arms, she displayed all the startled resistance of a fearful virgin.

Some days later, at a performance at the Teatro de São Carlos of *Robert le Diable*, just when the nuns, wearing short, full skirts and with their hair loose, were dancing in the 'cloister of Santa Rosália', Dâmaso came in, looking very pleased with himself. He threw his hat down on an empty seat, polished his opera glasses and examined the people in the boxes. In a box just above the stalls, Joana Coutinho gave him a simpering smile and discreetly beckoned to him. Dâmaso rushed to see her.

She was with a fellow called Lacerda, who had greying hair and a rather sickly look about him; he sat at the rear of the box, muffled up in his overcoat, sucking a cough drop.

Dona Joana Coutinho immediately said:

'Have you heard the news? Genoveva is getting married.'

'To Vítor?'

'To Vítor.'

Dâmaso blushed scarlet and affected a rather coarse laugh. Then turning his plump face to her and fixing her with his little eyes, he said:

'You are joking, aren't you?'

And Dona Joana Coutinho told him that she had spent the afternoon with Genoveva, that all the papers had been drawn up and they were to leave for France.

'Disgusting,' muttered Lacerda, between coughing bouts.

'What a fool!' exclaimed Dâmaso and smugly rubbed his hands. He had seen it coming. She was after Uncle Timóteo's eighty *contos*. But the old man was astute and very proud and quite capable of disinheriting Vítor.

'Does his uncle know?' he asked.

Dona Joana Coutinho was not sure. Of course, she thought marriage an excellent thing, a moral institution of which all Christians could not but approve. Genoveva may have made mistakes, but who among us has not? Marriage would wash all that away . . . She wished her joy. Genoveva was happy as a lark.

'Though, frankly, between you and me, she doesn't deserve him. She's got no manners, none at all.'

'No shame either,' said Dâmaso.

'And no delicacy of spirit,' added Dona Joana.

Lacerda cleared his throat loudly and asked:

'Has she got any money of her own?'

Dâmaso was about to say: 'Only what I gave her', but he restrained himself. He wanted to continue to be thought of as the man Genoveva had loved, and since Genoveva might have talked to Dona Joana about their relationship, he judged it best not to respond and pretended, instead, to be interested in the ballet.

'How was the funeral scene?'

'It was quite good today,' said Dona Joana. 'But the Spanish dancer, the big one, nearly fell over.'

Dâmaso sat for a moment twirling his moustache, then he got up and said goodbye. Out in the corridor, he lit a cigar and then left the theatre.

Vítor had not dared mention the portrait; Genoveva brought the matter up the following day, when she showed him a letter she had written to Camilo Cerrão, telling him she was leaving for France and regretted having to interrupt his work; she hoped he would keep the sketch he had done ready for her return; she had slipped twenty *libras* in notes into the envelope.

'That should console him,' she said.

Knowing Camilo's interest in the portrait was artistic rather than mercenary, Vítor thought that such an offer might merely increase Camilo's irritation at having to stop work. He made no objections, however, as he did not wish to appear overly concerned.

The following day, he was getting dressed at home before supper (he was going to the theatre that night with Genoveva), when Camilo Cerrão came into his room; he looked very fed up and seemed even more rumpled and dishevelled than usual. He began by removing Genoveva's letter from his overcoat pocket and placing it on top of the chest of drawers, saying:

'Give this to your good lady. What I've done so far isn't worth twenty *libras*; it's very kind of her, but . . . Anyway, we can talk again when she comes back . . .'

Vítor, who had coloured at this remark, mentioned the cost of canvas and paints, but Camilo interrupted him with a resolute gesture, and throwing himself down in an armchair, he began describing the life of the artist; he had come to the conclusion that he should change careers; in Portugal there was only a market for little art by little artists and a very narrow market at that, one that wanted iconography or illustrations for novels or serials; he regarded such things as a prostitution of his talent; he wanted to keep his talent pure and so had decided to go to Brazil.

'Why?'

He had a sister there, married to some very rich man, who, by some strange coincidence, was a great art lover; he was perhaps the only such person in the whole of South America. This lover of art was offering him bed and board, as well as an introduction to theatre directors and a few mad collectors. He could make his fortune either as a designer of sets or by obtaining from the Brazilian government a commission to go to Italy and make copies of famous paintings. As soon as he had made a small fortune, twenty or thirty *contos*, 'which, apparently, is perfectly possible', he would return to Portugal, open a studio, gather some disciples around him and live a dignified existence, surrounded by works of art and living only for his ideal. If he didn't make a fortune then he would die there. At least he would have a chance to experience the exuberance of Brazil's vast forests.

Vítor was carefully combing his hair; he coughed and asked casually:

'Are you going alone?'

'Oh, yes. Joana is becoming unbearable; she spends all day as silent as a statue and as gloomy as a mausoleum. The baby cries all the time because he's teething, and it's impossible to work. I'll leave them some money and send them an allowance every month. The woman seems rather pleased about the arrangement. I'm thinking of sending her back to Ílhavo. And then I start a new life.'

Sitting in the vast armchair, his head slumped on his chest, he had spoken in rather melancholy terms. Vítor, meanwhile, was meticulously tying his white tie. The resigned, indifferent way in which Camilo spoke of 'the woman' diminished any feelings of remorse Vítor might have had. He even said rather bluntly:

'Well, she wasn't the right woman for you anyway.'

'No, I see that now. An artist's wife should be an artist herself, she should have an artist's intelligence, understanding, taste . . . But perhaps the best thing is to live alone, as powerful and solitary as Alfred de Vigny's *Moses*.'

He rolled a cigarette between his fingers and, seeing Vítor putting on his tailcoat, said:

'Are you going out somewhere?'

'Yes, to the theatre.'

And Camilo immediately began praising Genoveva. She was, he thought, a supreme example of modern beauty, the embodiment of years of civilisation and of the genius of all the truly great prostitutes of the past.

When Vítor heard that word used to describe the woman who was to be his wife, he went as red as if someone had slapped him.

'Alas,' Camilo went on, 'these mean-spirited, constitutional times do not allow for the development of such a magnificent embodiment of dramatic sensuality. Before, especially in the sixteenth century, such a woman would have been the centre of intellectual, artistic and political life; all the great ideas and poetry of the day would have happened around her bed, on which she would have lain as if on an altar, a queen of grace and a goddess of beauty; poets would have written poems for her, the Titians of the day would have immortalised her in paintings; her words would have settled arguments between philosophers; in her bedroom, plots would have been hatched and wars declared; princes would have handed her slippers to

321

her; while she was dressing, she would have given audience to cardinals, who would have asked her questions about dogma; the great sculptors and jewellers would have invented for her the most sublime works of art; popes would have kissed her white feet; such women would have inspired the sailors on galleys, would have inspired great victories, would have been the muses of a pagan cult. But,' he added, 'today all they do is exploit some temperamental grocer, fall in love with a shop assistant and end up marrying some nincumpoop who is only after the money other men gave them, or who is dazzled by their first glimpse of underwear trimmed with Mechlin lace. We live in ignorant times.'

Vítor was by now deathly pale. He had gone over to the window and was looking out, so as to hide his feelings; every word had fallen on his ears like a scornful insult. He almost wondered if Camilo knew about him and Joana and was having his revenge with those disdainful remarks about his marriage to Genoveva. But Camilo was speaking very calmly, as if delivering a critical lecture. What would he think if he knew? What he said was like a fragment of the thoughts of all honest men.

Vítor walked about the room, looked at himself in the mirror, put his hands in his pockets and stared down as if studying his patent leather shoes.

'Passion justifies everything.'

'At least,' said Camilo, 'it lends our actions a suggestion of fatefulness that makes them interesting.'

He stretched, yawned and drew his hand across his face; he was about to get up when the bedroom door opened and Uncle Timóteo appeared.

'Oh, I thought you were alone,' he said to Vítor. 'I'll wait for you downstairs.' He closed the door, and they heard the sound of his wooden leg moving off down the corridor.

Camilo picked up his hat.

'But you're not leaving for Brazil immediately,' said Vítor. 'Who knows, you might change your mind.'

'No, I've had enough of this rabble. And I'd like to see the sea, the jungle and the vast rivers. After all, landscape is the noblest part of art; modern man lives so removed from the natural world, that an art which surrounds man with nature, which makes nature portable, bringing it into the dining room and the bedroom, interpreted and selected, does the greatest service to man; it puts him in permanent communication with nature. And nature is everything: it calms, consoles, elevates, refines and vivifies. Goodbye.'

Vítor remained for a moment in his room, worried. What could Uncle Timóteo want? He only ever came to see him in his room when he was ill. His heart beat a little faster as he went down the stairs.

He found his uncle in his study, looking stern and worried, his eyes red. He was sitting by the window and, as soon as Vítor came in, he got up and went over to his desk; the dull thud of his wooden leg had a grim solemnity; and Vítor, feeling slightly awkward in his white tie and tails, in the presence of that sad old man, asked rather unsteadily if he wanted anything.

Timóteo shuffled a few papers on his desk and said:

'I don't normally pay much attention to anonymous letters, but I would just like to know if this is true. Read it.'

And he handed Vítor an envelope. Vítor realised at once that the letter it contained must be about Genoveva, their marriage and departure for Paris; his first startled reaction, a timid one, was to deny everything. He opened the letter with slightly trembling hands and read:

Dear Sir,

A person with the greatest respect for your character warns you of the plans of a shameless woman who threatens to destroy for ever your name and your family. Your nephew Vítor is about to marry a certain adventuress who calls herself Genoveva, who is, to put it bluntly, a prostitute with whom your nephew has been living. Try to put a stop to this scandal while there is still time.

A friend.

323

'It's from that fool Dâmaso!' said Vítor. 'He wants revenge.'

Timóteo stared at him hard; the lines in his face seemed to have grown deeper; he looked rather pale and weary; his lips were white.

Vítor realised how distressing the news was to his uncle. He kept repeating awkwardly:

'It's from Dâmaso.'

'I don't care who it's from, I just want to know if it's true.' And raising his hand, he said with an intensity that Vítor had never heard before: 'Just tell me the truth. If I found out you had lied to me . . .' He stopped and gestured with his clenched fist. 'Be a good chap and just tell me the truth.'

Vítor was as pale as wax; he kept his eyes fixed on the floor. Realising that he could not lie and feeling the full force of Uncle Timóteo's accusation, he said in a faint voice:

'It's true.'

'Do you want to marry this creature?'

Vítor did not respond. Standing by the desk, he kept mechanically opening and closing a book.

'Answer me, man!'

And Uncle Timóteo's eyes flashed.

'Well, the fact is, Uncle, I gave her my word.'

'Idiot!' exclaimed Uncle Timóteo.

His lips were trembling with anger. He paced up and down the room, thumping his cane on the floor, then he stopped:

'So you want to marry a shameless hussy who has had more men handle her than a pack of cards, who will sleep with a man for a couple of *libras*, and who is only interested in my money.'

'Uncle Timóteo,' said Vítor indignantly, but he was frightened too.

'What? Are you going to deny that she arrived from abroad with a man called Gomes, that she lived with Dâmaso all winter, that she hired herself out at so much a night? Are you trying to tell me she's a decent person, an honest woman, a virgin?'

Vítor stammered:

'She may have made a few mistakes . . .'

324

'Mistakes!' bawled Uncle Timóteo. 'Does being a professional whore constitute making a few mistakes?'

Vítor slammed the book down on the table and in a voice shaking more with pain than anger, he said:

'If the only reason you called me in was to insult her . . .'

His voice broke and he slowly turned his back.

'Listen to me,' roared Uncle Timóteo in a terrifying voice, banging his cane hard on the floor. 'I have brought you up, clothed you, shod you, taken care of you; I have been a father to you; I think that gives me the right to speak to you when I see you about to commit a gross error.'

Vítor stopped and, head lowered, he approached the desk again; he was in such a state of inner turmoil that he could not utter a single word in reply. His brain weighed heavy and his blood ran cold in his veins.

'Close that door,' bellowed Uncle Timóteo, folding his arms. 'Right, tell me what exactly you think your position will be once you have married this creature?' And without waiting for a reply, he went on: 'I'll tell you, shall I? You'll be no better than a pimp! Yes, a pimp! How else can I describe a man who walks down the street arm in arm with a woman whose legs and every other part of her anatomy are familiar to the whole world? Even the petticoats she's wearing were bought for her by someone else! The supper you eat at her house is paid for with the money some other man left on her bedside table in the morning.'

Vítor went red to the roots of his hair. For a moment, he stared, eyes glittering, at Uncle Timóteo; then, in a strangulated voice, he said:

'I won't have you talk about her like that. If you weren't my uncle and an old man . . . You have no right to insult me. You can throw me out of your house. No, you needn't bother, I'll leave.'

'Leave, then!' shouted Timóteo and, his arms shaking, he added: 'Scoundrel!'

Vítor left, slamming the door. He went up to his room and, in the grip of anger, he decided to leave the house that instant. He dragged an old suitcase from beneath the bed and started piling clothes into it; he felt overwhelmed by violent anger; he hated Uncle Timóteo, thought him ungrateful, hard, tyrannical; certain things he had said still burned in his consciousness; he trembled at the truth he found in them and his mind was caught up in a storm of contradictions.

The door opened and Uncle Timóteo appeared. He was extremely pale; he stood leaning on his stick, looking at Vítor, who was surprised and slightly ashamed, holding a tailcoat in one hand and a pair of trousers over one arm.

'So, my boy,' said his uncle, 'are you really so madly in love with this woman?'

Those words spoken in a quiet, almost friendly tone, touched Vítor; he felt his eyes fill with tears; the very sacrifice he was making for Genoveva exalted his love for her, and in a passionate, almost desperate voice, he said:

'I am, I swear I am. We'll go to Paris where no one knows me, where no one will talk about us. It's the only way I can be happy.'

Timóteo came into the room and sat at the foot of the bed and, for a while, said nothing.

'Are you sure she would sacrifice everything for you too?'

'Yes, I am,' said Vítor passionately.

Timóteo gave a disdainful shrug.

'My friend, if I were to go to her tomorrow and offer her four or five *contos* to leave you and to leave Portugal, you can be sure that she would accept.'

'For God's sake!' exclaimed Vítor.

Timóteo looked at him pityingly, the way one might listen to the ravings of a lunatic.

'I don't doubt the woman loves you; you're young, you're pleasant company, etc. That's all very well, but apart from your face and your twenty-three years, which always make a favourable impression on women, I think she's in love with the eighty *contos* that people say I have and that I'll leave to you. Believe me. Of course, you give her a great deal of pleasure and she finds you absolute perfection, but it pleases her too that your handsome eyes are accompanied by those eighty *contos*. I can perfectly well believe that you were her reason for leaving Dâmaso, who, because he's a fool, gave her a fair bit of money, but that you should marry her! That is precisely what such women want. They want to find a young man they like, from a good, reasonably wealthy family, someone willing to give them his name. And since this doesn't happen every day, she does everything she can to bait the trap; what you take for passion is pure calculation. But even if she were truly in love with you and prepared to accept you poor, is that a proper fate for a decent man – to abandon everything, to destroy his relatives and his family, to ruin himself for ever by marrying a prostitute? And for what? In order to spend his whole life loving? Oh, Vítor,' and Uncle Timóteo's voice became affectionately solemn, 'if you want to travel, to Spain or Italy, you know I'll give you the money. Have fun; forget her. Before you leave, buy her a nice present. I'll even give you the money to do so; behave like a gentleman and you'll see how easily consoled she is. Just remember one thing; if you marry, you dishonour yourself and me. Since I cannot live with such dishonour, I won't blow my brains out, no, but I will shut myself up in my study and never see another living soul until I die. Other than that, I only hope that God or Fate or the Devil, or whoever it is up there, does not leave me to moulder very long in this wretched world. But that's enough sermonising. Think about it. You can have the money if you want it. Let's not fall out over it. Let's embrace and to hell with the woman. What do you say?'

Vítor was biting his lips in order not to cry.

'Well?' insisted Uncle Timóteo.

Vítor stammered out:

'I don't quite know, Uncle. I'll see . . . but suddenly to . . .'

Timóteo got to his feet and said sadly:

'The best decisions are the ones taken quickly, my friend. If you see her now, there'll be tears and scenes and everything will become muddied again. I'll tell you what. Let me talk to her.'

Vítor ran a hand over his hair and looked at his uncle.

'You won't be rude to her.'

327

'I'll just tell her the truth: that if you intend to marry her, I'll take my money and go and live in England, and leave anything that remains to the poor. And you'll see how that cools her ardour.'

'And if she doesn't care, if she proves she's not interested in your money?' cried Vítor. 'If she doesn't even want to marry me, if she only wants to live with me?'

Timóteo thought.

'If she wants only to live with you as your lover, then that's fine; I'll give you the money to pay for her and ruin us both.'

As he was leaving the room, he turned and said:

'And don't be silly, unpack that case.'

'My uncle is coming tomorrow to talk to you.' Those were the first words Vítor said when he arrived at Genoveva's that night. And he told her about his argument with Uncle Timóteo, slightly censored so as not to offend her.

'My lover?' she said. 'It's like a scene out of *La Dame aux Camélias*? I'll dress to play the innocent tomorrow. That will show him. Oh, you may laugh, but . . .'

She went over and placed her hands on his shoulders and, seeing him still gloomy and preoccupied, said:

'But, of course, if you don't want to fall out with your uncle because of me . . .'

She moved away and curtseyed.

His hands were shaking.

'Why are you so cruel? You know perfectly well that . . .'

Genoveva shook her head sadly.

'I know that's what you feel. Don't deny it. I can see it in your eyes. You're free to do as you please; I don't want you to turn against me when, later on, your uncle breaks off relations with you. Think about it. I don't want you to belong to me because of a decision based on exalted ideas, on mere fantasies. I want you to come to me spontaneously, having considered all the consequences, so that whatever happens, you cannot accuse me of having forced you to do anything or to say that I was your downfall.'

He put his hand over her mouth.

'Genoveva, you're mad. Whatever you choose to do, I'm yours for ever, for ever.'

The door opened, and Mélanie announced that supper was on the table.

'And you don't care about your uncle or his threats or his curses?'

'No!' he said fervently.

'And you're my dear little husband, the husband of my soul?'

Her lovely dark eyes shone with real passion.

'Yes, I am,' murmured Vítor, kissing her neck.

'Then, you just leave your uncle to me, and let's go and sit down to supper.'

Genoveva always seemed particularly alluring to Vítor at that hour of the day. They dined at a small table lit by the subtle, elegant light of an oil lamp. The supper was always excellent; Genoveva dressed very carefully; the light gleamed softly on her face, her neck, her décolletage and lent a gentle glow to her skin; she looked her loveliest then: the lace trim on her three-quarter-length sleeves, the various glittering bracelets she wore, the pretty flower pinned to her bodice. Mélanie laughed as she served them, looking fresh in her beret and her white apron.

Genoveva talked a lot; they would laugh and make plans; sometimes, during a pause in the abundant meal, they would squeeze each other's hands ardently; and that elegant, comfortable, warm, loving atmosphere filled Vítor with a sweet delight to which the Burgundy added a sense of languid well-being.

They would always round off the meal with liqueurs in the living room, where Mélanie would bring them their coffee; Vítor would light a cigarette and lie on the sofa listening to Genoveva playing the piano or singing a song by Gounod or Schubert in her warm, penetrating voice.

That night, they were to go to the circus. The carriage was waiting below. Genoveva went and sat on Vítor's knee and, putting her arms about his neck, she said in a low voice:

'It's so lovely living with you, so sweet!'

A tender sigh made her breast rise and fall; with her lips on his face, she murmured:

'If I lost you, I'd die!'

'So would I,' he said very quietly.

And his heart beat fast.

'Come along, then,' she said, getting to her feet and pulling him up by his arms. 'Come along, my dear, up you get and put your overcoat on. Do I look pretty tonight?'

She stood before him in her magnificent red and black dress and showed herself to him, slightly spreading her arms, her head turned towards him in a provocative, lasciviously humble pose.

'You look delicious,' he said and tried to put his arms about her.

She pulled away, smiling, crying 'No, no!' and ran into the bedroom to put on her cape and her hat, to glance in the mirror and dab on a little more powder.

Vítor drank a glass of cognac, thinking that no Uncle Timóteo could ever make him leave that woman.

There was only a sparse audience at the circus. When they went into their box, the stalls were almost empty, apart from a few people here and there; a man with his hat pulled down over his eyes was smoking lugubriously; two Spanish women dressed in green were frantically fanning themselves; some English sailors, slightly drunk, were fighting in the upper circle; and to the sound of the brass band, a white horse was lolloping monotonously around the ring, bearing a thin woman with scrawny, melancholy muscles, who was performing juggling tricks.

After a while, Genoveva yawned and declared she was bored, but she immediately brightened up when, in another box, she spotted Madame Gordon, the baron's mistress, with an elderly woman all dressed in black like a widow.

They waved enthusiastically and Genoveva gestured to her to join them in their box. The German woman did not delay; she too declared herself to be extremely bored; it was so tedious, there was no one there she knew and the circus was appalling. At that moment, a female acrobat mounted on a dark horse was striking graceful poses; she was very thin, and her hair was caught up in an ugly chignon, with ringlets threaded with silver-gilt ivy leaves and ears of corn hanging down her back; her low-cut costume revealed her collar bones; the classical poses she struck while poised on the broad saddle accentuated her gymnast's muscles; now and then, the music would stop and she would sit down in an affected manner, swirl her skirts and look around at the audience, smiling and revealing her bad teeth. A young man started stamping wildly, while others applauded; she bowed, and the English sailors cheered. The clown came over to her and blew her a kiss, athletically contorting his body into a grotesque caricature of passion; the ringmaster cracked his whip and the clown fell flat on his face; the audience laughed. The music started up again and the acrobat climbed back onto the saddle and stood pirouetting on one leg. The place was lit with crude gas lights as if in a tavern; the musicians in the band sleepily clanged out an accompaniment; people glanced down the programme, yawning, and the horse's hooves kicked clods of dry earth onto the seats in the stalls.

Genoveva said that it was 'absolutely dreadful'; they would be better off at home. They could play dominos or lotto.

The German woman could not go with them; the baron had promised to pick her up at the circus.

'Oh, these long Lisbon nights!' sighed Genoveva.

A tall, strange-looking man dressed in skins and striking satanic poses so irritated her that she got up and said to Vítor:

'Come along, my boy, this place is affecting my nerves. Such a bore!'

And they left the German woman, who had spent all night with her opera glasses trained on one of the Spanish ladies, a pretty young girl dressed in green, with sleepy, languid eyes.

As they left, they encountered Dâmaso, who was just arriving. Genoveva inclined her head slightly, and Dâmaso, turning scarlet, looked away, affecting disdain. They even heard him joking with the fat Englishwoman who was his companion.

It was a glorious night, the air was as warm and sweetly

serene as summer, the full moon shone like silver and the streets were filled with the melancholy that comes from the contrast of shadows and moonlight.

Genoveva wanted to walk and so they strolled slowly along the pavement. There was still some faint light from the shops; people were walking up and down; a woman wearing a veil approached them, glumly asking for alms; the tall buildings bathed in moonlight had an abandoned look about them.

At Largo do Loreto, they turned down to go home; Genoveva stopped; at the bottom of Rua do Alecrim, the Tagus glimmered beneath the vast, tremulous moon.

'Shall we walk along by the river?'

They went down to Cais do Sodré. Two boatman, smoking cigarettes and sitting on a large pile of stones, offered them a boat trip, very cheap.

'It's a real bargain, sir,' one said, smiling.

'My name's Manoto,' said the older man smugly. 'Speak English?'

'It's too cold,' said Vítor.

Manoto protested:

'Cold? The air's warm as a kiss tonight!'

Shortly afterwards, they were sitting in the boat and moving away across the still water.

'What a beautiful night!' Vítor said.

The city rose up before them, the façades of the buildings washed with moonlight, the windows glittering like sheets of silver; the gaslamps seemed to grow dim beneath that abundance of silvery light. The houses were silent and white as if immersed in some tranquil, ecstatic meditation. The full moon shone silent and serene; a brilliant trail trembled on the water, like enamel or liquid filigree; the rest of the water was sometimes pale blue, sometimes, farther off, smooth and mirror-bright. A luminous mist covered the shore on the farther side, and the shapes of the ships and their lights looked slightly blurred and dim. Beneath the cold, dumb silence of the sky, the boat was accompanied by the sound of the oars striking the rowlocks and the gentle splash of warm water.

They were sitting very close and Genoveva started singing Lamartine's *Lago*:

> One evening, do you remember? We
> drifted along in silence . . .

Vítor had often walked by the blue river, he had often seen the moon and the clear, tranquil water, but the Tagus and the moonlit night had never seemed so beautiful to him, as if his love heightened nature itself. He put his arm about Genoveva's waist; the contact of silk on silk filled him with elegantly amorous feelings. He recalled lines from Alfred de Musset. The moon lent her face a look of sweet, poetic beauty; her hands smoothing the folds of her dress glittered with rings, and her low, cool, musical voice filled Vítor with a kind of ecstatic somnolence. She rested her head lightly on Vítor's shoulder, and he wished they could go on like that for ever, caught in the marvellous sweetness of that poetic languor. She said nothing and, still sitting very close, they lost themselves in vague thoughts.

'What time is your uncle coming tomorrow?' she asked suddenly.

'Hm?' said Vítor, as if waking from a delicious dream. Then he shrugged and said: 'He can come when he likes and say what he likes. He's just wasting his time, isn't he?'

She sat for a moment in silence, then said rather loudly:

'There is nothing in the world that could separate me from you. Nothing! As long as you love me, I am your lover, your wife, your slave, whatever you want . . . anywhere and for ever.'

'What can he do, after all? He can cut me off, break off relations with me, but what does that matter? I'll work, if necessary, as long as I have you to console me and embrace me and give me courage.'

And they clung passionately to each other.

'You'll always have me, my love,' she said quietly.

The certainty of his love made her deeply happy, but she added, smiling:

'The worst he can do is to put a curse on us like that fellow at the circus!'

'God will bless us,' said Vítor, almost seriously.

'Amen,' she replied, laughing.

But the night was growing colder and they rowed back to the shore. The clocks were striking eleven o'clock as they walked up Rua das Flores. Genoveva leaned heavily on Vítor's arm; she was rather tired and she paused, breathing hard, to look up at the brightly lit windows on the third floor.

'We live awfully high up. It'll be quite an adventure for your Uncle Timóteo's wooden leg.'

She was very concerned about his visit. What could Uncle Timóteo want? Doubtless to stop their marriage, but how? With threats, pleas, promises?

'What do you think?' she had asked Mélanie, from whom she had no secrets, adding: 'Just in case, make sure the living room is tidy and put fresh flowers in the vases and wear your black silk dress and a clean apron.'

In the morning, while Vítor was bathing and dressing, she lay out the cards, but could gain no insight into the future beyond property, money and a letter from across the sea. Then she went to check that the living room looked suitably respectable and bourgeois and completed the décor with a few 'humble touches', as she put it. She placed the music for Rossini's *Stabat Mater* on the piano, put a muff on a chair and, beside it, a prayer book, as if she had gone to church that morning; and on the table she left the receipt for a weekly contribution to schools for poor children.

'Have you got a new duster somewhere that needs edging?' she asked Mélanie. 'Bring it to me, will you?'

And she put the duster on top of her sewing basket in place of her embroidery, to show she busied herself with useful jobs, rather than mere elegant pastimes. With the skill of an artist, she arranged the curtains in stiff folds and, looking contentedly around, said:

'It looks like the temple of virtue!'

Shortly afterwards, she went in to Vítor, who was waiting

for her in the dining room, reading the newspaper. She was wearing a black cashmere dress with sombre silk trimmings, a silver lace cravat and a rosebud in her bodice; her hair was very simply dressed and adorned with some English lace; there was about her manner and her bearing a natural reserve and an air of domestic propriety and maternal serenity.

'Well, do I look like a decent little woman?'

'You always do,' said Vítor, enchanted.

They were both very nervous though. They jumped when the doorbell rang and exchanged agitated glances. It was just the woman selling fruit.

'Perhaps he won't even come today,' said Vítor.

The tea cup trembled slightly in Genoveva's hands. She tried to laugh, mocking her own nervousness.

'He's not the bogeyman, he's not going to eat me.'

When they went into the living room, Vítor noted how intelligently she had arranged everything to create an air of tranquillity and order.

'It's a day of battle,' said Vítor.

Genoveva suddenly thought of something and went over to the piano to look out her book of Schubert lieder; she played the opening chords of 'Salve, salve, last morning of my life!' And seeing Vítor's surprise at the almost superstitious way in which she sang the melancholy words, she said:

'It's to bring us good luck.'

And she told him about a friend of hers, a young Frenchman, who had described to her how, during the terrible winter when the Prussians were besieging Paris, the soldiers in the fort of Monte Valesiano used to gather in one of the dungeons where they had installed a piano and how, before the sun came up and before the first shots of the day were fired, they would all sing that Schubert song as a kind of protection against death, because for one of them it could well have been his last morning. In fact, not a single man was wounded or killed. Ever since then she had clung to that superstition, and whenever she was faced by some decisive event, by one of life's problems, she would sing that protective song. She sang on:

Vítor went over and looked out of the window. It was a sunny day and already quite hot; the spring sky was a bright southern blue and the water cart was moving slowly along Rua do Alecrim to slake the dust in the street; the tall houses in Rua das Flores discreetly shaded the road and that part of the city seemed somehow quiet and private. Leaning out into the street, he could hear the melancholy notes of the song hovering in the hot air and he felt a vague oppression of the senses.

At midday, he picked up his hat and said to Genoveva:

'I'm going to walk over to the Chiado and see if my uncle's carriage passes by; I'll wait until he leaves and then come up to see what happened.'

He was about to go, but some strange, almost melancholy impulse made him turn and clasp her to him; they kissed each other tenderly and he left, feeling deeply touched, swearing that, whatever happened, he would be hers for ever.

It was one o'clock when Uncle Timóteo's ancient horses stopped at the door of the building. Standing in the corridor, her heart beating fast, Genoveva heard the sound of his wooden leg come thudding slowly up the stairs. She murmured: 'Open the door, Mélanie,' and then ran into her bedroom.

When Uncle Timóteo went into the living room, he glanced at the furniture, the paintings, the sewing basket and seemed rather taken aback to find Genoveva looking so respectful and dignified.

'You're Vítor's uncle, I believe,' she began, bowing and instinctively echoing the words spoken by Marguerite, *La Dame aux Camélias*, when she received Armand's father.

She sat down gracefully on the sofa, murmuring:

'To what do I owe . . .'

'First of all,' said Uncle Timóteo very respectfully, 'I must apologise for a moment of ill humour on my part, a short while ago, when I first had the . . . er . . . honour . . .'

He fumbled for the right words; Genoveva's attentive

eye, benevolent smile and humble, filial air troubled him; he looked at her hard, with a vague sense that he knew that face and had already seen those eyes . . . She made a kindly gesture:

'Oh, no, please, it was entirely my fault. I adore children and, believe me, I blush with shame and remorse to think that I caused the little angel to fall . . . But we all have our bad days, our "blue devils". I was rather upset at the time and . . .'

She bit her lip and lowered her thick black eyelashes, as if ashamed of her own behaviour. But she immediately looked up again and her eyes again fixed on Uncle Timóteo almost insistently; she too felt that his face and voice were somehow known to her; when had she seen him before, where?

Their eyes met and for a moment they stared at each other, both desperately asking themselves the same question. Then, either in order to break the silence or because he could not find the memory he was seeking, Uncle Timóteo said:

'Everyone who knows me, knows I am a man who says exactly what he thinks . . . I like to be frank.'

She nodded slightly.

'For me, frankness is the prime quality in a man, along with courage, of course.'

Timóteo liked that; Genoveva's beauty, her soft voice, her chaste, attentive attitude, were beginning to dissolve his anger. Still distrustful, though, and determined not to let her 'butter him up', he said rather brusquely:

'And in the interests of frankness, I will come straight to the point. I'm sure you know what that is.'

Her face bore a sweet look of smiling doubt and hesitation.

'Well, I presume you want to talk to me about Vítor.'

'Exactly.'

There was a brief silence which Genoveva broke, speaking with grave dignity, weighing every word:

'Vítor has spoken of his Uncle Timóteo, as he calls you, so often and with such affection and enthusiasm, that I am, of course, ready to give you my full attention.' Then she added after an emphatic pause: 'I know he owes you everything and that he loves you deeply.'

'Quite,' said Uncle Timóteo, 'it's only right that the boy should feel some friendship for me.'

'He adores you!' she said forcefully, moving slightly closer to Uncle Timóteo.

'Aha, a siren!' he thought, and after pensively rubbing his knee, he said:

'You will not be surprised, then, that I should come here to defend his interests.'

Genoveva seemed very surprised to hear him speak of 'interests'.

'Because, after all,' he shifted resolutely in his chair, 'what does he stand to gain from this relationship?'

Genoveva, twisting her lace handkerchief about her fingers and lowering her eyes, replied:

'What does one ever stand to gain from a relationship with the person one loves?' And she smiled adorably: 'Happiness, I presume.'

Timóteo looked straight at her and said in a slightly louder voice:

'My dear lady, I'm not one of those old uncles you find in bourgeois comedies, who are shocked and horrified that a boy should have a lover. Between the ages of twenty and thirty, all men have lovers; it's as necessary as taking a bath. I'd go further, it is a positive joy when the lover in question is pretty, intelligent, talented, elegant, and has a lovely apartment,' he glanced around him, 'good conversation and,' here he bowed, 'fine clothes. Absolutely. I would be the first to congratulate Vítor if this relationship were not a cause of grave difficulties.'

Genoveva said:

'But you're wrong; I demand nothing of him; I don't distract him from his duties. I am not that selfish. All I want is for him to come and see me . . .'

'And to marry you,' broke in Uncle Timóteo.

Genoveva blushed; a wave of anger swept through her, but she controlled herself and replied:

'We feel it is the pure and Christian thing to do to legitimise our relationship.'

Timóteo looked at her, astonished; he did not know

338

whether to laugh at the sheer affectation or to be shocked by the hypocrisy; he suppressed the curse that came to his lips and, thinking that he would wound her or upset her, he said calmly, placidly, with one eyebrow raised:

'You know, of course, that if you marry, I will not leave the boy a single penny.'

She bowed.

'That would be sad for Vítor because it would be proof that you had withdrawn your love, but it has no bearing on his decision; he's young, intelligent, he can work, and I have some money of my own . . .'

'Given to you by other men!' Uncle Timóteo exclaimed angrily, with a scornful shrug of his shoulders.

Genoveva turned pale, and her lips trembled. She dabbed at her eyes with her handkerchief and said with her head still bent:

'Your horror at my past life cannot be any greater than my own. The reason I seek this pure, noble affection is in order to forget my past and to wash it clean. Besides, it seems to me ungenerous on your part to try and humiliate me.'

Timóteo thought: 'She really is extraordinary!'

He bowed and muttered an apology, then added:

'I see I am talking to someone of great intelligence . . . but let me get to the point. Do you call it "love" forcing a young man into such an ill-sorted marriage? What kind of future will the poor boy have? He will be eternally ashamed of his wife, who can never merit the respect he wants for her; he will meet other men who know as much about your past as he does. Let me speak frankly. I am an old man; you and I both know what the world is like. It would be ridiculous not to be open about these things. He will never be able to appear with you in society; all careers and all ambitions will be closed to him. If you had children, your children would bear a terrible name. They would be constantly at risk of some cruel person telling them to their faces what their mother used to be.'

An anxious, despairing look crossed her face.

'But we would lead such a retiring, secret life . . .'

Timóteo laughed.

'That's pure romance! You can live like that for a year perhaps, but you can't live your whole life in a cottage, exchanging cosy kisses and gazing up at the moon. Do you honestly think you could live such a reclusive life, such a convent existence? You cannot change the habits of a lifetime as easily as you can a pair of gloves. Now, of course, you are under the sway of passion, but what will happen later on? Can you really resign yourself to such a modest existence, with no carriage, no parties, no suppers, no affairs?'

'I'm sorry,' she burst in, 'but you have entirely the wrong idea about my life. I have lived a life bereft of parties and affairs.' She lowered her voice: 'Believe me, my errors were born purely out of necessity. I come from a bourgeois family with bourgeois habits.'

Seeing the surprise on Timóteo's face and thinking he might be softening towards her, she decided to play her final card; she bent towards him, sitting almost on the edge of the sofa, and raised her hands to him:

'Listen, I'm going to tell you my whole life story; I trust you, I can see you're a decent man, a man with heart and intelligence, capable of understanding. I have never told anyone these things. Vítor knows nothing about it. He, like everyone else, thinks I was born in Madeira, that I ran away with an Englishman and that later, in Paris, I became what people term a *cocotte*.'

She gave a bitter laugh. A sudden breeze entered the room and Timóteo made as if to move out of the draught. Genoveva ran over to shut the window and, as she was bolting it, she quickly gave the bare bones of the story she was about to tell him. When she turned round, Timóteo was standing up; something about the way she moved had touched him and a vague memory was forming inside him; he could not take his eyes off her.

'Where are you from then?' he asked haltingly.

'I got married in Portugal.' She paused, blushing with shame: 'I ran away from my husband.'

'But where are you from?' asked Timóteo; he was breathing hard now, and his walking stick shook furiously in his cold hand.

'I'm from Guarda.'

Timóteo stood utterly still, his eyes wide; he muttered:

'Good God! Good God!'

'What is it?' she asked, deathly pale now.

'Your husband, who was he?'

She responded anxiously, her hands pressed to her breast, leaning towards him.

'Why? My husband's name was Pedro da Ega.'

'Oh, you poor wretch, you poor wretch!' roared Timóteo. He raised his trembling arms in the air; his eyes were wild. In a terrible, strangled voice he said:

'That young man is Vítor da Ega. He's your son! I am Timóteo da Ega.'

She raised her hands to her head in a gesture of horror; her eyes started from her head, her mouth opened in a silent scream; she leaned on the edge of the table, her arms grown rigid; she grabbed convulsively at her necklace and the clasp broke; she staggered about the room, trembling and uttering hoarse sounds, her arms beating the air, then she fell spreadeagled on the floor.

Timóteo shouted:

'Help, someone, help!'

Mélanie ran in, and rushed, screaming, to Genoveva's side. She went to open the windows and hurriedly loosened Genoveva's clothes. Half-crazed, Timóteo groped his way along the walls and down the stairs and hurled himself into his carriage; when the driver turned round, he was shocked to see tears rolling down Timóteo's cheeks.

Vítor had seen Uncle Timóteo go into Genoveva's house and had then walked down Rua do Alecrim and strolled around the Aterro. He was very nervous and agitated. He met Carvalhosa, who asked after Genoveva.

'She's fine, thank you.' And since almost an hour had passed, he thought he should return and so he accompanied Carvalhosa back up Rua do Alecrim. Carvalhosa talked about politics and literature. What did he think about that idiot Roma's latest book of poetry? He thought it pretentious and banal, with no ideals and no images. Vítor replied in monosyllables and with vague smiles. He gave alms to all the poor people they came across in order to bring good fortune. When he reached Largo do Quintela, there was no carriage to be seen. 'My uncle must have gone.'

'Literature is stagnant,' said Carvalhosa.

'It certainly is,' replied Vítor, his eyes fixed on Genoveva's window. He bade Carvalhosa a rather brusque farewell, then repented and asked him to come and dine with him and Genoveva.

'When?'

'Tomorrow.'

'At six?'

'At seven.'

And he ran into the house, taking the stairs four at a time. He found the door open and went in. It occurred to him that perhaps Timóteo was still there and that he had asked the carriage to come back for him. He tiptoed into the living room and carefully raised the curtain. He saw Genoveva sitting on a chair, her arms hanging by her side, her head lolling on her chest.

'Genoveva,' he said quietly.

He noticed that her hair was all dishevelled, her bodice unbuttoned, her face pale and suddenly old. He rushed in. She looked up, saw him and leaped back, her arms and fingers stretched out towards him.

'What's wrong, Genoveva?' he cried, running towards her.

She recoiled, her eyes wide, her body rigid, a terrible grimace on her face, her arms signalling desperately 'No, no!' She was breathing hoarsely, the stertorous breath of the dying. And her terrible, terrified eyes, like the eyes of the dead, were fixed on him with fearful persistence.

Vítor was petrified. He stammered:

'Genoveva, my love, what is it?'

He took a step forward.

342

But she, possessed by fear, shrank back and looked wildly about her with fierce, crazed eyes, for a door, a corner, some way out.

'Oh, my God, you've gone mad!' he exclaimed in a tearful, frightened voice. 'It's me, Genoveva, it's me!'

And he went towards her. She opened her mouth in a gesture of terrible distress and managed to cry out:

'Poor wretch, poor wretch!'

Then she turned and ran to the window and, with an awful scream, hurled herself over the balcony. Vítor heard the sound her body made as it hit the ground, a soft, dull sound like a bundle of clothes.

When they carried Genoveva's body into the room, amidst Mélanie's clamorous cries, they found Vítor lying on the floor; he had hit his head on the corner of a console table and a thread of blood was running from his pale brow onto the carpet, where it was slowly drying.

The newspapers were filled for days afterwards with 'the Rua das Flores suicide'. The police made a few desultory enquiries and, convinced that it was just a suicide, gradually forgot all about it. Dâmaso was, at first, as he said to his friends 'devastated'. He remained at home for a few days, but he was soon out and about again, plump and smiling, and declaring pompously:

'I always said something like this would happen. The woman was mad and bound to come to a bad end.'

During that time, Vítor was lying in bed with brain fever. Neither Timóteo nor Clorinda slept for twenty-five nights, and on the day when Vítor could take his first few steps around his room, leaning on the nurse, and managed to eat a little chicken, Uncle Timóteo flung his arms about him and wept.

'But why did she do it, why?' sobbed Vítor.

Uncle Timóteo said simply:

'I don't know. She was telling me about her past life and she suddenly fainted. Only God knows why she did it.'

He had aged; he spent his days near the armchair in which Vítor sat recovering his strength, and he smoked pipe after pipe, saying nothing, staring at the floor, where his faithful dog, Dick, lay at his feet.

One day, after a long silence, Vítor suddenly said:

'I was going to marry that woman. Do you think I should wear mourning when I go out?'

Timóteo suddenly got to his feet, paced about the room a little, stopped, tapped his fingers on the window sill and then turned, looking very pale.

'Yes, probably, but just a black band around your hat.'

But Vítor wore the full mourning of a widower. He wanted to travel and he did so. He stayed in Madrid and in Paris, where he found Genoveva's house, which he passed by every day and every night, staring up at the balcony; he felt that some part of his own past life lay in that place where she had lived. He even considered renting it and buying the furniture; the current tenant led a very jolly existence; sometimes, at three in the morning, the street rang to the sound of piano music; a waiter in a nearby café told him that a woman called D'Arcy lived there and, realising that Vítor was a foreigner, he told him she was very pretty and only charged four *libras*.

One day, coming round the corner into Place de la Bourse, he bumped into Mélanie. They embraced warmly. With the money Uncle Timóteo had given her, she had bought a small cakeshop in La Villette. She was doing well, and Vítor often went to see her; it was winter and they would sit in a dark little room on the carpet by the hearth, drinking coffee in the dim light of the wood fire; outside it would be raining or silently snowing and they would talk for hours about Genoveva, until Vítor, his eyes fixed on the flames, would fall silent, lost in infinite longing, his eyes full of tears. At eleven o'clock, though, he would have to leave because Mélanie's lover, who was employed as part of a claque at a theatre, came back at midnight.

Vítor returned to Portugal and found Uncle Timóteo older, sadder and more silent. Two weeks after his return, his uncle caught pleurisy. He died a calm, peaceful death. When he heard Clorinda talking about the sacraments, he said in a feeble voice:

'No, I don't want any priests. Don't spoil this last moment. It's the best moment in life.'

He left Vítor seventy *contos* in his will.

Two months later, Vítor was coming back from the cemetery where he had been to visit the graves of Genoveva and Uncle Timóteo, when he heard a little girl running after him, calling:

'Sir, sir!'

'What is it?'

'The lady on the second floor wants to speak to you.'

Puzzled, he followed the girl and found Joana in a wretched second-floor apartment; she hurled herself into his arms and told him her story. After Camilo left for Brazil, she had received a little money from him, but had had nothing more from him for six months and had now pawned everything she had. She no longer wore the yellow cotton gown, and a slight melancholy had given her a more delicate beauty.

Vítor set her up in a house and took her as his mistress, bringing up Camilo's son as his own. They say he's going to marry her. Somewhat consoled in his grief, he devotes himself to literary works and, some time ago, he published this poem in the *Ladies' Journal*, an imitation of a poem by Richepin:

> *To Genoveva*
> You were so deeply loved
> That my life will always be
> Perfumed with your dear memory.
>
> Others perhaps still love you.
> I, faithless and weak,
> Keep the receipts from roadside inns -
> Souvenirs of a single night.
>
> Yet even in the loveliest eyes
> It is you that I still see;
> Though others arouse desire in me
> I live, as ever, only for you.

Thus on the plains of Jericho,
The magus king surveyed the stars,
But followed only one.

So, even when, in ecstasy,
I possess the most desired of bodies,
I have only to turn away
To see you waiting there.

Dona Joana Coutinho, who read the poem and loved it, asked him some days ago, in the house of Senhor Seixas, where Vítor occasionally reads his work:

'Is your wife not jealous?'

Vítor smiled and said nothing. How could she be jealous? Joana, his wife, could not read.

Dedalus European Classics

Dedalus European Classics began in 1984 with D.H. Lawrence's translation of Verga's *Mastro Don Gesualdo*. In addition to rescuing major works of literature from being out of print, the editors' other major aim was to redefine what constituted a "classic".

Titles available include:

Little Angel – Andreyev £4.95
The Red Laugh – Andreyev £4.95
Seraphita (and other tales) – Balzac £6.99
The Quest of the Absolute – Balzac £6.99
The Episodes of Vathek – Beckford £6.99
The Devil in Love – Cazotte £5.99
La Madre (The Woman and the Priest) –
  Deledda £5.99
Undine – Fouqué £6.99
Misericordia – Galdos £8.99
Spirite – Gautier £6.99
The Dark Domain – Grabinski £6.99
Simplicissimus – Grimmelshausen £10.99
The Cathedral – Huysmans £7.99
The Oblate – Huysmans £7.99
The Other Side – Kubin £9.99
The Mystery of the Yellow Room – Leroux £7.99
The Perfume of the Lady in Black – Leroux £8.99
The Woman and the Puppet – Loüys £6.99
Blanquerna – Lull £7.95
The Angel of the West Window – Meyrink £9.99
The Golem – Meyrink £6.99
The Opal (and other stories) – Meyrink £7.99
The White Dominican – Meyrink £6.99
Walpurgisnacht – Meyrink £6.99
Ideal Commonwealths – More/Bacon et al £7.95